Acts of Love

Acts of Love

Susan Pearce

Victoria University Press

VICTORIA UNIVERSITY PRESS
Victoria University of Wellington
PO Box 600 Wellington
vuw.ac.nz/vup

www.susanpearce.com

First published 2007

National Library of New Zealand Cataloguing-in-Publication Data

Pearce, Susan, 1969-
Acts of love / Susan Pearce.
ISBN 978-0-86473-565-2
I. Title.
NZ 823.3—dc 22

Published with the assistance of a grant from

ARTS COUNCIL OF NEW ZEALAND *TOI AOTEAROA*

Printed in Singapore

For Dad

Contents

Part 1
New Zealand
2004

1

The name written on the back of the airmail envelope fixed Rita's feet to the driveway. She looked around for something that might rescue her, but the usual meanings of the russet-coloured gravel and the white letterbox, of Bill's roses and the neighbour's tabby balancing on the fence: all had rushed away, leaving the envelope the only solid thing in the world.

She flipped it over and began an intensive study of the stamps. The postmark—she could not help reading 'Minnesota'—had smudged them only a little. With effort she saw that the pelican was delicately watercoloured, and that the faces of the sculpted soldiers marching towards her from their war memorial were grim and determined. She could have gone on examining them forever if it meant she would not have to open the letter, but Bill called from the living-room window, 'Charlie?'

The envelope trembled. She shook her head and tried to smile.

'Not to worry. He'll email, most likely.'

He disappeared. Rita looked again at the letter. Bill did not know that in the first years of their marriage she had daydreamed constantly of Leland Swann. That Leland would write announcing the annulment of his mistake. That financed by some of those wealthy congressmen he would send a plane, or come himself to claim her.

She slipped her forefinger under the flap and made a messy rip. Inside the envelope a single sheet of onion-skin paper, dark inky reversals of Leland's handwriting showing through, was folded around the Order of Service for a funeral. Rita did not recognise the name centred on the heavy paper, and it occurred to her with relief that Leland had accidentally included her while notifying acquaintances of a relative's death.

Elizabeth Lois Swann
February 22nd, 1944 to December 23rd, 2003
Duluth First Presbyterian Church

Only one month older than me, she thought. Fifty-nine was awfully young to die, though she had known others who'd gone early. Several work colleagues, and three of Bill's Quaker friends. Car accidents and cancer. She never could get used to the passing of her own generation.

Then, as she began to walk towards the house, preparing herself to read whatever words were contained in this artefact of the man who had exiled them from the Centre (his fingers had brushed against this flimsy paper, squeezed the pen, his tongue had licked the stamps), another part of her mind continued to muse on the dead Elizabeth—

Betty.

Betty was gone. Gone from the world. After all this time, but so soon.

She dropped the Order of Service and stumbled to the edge of the drive, sitting heavily on its red-brick border. The bricks' sharp edges pressed through her skirt. A twitchy breeze nudged the pamphlet on to the lawn and towards the rhododendrons. For a few moments she let it drift; she'd have liked to see it tumble right off the property. But she knew that if Bill found it dirtied, softened by rain and glistening with snail slime, he wouldn't buy a tale about the wind whipping it out of her hand. He had liked Betty. Even if Rita could lie to him, he'd know it, and then she'd have to disclose her other secret: that she couldn't bear to think about her old friend.

She braced her hands on her knees and slowly stood, collected the leaflet from the lumpy soil beneath the rhododendrons and blew a tiny black spider off one corner. With a shivering intake of breath, she opened it.

The mourners had sung 'The King of Love My Shepherd Is' and 'Holy, Holy, Holy, Lord God Almighty'. Reverend Michaels of the Duluth First Presbyterian Church had welcomed them, and someone called Dustin Franks had read from 1 Corinthians 13. Aurelia McClure, Cousin, had given the eulogy. The congregation had been invited to partake of coffee and sandwiches after the service. It had all taken place two weeks ago, while Rita and Bill were sitting in deckchairs outside their caravan at Riversdale, munching on leftover Christmas cake and talking lazily about how it would be Easter before they remembered to write the correct date on cheques. Perils of growing old, they'd said.

The breeze cut at her arms. She folded the Order of Service back into the envelope, and carried it into the house. Bill was in the kitchen. 'What you got there?' he asked, and she had to tell him: Betty was dead. Cancer.

'No? Good God, terrible,' he said, hugging her close. 'Terrible news. Poor Betty.'

Rita buried her nose in the musty wool of his sweater, wishing she could stay there forever. He rubbed circles on her back. 'You all right?'

She straightened, and moving away from him began to tidy some papers on the counter. 'Sure. It's a shock, it brings back memories, but it's not like we . . . I mean, I haven't seen her in so long.'

It worked. He patted her again, and kissed the top of her head. 'Take it easy, eh. Have a sit down. I was just on my way out to pick a few of those cherry tomatoes.'

Obediently, she sat, but after the screen door banged behind him she stood again, watching through the window until he'd collected a pile of tomatoes in his frayed towelling hat and was crouched by the spinach, weeding. He'd keep at it until his creaky knees drove him inside. She licked her dry lips, tapping the envelope against her palm. Had Betty told Leland something before she died and he'd written to complain? The possibility of their joint criticism terrified her.

But the letter was short, with only a scant three sentences about Betty's death. Cancer again, its original location and progress unspecified. One line made her wonder: 'The self-

13

determined circumstances of her illness have rendered my loss all the more painful.'

What did he mean? What had Betty 'self-determined'?

His next words put everything else out of her head.

'My doctor has advised me to take a vacation,' he wrote. 'I arrive at Wellington airport on Tuesday 27th. It is close to your home. I would appreciate your hospitality.'

Tuesday the 27th of *January*, she realised, checking the calendar. In four days' time.

The letter mentioned a flight number, but nothing about the length of Leland's stay, or whether he planned to tour after his arrival. She pushed her fingers into her temples, then collected cookbooks from the shelf above the table, fetched paper and pen. Deep in menus, she didn't notice Bill come in, and he had to plonk the tomatoes by her elbow and ask twice before she heard.

'Oh! Leland's coming to stay. In *four days*!' She didn't turn to see his reaction.

That evening, after they had kissed good night and switched off their lamps, he said from his pillow, 'You all right then, Reet?' She squeezed his hand, but she was fretting that her insomnia would return and, if it did, how would she get through the cleaning and preparations? Hours later, though, she became sleepily aware that she was breathing slowly and deeply, and that her slow, deep breathing had manifested itself in a sliding weight along her hip and thigh, as though her whole body had transformed into a replenishing breath. When Bill, spooned behind her, moved his hand lower and pressed his fingers gently through her nightie, she emerged a little further into the bedroom's sludgy, comforting darkness. Deep in the shadows of her drowsiness, something she didn't want to remember threatened to make itself known. She wiggled to show Bill she had woken, and he kissed the knob at the top of her spine, and her neck and bare shoulder. She turned on to her back, hooking an arm around him. She had long loved these early morning assignations, when her drowsiness nudged out the internal chatter that ruled her head in daylight hours. Instead, her freed self rose to meet Bill from somewhere near her solar plexus, and she could move her luxuriously floppy, aging limbs with abandonment, forgetful of her skin tags and the slack muscle on her upper arms.

Tonight, she refused to remember anything at all, refused everything except the brief burn as he guided himself in, and his mouth closing over hers, and every soft and bumpy point inside and out where they joined. When the currents shivering through her belly threatened to bring her to full consciousness, she wriggled out from under him and pushed him on to his back, kissing him hard, sucking now and then on his lips, swirling her tongue around his mouth, catching it briefly on his broken tooth. Acting this way still felt somewhat daring, even though she'd been doing it since not long after Charlie was born, when she'd discovered it in a crazed, uninhibited state brought on by sleep deprivation.

Bill gripped her wrists and lifted her hands off the sheet, then loosened his hold and slid his palms against hers, propping her up so she could sit straight while she moved above him. She felt him smiling through the darkness, and returned his smile.

Afterwards, lying next to him, she straightened her leg and laid the sole of her foot along the smooth, bony top of his. She felt a deep steadiness, as if she had been lowered, vertical, on to ground that would never move. He whispered, 'Happy Almost-Anniversary, love.'

It hadn't taken her long to get used to him: his smell of leather soles and fallen tree bark and the inside of small tin boxes; the way he gurgled in his sleep, and on rising always drew the curtains right back, leaving the entire window frame exposed; his habit of scraping dead skin from round his toenails on to a newspaper he laid over the quilt. And then, in the second decade of their marriage, she decided she had never loved Leland. How could that feeling have been love, when Bill made it so easy for her to love him?

That didn't erase the fact that she had failed God: had failed

His Promise. (After all, who knew what profound feelings for Leland might have developed if she'd lived up to it?) She still believed in God's divine plan—it seemed foolhardy not to—and believed, with equal certainty, that forty years ago her inadequacy had spoilt it. She had never been able to confess to her steady, affectionate husband that in her very foundation, where wordless desires and terrors bumped blindly around in the dark, she feared dying in the knowledge that she had lived a second-best life.

Now, only moments after she and Bill kissed more quietly and said a second good night, and he subsided next to her, one hand still on her thigh, this fear crackled and flamed. A hectic, jumbled sense of the Centre roared into her head—the Movement's magnificent ideal: a perfect, painless world. The hope and vigour, the exhilaration of being part of the biggest, most important effort in history.

And she had failed it.

She knew Bill, snoring softly beside her, didn't feel the same, even though Leland had sent them both away. But then, God hadn't made him a special Promise.

Neither had Bill betrayed his best friend.

She fell into dreams of sole responsibility for an endless series of five-course banquets on which depended stakes as vague and high as world peace. She smeared mud across the table linen, or saw, too late, that the most honoured guest had sat on the cracked chair. She sprinted down the Centre's long corridors, chasing deliveries of sticky ribs that flew ahead of her, catching on the panelling. Betty hovered at the periphery of every dream, indistinct, her intentions unclear.

'Don't get het up, will you,' Bill said in the morning. 'He's an ordinary man, grieving for his wife. Poor Betty. Strange to think they were married right next to us in the chapel. And now she's gone.'

'Yes,' Rita said. 'Are you done in the bathroom?'

She didn't want to think about that double wedding, or what had led up to it.

16

Over the following days she planned menus, tweaked crispy leaves from the house plants, polished the indoor fig and regularly dead-headed every flowering shrub. On the evening before Leland's arrival she could not stop cleaning. Bill came to find her, and she said, without believing it, 'I'll relax once he's here.'

For the fourth time she straightened the spines of the *National Geographics* she'd arranged on the hall table. She tried to look calmly preoccupied, but Bill spoke again. 'Charlie's on your mind, eh. He'll be in touch. Give him time—you know what it's like with a wee one. Zane's probably not sleeping too well in that air-conditioning. But there's no way they'll miss the big do.'

For months, when Bill wasn't looking, Rita's forearms had cradled air, conjuring the sensation of baby Zane's bundled weight. It was all she knew of her grandson. Charlie had yet to make the journey home with his new family, and Rita and Bill, believing he would bring Noelle and Zane over for the planned Harper Family Anniversary Weekend (forty years of marriage! and Rita's sixtieth birthday, or near enough), had not diverted any of their hard-earned retirement savings into a Hawai'ian holiday.

There was a second reason to count on the presence of Charlie's little family at the Anniversary Weekend. Without Zane to cosset and coo over, she would have that many more awkward conversations with Stella, who would try to be sweet while giving away nothing, and with Stella's supercilious husband, Dan. It was a shame, she thought, rubbing a last dose of linseed oil into the table's wooden scrolls, that her overly educated son-in-law couldn't bring himself to be more civil. And ever since he and Stella had eloped to Fiji four years ago, her daughter had been even less confiding. Nonetheless, Rita fretted that Stella and Dan might stay away from the Anniversary Weekend. More than anything, she wanted the family together for the occasion—proof that her life had been worth something. Leland's impending visit had put her on notice. Somehow, her future, and the final verdict on her, would be decided.

When the time came the next day to collect their guest from the airport, they drove down the valley and along the harbour's edge towards Wellington. A changeable wind gusted back and forth, sweeping creamy comb-overs from the waves, and the sky was full of a bright, blanching light that seemed independent of the sun hanging over the mountains. Looking across the water, Rita could see the narrow isthmus that the runway spanned and a plane coming in low from the south. If Leland's plane took the same ocean approach, it would skim the boulders that protected the runway from the sea.

'Funny sort of a northerly,' Bill said. 'Hope he's got a strong stomach for landings.'

In 1964, when they had come here after Leland told them to leave the Centre, they too had landed from the south. Roaring, bone-shaking, the plane had seemed to Rita like a transport to Hell. She'd resented the air hostesses with their shellacked, bouffant hair, miniskirts rising up sheer-stockinged thighs as they reached into overhead lockers. Earlier, Bill had pointed out three white cylinders rising from a distant platter of cloud: 'Look, Reet, the Three Pillars.' But, as they watched, the cloud towers had toppled and dissolved.

The wind buffeted the side of the car, bumping it sideways.

She said, 'Don't talk about the war.'

Bill looked at her, raised an eyebrow.

'Or the occupation, or whatever you want to call it.'

'Relax. It'll be fine.'

She had not slept well the night before, waking with gritty eyelids every hour or so, aware of Leland's route as she had been since she started tracking it the previous morning. Then, he must have flown out of Duluth after breakfast. By lunchtime, with a good connection, he'd have been over the Midwest. While she and Bill ate dinner he might have shifted around uncomfortably on a moulded plastic seat at LAX—as far as they knew, the

Movement's richest benefactors had died or defected long ago. During the night, while he flew over the Pacific, she had felt him bearing down on her like a potentate wielding judgement.

'Round the bays, eh?' Bill flicked the indicator. 'Nice day for it. We've got time.'

She looked down from the overbridge at the ferry terminal and the gaudy tails of cars waiting to board. Square loading cranes loomed above container ships. Then Bill steered them on to the ramp, and they headed towards the slit-eyed grey wall of the sports stadium. She knew this city better than she knew St Paul, now. Had lived in its neighbour, Lower Hutt, almost twice as long as in her own birthplace. The last thing she had expected was for her old life—let alone *him*—to touch her here.

'Shame they never had any kids,' Bill said. 'Company for Leland. And Betty would have made a fantastic mother, eh. What's up? Are you feeling crook?'

Her voice wobbled. 'I'm fine. I forgot to thaw the roast.'

She could almost persuade herself that she was telling the truth.

At the same moment that Bill and Rita's car passed the ferry terminal, their daughter Stella, teetering by one of their potted daphnes, leaned backwards into the arms of a taxi driver. She let him lower her on to the top step of the white-painted concrete porch, then smoothed her skirt over her legs, resting her palm on the hard plaster encasing her ankle as if to prove that it didn't bother her.

The driver heaved her suitcase up the steps. The previous evening, the paramedics would have driven away without it if Stella hadn't yelled at them to chuck it in the back of the ambulance. At the hospital the nurses had joked that not many patients arrived so well prepared. She couldn't laugh. The furious tears with which she'd thrown her clothes together and marched out of the house weren't far beneath the surface.

The driver, whose badge said *Aziza*, balanced her crutches against a post and squinted at her. 'You okay? You don't want lift?'

'No, it's fine. They'll be back soon.'

Her mind was murky with the hospital's instant coffee. She needed to remind herself what she could and could not tell her parents. The accident would divert their attention for a while: how, descending too quickly the mossy, uneven steps from the home she'd until yesterday shared with Dan (no, leave Dan out), she'd looked an instant too long at the white spiders' nests patching the bracken on the bank, each polyhedron built around the central axis of the branch and penetrated in all directions by thorns that seemed to lift the silk walls like marquee poles. Still looking, she'd stepped on to a slope covered in brownly decaying camellia blossoms, turned her ankle with two audible cracks and sprawled sideways, shrieking, into the wild onions.

Damning Dan as selfish didn't help, although that's what she'd been doing in the hours since, beating him down a dark path into a cul-de-sac of distracting judgement—*selfish, selfish*—before lurching into frustration: if she'd known he'd be so cold-hearted, maybe she wouldn't have fooled herself that he'd ever change his mind. It was all 'what if' and pointless sorrow.

She tweaked a leaf from a geranium and rubbed it between her fingers, inhaling its spicy smell. Until she found somewhere else to stay—in Wellington, she meant, not out here on these alluvial flats shouldered by gorse-covered hills—this, once again, would be home. No broadband, but that was minor. It could be six weeks before her cast came off, and all her friends' houses in hilly Wellington had at least a few old, crazy steps like those she'd dived down yesterday morning.

She sat on her hands for a while to relieve her aching buttock bones. When she released them her palms were minutely pitted by the concrete. She flexed her fingers. Dan had relished her double-jointed skills, but he resented ultimatums, or any hint of betrayal. He would never go back on his final, caustic words, spoken before he picked up his bag and walked out the front door. 'You've lied. There's a lie at the heart of this relationship. Deal-breaker. Don't be here when I get back.'

Why had she stayed with a man who could say, with a serious face, *deal-breaker*? His pursuit of perfection had lured her in before it had begun to repulse her: he possessed the world's best recipe for hot chocolate (freshly pressed orange oil), the back-road directions to the North Island's only decent organic vineyard, the contact details for local manufacturers of titanium mountain bikes. Towards the end, wanting a child had kept her with him. That, and secretly hoping he too would change his mind. Staying put had seemed a smoother option than finding someone new.

Tensing her thigh, she lifted her plastered ankle a few centimetres, feeling its unfamiliar weight, then let it drop against the step, the pain a high, discordant screech in her bones.

'Fuck. *Fuck*.' She drummed her knuckles on the concrete. *Stupid*. Stupid to like him in the first place, stupid to fall for his act, stupid to stay and, most of all, stupid to think she could persuade him that, despite his avowals, in his heart he did want to be a father.

She had suspected the endometriosis since her mid-twenties, and a few months before she met Dan it was confirmed by a workaholic surgeon finishing her post-op rounds close to midnight. The surgeon described the migration, at some unknowable point in the past (possibly while Stella hung upside-down from a jungle gym), of endometrial cells from her womb into her lower pubic area and left fallopian tube: cells that were meant to stick to her uterine wall, sponging forth each month to create a fresh nutritious nest, but that once departed had no reason to return, building and flowering as regularly as ever in their new, random homes. There they nurtured not babies, but pain and scars.

During their first date, Stella had agreed with Dan that bratty, snot-nosed kids were a blight on life. She spoke with an assurance born of hidden anger—how dare bad fortune visit *her*.

She had convinced him, and managed to convince herself too, but the previous spring she had lost a cyst-riddled ovary. (A girls' weekend up the coast, she had told him.) After the operation, she woke knowing how much she wanted a baby. At first she did nothing except hope for Dan's impossible conversion. Then her monthly cycle had begun to lengthen.

Two weeks ago, silently panicking, she'd flown to Auckland three days after her period began (a computer conference, she told him), and visited a fertility clinic where an efficient, sympathetic doctor inserted a long plastic probe into her vagina and bounced sound waves off her remaining ovary.

Yesterday her cycle had entered its crucial phase, but Dan didn't care that the clinic's 'egg check' results had said pretty much soon or never, and that he was about to leave for a six-week business trip. He cared only that she'd misled him, that he'd been diddled. If she was that desperate, he said, she should display her wares in a bar or apply to a sperm bank.

No. Anonymous sperm wasn't for her. She wanted to know the father of her child. But Dan's refusal had got her thinking. Now, tired, headachey from the sun's glare, she saw that she'd wasted time, unwilling to push him away because at thirty-six-going-on-seven she couldn't be bothered to find a more suitable mate. She would have settled for him, believing more in nurture than in nature. Now she needed a friend, someone who'd gladly donate some fast-swimming tadpoles in exchange for a few good fucks or, even better, wouldn't care about the consequences. Someone who lived for the day, or was befuddled by lust to the point of—

And then she had it. A candidate.

A plan.

She would have to lie again.

❧

22

What was New Zealand to Leland Swann, flying down the west coast of the North Island towards Wellington airport? Somewhere in his thoughts was a Discovery Channel view of towering granite cliffs and waterfalls crammed up against rolling pasture. The camera crested the top of a green hill, and on the other side he saw the Harpers' suburb, much like his own back in Duluth, but with the addition of singing natives, the men's faces elaborately tattooed, the women slapping together white balls on strings.

He had not asked for their opinion, but his well-travelled neighbours, hearing of his plans, had dropped by to tell him that the driver on their most recent Australian coach tour had said New Zealand was behind the times, neither as sophisticated nor as riddled with crime. 'Like America in the fifties,' the wife said wistfully.

Over the intercom, the captain's honeyed voice advised passengers seated on the plane's right to view a mountain. Leland propped his forehead against the cold plastic of the window, peering down at a grey cone, its lower slopes covered in tangled, dark green forest. His sinuses throbbed. He had forgotten to pack his sleeping pills in his cabin luggage for the flight from LA, and had remained maddeningly alert and dry-eyed under the yellow benediction of his reading light.

The mountain passed behind them. He fell against the headrest, massaging his nose with thumb and forefinger, and here came Betty, young and tan as Nellie Forbush in *South Pacific*, garlands of scarlet and yellow flowers around her neck. She was singing 'Bali Hai', backed by a swelling chorus of high-pitched minor harmonies. Behind her, an island of black volcanic rock rose through pink mists. Betty undulated her arms like a Hawai'ian dancer, eyelashes fluttering. During an instrumental interlude she leaned towards him, her voice low and forceful. *I knew all along. You never fooled me.*

He twitched, but she would not release him. *You think you can get away by scooting off down here? Wrong, buddy. I'm with the Big Guy, and He's not happy with you.*

His head snapped forward. He cleared his throat roughly, startling the woman next to him. Betty had no right to be haunting his dreams. Her ashes were unclaimed in a locked cabinet at the funeral parlour; she should not be bossing him around, declaring her unfounded suspicions.

He dug a forefinger around his shirt collar. Dead, he reminded himself. Dead, and unable to halt him any more with her considering, withholding looks. He could rediscover his strength in this young and untried country. He could rise again.

✣

'Have you booked the place?' Bill asked.

They sat at a café table by floor-to-ceiling windows in the arrivals area, Rita with a clear view down the wide tunnel that led to the gates. Bill stirred a second spoonful of sugar into his tea. She raised her coffee to her lips, but returned the cup carefully to the saucer without taking a sip.

'No. I found out it's only got two double beds. The woman says she has twin beds at her house she can put in the second living room, but Charlie and Noelle will want Zane in with them for their "family bed", and Stella will get antsy if she thinks we're making her sleep even a few inches away from Dan, she's so defensive about that dumb elopement. If you'd agree to singles, pushed together – '

'Definitely not. It's our fortieth anniversary, Reet.'

A small boy and older girl ran beside the tables. They flung themselves on the low aluminium shelf in front of the window, hands and noses pressed flat against the glass.

'No, no-no-no-no, *oh*—'

'Oh-no, don't do it, please—'

'*Plee-ease* don't, and we love you! Don't!'

Bill said, 'Kids, eh.' He chewed on his lip.

'Poor things. Their parents must have split up.'

'No, they're playing. They've watched too much TV.'

She listened again, and realised he was right. They were making believe a soap-opera departure '—No, don't, no!'—cranking up the drama. Yet she could not stop hearing, in their pleading, the possibility of real griefs.

Bill hesitated. 'Love, I got . . . thing is . . .' He looked anxiously over his shoulder towards the gates and turning back to her, seemed to collect himself. 'Look, the house is a gem. Magnificent. We'll be happy as chooks.'

'No. The beds. It won't work out.'

'Reet . . .' Bill took her hand. 'Maybe this isn't the best time . . . but, thing is, Charlie emailed this morning. They can't make it.'

Immediately, tears came to her eyes. 'What! Why not? Why?'

'Pet, don't get upset. We'll see them, go later in the year.'

'But *why*?'

'Noelle's mum's being awarded an honorary doctorate on the Monday. She's still in a bit of a bad way after that surgery. Noelle feels she should support her. All her brothers have gone to the mainland now.'

'What if we make it the next weekend? Or the one before?'

He sighed. 'Noelle's teaching at a community college all semester, Saturday mornings . . . she has to deliver every lesson if she wants a chance at a better slot in the future. It's in her contract.'

He was reciting from Charlie's email, she could tell. She turned her head away, but thought of something else. 'Zane's still a baby! What does she do with him while she works?'

'Look, love, it'll be all right. We can go and see them as soon as you want. Before the weekend, or after. We might come in useful, if Noelle has to spend time with her mum.'

She didn't answer.

He stroked her forearm. 'It's not the end of the world.'

She knew that behind his level, kindly expression, and his refusal to respond to her point about Zane, he believed she was 'het up'. He would be sympathetic, but he was not on her side; he would think her wrong if she encouraged Charlie to reconsider. Oh, he thought he was all so spiritual, driving off every Sunday morning to his 'Meeting', sitting in silence for hours on end, but he lacked sensitivity. He had no feeling for the greater things in life, for transcendence or ceremony.

She snatched her arm away. 'It's time.' Rising, she almost tripped over the table leg.

'Hang on, love. You forgot your bag.'

She felt as though she were facing Leland's arrival alone. Alone, and without the promise of a family reunion to get her through his visit. Pacing down the corridor ahead of Bill, she swiped at her tears and tried to focus on the task ahead. Would they even recognise him? She could only bring to mind the framed clipping that she'd dusted and placed on the sideboard: a colour photo of Leland levering the hand of a slight, pinch-nosed man. The caption read: '*Mr Leland Swann (PUGC), having persuaded Sen. Harmell Stinson (R) to adopt the Three Pillars.*' Underneath the clipping, Rita had glued a second typewritten caption, now rising at the edges with age: '*Life*, August 1963'.

They arrived at the gate. Bill rubbed the small of her back and circled her waist with his arm. She stood stiffly inside it. The first disembarking passengers walked down the chute: a couple of businessmen, briefcases swinging towards the next meeting. She craned her head to see through the swelling stream behind them, but the people moved back and forth in front of each other, their jogging gaits preventing her from getting a good look. Leland would be upon them before she had a chance to prepare herself: he would have the advantage. She may as well shut her eyes.

Part 2
People Under God's Command
1963–1964

1

Before People Under God's Command arrived in St Paul—before, even, it announced extra tour dates for the Twin Cities—the *Star Tribune* ran stories, reprinted from the *Washington Post*, about their revolutionary play. 'Divine Instruction Protects Us From Reds'; 'Swann: "Listen and Obey"'.

Hilary Daley stood over the breakfast table, her aproned waist a couple of inches from her daughter's face. She laid the morning paper on the cloth and nudged it towards Rita.

'These kids don't mope around. They've got zing.'

Rita carried on spooning Wheaties and milk into her mouth, but her heart beat faster. She had only recently learned to ignore her mother. Mrs Daley retreated to the door that connected the kitchen to the breakfast nook. There she stood wiping dry a skillet, watching.

If the toast burnt, Mrs Daley ate and professed to like it. She did not shower or dress before Rita and Frank Daley left in the morning, Rita to Lambert's Secretarial Academy and her husband to Premiere Television & Phonograph Sales, but bagged their lunches and washed dishes in her old housecoat and slippers, a black hairnet covering her loose perm. When she carried a new dish to the dinner table and placed it before them, she mumbled, 'I'm sure this hasn't turned out the way it should.' There was nothing you could say that would make up for that. No chance of a simple, 'This is good, Mom.' It was easier to stay silent.

After a couple of minutes she stalked forward and propped the newspaper with a sharp thrust against Rita's glass of orange juice. Rita couldn't help but see the three-column photograph of young people, caught mid-song with mouths wide open, upper lips curled back from their teeth. They lunged, pointing into the audience, every face lively and eager.

She snatched the paper aside and drank her juice. Being tardy for shorthand meant spending the remainder of the class leaning awkwardly against the blackboard, gripping her notepad and scribbling while Mr Lambert dictated to all the poised, seated girls, interrupting himself to ask with oily concern, 'Miss Daley, did you get that? Are you up to speed?'

It was not that she wanted to argue with her mother. There was little pleasure in it—Rita flailing, jabbering; her mother tight-lipped, jaw working up and down so that dimples intended for a happier woman winked in the pouches of flesh that guarded her mouth. Even if Rita clenched her fists and shouted, or crashed down the hallway and kicked her bedroom door shut, then returned, crying, half a minute later, to justify her rage ('You keep *nagging* at me, I can hardly *breathe*'); even when provoked, her mother only turned away, stony, as if to suggest that Rita had hurt her beyond endurance, or laughed with no real mirth into the face of her daughter's fury: 'You think you have so much to say.' Worst of all, though, when Rita's mid-quarrel eloquence matched the intensity of her anger, her mother would slump, looking up at her with entreaty. 'I know I'm a frustrating woman.' (Yes!) 'Lord knows I try my best.' She'd stretch out her arms, tears in her eyes. '*Forgive me*.' Rita, choking on a rush of shame and unspent anger, could not move to grasp the proferred hands. She could not believe in her mother's remorse; at the same time she completely believed her, pitied her, was revolted, wanted to kill her, hated herself, wanted to rush forward and be enveloped in her arms. Her failure to respond merely stoked the fires for the next conflagration.

Frank Daley limped in from the marital bedroom, running a comb through his hair, his sideways glances suggesting that among mankind only he understood the wretchedness of the human condition. 'How are we this morning? My estimable wife? My indefatigable daughter?'

30

'Frank—I'm sorry to harp on, but—please don't moult over the breakfast table.'

'Oh, I apologise. I withdraw. Back to my haven of conjugal bliss.'

Early on, Rita had made up her mind that she loved her mother best; had found the answer to that troubling question of which parent she'd rather, if forced to choose, have dead. Once, ten years old and experimentally sassy, she'd tried to persuade her mother to stand up to him. Hilary Daley replied, 'If you look hard enough at the troubles in your life, you can always find some way you're to blame. God notices everything.'

Rita never forgot that, because it explained her mother.

Mrs Daley's capital-G God was a relative pushover, forgiving all, in the end, if one showed sufficient remorse. She set up a second, far more vengeful god in the form of Life itself, which aimed to destroy ignorant women with its traps, punishments, tricks and disappointments. To get through Life without falling prey to its vagaries, and then to be lifted beyond the pit after death, was all she hoped for. She took care of the second item with church attendance and by constantly promoting her own unworthiness, but the sole protection she had against dreadful Life was to be respectably married.

Frank Daley had been a travelling salesman for Myer Insurance, in whose poky offices Hilary, bitterly seasoned by romantic disappointments, typed up letters rejecting payout claims. They married on 30 November 1943. After Pearl Harbour Frank was quickly drafted into the Navy, and just as quickly took a hit of shrapnel in his right thigh. Until Rita was four, the family lived in one of St Paul's veteran villages; she remembered running around the cavernous Quonset hut, negotiating the oil burner's dark hulk and tripping on the rugs scattered over the chilly plywood floor. These days Frank was deputy manager of a TV store down on Payne Avenue, and they lived in a compact, single-storey rambler in one of St Paul's treeless new suburbs.

'Charm and efficiency,' Mrs Daley now said, fluffing out Rita's limp bangs and looking critically at her chin. 'They'll get you a long way. Work hard today.' Then she hugged her.

Her father drove in silence. When he dropped her off at the Academy, he said, 'Go wild, chicken.' She thought she would combust if she had to live with them for another year.

That evening, she went to the sideboard and sneaked a look at the newspaper article beneath the photo.

A New York audience of 800 rose in a standing ovation last night to a challenge from America's youth: let's listen to God and straighten out our lives, or risk Communist takeover.

Leland Swann, the group's 25-year-old leader, said, 'Communism is a cancer. It's crazy to say we can co-exist with it. God is the only cure. Unless we surrender ourselves to Him, America will become an immoral death-camp run by the Reds. Is that what you want for your children?

Leland Swann was pictured separately, shaking hands with a city leader. He had removed his jacket and rolled his shirtsleeves up to the elbows. Dark hair curled back from his forehead. Rita touched her fingertip to his cheek. He looked the antithesis of her father: vigorous and well built against Mr Daley's spindly, dried-out frame.

One month later, when *The Divine Instruction* came to St Paul, her mother readily agreed to accompany her. 'Maybe it'll wake you up,' she said, steering their Chevy through sleet and snow. 'The sooner you know the world's not arranged for your benefit, the better. I love you—that's why I tell you these things. You know I love you, right?'

Rita said yes, but her mind lurched away from the question, leery of its swampy, indefinite terminus.

The parking lot was almost full. A photographer and a man with a notebook huddled under the awning by the theatre's double doors.

'Ma'am, what do you anticipate—'

'Nothing to do with you, thank you.'

A steamy, wet-wool smell infused the auditorium. Rita used the press of the crowd to ignore her mother's instructions, and manoeuvred them towards two empty seats near the front, facing centre stage. Colour programmes lay in precise diagonals across the crimson velvet cushions.

'I see they've come into money,' said Mrs Daley, setting her purse on her lap.

Rita flicked through her programme. Here was the *Washington Post* story reprinted; here a close-up of chorus members, who twinkled at the camera as if singing Happy Birthday to a beloved friend. One whole page was taken up with a head-and-shoulders shot of Leland Swann; opposite, he leapt over a hurdle and slammed a tennis ball.

> Leland Swann: the man America's crying out for. He's young, but wise beyond his years. Already, statesmen and business leaders seek his advice. He attributes his tremendous drive and foresight to God: 'God tells me what to do, and I stick to it. He can't compromise, and neither will I.'

At seven o'clock, without any announcement, two lines of young men and women filed on to the stage from left and right. The audience hushed. The chorus members arranged themselves into a wide semicircle, smiled at the audience—now quiet—and on the next beat their voices resounded through the theatre.

> *God's people are certain people!*
> *Sure of their way in life.*
> *Seek his path, the one he's chosen*
> *And farewell trouble and strife!*

Many of the singers looked Rita's age, or barely older. The women wore full green or blue skirts with wide, contrasting waistbands, their hair in wavy bobs or French twists. Each bore the confidence of a homecoming queen. The men, co-ordinated in blue and white, seemed to be uniformly fitted out with Rock Hudson jaws.

The song finished. While the audience rustled and coughed, one of the young women walked to the front of the stage. She had dark brown curls and stood like a trained actress. Rita knew her face before she could work out the connection, and then, as her mother nudged her elbow—'Isn't she that floozy?'—she thought, with a start, *Margot*.

Sometime during a humid July night the year before, Margot had climbed on to her boyfriend's motorbike and freewheeled noisily away, leaving 'House of whores!' daubed in red paint along the street-facing wall of her parents' home. Although Rita liked to think of the romance in this story, she knew from the pulp novels passed around Lambert's Secretarial Academy that Margot's rebel boyfriend could not be a long-term proposition. Therefore Margot, by Rita's calculations, had no one but herself to count on. Since that time Rita had often thought that were she in that situation she would like not to care, just as she imagined Margot didn't care.

Now, however, Margot was groomed and serene, backed up by good-looking people who smiled affectionately at her. Surely, if she could find a home with them, anyone could.

'I hated my mom,' she announced. 'I ran away from home and got myself into some pretty bad trouble. Started on drugs. My Great-aunt Alice has been with People Under God's Command since the beginning. When they were in New York, God led her to the department store where I was a clerk. The first time I Listened, God told me, "Your bitterness will eat you up. Apologise to your mother." I thought *she* should apologise to *me*.'

Here she half-smiled, and the audience chuckled in sympathy.

'But my aunt told me God can't work through you if you don't obey Him. I said sorry to my mother for my hatred of her.

34

It was like being washed by a summer rain. Now I'm free, free for God to use me to make a new world.'

She returned to her place in the semicircle.

A boy came forward and began to talk about how he'd cheated on every test he'd taken. After meeting People Under God's Command he'd written to his former teachers, and his principal had invited him to speak at their school. It was swell, he said, being part of a team dedicated to remaking the world.

Another man described the torment of his impure thoughts: how they had kept him from his studies and stopped him from sleeping. He was cured, now, by working with People Under God's Command.

He stepped back into line, and the chorus sang that true freedom came only from obedience to God.

A man dressed in a suit left the front row and mounted the steps to the stage. He moved deliberately, seeming to welcome the audience's gaze. Rita's cheeks prickled. It was Leland Swann. He turned to face them, pausing before he spoke. The hall was silent.

'Ladies and gentlemen, good evening. Every one of these people—' he swept his arm back to indicate the semicircle of singers '—has a story equally as powerful as those you've heard. If you want to know how they did it, if you're looking to transform *your* life, may this prove to be a remarkable evening for you. I am Leland Swann, the leader of People Under God's Command. We're happy to present to you our first Twin Cities performance of *The Divine Instruction*. This is no ordinary play. We hope to entertain you, and we also offer you a new way to live.'

He gave a restrained smile. There was a sudden exhalation around the hall, as if he had permitted them to breathe.

'I hope this play will change your life as God has changed mine. I hope that together we will save America and ensure her future greatness. Ladies and gentlemen—' he paused '—*The Divine Instruction*.'

Hilary Daley said, 'I guess he's hoping a likeness to the

President can get him places. Might well do, for all I know.'

The chorus members applauded and fanned out, backing towards the wings. Three women in overalls carried onstage a sofa and a rickety fireplace. The right side of the fireplace swung off as they set it down, and one of the women grabbed it and slammed it back. Another received a potted fern from the wings and took some time arranging it on the mantelpiece.

Rita watched Leland Swann. He stood to one side of the stage, every line of him declaring that he was in full possession of his own authority. She thought she could smell cedarwood and oceans.

The play told the story of Joyce, a spoilt and disrespectful young woman. She had recently shoplifted a scarf and some perfume, and was terrified of being discovered. A sub-plot revealed her mother's preoccupation with another man and her consequent neglect of her daughter. Joyce's father claimed that his daughter baffled him. However, the audience discovered that he had more in common with her than he liked to think: the IRS was investigating him for fraud. All in all, Joyce was only a few steps away from a late delinquency. She blamed adults for the rotten state of the world.

The dialogue was alternately leaden ('There is nothing you could undertake to do that would make me obey you') and folksy. But Rita tingled from the moment Joyce, frowning and pouting, slouched from the wings. Like her, she wanted her life to count for something. She too covered up her unhappiness with glowering moods. And from what Joyce said, her supercilious, bad-tempered brother—away at school in Boston—made her feel as small as Rita did when her father used her as a strop for his wit. When Fred came home with apologies for the whole family '—Mom, Pop, I've lied to you about how I'm doing in school, and Sis, I've never looked after you the way I should'—Joyce's scepticism gave way to gratitude. Rita sat up. Fred was played by the man who'd just now spoken of his impure thoughts. What was his secret?

Fred said, waving his arms before the plywood fireplace,

'Truth is, we all want the world to change, don't we?'

Joyce's mom and pop tutted and fidgeted.

'C'mon, Pop, I've heard you complain about politicians. And Mom, you've always hated how Mrs Finnigan talks about you behind your back.' He turned to Joyce. 'Sis, I know you feel misunderstood. It's hard for us young folks to take on this tired old world. But cynicism isn't the answer.'

He paused. Rita clenched handfuls of her skirt.

'How can we expect the world to change without changing ourselves? How can we know how to change ourselves or the world unless we ask God? I met an unusual man at school. He told me God can help me live a life bigger and better than anything I could imagine. He can do that for all of you too! But we have to Listen to Him, and clear out sin from our lives.'

He held up three fingers. 'God's commands can be understood as Three Pillars: Perfect Truthfulness, Perfect Selflessness and Perfect Chastity. When we live according to those pillars, we discover His plan for our lives and for the world.'

His father blustered from his armchair. 'Look, son, I'm no better and no worse than most men. Besides, I'm not convinced God—if there *is* a God—takes all that much of an interest in my life.'

Fred grinned. 'I tell you what, Pop, why don't we give it a try. If you ask Him about the Three Pillars, and you don't hear Him speaking to you—mind you, His voice might sound an awful lot like your conscience—but if you genuinely get no results, I won't mention it again.'

He pulled pens and notebooks from behind the fern and handed them to his family. They froze, seemingly mesmerised by the stationery. Fred looked into the wings and coughed. The lights came up over the audience.

'Ladies and gentlemen, in real life, I'm Gus Driver. As you heard earlier, I've been cured of lustful thoughts. If you'd like to join us in this experiment, if you feel inspired to get right with God and with your fellow man, you'll find pens and notebooks beneath your chairs.'

37

Mrs Daley had stiffened with each successive minute. 'Self-indulgence, if an untaught woman may say so. God's already said what's what.'

At seven years old Rita had pulled a dining-room chair over to the mantelpiece, climbed on to it, and picked up a porcelain nest containing five porcelain eggs, an heirloom passed down from her mother's grandmother. The untended eggs, hand-painted in a mushroom beige speckled with blue, were glued to the twiggy nest, their smooth domes deliciously bumpy under her fingertip.

She broke it, of course. Her foot slipped on the chair's satiny edge, and she flung one hand over to the fireplace to steady herself. The nest—travelling along with her hand—smashed on the faux-marble.

An awful grinding seemed to precede her mother's arrival from the kitchen. Hot-cold with panic, Rita couldn't stammer her useless defence (*It was so pretty, I only wanted to hold it awhile*). She stumbled, trying to keep up with her mother's yanking arm. When her father returned home he dragged her out of her room, swung her upside down on his knee and spanked her twelve times.

Before bed that night she composed a list entitled, at her mother's suggestion, 'Things That Are Wrong With Me'. She had been told them often enough, and could write without any prompting:

I don't love mommy and daddy like I should.
I'm grouchy and to demanding.
I want to much attention. I am selfish.
I steal apples and cookies from the cuboard.
Sometimes I'm careless and brake things.

Not every item on the list was a transcription of her mother's complaints. Some Rita made up by herself, but she believed each one like she believed in her fingernails.

When she had finished, Hilary Daley slipped the list into her pocket. Later, after Rita had cried and cried in her room, her mom said she forgave her, and hugged her. But what was the point of being forgiven when you knew you would do something just as bad the next day, and that every time you messed up you would be frozen with despair, knowing your new failure was more proof you weren't fit to be loved?

No point, was the answer, but still, and even now, Rita pressed herself into her mother's twice-daily hugs: once before she left the house in the morning and once before bed. For those few moments—as long as she hadn't disqualified herself by talking back—she lived in a different world, protected by the arms of a loving mom.

Hilary Daley was Rita's only ally. Agreeing with her mother, even in the matter of her own unworthiness, helped to ensure (so Rita's seven-year-old logic ran) that she would not be abandoned to the darkness. 'Things That Are Wrong With Me' was folded away into her mother's papers, and into the back of Rita's heart, along with every other piece of evidence that proved she wasn't good enough, wasn't well behaved or clever or *right* enough.

She hadn't thought of it in years, wasn't thinking of it while she sat waiting for Gus Driver to speak. But the old terror sensed that Leland Swann's straightforward, decisive God might allow her to be at peace with herself and the world: if she did as He asked, she would be truly right. Right all the time, and therefore lovable all the time, not only for a few unreliable moments per day.

She opened her free notebook to the first page and waited for Gus's instructions, perspiring around her hairline. He stood at the front of the stage, legs wide, fists on hips.

'We in People Under God's Command find the best way to start in on Listening is to write the name of each pillar up at the top of a new page—or give yourself more room, if you think God might have a lot to tell you! That's Perfect Truthfulness . . .'

Rita wrote the words in block capitals along the upper margin of the first page.

'. . . Perfect Selflessness and Perfect Chastity. Remember, the pillar you least want to think about is probably the pillar God most wants to talk to you about!'

'Excuse me?' A portly man further down the row waved at Gus. 'Excuse me? What precisely is your theology? I guess most of us here are Christians, good Protestant Christians? What's wrong with what we got already, what we got in the Bible? And speaking of Christ, where *is* our Lord and Saviour in all this?'

Leland Swann stepped forward. 'We're obliged to you, sir. We welcome enquiring minds. Problem is, left to his own devices, man tends towards inertia and complacency. It goes without saying that the Bible is our guide. It is the Word of God. But from time to time our interpretation—what we *do* with that Word in our everyday lives—needs a shake-up.' He paused. 'The Three Pillars are the *distillation* of Jesus' Sermon on the Mount. Who can recite every word of that great Sermon? I'll count you out, sir, since you're so learned.'

'Blessed are the peacemakers. Blessed are the meek,' suggested a man a few rows ahead. A woman called, 'Love your enemies, bless them that curse you.' Another woman cried, 'A-*men.*' There was a hail of shouts from around the hall.

'They're out of control now,' said Mrs Daley. 'He's lost them.'

He smiled and nodded, smiled and nodded. The noise died away. A very thin man wearing a beaten-up felt hat was leaning forward at the edge of the orchestra pit, waving his fingers.

'I see you, sir. You've committed the Sermon on the Mount to memory? I invite you to join me and tell us—' the man scrambled up '—tell us exactly *how* God's commands have manifested themselves in your life?'

The man threw his head back. 'Blessed are the poor in—'

Leland raised a hand and looked benignly at the baffled man. He had regained most of his audience, the prospect of a testimonial triumphing over a mere recitation. 'It's not easy. Most who return to Matthew Chapter Five, even if they sincerely desire to remake their lives according to Jesus' words, find it difficult to understand what He intended.'

He had been projecting his voice into the auditorium while appearing to speak directly to his stifled volunteer. Now he turned and appealed to the audience. 'What does it mean, when we try to relate those mysterious words to our offices and kitchens and schoolrooms? That's why People Under God's Command is the cure that America needs. Yes—' the man retreated from the stage '—thank you for your input, sir. Because the Three Pillars are a *God-given modern explanation* of that great sermon, and they get results. Line up your life with the Three Pillars, and we guarantee that God will intervene.'

He dropped his voice. 'If you let Him guide you, He will show you a plan for your life more adventurous and purposeful than anything you could conceive of. I stand before you as a man who has been fortunate enough to discover God's plan for *his* life, as have all those in People Under God's Command. And it is not only your own happiness at stake. Think for a moment of the state of the world.'

'Hold on there.' It was the man who had first objected. He stood now, grasping the seat in front of him. 'I find this very cut and dried. Jesus said, "Follow *me*." Where's faith in this? Faith in the blood of Christ? In his wounds?'

'Sir, obedience to the Three Pillars—Chastity, Selflessness, Truth—that obedience to God *constitutes* faith. When you get in your car, you believe it will carry you to the grocery store, church, school. You turn the key in the ignition, you depress the clutch pedal, you move the gearshift and rotate the steering wheel. You obey the rules for driving the car: that's what makes your car go. You obey the Three Pillars: that's what makes your *faith* go. Unfortunately—' he smiled a little, and Rita's stomach twanged '—even if your car's an automatic, your relationship with God is not.'

The audience chuckled.

'Some believe their churches are their chauffeurs. They climb into the back seat and stop paying attention. But only you can

41

drive your car, and if you don't Listen to God, or you don't judge your motives and actions by the Three Pillars, then you're driving without a map, without a steering wheel, even. And worse, you're being guided—without knowing it—by evil men, and they *do* have a map: they want to take you and the whole of America, the civilised world, in fact, on a grand tour behind the Iron Curtain!'

'What about love?' The question came from a woman sitting on the right of the hall. Rita could see her hefty gloved hand waving from the sea of heads.

Hilary Daley snorted.

Leland walked to the side of the stage. 'Please stand, ma'am.'

The woman adjusted the tilt of her emerald-green cloche. 'In the Bible it says God *is* Love, but you don't even mention it. The Golden Rule is, Love thy neighbour as thyself.' She lifted her hands in an overstated shrug.

Leland said, 'People think love is synonymous with kindness. We believe God's Love is far bigger. His Love demands that we become like Him. How do we do that? By obeying the Three Pillars, and by Listening. When we obey God's commands, we're in constant communion with Him. That means He can act through us to touch others and remake the world. *That's* what we call love.'

Simple. If she Listened and obeyed, God's Love would flow through her, and therefore—inevitably—love would flow back to her. Looking at the grinning faces of the kids onstage, Rita reflected that obedience to God would be a lot easier in their company than in her parents'.

The disapproving man in Rita's row, still standing, called out, 'It's impossible to become like God through effort. We need the *blood* of Christ. The Cross of Christ. You'll have to answer to Him sooner or later.'

Leland let silence fall. He stood gazing at the man, his face unreadable. His hands were clasped in front of him; he did not move for almost half a minute. Even before he spoke it was clear to Rita that his wisdom far exceeded that of his questioner.

At last he raised his head and addressed the hall. 'Some folks are eager to claim acquaintance with the Cross of Christ. But they know it only as a symbol. They have not *experienced* it. They have not sacrificed. The Cross *does* call on us to sacrifice: our greed, our desires, our ambitions. You may be wondering, what have *I*—' he thumped his chest '—sacrificed at that wondrous Cross? Well, I brought my youthful sins to the Cross, shameful, saddening episodes—'

He lingered on the words, frowning. Rita felt he still knew the gravity of his sins.

'—and Christ wiped them from my slate. I brought my present self to Christ, and he readied me for His service. I brought my *future* self to Christ, not grasping then that He would mark me forever with a *purifying blaze*—' he thrust his fist towards the audience '—of his sword.'

He dropped his voice. 'The Good Lord caused in me, indeed, what seemed to my young mind a mortal injury, but in fact He *sliced* down my small expectations so He could lead me on to His paths and show me His desires for humanity.'

A mortal injury? What did Leland Swann mean? Had he wrestled with an angel? His torso stripped, half obscured in a sandstorm's ochre twilight, grunting as he bore his weight against—

On the stage, Leland raised his voice. 'How is *your* relationship with God, sir? What sin prevents you from knowing His will?'

The man blew out derisively. He pushed past Rita's knees and clumped away down the aisle.

Leland Swann continued with his speech. 'Imagine a world where every hearth is peaceful and happy.' He gazed into the centre of the audience, his arms outstretched. With his face turned in Rita's direction, it was easy for her to imagine that they were looking right at each other.

'Imagine a world in which no one goes hungry or is oppressed. Where honest men are rewarded, and nations, rather than waging war, work for the betterment of the human race. A world immune to the threat of Communism. This is what we can achieve when we Listen to God. *Individuals* controlled by God.' With each sentence he punched the air. '*Nations* controlled by God. A *world* controlled by God.'

Her fingers quivering, Rita filled eight pages with her sins past and present. Anyone, however clumsy or homely, could act on a thought from God and so alter a country's course! She could!

She was still writing when Leland stood and said, a little wearily, 'I hope you've seen that God is impatient for us to give up our old selves. Our lustful, lying, cheating selves. Our sullen, selfish, demanding selves. Our ambitious, grasping, greedy selves.'

It was at that moment the words came into Rita's head—not rising to the surface like the sins she'd just recorded, but flying in as though thrown, hard:

You will marry that man.

Leland had stopped talking. Rita held her breath. Her childhood God had sat at the far end of a bejewelled throne room, its azure ceiling as distant and hazy as the sky, a marble floor spreading like a continent, accommodating all the souls who had earned the right to stand before Him. The set-up was impressive. But although this God was supposed to have counted every frizzy hair on her head, she had never, until now, felt the heat of His attention.

You will marry that man.

Leland Swann was right: God did have a plan for her life— and he, Leland, was it!

She smiled. How funny, how circular, that he should be the one to help her Listen to God, and also, amazingly, the one God wanted her to marry. It was already happening: God had rewarded her Listening with a promise of love.

Leland let his eyes rest on each section of the audience. 'We must not stop at making ourselves holy. God wants us to build His Kingdom on earth. That means reaching our politicians, our church leaders, our educationalists. There's no time to lose. Our advisers in Vietnam are doing their best to keep Communism at bay, but the threat grows stronger daily. We need people who aren't afraid to venture where God sends them.'

Covering his chin with one hand, he looked down at the stage's bare boards. Rita, thrilled, imagined that he was receiving inspiration from God before their very eyes. But he looked tired, she thought, worn out, as if each word cost him something. She would look after him.

You will marry that man. She didn't need to write it down. She had a sudden, heady vision of herself standing at Leland's shoulder like a First Lady, greeting Presidents and leaders of industry.

Leland said, 'I would like to talk briefly about a down-to-earth detail of our enterprise. Until now, People Under God's Command has been constantly on the move. We have laid our heads down with gratitude in many private homes. We have laid them down even more often in boarding houses and cheap motels. Recently, we received a clear direction from the Almighty that He intends us to acquire permanent accommodation. God wants us to work at the highest levels—to make America truly "a nation under God".'

There was a smattering of applause.

'The Movement's home must be a place where men of stature feel understood. And we'll need space for all the people who feel compelled to turn their lives over to God. That may include some of you here tonight. Perhaps one of *you* will be the conduit for God's generosity—perhaps, during the Listening, one of you received a pertinent command. Don't ignore His promptings, for you never know what wondrous things He has in store for you.'

Rita kept her mother up for an hour while she confessed how she'd snuck into her parents' bedroom—not once, but three times—and stolen four dollar bills from Mrs Daley's purse. She looked her straight in the eye and described how she'd bought, with those bills, two lipsticks, a powder compact and

45

a romance novel. She didn't tell her that she'd read close on twenty romance novels already. Neither could she describe how, whenever she reached The Kiss, her insides buzzed, because Mrs Daley became restless once Rita started on Perfect Chastity. When Rita admitted that she'd taken to stuffing handkerchiefs down her brassiere, she interrupted. 'I'm disappointed in you. I thought we'd brought you up better than that.'

'Mom, I'm going to change, I really am. I *have* been demanding and moody and . . . and not a good person. I want to live for something greater than myself. Look!' She knelt by her mother's armchair and opened her notebook to Selflessness. 'Here. God gave me the idea: *Arrange for some of the church ladies to meet Leland Swann.*'

'Hm. No doubt this is his fun before he gets down to real work. There's no one can claim evangelising's a secure job. You're over-excited.'

Now that I'm perky, Rita thought, she *still* isn't happy. Her mother's next question dismayed her.

'How do you know this isn't another one of your crazes? Why can't you find a steady faith through the church? You were baptised, you graduated from Sunday School.'

'You heard what he said: faith's like a car! You have to get God's map!'

Rita had already been saved twice: once when she was eight, and again six months ago. On neither occasion had it worked. Most recently, she'd hoped the event would release her from the mess of gloomy moods that prevented her from finding a boyfriend or pleasing her parents. Afterwards, though, she understood nothing more about how to be happy, and neither could she convert others, as the preacher said they should in order to complete their own conversions. When she confessed her difficulties to her mother, Hilary Daley told her she relied too much on her feelings.

This was different, though. Leland Swann had set out such an obvious path that she was sure she could follow it. Listening to God and writing His messages in a notebook was a new idea.

Furthermore, God had already placed His seal on her life by promising that she would marry Leland!

Hilary Daley folded her hands together. 'Perhaps it would be more appropriate to invite some of the young folks to meet him. I've said it before, you should make more of the Youth Group. You hang around like a regular wallflower. A few of those young fellows have got their heads screwed on right.'

'Maybe, Mom. But God was specific. He said the older ladies.'

The "young fellows" knew every terrible secret of her childhood—how she had blown her nose too hard in Sunday School and clear gooey strings of mucus had dangled between her hands like a cat's cradle; how she'd once risen from an undersized chair with a dark stain on the back of her primrose-yellow skirt.

She shrugged, faking insouciance. 'He *is* the leader . . . I guess God maybe wants some of the well-connected folks to get to know him. Like Miss Toller.'

'Well . . . I guess I'd appreciate Miss Toller's opinion. But only five or six ladies. She won't want to participate in a convention.'

Although Hilary Daley liked to say that gossip was not among her vices, she did occasionally allow herself the pleasure of discussing Miss Leonora Toller, the seventy-something maiden younger sister of Julius A. Toller, one of St Paul's wealthiest men. *He* had played kissing games with Scott and Zelda Fitzgerald at the Commodore Hotel, and his wife had died in the early 1920s, moments after giving birth to their first child—a son, stillborn. She and the boy were buried in the Toller mausoleum at Summit Cemetery. Church rumours hinted at a mystery illness that would put Julius A. Toller there before many more years elapsed.

Rita suspected her mother had signed up to the church's flower roster in order to claim an acquaintance with Miss Toller, who in summer donated enormous bunches of roses and carnations from the Toller garden, and had a standing order with two city florists to provide all the calla lilies the flower ladies would ever need for their altar and pew arrangements. Uncharacteristically unified, Rita and her mother discussed the Toller's Summit Avenue mansion over many Sunday lunches, ignoring Frank Daley's protests. When he hinted that Rita was planning to gold-dig her way to riches, '. . . parading your scanty wares in front of the old man's still en-*thyoos*-iastic eye!', she refused to take the bait.

Julius Toller's father, the banking tycoon, had built his family home on a plot of land next door to his foremost business competitor. He spent over ninety thousand dollars on the house and its furnishings, and further thousands on the gardens. In 1890 he executed a shareholder's takeover of his neighbour's business, forcing him to sell his home at auction. Mr Toller bought it, had the house demolished with steel wrecking balls, and established a magnificent garden on the land.

Every summer Rita and her mother drove past the property two or three times, admiring the quartzite's pinky red glow, and the steeply angled gables, and discussing what they knew of the mansion's interior. Walk-in closets as long as a driveway, and a trunk room. How wonderful to own a trunk covered in stickers from Venice and Seville and Edinburgh, and to have someone carry it for you! And ten master carvers had worked for six months on the oak pilasters and balustrades in the front hall, and another six months on the chapel, which also boasted hand-made, stained-glass windows in the style of the Pre-Raphaelites. And the gardeners had grown orchids in a greenhouse.

They debated the number of rooms—forty *bedrooms*, or did that number include the other rooms too? They'd heard there was one set aside solely for the development of photographs. Julius Toller was a hobbyist photographer. One of the darker rumours related to his subjects. Not to matter: he was not invited to the coffee morning.

On the day, Leland, accompanied by Gus Driver, arrived at their modest house five minutes after Miss Toller. Rita, who had been distractedly attending to elderly Mrs Flett's lamentations about the damage wreaked on her floribundas by tearaway boys with catapults, was vastly relieved.

Mrs Daley showed him to a seat by the fire. Gus Driver stood by the door. The ladies settled. When Leland spoke, the quiet intimacy of his voice made Rita blink. He leaned his elbows on his knees, and each time he looked her way she had to breathe deep to stay upright.

He went one up—with the greatest respect, he said—on President Kennedy. In fact, he was sure that *this* was what the President had meant: Ask not what your country can do for you, *nor* what you can do for your country. Ask God what *He* would have you do for your country, and for the world. He spoke of housewives who'd found new joy in caring for their families; of hard-bitten business people who now met not to beat down the other but to work out solutions; of parents who had admitted their dishonesties to their children and discovered that the children grew more obedient.

Transformed from a genteel gathering into a small congregation, the women Listened together, Rita happily aware of her head start.

Afterwards, Miss Toller was the first to shake Leland's hand. 'I am a privileged woman. I've wasted that privilege.'

'God only asks that you live under His command from this day.'

'Yes,' she murmured. 'You must come and see my brother.'

'Without a doubt,' said Leland heartily, turning to the other ladies who were pressing towards him.

Ten days later, the news came that Julius A. Toller had signed over deeds to the forty bedrooms, the darkroom, the dining and breakfast rooms, the chapel and his gardens to People Under God's Command. Rita, overjoyed, waited for Leland to call and express his gratitude. He did not. But Hilary Daley picked up information from the flower committee: the Tollers had moved from the mansion to a much smaller home, leaving behind most of the furnishings. The gardeners would continue in their jobs, paid for by Miss Toller, who planned to visit daily in a supervisory role.

At Lambert's Secretarial Academy, Rita produced multiple variants on qiuck vrown foxes that hymped over lazy dofs. She put off asking her parents whether she could work full-time for the Movement, but Frank Daley saw through her.

'Lend an ear to this,' he said one morning, lowering his newspaper and peering over his coffee. 'You want to know from whence our Mr Swann springs?'

'Sure.' In the old days she would have shrugged, curled her lip.

'Wee-eell, now, what does it say?' Ostentatious bobbing of his head up and down the columns. 'Ahem. It seems a humble collection of Christians had for some time *gal*-li-vanted through various of our northern states, *pro*selytising, incited by an aged foreign gentleman who, despite his de facto leadership—' he glanced up, imitating academic concern '—I'm interpreting, naturally; the original text is somewhat graceless—where was I? Despite his leadership . . . claimed *not* to be their leader . . . it does seem that the group was on the verge of indigence—starvation, indeed—when our hero *man*-ifested . . .'

In the long pause, Rita crumbled a charred toast crust on to her plate. *You will marry him*, she reminded herself. In time, she would be his confidante, would know every little detail about his life, his childhood, as he would want to know all about hers—but she had to distract herself, pressing sharp crumbs between her fingertips, so as not to grab the newspaper from her father's hands.

'Well, maybe I'll take this along today. TV sales are middling slow, what with half the population of Minnesota developing calluses on their knees.'

He made as if to stuff the paper into his black briefcase.

'Dad—'

'Oh, you'd like it? You're *in*terested?' He bent down, his face close to hers. 'You think, maybe, he'll have some second-, third-string men might be satisfied with you?'

She slammed both hands on to the table and shot up, knocking over her chair.

'Dear me.' He smirked at his wife. 'I've said it before, these quicksilver conversions often prove short-lived.'

After the bathroom door closed behind him, Rita settled to the rest of the story.

In 1956 Karol Sadowski, a Polish immigrant, had visited with his followers the small town of Stort, Wisconsin, and there attended a church service presided over by the Reverend Swann. The Reverend's son Leland, obeying a divine prompt, invited them home for lunch, during which his spiritual wisdom surprised even his father and mother. He recognised the Three Pillars as the cure America and the world desperately needed. Impressed, the group accepted young Leland as its new leader, and thereafter grew as never before.

The next day Rita's pride was saved by a mimeographed letter. It began 'Dear Colleague Under God', and although it did not mention her central role in securing the Movement's new home it did invite her to become

> . . . a person thoroughly under God's command, who discovers the joys and riches of such a life. There are many rooms in this mansion, as in our Father's, and you are welcome to serve in the capacity best suited to your talents.

An enrolment form was enclosed, and a third sheet, stapled to the back of the letter, set out the Required Standards of Dress for Ladies. Blue jeans inappropriate. Skirt hemlines should be below the knee. Long hair to be tied back.

Mr Daley insisted that she should finish her diploma at Lambert's before beginning what he called 'this hamster-wheel ascent to the heavens', and so it was three more weeks until Rita packed her single, unstickered suitcase. Her mother oversaw the packing with a sceptical eye. 'Don't fold your blouses through the centre. And best clean that hairbrush, or your room-mate will think you're slovenly.'

When she said goodbye, Mrs Daley stood straight and silent as a knitting needle. Rita moved tentatively forward. Her mother lifted her hands to the shoulders of Rita's taupe wool jacket and smoothed away a wrinkle. Made reckless by this gesture, Rita leaned her forehead into the curve of her mother's neck.

'Mom? Do you think I'm doing the right thing?'

'Well. Hasn't God "commanded" it? Time will tell.'

But God, despite showing His new, promising face, had never hugged her. And now her mother did, bestowing a quick, fierce embrace. 'Well, you'd better get along,' she said, stepping away from Rita's pull. 'Get your coat on. No point in lengthy goodbyes. It's not like you're moving to China. Come on now, that's enough. Anyone'd think we were sending you away, rather'n it was your choice.'

Frank Daley was waiting on the stoop, rattling his car keys and humming a jig. Suddenly, Rita longed for her parents to clasp one another, necks bent, cheeks pressed hard against ears, hair. She shuffled out of the doorway so they could surrender to each other and weep, muttering their love.

'Don't sit up late,' her mother called. 'Remember to smooth your eyebrows.' She stepped back into the hallway and closed the door.

After he'd turned the key in the ignition, her father said, 'This is strange for your mom. Think she had it in mind that if you moved away you'd be round the corner, the two of you sharing recipes.'

He had never said anything so revealing, but Rita could not give it her attention. A new life awaited her.

2

Like most of the residences lining the bluff along Summit Avenue, the Toller mansion stood close to the boulevard, separated from the sidewalk by a strip of lawn and a black iron fence. Rita stood by the car, looking up at the mansion's high chimneys and ivy-covered façade. From his window, her father called, 'Don't let 'em steal your soul!' She turned back to him and raised a hand.

He drove away before she reached the foot of the driveway. The enormous entry arch stood like a dark and gaping mouth before her. A large banner was slung across its upper section: in white letters on a purple background it read, 'People Under God's Command' and, underneath, 'Making a new tomorrow!'

Wasn't tomorrow always new? Rita wondered. She gazed at the clustered pillars. The mansion wouldn't belong to the Movement if not for her. Hundreds of people, perhaps whole nations, would be redeemed by her small action, exactly as Leland had promised. It made a fitting start for the story of his future wife.

She lugged her suitcase up the drive, her arms charged with joy. Beneath the arch she rang the ship's bell, expecting Leland himself to open the great doors, tender in his declarations of gratitude and admiration, his face flushed with happiness . . . 'With you, I am whole,' he whispered by her cheek.

She rang again, and turned sideways a little, as if surveying the sprouting bulbs on the lawn. When she heard a door open she prepared what she hoped was a winsome smile, tilting her head.

'You aimin' to stand there all morning?' A stout old woman peered out. She wore a shin-length white apron. Her grey hair was drawn into a tight bun approached by a path of bare scalp across her crown. 'Let's hear your name.'

'Sorry. I'm Rita Daley. I have the letter—' She unzipped her bag, digging into it.

The woman produced a clipboard and ran her forefinger down it. 'You're not on my list. You girls who think you can sashay in, meet Mr Swann, how d'you do and be my beau. You get on home and give some consideration to the Three Pillars, namely, Truth and Chastity.'

'No, truly!' Rita pushed back against the closing door. 'Mr Swann met Miss Leonora Toller at my parents' home.'

The old woman's eyes narrowed. 'Over a month ago, that was. You've heard stories flying around.'

'Please—my folks wouldn't let me come right away. I've passed my diploma, at Lambert's—at the secretarial academy.' She bent again to her bag, ready to tip its contents out on to the granite porch.

'Don't start that. I don't want more undergarments littering the garden. Tell me your name again—Daley?'

'Yes. Rita.'

The woman flicked over the pages on her clipboard, tutting. 'Lists aren't my strong point. Here you are. Come in, then. I'm Martha Sands.' She clumped away across the entrance hall.

Rita, weak with relief, scuttled after, dragging her suitcase and staring around at the oak cherubims and gleaming marble fireplace. When Martha Sands stopped suddenly, Rita almost ran into her.

'You're of legal age?' She spoke over her shoulder.

'Excuse me?'

'You have a right to operate under your own steam, and so forth?'

'I'm eighteen. Nineteen soon. My parents signed the form.'

'Hmph.' She continued across the hall, muttering. 'Some girls don't have the slightest acquaintance with truth, let alone the *perfect* variety.'

They climbed a wide staircase that doubled back on itself. At the first landing they looked down two corridors carpeted in a burgundy and green paisley design. Windows, surrounded by deep stone sills, were set into the far wall of each corridor. Every door was shut.

'Courtyard,' said Martha Sands, nodding towards the windows. 'This panelling's all oak. Some of the mouldings are cherry. Plenty of dusting. Secretariat's down there. The corridor beyond it, that's Leland Swann's suite. Three staircases altogether. The other two're smaller.' She turned up the next flight. 'Bedrooms this floor. Except myself and some of the seniors on the second. You girls at the back.'

They walked down a long corridor. Rita swapped her suitcase from one hand to the other. Around the next corner the doors were narrower. Several were open, and as she passed she peeked in at twin beds and bare boards. Her room, towards the end of the hallway, was the same. White-painted tongue-and-groove panelling to waist height, then a faded paper of twisting forget-me-nots. By the window the paper was torn, showing brown scrim beneath. A rag rug marked the narrow space between two single beds. There was one white bureau and a free-standing closet.

'Used to be servants' quarters. Up in the attic, too, but they're unoccupied. You girls share a bathroom. You got feminine requirements, come and see me. I keep a stock in my room. Applications for clothing funds, travel, go to the Secretariat.'

'A Secretariat?'

'That's what Cynthia Chant calls it. Highfalutin name. You should know, if you're a stenographer.'

'I could offer my services.'

'Don't bother. You'll be kept busy enough. You know how to make hospital corners?'

'No.'

'I'll show you. A well-made bed sets you up for the day.'

Together they stripped and remade one of the beds, Martha Sands commanding, 'Now a sharp diagonal fold—pull and tuck. Pull.' After the last tuck she straightened, breathing hoarsely, and clutched the small of her back with both hands.

'Oh, you can see the roses from here.' Rita had not yet

thrown off her 'charming' approach. She leaned against the single window's frame.

Mrs Sands said, 'Bedrooms at the front, you can see the cupola of the Capitol. The Falls too. No room-mate for you yet. Now the other bed, show me.'

Rita yanked the sheets off and tried to flick them back over the mattress as efficiently as Mrs Sands. 'I'm sure I'll have a room-mate soon,' she said. 'It's vital that People Under God's Command flourish—vital for America.'

After several tries, Mrs Sands approved her bed-making and turned to leave. Rita thought she would linger in her room, readying herself to work with Leland. But the older woman called over her shoulder, 'Come along. No lollygagging. You can change out of that fine suit later.'

'Where are we going?'

'The kitchen. You're on vegetable detail first. Laundry for you tomorrow, if my memory serves me.'

Everything was in God's plan, Rita assured herself. Vegetables and laundry: she was not disheartened. She followed Mrs Sands' broad back down the stairs. 'Were you at the play too? *The Divine Instruction*?'

'Here in St Paul? I probably took your money at the door.'

'Oh, you were already acquainted with Mr Swann?'

'I've travelled with this group the last fourteen years.' Mrs Sands paused by a mirror and whipped a white handkerchief out of her apron pocket. She rubbed at the ornate gilt frame.

'But I thought it was new—I mean, under Leland Swann.'

'I'll tell you,' said Mrs Sands, still squinting at the frame, 'this group has been propelled by the good Lord since Leland Swann was knee-high to a grasshopper. Mr Sadowski endowed him with a grave responsibility when he made him his successor.'

'He's . . . he's *inspiring*. I'm sure Mr Sadowski chose right.'

They reached the ground floor. Mrs Sands said quietly, 'You won't hear much of Karol Sadowski, bless his soul. He was truly God's man. No doolallying about. No loud talk. It was in his silence God came to him.' She glanced at the carved ceiling and

56

made a little 'poh' noise with her lips. Then she looked right at Rita. 'If you're sincerely interested—'

'Oh yes.'

'—there's a tract. '

'Yes,' Rita said again, but Mrs Sands walked on without further explanation.

The kitchen was the largest unsanctified space Rita had ever seen, outside of her high school gymnasium. It was starkly clean, but smelt of burnt dust. Large cream tiles covered the floor. She glanced behind her, afraid her shoes would leave dirty marks.

'Refurbished down to the last skewer, care of Mr Toller's donations,' said Martha Sands. 'The old kitchen was a real antique.'

At one end of the room a gleaming stainless-steel counter ran in an unbroken L, partly enclosing three Formica-topped tables. Sheets hanging from wooden poles screened off another section. From behind them came hammering and the screech of an electric saw. Over by the windows three girls about Rita's age were sitting on stools around a table, chopping carrots and talking. Rita recognised Margot, who looked ordinary now, relaxed. She wondered whether Margot had truly enjoyed telling her story to a hall full of strangers. Martha Sands nodded in the direction of the noise. 'A dishwasher. We're praying for a rapid installation. Construction work is not conducive to food hygiene.'

She led Rita over to a tiled archway and gestured into a pantry the size of Mrs Daley's kitchen. Cans of Crisco and boxes of Pillsbury cake mix were stacked on nearby shelves.

'It's a motley assortment,' she said. 'When God leads people to donate food, He doesn't tend to provide them with a shopping list. Pay attention now.' She propped a hand on her knee and bent to open a cupboard door. 'I can't stand to have you girls always asking me where such and such is. These pans here? They're for meat only.'

'Sure,' said Rita, shrilling in her eagerness. 'I'm a quick

learner. And, my mom is on Miss Toller's flower roster at our church—'

One of the chopping women swivelled on her stool and stared.

'—and in my very first Listening I was led to host a coffee morning, to introduce some of the ladies to Mr Swann.'

The woman, skinny and pale, was still staring. Margot and the third chopper had noticed too. Margot winked at Rita. Mrs Sands' lips had all but disappeared. Her arms were folded high on her bosom.

Rita subsided. 'Do I start now?' she asked, scuffing the tiles with her toe. 'With those girls over there?'

Martha Sands leaned in close. She smelled of swampy violets. 'This kitchen—it's a one-in-a-million opportunity. It may seem like an oversized bunch of chores, but it's sacred work. Usually, a man tells you being in a kitchen's sacred work, you have to watch out. But in this case it's true. Down here's the heart of the house. We can't make a peaceful world, have people caring for each other, if we don't have peaceful homes. And I don't mean being nice. We've got to be the best we can, *care* the best we can—'

'Martha, are you talking the ear off another one of my workers?'

The skinny, staring woman had sidled up next to them, her expression falsely respectful. She shrank into herself, one arm wrapped across her body, the other hand repeatedly tucking wisps of her lank blonde ponytail behind her ear.

'Patsy. Rita Daley. Rita, this is Patsy Chant, head of your Work Team. It's rude to interrupt, Patsy.'

'It's only we're so darned busy with these carrots.'

'All in good time. There's a few more pans waiting to be introduced.'

It was not what Rita was expecting, and Martha seemed to know it. Her parting words, when she at last delivered her into the circle of carrot-choppers, were, 'It's a challenge, no mistaking it. God's looking to see what you're made of.'

Rita looked at the heap of carrots on the table. It must be a test, she thought. Once she'd proved herself in the kitchen, Leland would come and find her.

'Hi, Rita!' cried Margot. 'What a surprise.' She pulled out another stool.

The third woman introduced herself as Joan Jessom. A recent arrival, she immediately told Rita that her brother was working for the Military Assistance Advisor Group in Vietnam. While she talked, she rubbed at clown-patches of psoriasis on her cheeks.

'Don't *pick*, Joan,' Patsy snapped.

Margot's and Joan's smiles were candid and merry, with none of the studied appraisal Rita was used to. Everyone counts here, they seemed to say.

'So!' said Patsy. 'What were you bragging about back there?'

'Don't mind Patsy,' Margot said. 'She likes bossing us around. Talk and chop, that's what we do.'

Patsy said, 'I've been with the Movement longer'n I can remember—'

'Her mom's here too,' Margot said into Rita's ear.

'So!' Patsy said again. 'How did *you* meet the Movement?'

They looked at Rita, knives hovering. She would know, soon, the hunger for stories provoked by menial tasks.

'This is because of *me*,' she wanted to say, 'this grand house', but Margot's and Joan's openness, and Martha's speech about caring, made her pause. 'My mom took me to *The Divine Instruction*,' she said. 'I think she thought I should reform!'

The others grinned, and she knew she had said the right thing.

She was part of a twelve-person intake that week. By the end of the month, Martha Sands had eight all-female Work Teams to roster. The teams rotated around food preparation, serving, cleaning, polishing, laundry and flower arranging, but before the women began their daily work they met for Ladies' Sharing.

When the gong rang out at 7 a.m., they gathered in the library, having already completed an early Listening.

Men's Sharing met at the same time in the old smoking room. Afterwards, the men's sole housekeeping duty was to operate the new dishwasher. They sang and joked while they carried the heavy trays of dishes and glasses back and forth, the rowdier among them flicking tea towels at each other. They could be called on to lug crates of food into the cellar, or to shovel the last snowfalls from the front walk, but for most of the day they disappeared to read the newspapers and discuss strategy.

On Sunday mornings the Work Teams met separately, in rooms dotted around the mansion. Rita was surprised that the Movement did not make more use of the Tollers' chapel, but Patsy explained that it was costly to heat, and anyway, one could hear God more easily without the interference of tradition.

On Rita's first Sunday, her team met in the Lavender Room on the second floor. She dreaded getting lost in the unfamiliar corridors, but followed Margot's dark curls and arrived seconds after her. Martha Sands' measured gaze met Rita as she entered. She was sitting on the edge of a brocade sofa, her spine perfectly straight, and she looked no more welcoming than when she had opened the front door.

Cynthia Chant, reclining in an armchair, sang out, 'Good morning girls!' Pearlised balls the size of jawbreakers hung from her earlobes. She was a buxom version of pale Patsy, her cheeks long and rounded, her eyes a clear blue. She had spoken to Ladies' Sharing on Rita's second morning. 'Imagine your conscience is a forest pond. Over the years you've fouled it up and now it's scummy and green. Your work with us will clear it out, and as you live closer and closer to the Three Pillars, God's plan for your life will be revealed to you. The way to kill unhappiness and discontent is to serve others. Think for them, not yourself. How can you help *them* change? How can you answer *their* needs?'

Now she said, 'Margot. Your Great-aunt's sore throat has

turned into a cold. You should take some chicken soup up to her later.'

'Sure, Mrs Chant.' Margot pulled Rita down next to her on to the brocade sofa, and whispered, 'I know Great-aunt Alice better'n my own parents. My dad's out in Austin, Texas, looking after an oil company. And my mom's a drunk. Salvation skipped a generation, you could say.'

'But at the play, you said you'd forgiven your mom?'

Margot laughed. 'Forgiving someone means more than saying sorry. Sure, I forgave her, but you mean I called her a drunk? She still is. Me saying sorry didn't change that.'

Patsy hurried in, closely followed by Joan Jessom. 'Good morning, Mrs Sands. Good morning, Mom.'

'Take a seat, girls!' cried Cynthia Chant. 'Or a piano stool! Everyone comfy? Now, new girls, on a Sunday we always begin with a prayer.' She launched straight in, closing her eyes. 'Dear God, please show us your Will. Help us to grow ever more strongly towards your light. Amen.'

By the time Rita caught on, the prayer was half over.

There was no more talking. She flicked to the back of her notebook, the same one in which she'd written her eight-page self-assessment after *The Divine Instruction*. Since the successful coffee morning, her entries had been sparse, but here were notes on a slew of letters she had yet to write: apologies to girls at school whom she'd resented; teachers she'd hated; Mr Lambert of the Secretarial Academy, because once she'd seen a forthcoming test paper upside down on his desk and had failed to alert him. One to the St Paul Tram Company in which she needed to enclose a cheque for $16.50, that being the amount she'd cheated them of.

She looked around at the others, who were balancing their notebooks on their knees, their pen tips touching the paper, their eyes fixed on a point beyond, as though God might direct the very movements of their fingers. Joan Jessom sat across from her, plump and wordlessly noisy. She inhaled gustily and breathed out through her nose, twirled a brown strand of hair, then snatched her fingers away to scratch at her wrist. She looked up.

Rita's heart thumped. In the heavy silence, the meeting of their eyes seemed unlawful. She turned her head away. Already, she knew that Listening to God should be a bodiless activity, engaging only the mind, soul and heart. This was a problem for her. So far, the Listenings she'd attempted alone in her room had been beset with thoughts of Leland. Of his height, well over six feet. Of the way he pushed his fingers backwards through his hair after turning from a conversation. He rarely laughed, but she knew that after their marriage he would be affectionate and teasing. The day before, she had seen him stride up to a group of visiting teachers and shake their hands. He stood a head taller than any of them. One man said something that made him smile. Then he laughed, and the whole group laughed with him. After a moment he cocked an eyebrow and spoke, undercutting their laughter with his deep voice. Rita couldn't hear his words, but their tone resonated through her body. The teachers sobered, leaning towards him. She took a deep, wavering breath and returned to her work as warmed and fizzy as if he had turned his smile on her.

She could not tell whether any of the other girls were in love with Leland, but his influence was clear. If he was known to be studying, the women went about their work in a contemplative mood, a gloss of holiness shimmering off the ironing boards and preserving pans. When he was in strategy meetings, Patsy was almost autocratic, and Rita became unusually decisive and resourceful. When congressmen and church leaders visited, she felt as though she was dancing on top of an enormous gush of air, lifted so high that she could see how all the individual actions of God-led people would bring heaven to earth.

Her daydreams always began with a coincidental meeting in the garden, or in a sunlit, isolated corridor, and quickly moved to hot embraces and declarations of love. But here in the Centre she could not lie under the quilt fingering her nipples. She could not practice kissing her palm with 'yielding' lips and the tip of her tongue. If her thoughts wandered in that direction, a scowling Cynthia Chant materialised, brandishing the Pillar of Perfect Chastity like a battering ram, Rita's mother shoring up its other end.

In the dark, though, Rita revisited until she fell asleep the beginning of their wedding night: herself in white lace, waiting in the upper room of a stone tower in the countryside; a window looking down on a garden where fireflies played; her unselfconscious murmur, 'Aren't they pretty?', at which Leland, who had entered noiselessly, would wrap his arms around her and kiss the back of her neck.

She longed to be kissed on the back of her neck.

Cynthia Chant cleared her throat.

Rita closed her eyes. At first she heard only her blood pumping through her ears, and then she remembered to search herself for bad feelings. From Ladies' Sharing, she had picked up the convention of writing as if taking dictation from a no-nonsense, terse God. She wrote, *Be humble. Do not envy Patsy. You only think she is bossy because you are oversensitive. Be disciplined. Don't complain when the work is hard. Stop indulging in daydreams of Leland Swann.* (This in shorthand.) *Do not be glad to be away from your parents. Be thankful for them. Don't be scared or shy. Shyness is self-indulgent and does nothing for the other person.* (A surreptitiously scratching Joan had given a testimonial on that very point in yesterday's Sharing.)

She thought again of her parents. Hadn't her father sometimes boasted of sneaking a customer away from a junior clerk and pocketing the commission on a colour TV? Catching herself in this criticism, she scribbled, *You should apologise to your parents for not appreciating them. Do your best and be your best. You could have found this spirit when you were living at home. It is not their fault you didn't.*

She felt strengthened by God's severity.

Martha Sands was the first to address the group. She announced that she did not consider anything that had passed through her head in the last fifteen minutes worth sharing, but that she would read aloud a small essay she had been working on. Cynthia Chant's eyebrows lifted a fraction. Martha began in a low monotone, hunched over a loose sheet of paper she unfolded from her notebook.

'What God Means To Me. He gives me courage when I'm afraid. He makes me care for people when I would gossip about them. He helps me understand them when I would be self-righteous. He makes me tell them the truth when I would be soft with them.'

Rita remembered her first day, and Martha's curt instructions.

'He gives me victory in temptation, strength when I'm tired and a fire in my soul when I lack conviction. He tells me that this Movement is my family, my friends and my responsibility until I die.' She looked up, expressionless.

Rita's eyes were wet. Martha's words had startled her senses. She did not think to fix in her mind any specific thing that Martha had said—she was left only with an impression that the older woman enjoyed great intimacy with God. When her turn came to share, she omitted the daydreaming and Patsy's bossiness. As soon as she finished, Cynthia Chant said, 'Dear me, Rita, you seem to be aiming for immediate sainthood. It *is* sometimes useful to list our failings, and what we imagine might be their remedies, but what *God* says to us can have a somewhat more . . . *unexpected* quality.'

I know about unexpected, Rita wanted to say. *He promised me I'd marry Leland! And you're only in this mansion because of me.* But now Cynthia Chant had as good as told her that she was not in communion with God. Homesickness, acute and unexpected, struck her. No one had hugged her in days.

The door opened. There was Leland, only a couple of feet away. The air pressure seemed to change.

'Leland!' exclaimed Cynthia. 'How delightful! Do sit down. Henry said you might come and meet Patsy's new members. Over here's Joan. We've persuaded her to join the Chorus—she sings like an angel, a true soprano. And Rita.'

'Joan. Rita.' Leland's eyes skidded away from her. 'Do you have any questions? We believe in democracy.'

They laughed.

He seems stiff with us, Rita thought. *Maybe he's shy, deep down.* She could relate to that.

Joan, rubbing nervously at her neck, said, 'I've noticed we don't talk about God, unless we're Sharing.'

'Why would God want us to talk *about* Him, Joan, when we can talk *with* Him? When we're busy feeling spiritual, it's too easy to ignore Him. Better that we dedicate our energies to living a sin-free life, so God feels welcome.'

He looked straight at her while he spoke. Rita resolved to ask a question.

Joan said, 'Surely telling stories of Jesus—I mean, He shows us God in human form.'

'Ah. The man from Galilee. Yes, Joan, I sacrificed my former self at the Cross of Christ. So have you. His spirit is now incarnate in us. That's what we turn to when we ask for direction.'

'But—' Margot pushed a hand through her glossy curls, sceptical '—okay, I'm not new, but anyway—if His spirit is incarnate in us, why is Listening like trying to hear a voice outside myself? Why don't we talk about Listening to the voice *within* us?'

Leland took a deep, slow breath, leaning both elbows on his knees. 'Margot, I'll only answer these questions once. If we let this kind of speculation bother us, we'll crowd out God. His spirit opens our hearts and minds to the divine voice. Imagining that the voice of God resides within us is dangerous. We tend to pass off our miserable desires as His Own.'

But God's Promise had come from outside of her, Rita was sure. She had almost caught the timbre of it, as if it had been spoken aloud. She smiled. What would Leland say if she leapt up now and proclaimed, 'God said I would marry you! He promised me your love if I obeyed Him!' For he could not know, otherwise he would give her a signal.

'But what about the Eucharist?' Joan asked anxiously.

Leland was impassive for a few moments. 'That's the crux of it, Joan,' he said at last. 'That's why the Movement is the world's only hope. For almost two thousand years people have knelt at the altar rail, crunching those little wafers. Multitudes of priests and ministers are closet alcoholics from drinking leftover wine. What I'm about to tell you I won't say outside the Centre, because it's liable to be misunderstood. We want the churches to know we're on their side.' He paused. 'God has told me not to observe Communion. He said, *Do my will now. In the present. That will be your act of communion—the moment-to-moment obedience and the attitude of Listening.* The act of Listening is the new Communion. And how much more meaningful it is, that we leave it full of intent, knowing God's will for us.'

'But—' Joan had not surrendered her original concern '—how will we know God if we don't talk about Him?'

'Joan.' Leland's expression turned inward for a moment, as if he needed to find more patience. 'God knows the heart and mind of every individual. For better or for worse, He bestowed free will upon us, and what *that* means is, if *we* do not will it, *His* will cannot rule.'

For better or worse? Did that mean Leland didn't think God should have given humans free will?

'Um . . .' Rita tried to look intelligent. Perky. 'How often should we expect Him to speak to us? I mean, I know there's Listening in the morning, and we should kind of Listen all day, right, but—'

'Wait on Him,' Leland said, getting up from his chair. 'Wait on Him.'

'Um—?'

He turned back, at last fixing her with his gaze. 'You are a bundle of affectations. You need to forget about what others think of you. Get to work. God's work. Abandon yourself to it.'

And then he had gone. She did not know where to look. *A bundle of affectations*: he had pinned her down exactly. She furtively pinched the bridge of her nose while Cynthia Chant made concluding comments.

After they rose, Margot patted Rita's shoulder. 'Don't cry. He diagnoses all of us sooner or later. You'll get over it. It's not personal. We're out to change the world.'

Martha Sands walked beside her to the kitchen. '"Wait on Him,"' she quoted. 'Karol Sadowski said that.' She sounded angry, but her face was blank. 'No cause for you to gape like an Aunt Sally. Get along—don't you have chores?'

Rita scurried away, feeling like a chased hen. Later, during lunch, she recalled the tract Martha had told her about on her first day, and reminded herself to ask for it. Maybe it would give her the boost towards God that she needed.

3

By the end of Rita's third week she could make up ten guest beds an hour, every fold and tuck accompanied by the reassuring hum of divine approval, but when she tripped over the Movement's many Don'ts she came down with a thump. The Don'ts were conveyed to her in Ladies' Sharing and in 'friendly chats' with Cynthia Chant or Martha Sands: Don't draw attention to yourself. Don't give 'private looks' to people. Don't sigh, complain, or show tiredness. Don't leave water droplets around the sink after refilling vases; don't leave the undersides of tables undusted. Et cetera. As far as housekeeping went, the list was infinite. God was the most demanding of supervisors, and impossible to fool.

She tried to inoculate herself against criticism with rigorous Listening. Comparing herself to the Three Pillars was a constantly fruitful exercise, but since Cynthia Chant had put her right she'd known that her Listening was missing a divine quality.

Gratitude for being here. A chance to serve. Part of a revolutionary movement. Daily, something on that theme. Sometimes, if she'd done well the day before, she truly did feel grateful and excited. *Talk to Patsy about getting those pickles laid up.* Always some task to keep in mind. *Don't pretend you're perfect. Be honest with Margot about your irritation. Don't give in to envy or ambition.*

In Ladies' Sharing, she listened attentively when a new girl asked, 'When you get an idea during Listening, how do you know it's God?'

Cynthia Chant smiled from the platform. 'Does anyone care to answer that?'

Patsy stuck up her hand, twisting in her seat to address the girl. 'Measure it against the Three Pillars. If it's not Truthful, Chaste or Selfless, it isn't God.'

'Also it helps if you've prayed first,' said another woman. 'Asked the Lord to guide you. Then the Devil can't get in your head.'

There was a moment's laden silence. People Under God's Command had already won, it said. All that remained was for the rest of the world to wake up to the cure. It seemed distasteful to invoke the Devil in such victorious circumstances.

Rita fidgeted. If she was brave enough to declare her longing for God to give her a voice-in-the-storm, writing-on-the-wall indication of how she could become good enough to marry Leland, Cynthia Chant and the other seniors would only recommend humility and patience.

'I don't know,' the girl said. 'It all seems kind of vague.'

Cynthia Chant said, 'You need a good dose of action. Action and *service*.' She smiled triumphantly. 'Service *in* action!'

The meeting dismissed, Martha Sands elbowed Rita as she turned down the corridor towards the kitchen. 'Saw you paying attention during that theological to-and-fro. Got something here might provide food for thought. And someone who requires your care. You do an about-turn and come to the front door.'

'I'm s'posed to start on the vegetables before breakfast.'

'People come first, not potatoes. Here, you asked for this.' From her capacious pocket Martha dug out a thin grey booklet, mimeographed, its staples rusting. The cover bore a line drawing of three columns supporting an upside-down saucer. Rita took it cautiously between two fingers. It was the tract Martha had talked about, but decrepit and tatty, unlikely to harbour the secret of how to get close to God.

She tried to be politely interested. 'Are those the Three Pillars?'

Martha looked pleased. 'So you'd think. Put it away now, it's not for everyone to see.'

Cheerful voices filtered towards them as they neared the entrance hall. One of the young men was talking to a tall, smiling woman in a navy coat and a pert pillbox hat around which her honey-gold hair shone. She held white gloves in one hand with casual grace.

The man turned. 'Morning, Mrs Sands.' He nodded at Rita. 'Morning. I've been keeping our new arrival company. She's all fired up to go.'

'You get along now,' Martha said, frowning. 'Your new room-mate,' she said to Rita. 'Betty Wallace. Betty, Rita Daley. Betty's making up your Work Team to five. Now I'll leave you two to get acquainted. I've got to go decide on those new towel sets.'

Rita led Betty up the wide and curving staircase, self-consciously instructing her on the significance of the furnishings. 'The vase in that alcove was given by the Minneapolis Chamber of Commerce in gratitude for a speech Mr Swann made to them . . . this Persian rug was donated by Freddy Markham, the industrial tycoon.'

'Uh huh,' said Betty, and, 'I see,' but once they reached Rita's room she became more expansive. 'What charming wallpaper! This is wonderful. You've taken the bed by the window?'

'Yes.'

'Perfect. Morning light disturbs my sleep. But I guess we rise early for Listening? You must be an old hand, you can give me some tips.' She threw her case on the other bed and flung her arms up. 'This is peachy! I'm glad we're room-mates.'

Rita smiled awkwardly. Betty could not be genuine: it was the kind of thing someone like her said to ease her way through life. She had a scar, a small irregular crater, interrupting the translucent curve of her forehead.

'Looking at my third eye?'

'I beg your pardon?'

'My last boyfriend was a natural history professor. He called it my pineal eye. Reptiles have them. They're not like real eyes, they can't see through them.' When she spoke her hands circled, waved, plucked, pointed. 'It's only an old chickenpox scar. Don't pay me too much attention, I'm kinda jittery, you know, new place and all.'

70

The morning sunlight slid along her brow and jaw, picking out another dark line.

'What about that one?' Rita pointed to the corresponding place on her own chin.

Betty rubbed it. 'It's . . . old. Nothing.' Her hands dropped to her sides and her smile vanished. She turned away.

Discomfited, Rita fiddled with Martha Sands' tract, still in her hand. What a nuisance. She would have to read the thing and perhaps talk to Martha about it. Furthermore, it seemed from what Martha had said that she wasn't supposed to have it, and she didn't want to get in trouble. She tucked the tract underneath some Movement magazines on the shelf below her nightstand.

'Were you and the professor . . . serious?'

'Let's see if I can get through this without wailing.' Betty took a deep breath, grabbing a pink angora sweater from her case. 'Until three weeks ago, I thought he'd propose. But then a friend told me she'd seen him holding an umbrella over another girl's head. It was very small—the umbrella. He was underneath it too. When I asked him, he didn't try to pretend. I think he wanted to get away from me. Me and my pineal eye.' She squashed the sweater into a drawer.

'It's not noticeable.'

'You noticed. Don't worry, it doesn't bother me.'

Rita watched her put away more clothes. 'How did you hear about the Movement?'

'Oh, I've been scared out of my wits ever since they found those missiles in Cuba. If it's so easy for us to get to the edge of a nuclear war, what if we trip over it next time? When I heard Leland Swann talk about making a new world, I knew I had to join up. Any more hangers? Can you double some of your skirts?'

'Sure. You have a lot of clothes.'

'Borrow anything. We could pin the hems.' Betty held a lilac dress to Rita's shoulders, exclaiming over its effect with her dark colouring.

'Have you had many boyfriends?'

'One or two.' Betty caught her eye. 'Oh. Perfect Truth, right? Three. I went steady for a while with a boy in high school. Then in the summer after graduation I saw a pianist—he played lunchtime sessions in a department store. I loved the music, but he bored me.' She sighed, fingering a strap on her suitcase. Then she seemed to recall herself, flashing a smile at Rita. 'After that I didn't date. But Mr Natural History came along. For a good long while he seemed like The One. And now I'm here! I want better things to do than fret over the whereabouts of my future husband.'

Rita could not ask Betty whether she was a virgin, but she was curious. The pulp novels had not provided her with any significant information, and the frayed and nervous girls she had counted as her friends were no more sophisticated.

She made room on the narrow dresser for Betty's hairbrush and jars of cream. 'We should go down for breakfast,' she said. 'You can't hear the gong round this side of the house. Alice Maniaty's probably found a place for you in the seating plan.'

Like all the other young women in the Centre, Rita was one of a set trio that moved to a new table for every meal, proceeding around the dining room as if in a slow barn dance, welcomed by each table's resident trio of young men and pair of chaperones. Appropriate conversation covered US and world news, gleaned by the men during their daily study of the newspapers and *Life* magazine. The men always sat along the side of the table that faced into the room; therefore, for seven meals out of nine, the women's view was of their dining companions and the embossed wallpaper. Every three days, inasmuch as they could see past the heads of their male counterparts, they could observe the occupants of the Long Table for two consecutive meals. At the Long Table, Leland sat with his back to a row of windows that looked out on to the terrace where narcissi now bloomed in tall urns. He was flanked on either side by the senior men, like Jesus and his disciples in Da Vinci's Last Supper.

At this breakfast, Rita knew, she would be facing the Long Table. If she and Betty hotfooted it, she might be able to nab the seat closest to Leland's direct line of sight. But by the time they scuttled through the carved oak doors of the dining room everyone else had sat down. They checked the noticeboard, and at Betty's table Rita introduced her to its two chaperones in suitable tones of respect: Cynthia Chant—'Mrs Chant is Patsy's mother, Patsy's head of our Work Team'—and Henry Allerton, the Chorus Director, who sat hunched over his plate of eggs and hot biscuits.

Rita did not meet Mr Allerton's caustic eye. She had attended several Chorus rehearsals on the new stage in the great hall, hardly opening her mouth at first, so intimidated was she by Allerton's barked commands: 'Smile, don't grin! You look like deranged skulls! Heads up! Heads *up*! Arms relaxed!' He made them laugh, though, when he pranced below them, wailing and yowling in imitation of The Chiffons or The Crystals. '*Ron de doo de ron, lee-oorve, doobie, dum dum loodle oo-oh.*' Gradually, she had begun to derive a peaceful pleasure from getting it right, pretending the crown of her head was suspended from the ceiling by an invisible thread, letting her arms hang by her sides, slightly turning out her toes. She learned to emphasise the last consonant in every word, breathing the soft extra syllable into the end of it. Enunciation was paramount. If the audience missed the message, they may as well be at home watching Ed Sullivan.

> *God's pee-ople are cer-tain(a) people,*
> *Sure of their-rr way in Li-fe(h)*
> *Find your p-ath(a), the one he's or-rr-dered(a)*
> *And farewell trou-ble and stri-fe(h) . . .*

But just when Rita was getting comfortable she held a wrong note a second too long, yodelling a flat 'A' into the corners of the great hall. Henry Allerton identified her immediately and instructed her to leave; she descended the steps of the stage under the silent gaze of the remaining, tuneful Chorus members, letting the door slam behind her. Later, Mrs Chant had chastised her for that show of temper.

One of the young men at Mrs Chant's table shot up from his chair and ran around to pull out Betty's. Betty thanked him and sat down next to Margot, who grinned at her and said, 'We're going to be teammates. Hope you brought hand cream—we're peeling four sackfuls of potatoes this morning.'

Cynthia Chant said, 'Mr Allerton's been telling us about plans for the new production. The sequel to *The Divine Instruction*. He's setting up a playwriting committee. He'll compose the music himself, naturally. Rita, aren't your breakfast companions waiting?'

Betty's voice rang out before she had a chance to reply. 'That's so neat! I love theatre—I studied it for a little while.'

Typical, that the most beautiful girl in the Centre would have an easy entrée into the Movement's higher spheres while she had been excommunicated from the choir and was stuck in the kitchen. Rita walked to the buffet where the duty Work Team was beginning to clear away the hotplates, and served herself some cool scrambled eggs on woody slices of toast. At her table she had to sit between the two other women, and the man opposite obstructed her view of Leland. She tried to shift her chair to the right, but jostled Nadine Strassman, who teased her: 'Elegance, dear Rita!'

Nadine, sleek and dark-haired, was well known in the Centre because a part of her pre-Movement life, a published volume of poetry, had received a good review from a professor in *The New Yorker*. Cynthia Chant, a literature graduate, had read the collection and pronounced it 'Not nihilistic, not bitter, not pretentious'.

'Good morning, Rita.' Gus Driver, the ex-pilot who had confessed to lustful thoughts and played Frederick in *The Divine Instruction*, greeted her. 'It's not like you to be late.'

'I was showing around my new room-mate.'

'Mr Driver?' Nadine raised her chin towards him. 'Tell me,

what do you think of the anti-Communist movement in this country?'

Excused, Rita concentrated on her food. For a moment, she didn't realise she'd been spoken to by the man who blocked her view of Leland. 'What? I mean, pardon me?'

'I've been working on some—um, some sayings. I could do with another opinion?' He spoke as if his vowels had got lost in a cavern at the entrance to his throat. Even though it wasn't yet nine, he had a five o'clock shadow, and on his right cheekbone the hard brown embroidery of a scabbed graze.

'I used to be a fireman. Thing is, Leland's told us to come up with vivid sayings—type of thing to grab hold of people's imaginations.' He laid down his knife and fork, placing his fists on the table. 'Give this a go: "I used to quench fires in people's homes. Now I help God light fires in people's hearts"?'

'Good. It's short. That's good.'

'Right. Is "quench" all right? I had "put out" before—you know, "I used to put out fires".'

'Yes. I like "quench".'

'Right then.' He took his fists off the table and ate two mouthfuls. 'I've got another for you. It's a bit lengthy. But might be good for speeches. Here goes: "There's chaos in a burning building, like the moral chaos that wants to bring us to destruction. If a fireman ignores the basic rules of firefighting, people lose their lives. If we ignore *God's* rules, we lose our souls."'

'I like it,' she said. How clever of Leland, knowing how to bring out the best in people. When she was married, it would be part of her job to help men like this feel at ease.

'Where are you from?' she asked.

'New Zealand. Down by Australia.'

'I've heard of it.'

'Great.' He grinned. 'Sorry, should have introduced myself. I'm Bill.' He pointed at his nametag. 'Haven't been called William since my mum caught me tucking daddy-long-legs into her bed. I saw you in Chorus practice—I got chucked out too, the one after you.'

'I'm Rita.'

'Good as gold, Rita.' His eyes—brown, dark-lashed—were level with hers. He was shorter than Leland. Definitely not as handsome.

He waved a hand at the room. 'This is posh, eh? Chandeliers. White tablecloths every meal. Silver.'

'It's the Toller family silver.' Leland had instructed them to become accustomed to elegance, so they would not be overwhelmed when mixing with ambassadors and statesmen.

'Money flows upwards sure as rivers to the sea. It's a far cry from where I grew up. Tell you what, I'd give a few fingers to've been with the group when it was hard yakker, travelling round the place, bit of adventure.'

'Me too.' Leland next to her in a Greyhound, confiding his hopes and dreams, his hand lying on his thigh, only inches from hers. She sat next to the window; he bent over her lap to point out a full moon rising above silhouetted poplars . . .

Gus Driver said, 'Bill, listen, you know Miss Toller? I met her by the tennis courts. She gave me a letter for Leland.' He twisted and pulled a creased cream envelope from his trouser pocket. Rita glimpsed spiky black handwriting, less graceful than she'd imagined Leonora Toller's would be.

'You seeing him later?'

'Yup. I'll hand it over.'

Nonchalantly, Rita straightened, and caught sight of Leland digging a finger around the inside of his tie. Her breath stuck in her throat. She wanted to own those moments.

Gus Driver winked at her. 'Sore neck?'

'Oh . . . no.' She turned to check on her new room-mate. Betty was talking, but had toned herself down, keeping her hands below her shoulders. Even so, her surplus energy—her 'zip', as Hilary Daley would have said—threatened to burst out of the walls.

Happy anyway were the words that came to Rita. Betty would be happy even if she'd never met the Movement. You weren't supposed to be happy anyway. Everyone outside People

Under God's Command needed fixing: that was the unspoken rule. Besides, individual happiness was too small a goal.

'Thing is—' Bill chewed fast, swallowed '—I thought a fireman's life was exciting, but it's nothing on this.' He chuckled, the skin around his eyes crinkling. 'You and me, we're ordinary types, but we're in on a blow-your-britches secret, excuse my French, but, y'know, this . . . time bomb of a cure that'll capture the imagination of every soul on this earth. And we're in on it almost from the start. I reckon it'll be the ride of our lives.'

His face blazed, and Rita caught in a flash what it meant to forget yourself in the exultation of changing the world. They grinned at each other.

A shred of wilted lettuce lay on Bill's white shirt-cuff. Without thinking, she stretched across and picked it off. Even before she had retracted her arm, she was smothered with embarrassment. She sucked nervously on her lip, staring at the gold rim on her plate. At both ends of the table, the conversation paused.

Maintain some class, said her mother. *For goodness' sake.*

'How did you get here, Bill?'

'Cargo boat. Auckland, Hawai'i, Los Angeles.'

'I mean, the Movement. How did you meet People Under God's Command?'

'Whoo. It's a long one. I've been practising, but . . .'

Sixty to ninety seconds: that was the recommended length for conversion stories. Like a good commercial, Henry Allerton had said.

'Right. Here goes. I was a hard-bitten bloke, out to protect my own back. Loved to talk about what the men at the top were doing wrong—I ran out of willing listeners, so I had to buy a ticket to America.'

Rita smiled. Self-deprecating humour was expected in conversion stories.

'Wasn't long before I was as cynical about America as I'd been about New Zealand. I prided myself on being well informed, but my point was to show how right *I* was about how wrong everyone and everything *else* was. No one could say a thing without me pulling out some fact or figure to show I knew better.'

He took a gulp of water. 'I met Leland at a bus station in Chicago. He was parked down the other end of the bench from me. Two or three more blokes standing around, talking about Korea, Russia, Spain, all that. They said something that made me snort. Leland heard. Stared at me. I thought he was looking for a fight. Then he said, "Are you going to be another fly feeding on the stinking mess we're in, or part of cleaning it up? Are your children going to be proud of their father, or as cynical about you as you are about every other fellow?"'

'I wish I'd been there.'

'Yes. He's one out of the box all right.'

Leland's questions to Bill had been a Challenge. The Challenge was the Movement's key conversion tool, prompting people to focus on their sin and its dreadful magnitude. A successful Challenge depended on an accurate Diagnosis, like the 'bundle of affectations' Leland had seen in Rita. Alice Maniaty, Margot's great-aunt, had given a talk on Leland's Diagnoses, beginning with his Challenge to her: 'Why are you clinging to your shyness when the world needs you to fling open your heart?' To Cynthia Chant's late husband he'd said, 'Your wandering eye is destroying your wife. Are you man enough to change?' And to Martha Sands: 'You like to tell others what to do. Will you let God tell you what to do?'

Why, Rita wondered, had Leland's Diagnosis not transformed her? Here she was, surrounded by cheery, galvanised men and women who quivered with readiness to take on the world at Leland's signal. Sometimes she could wrap herself up in the excitement and roll along with it—she did not doubt her happiness then. Afterwards, though, she felt blurred at the edges, as if something essential had flown out of her body and would not return until she fell asleep.

One of the chaperones, an elderly man with a mole under his eye, asked, 'What did you say when he Challenged you?'

'I didn't say anything,' said Bill. 'My mind went blank. I tell you, I felt like a dork—I wanted to get out of there. Then he said, "What is the sin that stands between you and God's plan for your life?" It was news to me that God had a plan. So I told him. I hated a man. I wanted to defend myself—I was convinced the other bloke was wrong!—but he said, "God can free you from that hatred." In fact, when I Listened later, God told me, *Hate is only a seductive, self-righteous form of selfishness.* I asked Leland, "Who are you blokes, anyway?" He said, "We're ordinary men remaking the world." I couldn't stop hating then and there, but I was curious. I changed my ticket and went with them.'

'Who was the man you hated?' Rita asked.

'Chief of my station.'

'The fire house?'

'Fire station, yes.'

'Do you still hate him?'

He paused. 'No. I forgave him. He'd blamed me—we were on a call. A man died. My best mate. Big fire, in a shop. We got stuck out on our own. Second floor. A backdraught got him. The boss blamed it on me. Some of the other blokes believed him.'

'Was it your fault?'

'Not in my book. I reckon another witness would've backed me up. There was an enquiry.'

'An en—? Oh, an *inquiry.*'

'You say to-may-toe, I say to-mah-to. Anyhow, that's my story. What's yours?'

'I went to a performance of *The Divine Instruction.* Afterwards I apologised to my mother. For stealing money. And lying.'

Bill beamed at her as if her story had the power to change millions. 'Men right here in this town need to hear that. If people could get honest with themselves and each other, America's industries would see productivity go into orbit. You never know, we might get a man up there too, to keep the Russians company!' He leaned across the table. 'What we need is for heads of industry and unions to get together away from the racket of the factory floors and red tape, with people who can inspire them to honesty and . . . and a willingness to take on a new, generous spirit, and I'm not only talking about getting a fair day's wage for a fair day's work, though that's part of it—'

'You at your socialism again?' Gus nudged Bill's elbow.

'It's more than socialism. Socialism thinks we can do without God, thinks men will naturally treat other men fairly when they're living in a fairer system. I don't agree. What's natural to us isn't fairness, it's greed and envy and spite. We need God to lift us above ourselves, so we can let go of our self-concern—whatever it is stopping us from caring properly for the other person.'

Nadine said, 'You're quite the orator, Bill.'

He looked bashful.

'No, go on,' she said.

He looked around the table. 'Men and women need people who don't just talk God on Sunday, but who'll tell them He cares about their work and their lives. If we can inspire those people, we'll get workers working with their whole hearts, and owners who care for their employees. Then America really *will* be proofed against Communism. The other day a factory owner I'm in touch with came to one of our performances. He used to employ forty-five folk, before his factory burnt down. Right this minute he's knocking on doors, getting written promises of new jobs for his people. He rings me every evening with updates.'

Gus said, 'That's great, but it doesn't prove that People Under God's Command should have a special focus on labour—I know that's your beef. It could look an awful lot like Communism to some people.'

Bill nodded. 'Thing is, I don't mean to criticise. We have trouble in New Zealand too. But America's got labour woes enough to keep the Movement busy for years: strikes in Californian construction, troubles in aerospace, disputes at missile sites, the auto guys, the docks, the railroads. The bosses reckon the unions are too powerful, and the unionists reckon the bosses are unjust. If they could see that at the heart of every war or strike there's people who aren't right with God—I know what you're thinking, Gus, but imagine a union where every man was thinking how he could help every other man. Not much room for Red agents there.'

'That's great, Bill,' said Nadine.

They sat in silence for a few moments.

Across the dining room, the men at the Long Table had risen. Leland strode across to Betty's table and stood talking to Henry Allerton, counting off points on one hand. As far as Rita knew, everyone in the dining room had a story like Bill's: they had been bitter, dishonest, dissatisfied, promiscuous, self-indulgent or aimless before meeting People Under God's Command, and after their first Listenings and consequent repentance became energetic world-changers, untouched by doubt, immediately able to convert their families, colleagues, enemies and friends.

Leland walked towards them. Bill, noticing Rita's stare, looked over his shoulder. His hand flew to his jacket pocket where he had stowed Leonora Toller's letter.

'Bill. You all set for this afternoon?'

'I'm your man.'

Leland's hair was newly cut—who had touched those glossy strands? Pale strips of uncovered scalp showed up over his ears. He greeted one of the chaperones, a nervous man with a narrow face.

'I'll come up later, Leland—I have to write—'

'That's fine, take your time. We have enough to be going on with.'

Going on with what? No wonder Bill was so eager: it must be much more fun remaking the world if you were in touch with the nitty-gritty.

'Well. Onward and upward.' Leland walked away.

Gus Driver caught Bill's eye.

'Yup. I'll give it to him later.'

'Swell.'

They rose from the table.

'Pleasure to meet you, Rita.'

'Sure.'

She watched Leland disappear into the corridor. Behind him, Betty was walking and laughing with Margot. Henry Allerton and Cynthia Chant were standing in a corner, looking at Betty. Henry lowered his eyebrows and said something to Cynthia. She nodded soberly.

Rita hurried towards the kitchen, glad she was not the focus of their disapproval. Yet she wondered: maybe it would be better to be judged than to be so easily ignored.

4

In line with the tradition for the Movement's recently joined women, Betty gave a 'Welcome Talk' in Ladies' Sharing, so named even though the audience, rather than the speaker, did the welcoming. She stood to one side of the pine lectern, pale, her shoulders back and chin tilted as though she'd spent hours balancing books on her head. A deep rosy flush crept above her collar and up her neck.

The previous afternoon, as they dug the sprouting eyes out of winter potatoes, she'd asked Rita what other women had said in their testimonials. Rita recited what she could remember: Margot's drug-taking; Patsy's childhood shoplifting; an abundance of lies to parents and teachers; widespread bitterness towards relatives; the cheating of bus and tram companies and the IRS, as well as of employers, movie houses and any number of other public institutions; even a couple of unspecified carnal acts with boyfriends. Betty listened avidly but afterwards said little, as if she had not found any reassuring precedent for what she needed to admit.

A drop of perspiration quivered on her upper lip. Suddenly, she spoke. 'This Movement has saved me from a life of selfish boredom.' She caught Rita's eye and grinned.

Go on Betty, Rita thought. *It can't be that bad.*

Betty seemed to relax. She'd grown up, she said, believing she was entitled to attention. Boys called round with bouquets and chocolates, but she complained to her girlfriends—comically, wryly, because she didn't want them to think her a sourpuss— that none interested her. 'What I meant was, they didn't flatter me enough. This is mortifying . . . I was nice to them, because I didn't want to seem stuck up, but in my heart I took those boys for granted. I didn't see a single one of them as worthy of my care and attention.' She glanced towards the large bay window blurred by rain. 'My high opinion of myself gave me the idea of being a film star. But my pop insisted I get educated, so I started a theatre major. It was high school all over again, but with beer and cigarettes, and I got to be even more callous about how other people felt. What I want to tell you—'

She dropped her head and stared at the platform. 'I know you're all kind, wonderful people . . .'

Here it comes, Rita thought. *What's she done that's so awful?*

Betty touched the tip of her tongue to her lips. There was an expectant silence.

'I . . . I changed, after a while. I decided it wasn't for me and dropped out. I wanted someone who'd make me feel, you know, needed and . . .' She breathed unsteadily for a few moments. 'Someone who'd make me feel good. I did *believe* in love, but I thought it should come to me by rights.' Her voice broke. She sniffed hard, cleared her throat and continued, speaking quickly. 'Looking for a husband, to put it bluntly. Anyway, then *The Divine Instruction* came to my hometown and, this'll sound corny, but something inside me said, This is it. This is how more love could come into the world. So—I'm thrilled to be here.'

She stepped down from the platform, her face pink. Rita was sure she had not divulged whatever it was she had been afraid to confess.

Cynthia Chant stood. 'Thank you, Betty. We must all remember, if you're hunting for a man, you're not in God's plan!'

Betty, breathing shallowly, took her seat beside Rita. Rita checked the room: no one else was looking in their direction. Women often cried or berated themselves in Ladies' Sharing, and Betty's forthright admission that she had been chasing down a husband would be taken as more than enough reason for shame, especially given her easy beauty. It was the unspoken rule in the Centre that God's intentions regarding marriage would be transmitted through the men alone. A man in receipt

84

of such an instruction would then check with his most trusted friends and some of the senior men. These confidants would in turn check back with God, thereby ensuring all proposals were divinely planned. The proposal's recipient and *her* advisors should bear this in mind when deciding (with Listening) whether to accept or refuse. Only last week a girl from New York had left the Centre two hours after refusing a man who'd once let a whole trayful of stacked dinner plates topple and crash while he paused to discuss a baseball score. She had dismissed him so quickly and firmly that it was felt she'd followed her own will, not God's.

Cynthia Chant said, 'Now, Miss Alice Maniaty has met with Mr Henry Allerton to discuss preparations for our next theatrical production, and will update us.'

Margot's great-aunt walked to the platform, rustling some papers. She exchanged one pair of spectacles for another, and held on to the sides of the lectern like a tiny preacher. 'Come summer, Mr Allerton and Mr Swann will begin a tour of the country, meeting with mayors, congressmen and senators, and building our support. They are . . .' She paused, holding her notes up to her eyes. 'They're building a force from within. We will be—I'm sorry, this got a little smudged—oh, we'll be *unstoppable*. America will be swept by a transforming wave. Beatniks will find new purpose. God *will* return to our schools!'

The women applauded.

'As a result of these travels, Mr Allerton will not be consistently available, so he's appointed little old me as head of the Production Planning Committee. Bill Harper has volunteered to advise us on pertinent issues of the day. Our very own published poet Nadine Strassman will also join us. *And*—' she twinkled in Betty's direction '—I think we might have found the theatrical expertise we need in Mr Allerton's absence!'

She stepped down, and the meeting concluded. Rita turned to Betty, curious whether she would choose to confide, in private, what she could not bring herself to reveal in her Welcome Talk, but Alice Maniaty swooped in and took her by the elbow: 'You're my girl!'

'I don't know,' Betty said. 'I dropped out after a couple of semesters.'

Alice Maniaty continued as though Betty had not spoken. 'We're aiming to get the script ready in time for rehearsals to start near the beginning of next year, and to launch a national tour next summer. We're meeting for the first time this afternoon, in the old drawing room cattycorner from the Secretariat. But we won't get started for real until later. You'll be all settled in by then.'

Rita felt a familiar, queasy ache. To work across the way from the Secretariat, around the corner from Leland's suite!

The Secretariat was the base for the Secretarial Corps, a group of four women managed by Cynthia Chant who could be called upon at any time of the day or night to take dictation and type up letters and memos. Margot had stopped near it a few days before and pointed down the hallway of the southeast wing. 'That door facing us at the end? That's Leland's den. The senior men meet in there for briefings.' From where they had stood holding their buckets and mops they could see the leadlight windows set deep into the stone wall. On the other side of the hallway were four doors: the Secretariat and, Margot said, Leland's bedroom, dressing room and personal study. Margot liked the den best of all the rooms in the Centre. A continuous dais ran around its perimeter. Built-in bookshelves covered four of its eight walls, alternating with tall, arched windows; beneath each of these a high-backed chair faced into the room.

'Let's take a look,' Rita suggested. 'Leland's out, I heard.'

Margot chuckled. 'You've got more chutzpah than I thought. Hear that typing? Cynthia Chant's got more eyes than Medusa had snakes. I'll tell you something, though,' she said, setting off towards the north wing where they were to clean skirting boards. 'That room was in a ruinous state when we arrived. So dark my Great-aunt Alice fell off the dais and sprained her ankle. Mr Toller had nailed boards up over the windows. It smelled loathsome—sour.'

His darkroom, Rita thought.

'Bill Harper and Leland found evidence of his wrongdoings inside an old desk. Leland undertook a prayer vigil to cleanse the room of filth and evil. Prayed non-stop in there for a whole night and day. No nourishment or water; down on his knees on the bare boards.'

Rita had taken in the information with a shiver. This man, with his extraordinarily intimate knowledge of God—he would keep her safe from the darkness.

That evening, while they cold-creamed their faces and prepared their clothes for the next day, Betty gushed about the Production Planning Committee's first meeting.

'We didn't get into any real plotting, but I can tell it'll be the opposite of college. There everyone yak-yak-yakked and tried to get one up on everyone else, and I was the same, though I made nice about it. But here we start off with Listening and then share.' She jumped up from the rag rug where she'd knelt, using her mattress as an ersatz ironing board. 'Ow! Look, my kneecaps have little dents! Alice sure has her work cut out taking notes. She forgets to, half the time. She's crazy about Shakespeare. "Our Bard of the human heart." That would've driven me wild a couple of years ago, but now I know it doesn't matter, because God has a plan.'

She seemed to have recovered from her speech in Ladies' Sharing.

Betty said Bill Harper had been so eager to contribute that when she and Nadine and Alice arrived in the drawing room they found him already sitting at the table. Bill had said straight out that he didn't know the first thing about putting on a play— putting *out* fires was his specialty. 'Then,' Betty said, laughing, 'Bill said that "Production Planning Committee" sounds like we should be wearing fur hats in Moscow. Alice got worried, so we Listened and renamed it "The Playwriting Committee".'

They had Listened too, Betty said, for clues about how they should proceed. God had told Alice only to enhance the existing *Divine Instruction*, because they 'didn't have the noodles' to write a whole new play. Nadine wasn't sure about that, but thought the language should be clear. Bill said it was all-important to touch the heart of the working man.

'What did you hear in your Listening?' Rita asked.

'I couldn't stop thinking, Make something amazing!' Betty threw her arms above her head. 'Something that'll show them God is beautiful and glorious as well as being . . . you know, the right way to live. Trouble is, I didn't have a single concrete thought about how to do that.'

She didn't often talk about God. Rita assumed, though, that her Listenings weren't fraught with doubt; that her 'happy anyway' quality meant she must always have been close to God, just like some kids got on well with their parents.

Betty plopped on to her bed, sweeping aside a sewing kit. *'The Answer* could turn out a pretty straight play. *The Divine Instruction* wasn't exactly naturalistic, with Gus interrupting the story like that. As if Joyce and her family were nothing but fodder for the message. I want to bring it up, but I'm kind of scared of what Henry Allerton might say. Though I guess it's wrong to predict other folks' reactions, isn't it—like Margot said, it means you're denying God's ability to inspire them anew? Oh—I don't mean Mr *Allerton* needs to be inspired anew. Have you seen *Our Town*? Thornton Wilder?'

'No. I haven't.' Rita did not like being a spectator of Betty's new, exciting role. She said, 'Did I happen to tell you about the Promise God gave me after I saw *The Divine Instruction*?'

'No! What? Tell me!'

Rita hesitated for show, but could not wait long before describing the voice that had flown into her head.

'Omigosh! Imagine! There's a few girls here I might not believe if they told me that—not that they'd lie, but . . . you know what I mean, you're so level-headed.' Betty hugged Rita, keeping hold of her hand when she released her. 'I can't believe it! Why didn't you tell me before? Are you in love?'

Rita smiled shyly at the floor. 'I guess so—it's hard to say. I think God's planted love in my heart.'

'It's so romantic! And you're perfect for him, the warmest, kindest person . . . I can just see you making all those important people feel welcome. Wow! Are you going to tell the others?'

A few days earlier, Margot had invited the Work Team back to her room after a silver-polishing session and confessed that Gus Driver might have been entertaining 'some more than friendly' thoughts about her. 'I didn't think of him until he popped into my head during Listening yesterday,' she said. 'But he arrived there with a kind of a zing, and suddenly I felt convinced that . . . that he might *like* me.'

They had Listened together, perched on the narrow beds. Afterwards, no one had a definite 'No' for Margot, though Patsy advised her to stay out of Gus's way (none of them mentioned his previous problem with lustful thoughts), and practical Joan said to make certain it wasn't a coincidental attack of dyspepsia.

'I'm not sure,' Rita said now. 'Leland's not any old body. If word got round—'

'Tell you what, I'll pray.' Betty closed her eyes, lifting her face to the ceiling. 'Dear God, thank you for choosing my darling friend Rita for Leland, because her presence at his side will help the Movement. We pray that you will guide us in how to live wisely with this knowledge. Amen.'

As soon as Betty ended her effusions, bestowing more hugs and moving away to fetch her toothbrush, an obscure dejection spread through Rita. She shook it off, reminding herself that moodiness was her downfall. She had to believe in the Promise, and not surrender to doubt just because she sometimes felt blue.

Later that week, she climbed the grand staircase to the corner of Leland's wing and approached the rattle of typewriters in the corner office. The smell of typewriter ink transported her back to the classrooms of Lambert's Secretarial Academy. Peering around the door, she saw Cynthia Chant and Alice Maniaty seated at facing desks, flicking their noses back and forth between piles of notes and their machines: the latest Olivettis, she noted. Underneath the window, a long trestle table supported boxes of envelopes and batches of files. Three stacked trays bore the labels 'DONATIONS RECEIVED', 'CCs ACKNOWLEDGEMENTS' and 'NEWSLETTER REQUESTS'.

Cynthia Chant swivelled on her chair. 'Rita. Yes?'

'Mrs Chant, I . . . I have a secretarial diploma from Lambert's—my shorthand's pretty good and I can type sixty-five words a minute.'

'Did you Listen before you came to speak to me?'

'The idea came to me over lunch. Leland says God can speak to you any time.'

'Your idea, not God's, and not mine.'

'But sometimes you must have a rush on?'

'Have you subscribed to a fourth Pillar? The Pillar of Perfect Obstinacy?' Cynthia Chant made a rueful moue at Alice.

'Mrs Chant, I don't mean to be impertinent, but please excuse me . . . Miss Maniaty, Betty told me you have a tough job taking minutes and running the meeting at the same time. Could I help you?'

'I'm sure Miss Maniaty is perfectly capable—' Cynthia Chant interrupted herself, looking distractedly over Rita's shoulder. 'Leonora! . . . What a pleasant surprise.'

Rita stepped aside, but Leonora Toller caught her eye and smiled. 'Rita dear, I'm so pleased to see you. How's life with People Under God's Command?' She was wearing a long brown skirt, muddy around the hem, an untucked man's dress-shirt, sleeves rolled halfway to the elbow and a wide-brimmed straw hat. A white envelope was in her hand.

'It's great, Miss Toller. It's very rewarding.' She nodded enthusiastically. 'How're you?'

'I'm well, thank you. And grateful that the Movement puts up with my attentions to the garden. I don't know what I'd do with myself if I couldn't dig my fingers into this soil.'

Cynthia Chant gave a breathy, dismissive little laugh.

'The daffodils by the back gates are splendid right now,' the older woman continued. 'Have you seen them? I guess you don't get out often. Cynthia, I'd like to make an appointment with Mr Swann. For tomorrow, or later this week? He's in town, isn't he?'

'Um . . .' Cynthia Chant peered anxiously down the corridor towards Leland's rooms. 'I'll get his appointment book. Come into the drawing room—' She took Leonora Toller by the elbow and hustled her away.

Alice Maniaty stood and came towards the doorway. 'It never occurred to me to ask for help with the meetings! I did pray about my workload, and I Listened.' She giggled, grabbing Rita's arm. 'Complained to the high heavens, asked Him, "How much do you expect me to do? I'm a little old lady!" Guess what He said back? He said, "I expect you to do as much as I care to give you."' She dropped Rita's arm, looking worried.

'Maybe He's letting you rest a little. So you can use your greater talents. Betty said you like William Shakespeare.'

'Yes! The Bard! "Heap of wrath, foul indigested lump!"'

Rita drew back, startled.

'He's a tremendous help if you want to cuss without cussing. Though you have to ask forgiveness straight after, naturally.' She winked.

But if you know cussing's wrong, Rita thought, isn't it doubly wrong to cuss and then expect God to forgive you? It struck her that Alice Maniaty took the Three Pillars more lightly than she did. Maybe she was like Betty—happy *anyway*, comfortable enough in her own skin that she could line herself up next to the Pillars without getting flattened underneath them.

The door opened across the hallway, and Cynthia Chant ushered Leonora Toller out. 'I'm sincerely sorry, Leonora.'

'I don't understand! This constant prevarication . . .'

'No. Ours is not to reason why. You can leave that with me.' Cynthia took the letter from her, and Rita caught a flash of the same black, spiky writing that had graced the letter Bill Harper had undertaken to deliver. 'I'll see you to the door.'

Leonora compressed her lips. 'Goodbye, Rita dear. I'll tell your mother we chatted.'

Cynthia Chant turned the older woman towards the staircase. 'Come point out those daffodils to me.'

'*Such* a tricky situation,' said Alice, looking after them. She turned back. 'I appreciate your offer, Rita. You'll be an ornament to the committee. Now, we'll begin the real work in the summer. Who's your team leader? Patsy? I'll fix it up with her. I believe Bill Harper has a few ideas for the plot already, although naturally every element will have to pass the taste of our esteemed choral director.'

'Naturally,' Rita echoed, but she shuddered at the thought of having to work with Henry Allerton. At least she would be closer to Leland.

Towards the end of the month, Martha Sands asked Patsy's team to wait at the tables during a senator's visit. She gathered them beforehand in the Jericho Room, taking over Patsy's role and paying no mind to her hurt pride. She reminded them of the standards they applied at every meal. 'Don't call attention to yourselves. Silver service, good as he'd get in the White House. Serve from the right, collect from the left, and don't any of you ever, ever stack dirty plates near the diners.'

To Rita, known for her steadiness, she gave the task of carrying a tray of gravy boats to the Long Table. Rita aimed to settle the first a quarter of the way up the white linen cloth. As she leaned in, Henry Allerton said to the senator, 'More people than you'd think give credence to the idea the Domino Theory's a parlour game.'

The second gravy boat needed to be somewhere near the senator. Rita stepped into the gap between Leland and Bill Harper, preparing to put it down.

'Trouble is,' the senator said, 'McCarthy's self-indulgence on personal fronts, if you get my meaning, and his loose mouth— well, we lost a good deal of support over it. We'd be in a far better position now if he'd had your discipline, Leland. Shame the Movement didn't rise up a decade ago.'

Waiting until he'd finished speaking, Rita spaced out the remaining gravy boats on the tray and slid one hand further underneath it. As she did so, Bill Harper reached over and lifted the lid on the roast potatoes, waving it above the space she intended for the second gravy boat. She leaned sideways—over Leland, Martha later pointed out—to find another spot for it, swaying her hips so she wouldn't brush his arm with her behind. Under the tray, her hand slipped, and two gravy boats crashed on to the table, swamping Bill's plate and sloshing brown lakes around the dishes of peas and potatoes. A third landed in Leland's lap.

Horrified, Rita scooped up the gravy boat and tried to sweep some of the gravy away with her hand.

'Get *back*,' he hissed, leaping to his feet. 'Get away.'

He must have been in some pain all right, Patsy mused later. What control.

He was forced to go upstairs and change his trousers, missing the first twenty minutes of dinner, and Gus Driver, on the senator's left, while an adequate conversationalist, was not Leland.

In Ladies' Sharing the next morning Rita was called upon to explain herself. There was no such thing as an *accidental* accident, said Cynthia Chant. Rita could hardly have chosen a worse moment. The senator's good opinion was worth a great deal, bearing in mind that Leland's talents could take him at least as far as Congress.

All day, she kept busy to the point of frenzy: checked every skirting board for dust, took down and cleaned the Lavender Room curtains, hunted for the missing coffee jugs. In the evening she broke a vase and let a serving platter go through to the dining room with gravy on its rim.

'You can slow down now,' Betty said when they were in the bathroom after dinner. 'God doesn't care how fast you brush your teeth.'

'He's not having much luck with me.'

'Well hey, I should tell you what happened to *me* this morning.' Betty threw her toothbrush into her bag. 'At the time I thought it was stupid, a hoot, but now I'm furious, and . . . and I don't know what.'

They returned to their bedroom. Betty described how Cynthia Chant and Henry Allerton had invited her into the Garden Parlour after breakfast. When she reported Henry Allerton's opening comments—'Miss Wallace, we find ourselves perplexed by your demeanour'—Rita slipped under her quilt and pulled her knees up to her chest, relieved that she was not the only one in trouble.

Betty had asked them what, specifically, they would like her to do differently. Henry had made a few vague comments, and then said he'd leave the rest to Mrs Chant.

After the door closed behind him, Cynthia covered Betty's hand with her own. It's a woman's duty and honour, she said, to be an *in*-spiration, not a *tempt*-ation.

Betty said that's what she already tried for.

Perfect Chastity, said Mrs Chant—that is, purity of mind and body—will inspire men to be and do their best, *and* will attract the right sort of man to you. Remember, Betty, it's *chaste*, not chase! She had laughed, her throat taut.

Betty had asked again how they would have her change her appearance. Mrs Chant talked about Betty's butter-coloured hair, twisted into a chignon at the base of her neck. There is something insidious and *showy* about it in that spot, she had said. It beguiles. Arrange it on the crown of your head and it suggests a different, more demure sort of woman.

And then there was the matter of her posture.

'You know how I sit like this?' Betty said, plopping on to her bed and crossing her legs, her knees to one side, one calf lying along the other. 'I mean, for gosh sakes, the First *Lady* sits this way. But when I told Mrs Chant that, she said I'd been trained to cause men *mental distress*. The way I see it, it's not my fault if men think like that. And cross my heart, I haven't set out to

94

attract a man for . . . in a long time.' She stood and walked to the window. 'I feel like I've eaten a bushel of snakes. I've tried Listening, but I can only hear Mrs Chant. Does that mean God agrees with them? Are they right about me?' Tears broke apart her words.

'Maybe,' Rita said, clutching her soles. 'I mean, could you be acting sexy without knowing it?'

Betty cackled. 'Subconscious come-hither eyes? Why doesn't God change me, then?' She sighed. 'I guess the Movement'd say today was God's way of telling me to change. Maybe I should dye my hair *brown* or something. Oh, sorry, Rita. You know what I mean, though.' She yanked back the faded curtain. 'I could punch out this glass.'

She doesn't know her luck, Rita thought. Betty should have been reassuring *her*, retelling the whole gravy farce as a comic chapter in Leland's courtship. All the most intoxicating pulp romances had the hero getting mad at the heroine before he succumbed to her charms.

Betty turned from the window. 'If I start triple-guessing myself, I'll go cuckoo.'

'Uh-huh.'

'Oh, I'm sorry, you must think I brought your day up so I could talk about myself!' She bounced on to Rita's bed. 'Now, you might hate me for saying this, but when Leland zoomed up out of his seat yesterday, I had to laugh. I've never seen anyone move so fast. Don't worry, God knows what He's doing. There's always His Promise, right?'

Rita shrugged again. Unless efficiency, shorthand and typing counted, it wasn't as though she had a bunch of charms that would win Leland over.

She began to set her alarm for 5.30, struggling into wakefulness and switching on the bedside lamp against Betty's croaked protests. Collecting her notebook and pen from the nightstand, she plumped her pillow and shut her eyes tight. Her heightened fervour did not help: she could only dredge up the usual lists of owed correspondence and household tasks. One morning she threw her notebook and pen on to the quilt and rocked her head back against the wall. Through her frustration, she heard Betty's even breathing, and for want of anything better to do she followed it up and down with her own breath for a minute or two. Then she noticed her beating heart, and the light from the lamp glowing through her eyelids, and a voice inside her, low and quiet. 'Oh. Oh. Oh.'

Her sinuses began to tingle; she thought she might cry. She hoped the voice was God's, but knew that it was not. It seemed to be lodged in her diaphragm, dark and heavy. It had been there a long time. How could she be unhappy when she was part of a world-changing force and, despite her fumbles and disasters, in receipt of God's Promise that she would marry Leland?

Her eyes flicked open—a tiny liquid sound of soft tissues separating. She looked at her hair-curlers on top of the dresser, at the brass surround of the light switch. Was this what the romance novels meant by 'pining'? Was she pining for Leland? But she knew this had nothing to do with Leland, or with the gravy disaster.

She saw the rest of her life: the constant anxious scrabbling. Never to stop, to look around and say, *Here I am, and it's good*. It was like being dead while she was still alive.

She bit her lips together and abstractedly picked up Martha's tract. She had skimmed it a few days before, during a bored Listening. She fiddled with a loosened staple, and, soothed by the wire's repeated pricking against her fingertip, let her mind wander across what she remembered of it: how, on the day Karol Sadowski was released from Ellis Island, the thirty-five-year-old Pole had gone walking through New York, looking for architecture that would remind him of home. In the late afternoon he had carried his cracked leather bag into St Paul's of the City, an early nineteenth-century church built with traders' money and echoing, in its transepts, Europe's powerful gothic structures. Halfway down the marble aisle he stopped to gaze at the rose window above the altar. In a pew beside him an elderly woman stroked a Bible with swollen hands and murmured aloud.

The tract claimed that he heard her say, 'Him that overcometh I will make a pillar in the temple of my God.'

At that, it said, the air rushed around his ears and a circular temple with pearly, translucent walls appeared floating before the stained glass. Karol Sadowski was felled, his cheek against the marble tiles. The temple descended, growing larger than the ocean he'd sailed across, larger than the sky. St Paul's vanished. Karol saw that the temple was empty: there was no altar. Three enormous round pillars set at equal distances around its circumference rose to a domed roof. Each pillar was engraved down its length: Selflessness. Truth. Chastity. Karol Sadowski heard the words resound. He lifted his gaze to the temple's dome, and understood that there was, after all, a sort of altar: the golden light that fell from above, diffusing evenly and thickly through the air. The dome was not engraved, but Karol knew instantly that it was composed of Perfect Love.

'Take my instruction daily,' he heard. 'And you will be a pillar for America and the world. You and your followers will hold up the Roof of Love.'

Rita squeezed the staple back together. Her eyes caught the edict: 'SELFLESSNESS. TRUTH. CHASTITY'. She breathed out hard, pressing her ribs down on that space in her chest, and swung her legs out of bed. Betty grunted and turned over.

She unzipped her leather writing case and stuffed the tract into its most inaccessible pocket. It was unthinkable that she could be deep-down unhappy. Despite her recent catastrophes, the Promise and the Movement should give her hope. And what use was an obscure pamphlet's Roof of Love? If she could ever become good enough for Leland, he would bring her all the love and happiness she had ever wanted.

But she flailed around as she dressed, unable to lose the keening voice. Before she had finished she'd knocked her water glass off her bureau and woken Betty, who muttered and pulled a pillow over her head.

5

The Movement dealt trenchantly with those who indulged in unhappiness. To admit to it invited scrutiny of one's sins; its cause would then be identified as lack of purpose, disobedience or an ill-disciplined mind, and the following remedies prescribed: selfless actions and a close inspection of motives and behaviour, always ending with apologies and restitution. Rita drove herself into a manic state of faux-enthusiasm, reorganising the laundry roster and establishing a cardfile for cleaning duties, floors, furniture and woodwork cross-referenced by room. Each morning, when Betty yawned and picked up her notebook, she shuffled her rear end against the headboard of her bed and pretended to be in communion with God while she doodled on page after page.

In October she accepted her mother's invitation to return home for Memorial Day, determined to show forbearance, be magnanimous; to demonstrate that whatever the irritations, she could rise above them, even if she did not yet have the experience to Challenge and Change her folks. However, when she walked in the front door, the dent in the rim of the brass tray on the hallway table, and the way the fringe on the floor-length camel curtain grew like a row of bendy toothpicks from the carpet, announced themselves to her as far more powerful than anything she might have encountered since she last saw them.

Her mother kissed her on the cheek. Her father chucked her under the chin and asked, 'Does the Good Lord carry messages from Mr Swann when you're absent from HQ? Does he act as a telephone service?'

She set to work in the kitchen, but her effortful serenity lasted only a few minutes before she began to snap at her mother, who sought to ensure that Rita knew the best way to peel a potato, whip cream, roll pastry. 'I know, I *know*, what do you think I've been doing all this time!' Or through gritted teeth: 'I was *just about* to do that.'

And then her mother's raised eyebrows, and the hurt look, her bosom rising and falling in a little sigh.

'Mom, I'm sorry, but if you could treat me like an *adult*.'

'Well, *I'm* sorry *too*, but if you'd *behave* like one . . . I know I'm hard on you, but haven't I always treated you the same way I did the day before, so you know where you stand? That's what my love is, even though it's not good enough for you. Other folks'll be soppy one minute and turn on you the next. I'm getting you ready to take care of yourself when I'm not here.'

'You don't have to worry. People Under God's Command is my future.' *Leland's* my future, she wanted to say.

'You think because I don't have to clean and cook for you any more, I don't worry? You think *because* you're not sleeping under our roof, I don't worry? I can't imagine not knowing where you are. You wait till you have children of your own, then you'll understand.'

Her father began his campaign as soon as they sat down. 'You're marvellously silent for someone who leads such an exciting life. Will you be joining this tour the newspapers are beginning to caw about?'

She shook off her defensiveness. 'Maybe, as a secretary.'

'Is it allowable for you to drink a little wine?' He waved the bottle at her.

'No thank you.'

'Are you on the wagon?'

'We don't drink in the Movement.'

'Refresh our memories.'

'If we do, we can't help people who have a problem with it.'

'With what?'

'With alcohol.'

'But—' he held the bottle over her glass, tipping it so that the red liquid slid down the narrow neck '—you're not suggesting that *I*—?'

'I understand,' said her mother. 'It's a matter of principle.'

'I don't,' said Frank Daley. 'Have you met any alcoholics, Rita? Have a couple of drunks come stumbling into that big kitchen of yours?'

'No.'

'If what you're doing doesn't change this stinking world by one iota, then why go on doing it, pretending you're better than everyone else?'

'We *do* change things. Change people. We're going to change a lot more, too, once we start touring again and the new Centres open. The new play'll be a hit—' She talked fast, relating the plot Bill had described to her the last time they met over dinner.

His idea was to set the play in a town shut down by a strike in its only factory, and to have two families, their fathers at loggerheads. One family would be headed by the union chief, a gruff man further incensed by an injury received on the picket line. His teenage daughter is secretly dating the rebellious younger son of the other father, the supercilious factory boss. That rebellious son is resentful towards his caustic brother, away at college. But the older brother comes home different: direct, loving, repenting the hurt he's caused. Rebellious son Listens, feels uncomfortable about deceiving his own and his girlfriend's parents, persuades her they should come clean . . .

Describing Bill's plot, Rita could almost become the openhearted daughter she knew she should be. 'So at the beginning, everyone hates everyone else, the dads opposing each other in the factory, the husbands and wives arguing, and then they begin to change. Everyone has to be willing to be different. That's how they find a solution to the strike.'

'Makes sense,' said her mother grudgingly. 'The fault does always lie with the individual. It's not a new idea. I don't see that they have to make a fuss about it.'

Her father frowned. 'And in the meantime you slave away in that kitchen, your certificate going unused, taking instruction from God on every cup of coffee?'

'I *am* using my certificate! I take shorthand in the production meetings—I will once they get started. I'm going to type up the minutes!'

He rolled his eyes, setting off her tears.

'You never believe the best of me! You always assume I'm doing something wrong!'

'Is this emotionalism encouraged in the "Move-ment"? We're trying to have an adult discussion with you.'

'I'm doing okay! I'm doing what God wants me to! I'm living in His plan for me!' She was almost inarticulate—from a distant, appalled point she observed that she seemed less capable of living harmoniously with her parents than she did before she'd left.

Hilary Daley said, 'I know I'm not the smartest cookie in the jar, but this "God's plan for me" malarkey seems like the crowning self-indulgence. God's set out our path plain enough in the Bible. But I don't expect you to listen to me. You get riled up by the tiniest criticism, hate to be told you're wrong.'

Defeated, knowing that she proved both of them right, she flew from the table to her father's resonant: 'A nice way for dinner to end.' She escaped her parents' house that evening, a whole day earlier than she'd intended.

So much for the transformed, mature Rita.

Things were better at the Centre, despite her recent humiliations. On Tuesday morning Leland Swann unexpectedly entered Ladies' Sharing after Martha Sands had run through her housekeeping reminders. Betty, who seemed to have recovered from Cynthia's criticisms, touched Rita's sleeve. 'Your future husband!'

Patsy, sitting in front of them, swung around and stared at Rita: 'Shhh!'

Leland's cheeks were flushed, as though he'd been out walking in the frosty morning air. Pacing up and down the stage, he seemed to take ownership of the room. 'I am here to let you know your efforts are not in vain: we are expanding the Movement daily and are talking with wealthy citizens who wish to fund further Centres in Washington, and also on the West Coast, where, you will agree, our revolution is sorely needed.

America is under serious threat from Communist organisations. These Machiavellian naysayers want to emasculate our military and weaken the public's resolve. They do not trumpet their true nature, but undermine our traditional Christian roots with a materialist philosophy that elevates to the highest value the satisfaction and gratification of carnal appetites—thus denaturing American youth to the point that they are rendered unwilling to die for any cause. If the Communists succeed in this work, America will fall without a fight.'

His glance passed over Rita, as quick and light as an airplane's shadow.

'God has shown me it will not be long before we launch People Under God's Command internationally. Already, we receive weekly requests and compliments from England and across Europe, and from as far away as Australia. We also hear desperate pleas from those in regions where Communist agents and backers are active. I'm speaking of such places as Brazil, British Guyana, Kerala and, as you would expect, Vietnam.'

He stopped abruptly then, staring at them as if he had just recalled their presence. He thrust a folded sheet of paper into Cynthia Chant's hand and left the room.

Cynthia read the note. 'Ladies, it should go without saying that *any* correspondence addressed to Leland must be routed through the Secretariat. Even a memorandum hand-delivered by the President himself should not be given directly to Leland. You are dismissed.'

Rita remembered her accidental meeting with Miss Toller outside the Secretariat, and wondered if Miss Toller's letter had reached Leland. And what had happened to the letter that Bill Harper had tucked into his pocket? It was odd, she thought, trailing down the corridor behind Joan Jessom, that Leland did not, apparently, want to see Miss Toller. She recalled what Margot had told her about Leland and Bill's discoveries in the old darkroom, now Leland's den: evidence of Julius Toller's past sins. Surely, though, God must have forgiven Julius Toller after he donated his mansion to the Movement.

In front of her, Patsy turned at the door to the housekeeping room. 'Get a move on, Rita!'

Maybe, Rita thought, settling herself behind the old deal table, *Julius Toller doesn't feel any more changed than I do.*

Patsy checked over the clipboard in her lap. 'First up, a grateful store owner's delivered ten dozen cartons of canned tomatoes and beans to the back door. Yes, I know, ten dozen. He's grateful. His clerks paid him back for stock they stole.'

She turned to Rita. 'I have a sense we should work together, so we'll get on with putting those cans away once the men bring them round.'

'I have a sense' was Listening-speak for 'God told me'. Rita nodded.

'Betty and Joan, Martha wants you folding one hundred linen napkins into water lilies for the Minneapolis Methodist clergy's dinner tonight. Margot, there are pots soaking since last night.'

Once they were in the pantry, Patsy kept up a flow of gossip gleaned from her parents. Bill Harper, apparently, had been refining his elocution ever since Leland told him that the way his voice lifted at the ends of sentences made him sound uncertain and thus untrustworthy. Bill, Patsy laughed, was now notable for his growling emphases at the conclusion of the most trivial statements: I've run out of *toothpaste*. We should take the *Cadillac*.

Finally, stooping to break open another carton, she said to Rita, 'God told me I need to say sorry for being mean to you on your first day here. I can get kind of antsy—jealous, I guess. My mom's always telling me we have to adapt now that Leland belongs to a whole heap of people, not only our small crowd. Got to be Selfless.'

'Thank you. I thought you were planning on Challenging me.'

'Would that be so bad? Aren't we here to be the best we can?'

'Yes. I'm sorry too.'

'Maybe we can start over.' Patsy smiled at her and switched her attention back to the shelves. 'Leland's a terrific leader, isn't he? Got all the attributes to take the Movement far. When God takes away, He sure makes up for it.'

'What do you mean?'

Patsy adjusted some cans so all the fat tomatoes on the labels faced outward. 'Oh gosh. I don't know. Maybe God didn't mean for me to tell this part. Maybe I should Listen again.'

Rita shrugged. They worked in silence for a few minutes.

'It's very sad,' Patsy said. 'If you look at it one way. But God knows what He's doing, I guess.'

Another long pause.

'It's been weighing on my mind. Because I'm the only younger person who knows. And there might be a time when it's important—in order to save Mr Swann's feelings—to lead talk away from certain matters.'

'It's up to you. We could Listen now, if you want,' said Rita, though she hoped Patsy wouldn't take her up on the idea.

'Well.' Patsy shoved some cans to the back of a shelf and wiped her hands on her apron. 'You'll see why I'm being so careful. It's a delicate subject. Before we came to Minneapolis—a few months before my dad died—Mr Sadowski had a leading from God, saying we should attend a revival meeting. It was right over in Madison, and we were nowhere near it. No rhyme or reason, but we were used to that kind of thing. Once—' she lost her preachy tone and began to talk fast '—we were driving on the highway, in our bus, and Mr Sadowski suddenly said, "Stop at this diner," even though not a soul among us had any cash. My dad was driving and he didn't want to stop—they'd promised us dinner in Emmersburg if we got there before nightfall. But Mr Sadowski was real insistent. He kept saying, "Stop. You must stop," in his funny accent.

'So my dad pulled up and we got out of the bus, but the sign on the door said Closed. And my dad said, "Well, that's it, Karol, best get on." But Mr Sadowski went right ahead and pushed open the door, so we followed him. And inside—' Patsy smiled at Rita '—thirteen places were laid out at a long table, and an old woman was crying behind the counter. Mr Sadowski went on up to her and put his hand on her shoulder, and she looked at him and whispered, "They didn't come." And he said to her, "God sent us instead." And she looked at him for an age, and we were all standing around like doofuses, and real hungry because we could smell roast pork and biscuits, and then she smiled and got up off her chair and flung out her arms and said, "Sit down, everyone!"'

Patsy rushed her words, as though she'd been waiting to tell the story and was afraid her time would run out.

'So we sat, and she served us the best meal we'd had in months. Chowder with fresh baked bread, and the pork all crispy, and butterscotch cake and ice cream. Turned out she was seventy that day. She hadn't seen her children in years, and they'd promised to come for her birthday dinner. With her grandchildren. But just before we got there they'd all rung, one after the other, and made excuses. Now how could Mr Sadowski have known?'

'That's awful,' Rita said. To be forgotten by your own children. At the end of your life, after all that work. The lurid tomatoes on the labels blurred.

'Yes,' said Patsy. 'She was all right though. Mr Sadowski talked to her—he hardly ate a thing—and when we left she was grinning all over her face. And it turned out, when we got to Emmersburg, the people there had let us down and there was no food at all!'

'I wish I'd met Mr Sadowksi.'

'He never made you feel badly, you know? Just like you could be someone . . . bigger. And he never forgot a single thing. Like, he always remembered the names of my junior high girlfriends from the stories I told him. And amazing things would happen, like that time at the diner. That's why we scooted along to the revival meeting when he said to.'

Patsy had once again begun to sound as if she were instructing Rita.

Rita said, 'He had a vision, too. The Three Pillars in a temple.'

'What? Where did you hear that?'

'Martha Sands lent me a tract. It was very educational.'

Patsy tossed her ponytail and laughed self-consciously. 'It's a shame she wasted your time. She should know better. That tract's inaccurate. And . . . don't go yapping about what I told you. We've got to focus on the present, with the Movement growing so fast and all, and Leland getting noticed by senators and . . . and other important people. It would be wrong to get hung up on a dead old man. You've heard how the Movement began, right? Karol was looking after us until Leland was old enough to take over.'

'But what about the other part?'

'What other part?'

'The other part of the temple—the Roof of Love?' Rita did not know why she'd brought it up. She had not thought of it since she'd read the tract. She only wanted to argue with Patsy's superior tone.

'Well, what about it?' Patsy stuck a hand on her hip, her lips curling in an arch little smile.

'I don't know. Why don't people talk about it?'

'For heaven's sake.' Patsy turned away and continued pushing cans on to the shelves. 'Aren't there enough woolly-headed beatniks mooning around, carrying on, lovey this, lovey that?'

Rita recognised the tones of Mrs Chant.

'Anyway, I want to talk about Leland.' Patsy stacked more cans. 'You sure there's no more history weighing on your mind?'

'No. I mean, no more history.'

'Okay. So, ten days after the revival meeting Leland and me came down with the mumps. Leland and I,' she corrected herself. 'There were a lot of kids, so I guess one of them must've had it. We stopped where we were for a few days. I got better quick, but Leland had it real bad.'

Patsy made a face as though she was trying to say something behind a teacher's back. Rita didn't get it.

'He can't have *babies*,' Patsy whispered. 'No one else knows. Not among us young folks, I mean.' She raised her voice. 'But maybe—I wonder if you're really with us. Getting swayed by olden-style tracts and all. I was hoping I could count on you.'

'You can count on me. I want the best for Leland. For the Movement.'

So this was his 'mortal injury' he'd talked about the first evening she laid eyes on him. His sacrifice to the Cross of Christ. It was clear to Rita that God had engineered Patsy's disclosure so that when Leland made his proposal of marriage she would receive this information with grace and kindness—how moved he would be. She wished she could discreetly signal her knowledge to him right away. It was romantic to be in possession of your beloved's secret, as long as you didn't think about the mumps.

A few hours ago the prospect of childlessness would have filled her with sorrow. Now she felt only a brief throb of pain. As she pushed cans to the back of the shelf, she reflected that Patsy's message constituted an unmistakeable sign. God hadn't given up on her. She must have been doing something right after all.

In the final months of 1963, the Centre hosted, several times a week, groups of school superintendents, gubernatorial staff, philosophers, theologians, contemplatives, civic leaders, clergy and lawyers. They stayed for dinner, or for several days. Margot and Bill and some of the others with arresting conversion stories were let off duties or Chorus practice to address them. At the behest of neighbours who resented the automobiles clogging Summit Avenue, the driveway's box hedges were uprooted and the driveway widened to accommodate more parked cars. Patsy reported that the Secretariat was working overtime to send out press releases following each new visit. Often, these were reprinted verbatim in the *St Paul Pioneer Press* and other Minnesota newspapers: 'Head Superintendent: PUGC to reinvigorate Michigan schools'; 'Fire Chief: Three Pillars Prevent Roof Collapse'.

Journalists were intrigued that Leland Swann presided over dozens of single young men and women living under the same roof. The Movement invited two middle-aged newspapermen from the *St Paul Pioneer Press* to stay for a weekend. They roamed around under the scrutiny of Henry Allerton, attending Chorus practice and some of the less confidential meetings, and sitting at the Long Table with the senior men for meals. After their visit, they ran a story comparing the Centre favourably with the rumours about Timothy Leary's New York commune: 'Swann says Turn On, Tune In to God'. Betty said the journalists had asked her, 'You date any of these fellows? You let them buy you sodas?' But they found no sex at the Centre, not even a hint of it. They wrote about the 'clear, joyful gaze' of the Movement's young people, and concluded Leland Swann 'might be on to something fresh'.

The absence of unauthorised sex had become, without any open acknowledgement, the Movement's defining principle. It was rigorously upheld, even in the smallest part. '*Flirt*-ation is one of the primary tools of *tempt*-ation,' Cynthia Chant announced in Ladies' Sharing. When Betty and Joan were caught giggling over a fallen soufflé within earshot of a male washing-up team, Betty was reprimanded; Joan was not. 'I guess they don't think of me as capable of flirtation,' Joan remarked to Rita.

Now that Betty knew of the Promise, Rita assumed her romance with Leland was bound to move along. That was the way things worked in the Centre. Margot had become engaged to Gus Driver in early November, three days after Gus's friends had short-sheeted his bed and sprinkled sugar between the sheets with a note: 'Gus, we've made your bed for you! Now go lie in it!' (The indiscretion was allowable; everyone knew it was metaphorical.) Margot and Gus's wedding was scheduled for spring 1964, shortly before *The Answer*—still to be written—would begin touring.

Leland had begun to take meals in his room. 'He's in agony for America,' said Patsy. 'You know why? It's the new contraceptive pill. My mom told me. A woman takes it every day and then she can . . . go with anyone she likes and won't have babies. It's unnatural.'

'All it means is women can act the same way men always have,' said Margot.

'Is that meant to be a good thing?' Patsy's look said that *she* knew what Margot had been up to before she met the Movement.

They were in the old butler's pantry stacking dishes that had been used during a luncheon for the Twin Cities' Congregational clergy. Through the servery door Rita could see right across the kitchen to the windows. Another Work Team was wiping down the preparation tables for the evening shift. It was late afternoon, and the lights were on.

Patsy said, 'One thing I know for sure, Leland wouldn't like to hear you say that.'

Rita did not turn to observe Margot's response: she was watching Alice Maniaty totter into the centre of the tiled floor, her hands clasped over her cheeks, shaking her head wildly. Nadine supported her elbow and led her to a stool, leaning close while Alice sobbed words Rita couldn't hear. Then Nadine straightened and took several steps backwards, beginning to weep. Other women gathered around her, their faces limp with shock.

Rita's heart thudded. If Leland was sick, or dead, and the Movement closed down, she would have to return to her parents. Margot and Patsy had joined her at the pantry door. Nadine walked towards them, her mouth stretched wide in grief.

That evening, gathered in the candlelit chapel under the darkened stained glass, they prayed for America and the First Family. Tears ran down Rita's cheeks for the little boy and girl who would never see their Daddy again. Beside her, Betty choked with sobs, her head almost on her knees. On Rita's right, Joan Jessom's hands were folded in her lap. From time to time she scratched her wrists, and the insistent noise of her scratching filled the pauses in the service. As they'd filed into the chapel, Joan had whispered in Rita's ear, 'All I can think about is whether this'll make things worse for my brother.' Rita looked at her blankly. '*Stan.* My brother in *Vietnam.*'

Rita frowned. It seemed selfish of Joan to be concerned for her own family.

Henry Allerton spoke from the pulpit. Dark times. The senior men had sent condolences, on the Movement's behalf, to the White House. Behind him, Leland sat grim and motionless near the narrow oak pulpit, his gaze fixed on the two candles flickering on the altar. When Henry Allerton began to describe how the Movement would return every country to God, he stood, mounted the steps to the pulpit and positioned himself immediately behind Henry's shoulder, apparently oblivious to the sermon, which was building to a thunderous climax: 'One after the other, every country behind the Iron Curtain has failed. And thus we—ah, Leland.' For a moment, Henry and Leland faced each other, then Henry pushed past him and descended the few steps.

Leland gripped the lectern. 'Let us remember that while we have lost a man who perhaps wanted to be a good man, and who has left, tragically, his wife and two innocent children—let us remember that this man did not want goodness *enough* that he could be persuaded to honour every one of God's laws. This was a President who hosted Frank Sinatra and the rest of that Rat Pack on the presidential yacht and at the White House. Who consorted with silverscreen tramps and floozies only famous for the magnitude of their . . . mammary glands. Let us not set up false saints in our mourning, when our mourning should be saved for the morals of the United States of America.'

It seemed irreverent and unfeeling of him to speak ill of the dead President. Maybe ordinary standards did not apply to Leland. Rita tried to continue with this idea, but her mind would not comply. She looked sideways at Betty, but Betty, upright now, was staring straight ahead, one fist pressed against her mouth.

Leland had paused. Towards the back of the chapel a man coughed, but otherwise the silence was complete. He continued:

'Our President's assassin was no solitary madman. He might have acted alone, but he was not without his backers, his sponsors, although we may have to look beyond this world's powers and principalities to find them. What does this tell us? It tells us that in order to fight the battle on an ideological basis, we must look to the causes of evil. We need to divine that which connects apparently unconnected events. The cowardly assassination of our leader. The British Prime Minister's tainted resignation. Men brought down. Men *diminished*.'

Rita recalled that back in the fall they'd heard of the scandal Leland was alluding to. Margot had saved a day-old newspaper from the trash and spread it out on the table in the housekeeping room. There'd been a man whose name evoked cigar smoke and heavy, suggestive perfume. In a flashlit photo taken at night, a call girl climbed into a black taxi cab, looking over her shoulder. Her lips were pale and frosted, and she wore a miniskirt, her long hair loose down her back. There were spies in the story, and the ever-present threat of Communism. Martha Sands had whipped the paper off the table and said, when Margot questioned her, that there was a reason why Godless publications were confined to the library.

Leland crouched over the pulpit. 'They were young, these women. So young, so dewily youthful they might have been mistaken for innocents led astray. Yet they were hardly younger than those in the Movement.' His voice was hoarse. 'We are obliged to have them among us . . . but we will know them by their fruits.'

'Leland?' Henry Allerton climbed halfway up the pulpit steps and pulled on his arm.

Rita looked again towards Betty. She gave Rita a wobbly half-smile, but her face slackened. 'It's the death of goodness,' she whispered. 'That's what it feels like, on top of—I'm very selfish. Too selfish.'

On top of what? Once she and Betty had returned to their room, Rita asked her, 'Why did you look so . . . so stricken, when Leland was talking tonight?'

Betty, who had recovered a little, huffed through her nose. 'I'm doing fine. Sometimes . . . he's very challenging, the things he says, and then I have to go back to God and ask Him to help me accept it. Leland wouldn't be leading us, would he, and the Movement wouldn't so successful, if he hadn't been chosen by God? I have a lot to learn, that's all.'

She stood and walked to the mirror. Her back was straight, but something in the way she dragged her brush through her hair and muttered at the tangles made Rita uneasy, and reminded her of Betty's Welcome Talk, when she had seemed to keep something hidden from them.

'He worries me too,' Rita said, trying to sound mature. 'He seems to be under a lot of strain. I wish he would talk to me,' she added in a rush. 'I wish I could help him.'

'Yes. He needs someone to look after him. Some days he doesn't even eat a hot meal. Everyone expects the world from him and, you know what, I don't get the impression he's a naturally gregarious man.'

Rita jiggled the heels of her slippers against the rag rug. She should be the one making pronouncements about Leland's character.

Betty said, 'I guess he'll expect the same from you, when you're married. He'll expect you to forget yourself completely because . . . all that matters is making the world a better place. He probably won't even tell you that's what he expects . . . he'll just expect it.'

'If it ever happens,' Rita said morosely.

Betty laughed. 'If he doesn't get the nudge from God, *you* could always propose to *him*. He can't have any doubts about your purity.'

'I couldn't!'

'Sure. Next year's a Leap Year. Valentine's Day. It's allowed.'

Her words were too crisp. Rita did not believe that Betty was, truly, 'doing fine'.

6

Rita leapt at Betty's invitation to go home to Montauk with her for the Christmas holidays. The Wallace family was sure to be far easier company than her own. And it was fun, although Betty was unusually quiet in their bedroom and came to life only during the Wallaces' raucous family dinners. Mrs Wallace said Rita was a gem, a darling. She marvelled at her helpfulness and culinary skills. When they left, she hugged Rita for a full minute and said tearfully that she was glad Betty had such a wonderful friend at the Centre. For Rita's part, she would happily have stayed in Montauk for ever, playing Parcheesi with Betty's younger brothers and walking along the chilly beaches, daydreaming that Leland would approach her from the dunes and sweep her into his arms, solicitous and full of remorse for having taken so long.

However, when she and Betty got back to the Centre Martha Sands told them that Leland had only that day returned from a congressman's house on Lake Vermont, where, accompanied by Henry Allerton, he had been recuperating from nervous strain. He was still delicate, she told them. They should not seek him out.

Another person was still absent. Joan Jessom had not returned. Her brother, Stan, had been killed during a guerrilla attack on the Saigon headquarters of the Military Assistance Advisor Group, and it was not known when or whether she would feel ready to leave her family.

'They'd talked to him Christmas day,' said Patsy, her face sombre above her clipboard. 'His folks are travelling to meet his remains. Joan too.'

Betty blew her nose. Her yellow hair was caught up in a messy ponytail. She angrily pushed back strands from her cheeks. 'How many more people'll kill each other before we change the world? We're meant to start rehearsals soon, but the Committee hasn't met once since the assassination.' Rita knew, from conversations in Montauk, that Betty suspected Henry Allerton of being reluctant to delegate the script.

'I know what you mean,' said Margot. 'Changing people one at a time seems too slow.'

Rita had often wished for a brother or sister who might have deflected some of her mother's attention. Now Joan was an only child, like herself. How awful it would be for her, knowing what—no, knowing *who* she missed.

It came to her later, what she should do.

'Say sorry to your parents. You have never acted on your Listening to apologise to them. Put right your childish anger and resentment. Your sullenness. Hold nothing back. Demand nothing from them.'

She announced her intention in Ladies' Sharing, looking forward to the moment when she could report to them that the apology had gone well. After she spoke, Alice Maniaty announced that the Playwriting Committee would meet at eleven that morning. She dismissed them, and the gathered women began to move out of the room.

Nadine Strassman approached Rita and Betty.

'Hi, girls. Betty, you still planning to lobby for the cause of art?'

'Yes, I guess. Yes.'

'I don't know. Whatever our opinion of *The Divine Instruction*, it touched a lot of folks. You and I worry the play'll be too blunt. But I think the Movement says our message is that we don't have time to make . . . *beauty* . . . that lets people be complacent.'

'What do you mean?' Rita asked.

Nadine shrugged. 'Maybe we lose art as soon as we begin to talk about the Three Pillars. But you can't remake the world twenty-four hours a day. I can't, anyway. I'm free this morning and reading poetry.'

Rita thought of Joan's brother. Had Joan been right? Had the President's assassination made Stan's work more dangerous, or was this simply another bad thing that happened when people didn't Listen to God? People Under God's Command might have prevented his death if . . . if what? If the Movement had somehow transformed the soldiers and they had put down their weapons? Or if enough presidents and politicians had had seen *The Divine Instruction*? Or if there was no Communism for them to fight over? No wonder Leland wanted a strong force before beginning the 'push'. They had so much work to do.

Patsy complained about losing two of her workers, but Betty and Rita left the Team before eleven, met up with Nadine and made their way to the drawing room near the Secretariat. Bill Harper grinned when he saw them. Alice Maniaty led them in a short prayer. As soon as they had settled down to Listen, Henry Allerton threw open the door. He said, 'A very Happy New Year to you all.' They murmured in response. He crossed one knee over the other, balanced his notebook on his thigh and uncapped his fountain pen, which he held poised over the paper. Every so often he nodded, as though agreeing with what he heard.

Bill Harper snorted into a white handkerchief and winked at Rita.

She wrote down some thoughts, steadying her notebook on her leather writing case. She didn't strictly need it, but it made her feel more substantial, especially when she fingered the brass zip that curled around its corners. Before she left her room, she'd torn some sheets from its foolscap pad and slid them, folded, into the side pocket so as to bulk it out. Now she admired the gloss on its eggplant-coloured cover.

Henry Allerton said, 'I'll set the ball rolling. While I was on vacation I finished most of the compositions for the new production.'

Bill laughed. 'You must have advance knowledge. We haven't finalised a plot.'

'My songs are on general themes. Character-based lyrics, easily adaptable.'

Betty opened and shut her mouth.

'Do you have something to say, Miss Wallace, or is that a new beauty exercise?'

Rita, to her surprise, spoke up. 'What did your Listening say, Mr Allerton?'

'Miss Daley? What are you doing here? I wasn't aware of thespian qualities in that unmusical little head of yours.'

'I'm taking notes.'

'Ah, the amanuensis.'

'Your Listening, Henry?' Alice asked.

'Yes. Apparently our little Committee is the subject of great speculation in the household, of how the next production may be more "jazzed up" than our serviceable *Divine Instruction*. God is telling me to act as a steadying hand.'

Alice nodded. 'Yes. *I* thought, "Slow and steady wins the race." We mustn't ask questions that we can't answer.'

Henry spoke again. 'The play itself will be but an element in the production, lean and spare, a fable, *per se*.'

'Yes, but—'

'Now, Miss Wallace, is this your *Listening* or your longings?'

She sighed. 'I don't know, to be honest. I think God loves real art. Sure, let's have spare dialogue, but let's make our characters real. And maybe let's *imply*, instead of lecturing.'

'But we do let our audiences make up their own minds,' said Alice. 'Scads of people walked out of *The Divine Instruction*. We didn't chain them to the seats!'

Betty said, 'I guess I'd like us to respect our characters' wills, at the same time as we bend them to our uses. I'm not great at explaining it.'

Henry Allerton asked, 'Who inspires you, Miss Wallace? Among playwrights?'

'Well, Arthur Miller's *Death of a Salesman*—'

'Hah.'

Alice sniffed. 'He married Miss Monroe, didn't he? May she rest in peace, because she surely didn't find much in life.'

116

'Let's hear Betty out,' said Bill.

'Has anyone seen it? It tells us about America through the story of one man. A tragic man.'

'I saw the movie.' Henry Allerton waited for their attention. 'Wanted to assess whether Miller had anything worthwhile to say. You assert he tells us about America, Miss Wallace. I found his so-called hero an irreparable lunatic. Even the picture company—Columbia, was it?—were wise to it. They ran a short along with the main picture—*Life of a Salesman*, if I remember correctly. It showed a bunch of real-life average Joes working hard for their families. I don't need to spell it out for you, but those men proved our hero's misery was nothing but a front for Communist conspiracy. Anti-democratic hogwash. The arts boast more than enough vulgarity already, what with Mr Faulkner and Mr Williams and—' he turned down the corners of his mouth '—*Señor* Picasso saying art's sole purpose is "self-expression". Human nature being what it is, self-expression will drag the rest of us into the mud. We appreciate your theatrical expertise, Miss Wallace, but we don't need to sniff after some scrofulous, alcoholic writer who can't run his own life straight.'

The skin around Betty's mouth was tinged yellow-green. Her chest rose and fell quickly.

'Running your own life straight is the tricky bit,' said Bill. 'As I see it.'

'This isn't the place to experiment with highfalutin ideas,' said Henry Allerton, wobbling his head on 'highfalutin'. 'Miss Daley, do you have any thoughts to share with us?'

'I need to concentrate. Also, type up the minutes by the following day—'

'Very practical.'

She took a breath. 'And I agree with Betty. People like to learn from other people's stories.'

Betty said, 'Arthur Miller's personal morality, maybe he's trying to find his way—'

'That's the point. We *know* the way, and we must present our audiences with a clear choice. Miss Strassman?'

Nadine glanced at Betty, who had sucked her cheeks in as though she held back tears. 'Oh, I didn't get many thoughts. I guess, though, God would want us to move forward together. A team.'

Henry Allerton took the floor for some time after they'd shared, describing the musical numbers that would open and close the show. He'd written songs for all the main parts, based on dissatisfaction, fear, greed and so on. 'Our advertising will carry recommendations from well-known men. Leland's procuring sponsorship from major corporations. Big money. Big names.'

'Like who?' asked Nadine.

'A couple of lines from Pat Boone or Walt Disney would be worth hundreds of column inches. That's the calibre of man I'm talking about.'

After Henry Allerton left, Bill said he reckoned a plot diagram could be in order. Did anyone have any paper? Rita unzipped her writing case to get at the foolscap. She whipped out the whole lot and handed it to him. Other grey and tatty papers fluttered out of the pocket and on to the centre of the table. Bill began to hand them back, but he looked again.

'Are those the Three Pillars?'

It was Martha Sands' tract, in an even worse condition than when Rita had rejected it months ago. There were several small ruptures around its staples, and it had softened on the spine almost to the point of disintegration, as if she had been fingering the few pages constantly rather than not thinking of it at all.

'Gracious! I haven't seen one of those in the longest time!' Alice's initial tone of astonishment faded into reflection. She slid one brown-spotted hand towards the tract but withdrew it and twined her fingers together.

Bill, grinning, turned the cover to face the others. 'A flying saucer on stalks!'

'*The Vision of Karol Sadowski*,' Nadine read, peering over Bill's shoulder. 'The man who began the Movement? Where'd you get this, Rita? Is it from the Secretariat?'

'Goodness, no,' exclaimed Alice. 'Those tracts were printed long before we even *had* a Secretariat.'

'Martha Sands gave it to me,' Rita said. 'It's out of date, though,' she added quickly.

Bill read aloud from the first page. '"Karol Sadowski and we who follow him like to talk with everyday folk, sharing their trials and joys. We too have stories to share, of how Mr Sadowski's vision has changed our lives, and how making ourselves available to the God who gave us the Three Pillars and the Roof of Love . . ." Phew, wordy, eh?'

'*Making ourselves available to God*,' Nadine quoted. 'He sounds like an employment bureau.'

'That's how we used to describe Listening,' said Alice. 'Before Leland was in charge.'

Nadine held out her hand. 'Let me have a look.'

She read aloud the vision. Rita saw again a shabby Karol Sadowski gazing up at the huge rose window and, in a nearby pew, an old woman hunched in prayer while the temple of the Three Pillars and the Roof of Love descended.

When Nadine had finished reading, she looked up at them, openly surprised. 'This feels like the moment I realised my parents had another life before I was born. This is the beginning of the Three Pillars? And Listening? The beginning of everything?'

'Well,' said Alice. 'That was the *official* version, for quite a while.'

'Wasn't it true?' Bill asked.

'Of course it was true—what I mean to say is . . . if Karol were here you'd understand.' She smiled sadly. 'You'd understand everything, right away. But now we have to *make* people understand. It's a different game, nowadays. More serious.'

'Nowadays we don't tell them about the Roof of Love, eh?' Bill grinned.

Alice rallied with obvious effort. 'Love! Everyone talks about love, but does it do any good?'

Rita recalled Leland's riposte to the man at *The Divine*

Instruction who'd enquired about love. It didn't do any good to talk about it. You had to live in God's Will.

'Who's E. Cray?' asked Nadine, looking at the back page.

'E—?'

'Yes. "Enquiries and requests for appointments care of E. Cray, 16—"'

Alice brightened. 'Oh, *Esther*! Legs all twisted with polio, so she couldn't travel with us. Dealt with our mail. Cabled to let us know who wanted us where. I never saw Karol look happier than the days we arrived somewhere and there'd be a box at the post office from Esther. But he was always *detouring*, you know, haring off all over, consequently half the time we were tardy for our appointments. After they met Karol they always forgave us, most of 'em . . . still, though, Leland wasn't at all in favour of us being late. Anyway, Esther's darned lemon cake had greened all over its base by the time we got to it . . . it was an awfully moist recipe. Only kept a day or two, specially in summertime. We suggested to her that a fruitcake'd keep better, but she wouldn't entertain the notion. Stubborn, both of 'em.' She sighed. 'Best put that away now, Rita. Or better, give it to me to dispose of.'

Bill interrupted. 'May I have a closer look? I'll bring it to you later, Alice.'

He and Nadine discussed a few more ideas for the plot—it seemed to Rita in danger of becoming too involved—and then the meeting ended.

Betty, who had not spoken since Henry Allerton left, hung behind and caught Rita's arm on the way out.

'I need to talk to you, Rita.'

'Sorry, Betty, but I have to run down to the front door. Remember, my folks are coming in so I can apologise to them? I'll catch up with you later. After lunch?'

Her lips twisted. 'Okay.'

But the Daleys were late. Rita tried to be patient, then she fumed. After waiting a half hour in the entrance hall, she marched upstairs to the Secretariat, where the Work Team was stuffing envelopes with the Movement's new pictorial magazine.

120

Betty did not raise her head. Five minutes later, Martha Sands puffed in to inform Rita that her parents were in the kitchen and wondering where she was.

The opening minutes of the meeting were predictable. Her own panicked scolding: 'Why *wouldn't* you come to the front door? Isn't that what a visitor *does*?' Her mother's sniffy apology: 'We didn't think we'd have to stand on ceremony, seeing as how we have family here.' Her father's cheerless insults: 'You found a beau yet? No? Poor boobies. I should warn them.' And when she invoked Perfect Chastity to show him that she was beyond that: 'Oh, anyone can see you're not a danger to 'em. Just joshing. Can't you take a joke? Have they leached all your laughs out?'

'This room's only reserved until eleven. I thought we could relax, talk naturally.'

Her mother tutted. 'You've always been such a fatalist. I've told you before, fretting wastes your energy. That's why you don't have pizzazz.' She beckoned, drawing a handkerchief from her purse. Rita instinctively stooped. Her mother rubbed at her cheekbone. 'Don't they allow you time for grooming? Oh, you're not my responsibility any more.' She tucked the handkerchief up her sleeve.

'Mom, I'm almost twenty!'

Her parents sat on either side of her. 'Mom, Dad—' Rita turned from one to the other like a tennis spectator, feeling ridiculous. 'I know you did your best for me, and I didn't appreciate it. I want to apologise for all the times I've been ill-tempered with you.'

'So do you?' her mother asked.

'Do I what?'

'Apologise.'

'Yes. I'm truly sorry.'

Hilary Daley sighed. 'I won't deny you've always been difficult. Take your behaviour the last time you were home. Well, it's true, and you know it. My, I don't think this "Perfect Truth" is going well for you if you can't accept a little honest criticism.'

Rita yanked the tie off her ponytail, shook her hair loose, gathered it back in. Her father said, 'You do that when you're mad as all heck about something but don't want to say it.'

In Movement stories, an honest and straightforward apology always opened a chink in the soul of the sinned against; that person was inescapably moved, no longer able to summon up bitterness, and converted to People Under God's Command shortly after. That her parents were not following this rule seemed an incomprehensible act of malice.

'I apologised back there! Doesn't that *mean* anything?'

Her mother uncrossed her ankles and re-crossed them in the other direction. '*I'm* sorry you're dissatisfied with our response. We appreciate that you're contrite. It always was disconcerting to live with your bad temper.'

'I know I haven't been loving enough,' Rita said.

'Well, and how do you think you could be *more* loving?'

She said, haltingly, that she wouldn't get angry, that she'd listen more, that she'd always be courteous and gladly tell them about her life, but also, maybe, they could be more loving too.

'Another complaint? How can this be love, when you're always harbouring a complaint?'

'You think I'm a terrible person!'

'Now you're being melodramatic.'

'Do you love me?'

'Obviously we do,' her mother said. 'How can you ask, after all I've done for you.'

Rita lifted her hands to her ponytail but remembered in time to leave it alone. 'Dad, tell me about your job. I've never asked you about it. I'm sorry.'

'No point pretending sentiment where it don't exist.'

'Tell me, okay? I'm asking now.'

'You've seen the place. Mac's still boss, won't leave until they build the coffin around him. There's a couple of kids started, old story, think they understand "the psy-*chol*ogy of the customer". One's not so bad, probably'll go places, could've introduced you if you hadn't taken up with all this. Anyway, you'll have the house when we go. Won't matter if you're an old maid, long's you've got a roof and a couple of spare rooms. You can take in lodgers.'

She would rather die. 'I'm going to be fine. Leland says God will provide.'

'So did the pioneers. Some of them didn't make it.'

'Well,' said her mother. 'But the pioneers didn't have Mr Julius Toller as their patron.'

Her father said, 'I hear Mr Toller maybe isn't too enamoured of his decision, any more. Maybe feels he's had a raw deal.'

Her mother sniffed. 'Julius Toller should be grateful for any opportunity at penance God's given him.'

'How about Listening with me, Mom? Dad?'

Her father grunted. 'I know what that's about. Getting you to apologise left, right and centre. There're some people I won't apologise to. They're out of my life, and I don't see any reason to have them back in it.'

'Dad, it's wrong to hold grudges. Would you and Mom pray with me? Then we could Listen.'

'I'm sorry, but there are some people I trust to lead me in prayer,' said her mother. She held firmly on to her purse.

'Don't you think I'm good for anything? I can't even say a prayer for you?' Convinced of her own pure intentions, she cried hot tears.

'You said you wanted to pray *with* us,' said her father, 'not *for* us. It always did get my back up if anyone said they would pray for me.' He stood and moved to the piano, raised the lid and tapped out a bass note: *da*, da-da-da-da *da da*.

'It doesn't seem appropriate, here,' said her mother. 'I'm sorry, but this isn't a sanctified space.'

'Leland says we can Listen anywhere. But, if you prefer, we can go to the chapel!'

'Leland, eh.' Her father ran his index fingernail all the way up the keyboard. *Drghrrrfllweeeet!*

'Don't shout, Rita, you're getting carried away. This hysteria . . . it seems to me this is more to do with your ego than that you want God to look after us. It's in the service of your pride, your demanding nature.'

'It's not. I don't.'

'Stop crying, now. Someone will hear you. Tell me—'

'Mom, why didn't you and Dad have any more kids? After me?' She had not thought of the question until she spoke.

Her father stared. 'What in God's name—?'

'I don't object. Though it's bad manners for you to interrupt, Rita, I'm sure you're more emotional these days.' Her mother's lips trembled, but her voice was steady. 'We tried to give you a brother or sister, but I miscarried. And then my change came early.'

'In other words,' said her father, 'I didn't marry no spring chicken!'

'It doesn't matter,' said Rita quickly. Did it hurt, a miscarriage? Had her mother been in pain? 'Leland's an only child too.'

'Is he, now,' said her father.

'Anyway,' Hilary Daley said, 'as I was about to ask, are there any opportunities for you and all these young men to get acquainted? Don't mind your dad.'

Rita told her about the chaperoned mealtimes. Her mother said good listening was the key. And perkiness. 'What about that Committee you're on?'

'There's one man, but he's from New Zealand.'

'I'd sure like to see some pink in your cheeks that's not put there by crying. I'm glad you're using your diploma,' her mother said, veering on to another favourite topic. 'If this doesn't work out at least you'll have some experience.'

'No.' A job in an office with people who cared only for making money or getting a good manicure, where nothing mattered except typing up clean letters and keeping the coffee hot—she could not settle for that now.

Her father turned from the window. 'Couldn't work among us heathens? Mac'd give you a job if I asked him. Hire purchase forms. Accounts.'

'No thank you, Dad'

He limped back across the room and bent to her level, his smoky breath in her face. 'Shouldn't that be your aim? Reach the unconverted? Persuade them you're right?'

Her mother had not finished with her line of questioning. 'So Rita, you're telling me in all the months you've been here, there's not one single fellow you've . . . felt *sparks* with?'

Sparks? Yes, when she looked at Leland—a thrill (she thought of the pulp romances) to 'the very centre of her being'. And awe. And hope that the laughing and affectionate man she knew in her imagination would show himself.

Her mother's eyes widened. 'There *is*! But is it real or another one of your crushes?'

'No! It's—' She smiled. For once, she felt charming. 'It's not a crush. I heard it from . . . someone else. On good authority.'

'Good. Who are his family? Does he have a profession?'

She had always longed for this interest. 'I can't say who it is, Mom.'

'Why not? Is it a secret?'

'Kind of.'

'*He* knows, and *you* know, and this "good authority" knows, I guess—'

Rita laughed.

'Well, I'm sorry if I seem . . . *rattled* . . . but I'm a little hurt you can't tell your own mother. Are you sure this "good authority" wasn't making fun of you? You know it wouldn't be the first time.'

'No. This . . . person . . . definitely wouldn't do that.' She was in deeper than she had meant to go.

Her mother gave a bitter laugh. 'I must have been a poor mother, or you'd tell me. But you've always been secretive. Miserly. You can at least say who your "good authority" is. *That's* not confidential, surely. Oh—is it your room-mate? What's her name, Betsy?'

'Betty. No.'

Her father struck a couple of chords on the piano. Ta-*da*. 'It's

Mr L. Swann,' he said, without turning around. 'I'd bet my dead grandmother on it.'

'It's just your luck to be rooming with a pretty girl,' her mother said. 'Do you have to eat at the same table, too?'

'Mom, pretty, homely, we don't *talk* about those things here—'

Ta-da-*dum. Dum.* 'Mr. Leland. Swann,' said her father. He turned. 'Isn't it. End your mother's anguish.'

'What? Leland Swann? He told you that someone likes you?'

'No,' said Frank Daley. 'He's the one.'

There was a pause while her mother digested this information.

'Oh, Rita. Oh, this is *so* like you.' She clenched her fists, slowly beating them against the wooden claws that finished the arms of her chair. 'Darn you, *darn* you for stringing me along.'

Where were their astonished, newly respectful faces? Where was the celebration? Rita foresaw, suddenly, that she might never be reconciled with them, that they might die without once having treated her as an adult.

'Enough hysteria,' her father muttered, making for the door. 'I need air.'

'Mommy, please stop crying. Why's it so hard—'

Her mother gripped Rita's face between bruising fingers. 'You tell me now, tell me *right* now—' she glanced wildly at the ceiling '—where are you going to end up? Tell me that.'

Rita detached herself. 'I don't want to be like you. I want to be happy.'

Her mother stared at her, and her quivering mouth hardened.

'Whaddya-know,' her father said, holding the door open. 'Look who's coming our way.'

Leland entered, speaking over his shoulder to Bill Harper, '. . . plague of permissiveness, *that's* the threat.'

Bill said, 'But we're asking them to be perfectly honest in a system that isn't.' His eyes met Rita's.

'Now would be an appropriate time for you to clarify, I think,' murmured her father.

Hilary Daley whipped her compact out of her purse and began to dust her nose and cheeks with orange powder. Leland spoke as impassively as if ordering a train ticket. 'We've booked this room.'

Her father stretched out his hand. 'Mr Swann. Frank Daley. I'm intrigued to make your acquaintance.'

'If you'd like to contact one of my secretaries and make an appointment, I'll be glad to speak with you.'

Her father smiled at the carpet. 'Consider what might transpire from an *unscheduled* appointment! What mysteries might the Lord be nurturing for this very moment? My daughter, Rita here, is on your staff. Works many long hours for you, unpaid. Nonetheless, appears to hold you in vee-ery high regard. Indeed, tells us your inimitable wisdom has been brought to bear on her marital hopes.'

'Dad!'

Her mother had stood. 'Mr Swann, how lovely to see you again! You remember? You attended a coffee morning in our home. At which you and Leonora Toller made your first acquaintance.' Her eyes were still red, but she held her head high, blinking. Rita saw with terror that she was being 'delightful'. Now her father was reaching past Leland to shake hands with Bill, talking incessantly. Theological considerations . . . the plight of modern man . . . the corrupting effect of power . . . the Movement's role in—

Her mother hissed in her ear, 'We'd better have that get-to-know-you talk with our future son-in-law.'

'No, Mom!' She grabbed her arm. 'Let me explain.'

'Stop it. Your face gives you away. It always has.'

'No, but he's the one I told you about—the one who told me . . . the authority, Mom, the good authority. ' The Pillar of Truth rushed towards her, mowing her down.

'So that dreamy expression on your face before you were so hateful to me—no, don't try to take it back, I know what you meant. That dreaminess wasn't about him? Well, I hope you learn what love is before you *do* get married and make your husband miserable.'

'Excuse me, gentlemen, while I get the latest from the front.' Her father turned towards them. 'Rita, did I hear right? I've been buying you a little time here. Is Mr Swann—?' He cupped a hand under Leland's elbow, and allowed a predatory pause while she ran to his side and grabbed his arm.

'Daddy, please!'

She caught her mother's falsely superior smile, and was enraged, but in the next instant noted the defeated slope of her shoulders and knew her misery as well as if she had been standing inside her body.

Leland was gazing at her, his lips thinned. A sob burst up from her belly.

Her father said, 'We'd better let these fine men get on with their business.'

Rita let go his arm, planning to slip behind him and yank open the door that Bill had considerately closed. But she bumped into her father who, as if reading her mind, had taken a contrary step backwards. She pushed in front of him, tripping over his foot, falling awkwardly and shoving her shoulder against Leland's side, her head cricked sideways against his collarbone, her feet tangled, one arm constrained between their bodies—she righted herself by digging her elbow into his ribs, and planted a hand against a lower region that, she knew instinctively from its squashy curve, was somewhere her hand should not be.

There was no one in the hall, or on the grand staircase.

Was it possible to alter God's will? By failing him, to change His mind?

No one to see her race, panting, down the corridors.

She could not know, could she, because she was patently not close to God. Nor to her parents, nor to Leland.

Her room was empty. She collapsed on to her bed, wailing.

No one to moor her, to keep her from falling off the world and spinning in dark space like the lost Russian cosmonauts.

She spent an hour or two wetting her pillow with tears. Her stomach gurgled, but when Betty came to find her, Rita told her she 'couldn't face' lunch. Betty said anxiously, 'We'll still talk afterwards?' and seemed satisfied with her reply.

After some time, Rita smeared her face across her sleeve and considered. Whatever happened, she would still be herself. Whether she stayed at the Centre for ever, decorating butter pats with shaved curls of chilled butter and folding linen napkins into swans and water lilies, or grew old in her parents' house, dragging veined legs around the kitchen as she cooked dry meals for lodgers, or married Leland and entertained heads of state in glittering capitals, she would take herself with her.

The other girls—except maybe Patsy—looked out at the world with degrees of assurance. They talked about God as though they believed He noticed them. Even if their pre-Movement days had been riven by drugs or bitterness or uninvited terror, they were all a little 'happy anyway', believing, at their core, that they were worth something.

She saw that if she did not take action, she could, despite her earlier declaration, end up like her mother: resentful and self-hating. She could not stand to be so miserable.

She found her notebook and wrote down the date, then stared at it: 1964, the new Leap Year. Valentine's Day was weeks away. But months ago she had heard a Promise. God could not have been playing tricks on her. If it was in His Plan that she and Leland should marry, then surely she could bend some old traditional rule in order to get things moving. And God had led Patsy to tell her about Leland's infertility. He must have also led Betty to remind her about the Leap Year. In which case, Betty wouldn't mind if her own mysterious woes, whatever they were, had to wait until after Rita had spoken to Leland.

She splashed cold water over her eyes and combed her hair. Most people would still be at lunch. Leland, though, had continued to take his meals alone, and might be in his den, deep in contemplation, ripe to hear God's word from an unexpected source. She pulled on fresh stockings, changed into her prettiest jersey and, heart thumping, set off in the direction of the south-east wing.

Part 3

New Zealand

2004

1

On the way back from the airport, Leland sat in the front passenger seat. Rita sat behind Bill, straining forward against the car's momentum so she could check Leland's expression every time she made a cheery comment about the scenery. Occasionally he nodded in response. She longed for the trip to end. When Bill at last turned into their driveway, she began a nervous commentary on the native grasses they had recently planted. Their home was at the back of what had once been a double section, hidden from the road by the original weatherboard house. Their driveway passed by this first house before turning towards the garage. Rita couldn't see the front door from where she sat, so it was Leland, peering through his window, who said, 'There's a woman sitting on your porch.'

Bill gave a grunt of pleasure. 'Stella! Hang on—what's she done to herself?' He braked, lunging from the car. 'Pet? Stay put, don't move—'

Rita scooted across the back seat. The heavy green cast on Stella's leg sent a spasm lurching up from her belly, ratcheting against her lungs and constricting her breath. What terror had passed close enough to injure her child? She climbed out of the car and walked with Leland towards the porch, where Bill had clamped his arm around Stella's shoulders.

'Goodness,' she said, feeling the inadequacy of her exclamation. 'What happened to you?'

Stella smiled tightly, leaning in to kiss her cheek. 'Hi Mum.' She nodded at Leland. 'Hi. Let go, Dad. I can't balance.'

'What happened?' Rita repeated.

Bill said, 'Leland, this is our daughter, Stella. Stella, Leland Swann.'

'Hi. I'll tell you inside. I've had enough of this sun, and my bum hurts.'

Bum?

Before Stella turned on her crutches, Rita saw in her eyes a sulkily resolute expression that reminded her of the various extravagant ways in which her daughter, throughout childhood and adolescence, had exercised her will. She kept her eyes on Stella's bare, magenta-tipped toes, and hoped she would not give voice to *too* many of the slang words they had mistakenly allowed in the house.

They crowded on to the porch while Bill unlocked the door. Without a nod to Leland, Stella manoeuvred her way over the step and into the house. Leland followed her, and without any ceremony or space in which he might notice the miniature Stars and Stripes in the brass vase they all traipsed down the corridor to the lounge. There, Stella flung down her crutches and backed into one of the armchairs, letting her arms hang limply on the cushions.

'Take a pew, Leland. I'll fetch your bags.' Bill jangled his car keys.

Leland sat down opposite Stella, crossing his legs. He nodded at her.

'Hi,' Stella said.

He hesitated. 'Do you live here also?'

Rita observed him while he made conversation with her daughter. His hair, as thick as ever, now almost entirely silver-grey. The line of his jaw still sharp. In a navy polo shirt and casual jacket, he looked, she thought, like a man who might have lived the very best kind of life. But why so stiff and quiet? Where was his old charisma?

Jet lag. Of course. He would soon recover. Again, she felt the anxiety that had clutched her after she received his letter: how did her own life measure up? And there was Stella, lolling, uninterested to the point of discourtesy in how she might appear to him.

'You remember, dear, Mr Swann led People Under God's Command.'

'Oh, right. Yes. The Three Pillars. I remember them well.'

'And Listening. We often Listened as a family,' Rita said, covering Stella's ironic tone. 'To sort out our little differences.'

She heard her own coyness, and blushed, catching Stella's smirk. How frustrating that her daughter could see right through *her*, when she could so rarely penetrate Stella's nonchalance.

'Are you, um, Mr Swann as in Aunt Betty's husband? Is she here? Do I finally get to meet her?'

Rita interrupted. 'What about your leg, Stella? Your poor leg!'

'I fell on the steps—'

'Oh, no.' She could picture the scene too well.

Stella turned back to Leland. 'Is she coming?'

Rita homed in on the end of the sofa closest to him. 'Those steps, Leland! They're awful, higgledy-piggledy, real death-traps, nothing like the outdoor staircases in St Paul. Is it your shin bone that broke, sweetheart—what do they call it? Do you want an aspirin?'

'No thanks. It's the ankle, a couple of bones. I got a prescription at the hospital.'

'How long do you have to keep it on?'

'Ages. I broke some really small bones.'

'And your cast—*green*! Very smart. Bottle green. I didn't know they did them in green.' If she said 'green' one more time, she thought, she might strangle herself.

Stella sighed. 'Yup, they've got the range.'

'Good on you, pet,' said Bill, perching on the arm of her chair. 'Bag's in your room, Leland. Down the corridor, second left. Anyone fancy a brew?'

'I'll make it. You talk to Leland.' But Rita hovered, glancing at Stella's bag. 'Are you on your way somewhere, dear? A business trip?' Now that she had begun to recover from the shock of the cast, she wanted to open out a space in the world for the uncomplicating possibility that Stella's impromptu visit was but a break in a longer journey—to a distant interview, perhaps, or a conference.

She turned to Leland. 'Stella works for a bank. Computer

programming, and her husband's an architect. Charlie, our son, lives in Hawai'i. We have a grandson, did I tell you? Three months old! Yes, both of our offspring are married. Sadly—' she rattled on, wishing she could shut up '—we couldn't be present at Stella's wedding. They decided to tie the knot in Fiji.' *Before we knew it*, she thought. 'Dan should have designed you some better steps, Stella.'

'He's an *interior* architect. Anyway, the steps are on council land. So, have you heard back from Charlie? About the Harper Anniversary Weekend thingie?'

For a moment, Rita could not speak. She was aware of Bill's eyes on her. 'Charlie's not coming,' she said, as steadily as she could. She would not show her grief to Bill. 'None of them are coming.'

'Seriously?' Stella sounded distressed. 'Are you sure? You know what Charlie's like with dates and birthdays and stuff. Has he remembered it's your anniversary and everything?'

'Yes, I'm sure,' Rita said, unable to keep her anger from her voice.

'It's out of Charlie's control, love,' Bill said. 'We'll explain later.' In an aside to Leland, he said, 'We've been organising this family get-together thing.'

'*God*,' said Stella. 'I was really looking forward to seeing him. And Zane and Noelle. God. It won't be the same.'

'No,' Rita said. She caught the restraining glance Bill sent Stella, and knew that if the conversation continued she would begin to cry, or shout. 'Can I get you that drink, Leland? Tea, coffee? We have orange juice?'

His head jerked. 'Coffee, thank you. With milk.'

'We have semi-skimmed, if you're being careful. You can't order a simple coffee here. The wait-staff look at you like you're an idiot and make you choose from a list as long as your arm.'

'So,' Stella said. 'Is Aunt Betty arriving later?'

'Love, Betty's passed away,' Bill said.

Stella exhaled with a disbelieving puff. 'God. I'm beginning to wish I hadn't come. Oh, I'm sorry, that was really . . . She's *dead*? Since when? I didn't—no one told me. Sorry, this must be a bit weird for you, hearing me go on, it's just . . . her letters were great, I really liked her. Oh—' she swiped at one eye '—wow, this is . . . for someone I never even met . . . when did she die? Why didn't you *tell* me, Mum?'

Rita laughed uncomfortably. 'Not everything's . . . suitable for email.'

'You could've phoned!'

Bill spoke again. 'She passed away before the New Year. We've only known a few days. Sorry we forgot to tell you. We've all had a shock.' He said to Leland, 'Betty sent Stella presents when she was growing up.'

Rita watched Stella relax. Bill had always had the knack, she thought, whereas she only seemed to rile her daughter.

'She was my favourite proxy aunt, by virtue of fantastic presents. And the letters.'

'It's years since they were in touch,' Rita said quickly.

'No, she still sends Christmas cards. Sent. Not last year, though. Was she sick then?' Stella asked Leland.

His eyes were half-lidded. 'Well . . . this vacation will surely rejuvenate me.'

Stella's eyebrows lifted.

His dazed non-answer unnerved Rita too. 'I'll make the coffee,' she said. 'Stella, you should ask Leland about People Under God's Command.'

'Actually—' Stella heaved herself out of her chair, wobbling. 'Hang on.'

Rita heard, behind her, the clump of crutches. In the kitchen Stella hissed, 'What's up with you? Maybe he doesn't *want* to discuss his failed career! His wife just died!'

Rita turned from filling the kettle. 'I'm sorry I didn't tell you! I didn't know myself until three and half days ago! What if we hadn't been here?' She waved a hand in the direction of the lounge. 'My head's been full of preparations and details and menu plans.'

Stella was placated. 'Yeah . . . I'm sorry Charlie's not coming.

You must be gutted . . . And Betty was one of your best mates, right?'

Rita busied herself with the coffee plunger. 'We weren't especially good friends. We roomed together.'

'At the Centre? But you had that double wedding. I remember Dad saying you were close.' Stella lowered herself on to one of the red vinyl-covered chairs.

'For a few months. Not long.'

'What did she die of?'

'Cancer.'

'I can't believe . . . it's years since I've, kind of, given her much thought, except for getting those Christmas cards. But her letters were always . . . she seemed like a really *big* person, you know? Was she like that at the Centre?'

Rita wished that if Stella were to get confidential she would choose a different topic. 'It's so long ago. We were very young, different types. We lost touch fast. I guess that proves how superficial we were.'

'Are you okay? Your shoulders are up round your ears.'

'I'm dandy. Fine and dandy,' she whispered hoarsely. 'It's only . . . wondering what he eats, and making the house nice, and sorting out the junk in the guest room, and no time to sit down and plan properly—I dug out my old Fannie Farmer cookbook, and *The Joy of Cooking*, but they're Greek to me now. Your dad's always been happy with chops or chicken and potatoes and veg.'

How could she have kept all that cuisine straight, living amongst people who called biscuits 'scones', real scones 'pikelets' and cookies 'biscuits'?

She continued, 'I'm making Beef Wellington tonight. A food pun? Is it too cute?'

'No . . . Mum, I need to stay a while.'

'Stay! Here?'

'I can't manage the steps at home. I'd break my other ankle soon as.'

'Well, Leland's in the guest room for—I don't know how

138

long. Isn't Dan looking after you?'

'He's in the Philippines. I told you last week he was going.'

'He should come home!'

'What would he do, piggyback me up and down eighty steps a day? He can't abandon his clients. I'll sleep in the laundry till Leland takes off for the scenic south or whatever he's got lined up.'

'Maybe you should call him "Mr Swann".'

Stella looked at her strangely. 'Right. Are those old camp beds still in the garage? How long's he staying?'

'I said already, I don't know. How long do *you* want to stay?'

'Not long. I'll look for a flat.'

'Rent an apartment? Can you afford it, on top of the mortgage?'

'It's a tide-over. We had plans to sell the house anyway.'

'*Did* you? For a larger place?' An odd, intense excitement propelled Rita onwards. 'Sweetheart, did I ever tell you, the reason I didn't have any brothers or sisters is *my* mom's, um, "inconveniences" finished early. That and she got married late, or late for her times. My change came early too. I've always been glad your dad and I got started with you two when we were young. You never know how lucky you are to have children until you've got them.'

Finally, she could stop. She cringed. How many times had she told herself to keep quiet about it, ever since Stella, Dan disdainful at her side during a family Sunday lunch, had mimicked her tones precisely: 'Mum, do you know how many times you've gone, "Oh, I hope you don't leave it *too* long to have children"?'

'Well,' she continued, looking away from Stella's set face, 'and Dan'll be back in time for our Anniversary Weekend?'

'I don't know.'

Rita turned. 'What do you mean? It's three months away. You two *have* to be there! He can't stay in Thailand that long.'

'The *Philippines* . . . so can I stay? Please?'

From the moment of Stella's birth, Rita had fantasised that they would be best friends. The girl whom Rita had always wished to be bloomed in her daughter: feisty, apparently uncaring even of her peers' opinions. Rita worshipped those qualities along with Stella's curving beauty and the cinnamon-dark eyes she'd inherited from Bill. But as soon as four-year-old Stella fluttered her lashes at a jovial bus driver, Rita had known she had trouble on her hands.

At nine Stella insisted on picking out her own clothes, bringing home from op-shops a new abhorrence every couple of weeks. Rita remembered the trousers in shiny, textured materials, sharp pleats clustered at the waist, and the cream linen jacket that Stella wore over T-shirts, its collar turned up and cuffs rolled—Don Johnson of Lower Hutt, seeking out vice on Petone Esplanade with her German Shepherd, Petrol.

Stella and Petrol ran away to sea one windy afternoon in a dinghy stolen from the foreshore. The police launch found it drifting, capsized among the harbour's choppy waves. Stella was alone, sprawled dripping over its hull, her knuckles blue around the mooring line. She said, through tears for Petrol, that she'd planned to camp on Somes Island and row to the first big container ship that chugged past in the morning. The captain would pull her up, her plan went, and take them on as ship's girl and dog while they made their way to Miami, where she would hunt down real criminals.

It made the papers and TV news. Stella cried for an hour, and came close to convicting herself. 'Did I kill Petrol, Mum?' she asked that evening, lingering by Rita's elbow at the kitchen counter, averting her eyes from his food and water bowls.

Rita, still trembling from her near loss, had tried to find the right balance between love and truth. 'No, sweetheart, you didn't kill him. He wouldn't sit down in the boat, would he. But if you hadn't got into that big sulk and run away, he'd still be alive.'

That would have felled Charlie, always alert to his portion of blame. Stella did opt out of dinner, sitting next to Bill's carrot patch, drawing circles in the earth with a stick she'd picked off the compost heap. But afterwards she came swinging through the screen door. 'It's okay. Petrol said he's really glad I took him in the boat. He loved swimming. He doesn't care about being dead. He's got lots of pigeons to chase. He misses me, though.'

The Day of Resurrection had arrived early for Petrol.

Rita called for Bill to fetch the coffee and cakes. She could not face Leland now. Here in her kitchen, wiggling a set of naked toes, sat the one who represented her acutest failure. How could she have produced a child who hadn't so much punctuated as lined her adolescence with unwashed boyfriends and hickies, and who, fourteen years after moving out of home at the first possible instance, had *eloped* with her 'partner' of the day, selfishly stealing from Rita the joy of her own daughter's wedding? Neither of Stella's *fait accompli* excuses (Dan's 'trauma' over his parents' divorce, and their unwillingness to spend up big on a proper wedding) had explained why she would marry secretly in a Fijian resort. The hurt of it could still, four years later, bring Rita to tears, although never in front of Stella.

'How about it? Are the camp beds still in the garage?' Stella tapped her uninjured foot.

She did not look happy, Rita thought. Was it only the ankle? She could not ask her to name the problem, but if they spent more time in each other's company, away from the influence of snide Dan, maybe Stella would learn to trust her.

'They're on the right as you go in. Ask your dad to take one through for you. I'll throw some sheets on later.'

'Thanks, *Mom*. I appreciate it.' Stella grinned and hoisted herself upright.

Rita remembered that earlier she'd imagined Stella was scheming. She batted away her apprehension. Her daughter might have been headstrong in the past, but now she was a married professional woman, newly hobbled: not likely to indulge in worrisome antics.

᠅

One year ago, before Stella had joined the financial services company now employing her, she had worked for IT-chieve (pronounced as a narrow-mouthed version of 'achieve') Software Consulting, a sweating, badly managed little unit. Various glitches and follies led to its eventual crash, but the most pointless was the spuriously titled 'Team Building Weekend' held at Cascade Lodge, a lavish conference venue in the central North Island. As well as the unlimited bar tab and five-course dinners eaten under the dead gaze of stuffed trout, IT-chieve's manager had commissioned, from the Lodge's in-house Team Building Coach, activities designed to bind his indifferent employees.

During the first Visioning Session, while their manager directed them to 'zoom in on interoperability issues', Stella had scanned the hungover faces around the oval table. Their receptionist, bored, pierced and gelled. The two youngest programmers shading their eyes from the light that seethed through panoramic windows. Their project manager, a tall man with dark sideburns who avoided personal conversations but enjoyed his own jokes. More programmers, and, sitting furthest from the whiteboard under a brashly flourishing yucca tree, the disillusioned account manager who, in the bar the night before, had boasted of his early punk credentials. Stella had failed to imagine his grey comb-over glued into a mohawk.

Their manager stood aside while the Team Building Coach outlined a 'psychological instrument' which would deliver instant self-knowledge and sales-increasing empathy with customers. She required them to identify with water, fire, earth or oxygen, chivvying them into place under one of the signs she had tacked high on the walls. Stella ended up with the receptionist and the project manager, Adrian, beneath the flame.

After labouring through analyses with the adherents of other signs, the coach turned to the flame and suggested that it looked a lot like—*which* geometric shape?

A triangle, Stella volunteered, hoping a single contribution would suffice.

Same, said Adrian.

And if they engaged in some free association around the idea of a triangle, what occurred to them?

The receptionist suggested a pyramid. The coach laid out her hands like a Buddha. Yes! A mythical shape, representing our deep desires for harmony and beauty! She stayed in that position for a few moments, silent. Adrian caught Stella's eye and winked at her, stroking one of his sideburns.

The coach began to talk about their next planned activity: competitive sheep-mustering. Adrian leaned in and whispered, 'Did you know, sheep commit suicide more often than any other animal.'

'Really.' It was not the first time they had exchanged water-cooler badinage.

'Apparently . . . insofar as repeated suicide is an option for any organism. They walk into ponds and dams and drown themselves. Jump off cliffs.'

'I've heard they're a very well organised society in the wild. Matriarchal.'

He smiled, but glanced around the room. Stella sighed; his self-preoccupation limited his amusement value.

Outside, the coach divided them into two teams. The ex-punk account manager took it upon himself to lead Stella's group. 'You got what she said? Red collars left, yellow right, four each. Stella, you straddle the passage, get ready to sort them. Rob, you go down the hill in case they head that way. Adrian, with me. Let's roll!'

But as soon as they climbed the fence the sheep galloped to the bottom of the field, moving in a steady constellation. *Dad would laugh*, Stella thought. He had mustered sheep for real on his father's farm until he left to train for the fire service, and churned milk in a contraption no doubt very similar to the one displayed on a polished kauri table in the Lodge's conservatory. Stella had never set foot on the family farm. By the time Bill and Rita returned from America, her granddad, shackled by arthritis, had sold it.

'Get in behind, Rob! Not straight *at* them, man, get *round*, get in *back*!' The account manager took off down the slope, his forearms waving like mistimed windscreen wipers, grey wisps trailing over his scalp. 'Adrian!' he yelled. 'Get halfway up!'

Stella hauled herself on to the pen's boundary fence and watched the action. Once at the bottom of the paddock, the sheep swerved to avoid Rob, thudding along the far fenceline.

'Adrian!' the account manager shouted hoarsely, stooped, hands on knees. 'Get them!'

The sheep paused, held in equilibrium between Adrian and the other men. The account manager and Rob began to trudge back up the hill. Adrian raced towards the sheep, flapping his arms.

'Gitaway, ya bastards,' Stella heard him say. 'Gimme some space.'

They wheeled, and scudded back down the slope. The account manager stopped and clutched his hair. 'What the fuck are you *doing*?' he shouted at Adrian.

Adrian marched over to Stella, wiping his forearm over his brow. The force of his stare made her lean backwards on the fence.

'I think the boss would call this an ongoing crisis situation,' she said, trying to joke.

'I need to talk to you. My wife—um, Louise, she's . . . got problems, she hasn't been good for a while, things have got a bit crazy, oh, Christ, I shouldn't be going on about her, you must think *I'm* crazy.' Talking very fast. 'Not that it matters. Yes it does. I reckon she's seriously depressed. She won't go to her doctor. I don't know who the real Louise is, the girl I married or—she's been like this almost the entire time.'

'Effect of being with you?' She raised an eyebrow.

'Adrian, you arse—' The account manager's shout cracked into coughs.

'Do you need to talk to someone?' she asked.

He looked at her with concentration. 'I need to talk to *you*. I know her depression's not a reason—' He pounded the fence. 'I've started at the back end. Stella, you're like . . . a cool river and I want to jump in. When I think of you I . . . I relax. Coming to work, talking to you, it's the highlight of my life. Apart from my kids, but when I'm with them Louise is always around . . . I know you've already got some kind of set-up.'

Hell, she thought. This was the end of the light amusement. She jumped down from the fence. It was bad enough, him talking like this, without having his face turned up to her like some importuning Romeo.

Halfway down the paddock, the account manager was in a face-off with the sheep. Rob approached them. 'What a cock-up, eh.'

'Yup.'

He raised an eyebrow but vaulted across the fence and walked towards the Lodge.

Adrian said, 'I can't leave her yet. Got to wait till she's a bit stronger. It's a done deal, though. The way it is, it can't be good for the kids.'

'Mm. How many've you got?'

'Two. Girls. Five years old and three years old.'

Her fingers searched the fence for splinters. Below them the account manager circled, tied his shoelace in pretended nonchalance and straightened to run at the sheep. They capered towards the far boundary, separating into pairs.

She said, 'You're right, I'm with someone . . . anyway, I'm leaving soon.'

'Leaving IT-chieve?'

'Yes.'

'Oh, Christ. Bloody hell.' He braced both arms against the fence and hung his head.

'Look . . .' She searched for something to say. 'I'm really flattered.'

'When're you leaving?'

'About three weeks. I've resigned, but El Capitan said to keep stum about it till after the team building. Worried about morale.'

'So he should be.' Then he said, 'Probably better if we don't see each other after you leave. I'm tempted to suggest coffee, but it would be too hard.'

'Right. Okay.'

'. . . What're you going to do?'

'Contract to a finance company. Data warehouse for their funds.'

'Wellington?'

'Yes.'

The account manager, sending a final, accusing glance in their direction, left the paddock from the adjacent fenceline.

Adrian straightened. 'Well. I had to give it a shot. If you weren't already with someone, would you . . . ?'

'I hope your wife gets better.'

He gripped her forearm. 'Stella. If it doesn't work out with your current bloke, promise you'll get in touch. Give me a chance. This is the real thing.'

'Um. Okay. Thanks.' She removed her arm.

In the event, Adrian left IT-chieve before she did, hastening the company's demise. She had not often thought of him since. Even when Dan provoked her to remember her options she had decided that Adrian would be too high maintenance. And, to be honest, she'd never been turned on by easily acquired men.

Now, lying on her camp bed, she shut her eyes and reconsidered. From what she could recall, he was reasonably attractive. She thought she could tolerate his mild narcissism—he couldn't be worse than Dan.

She dangled an arm over the edge of the thin foam mattress and scratched at a paint pimple on the metal strut. The odour of the utility room pressed on her like a scorched, damp blanket. Her dad had set up the bed a few feet from the white wall of appliances, on a square of old carpet retrieved from the garage. In patches it was its original bright gold. It lay on streaked beige linoleum that ran out halfway down the room, leaving the remaining concrete floor bare. Storage boxes lined the other walls, some containing the detritus and treasures of her childhood.

Over the years she'd watched her mother and father change for the sake of each other: Rita less critical, Bill a little tidier; Rita less prone to proclaiming catastrophes, Bill restricting his commentary on her rather good driving. Recently she'd seen Rita struggle out of a sulk for his sake.

In contrast, she and Dan had preserved all their flaws perfectly. Beyond a few pragmatic compromises, neither had given up a speck of their particular, cherished domains. They often agreed on the other's opinion (restaurants, acquaintances, airlines, light fittings, music, etcetera), and she was further bound to him by their secret: the 'elopement' in a Fijian resort nothing but a lie, supported by cheap rings and a few photos, perpetrated in order that Rita would not have conniptions when they moved in together.

Stella thought, now, that she had changed very little in the years they'd been together.

Emailing on her birthday, Charlie had written, 'Sorry no card, Sis, parenting is the most loved-up experience ever, totally cracks open your life, makes you live in the here and now, no time for writing tho.'

Stella wanted her life cracked open. She wanted a baby.

She sat up, moving her shoulders, hips and cast in slow succession so the bed wouldn't tip and roll her on to the floor. In her wallet she found the business card Adrian had given her (with a long, soulful look) at his leaving do almost a year earlier. True to his promise, he hadn't contacted her. Project managers moved around fast in Wellington's tight market. He might have taken his unhappy family elsewhere.

It was a mistake to speculate. His wife and daughters flicked into her mind like flat cardboard figures in a pop-up book, the daughters' hair in plaits, wife in a frumpy blouse and A-line skirt, her face a blur. She flapped them away. Conventional guilt: the squirming, childish kind.

She would not fall in love with *him*, she was sure of that. A straightforward exchange: satisfaction of his lust for a few shots of semen. She had a couple more fertile days. If she could meet him tomorrow, and get started immediately, they might even hit her ovulation.

In the corridor, Rita's voice wandered past: '. . . the washing machine, Stella will be in there for a day or two, leave your laundry in the basket . . .'

Her hand, halfway to her cellphone, paused.

Ever since she'd moved out, it had been one of her priorities to no longer hurt Rita. The way she saw it, her mother couldn't help being naïve, overly idealistic, prone to religion. Stella had acquiesced to the fake elopement only after extricating Dan's solemn promise that he would never smirk during the anniversary dinners she knew Rita would cook for them. The endometriosis, too. Stella had told only her two close friends about it (both now baby laden, hard to pin down for coffee). She had feared Rita would believe the disease was the result of premarital sex. However, while lying in hospital after the removal of her ovary, she'd begun to realise how upset Rita would be that she had not confided in her.

It was too late now. Better to appear before her pregnant and glowing. She could say that Dan, caring nothing for the baby, had left. With luck, Rita would never bump into him.

She balanced the business card on her knee, and dialled.

❦

Leland stood in the kitchen doorway, watching his hostess slice something up. She had her back to him. Every so often she shrugged, as if she were holding a conversation with herself. In his head were the words about Betty that he had been planning to say since he booked his tickets in Duluth.

The only sounds were the knife hitting the wooden chopping board, and through the open window the rattling, rasping noise of cicadas. He found it enervating. His hostess—*Rita*, he thought, impressing the name upon himself once more—threw some chopped mushrooms into a skillet. They sizzled. She opened the refrigerator and removed a bowl covered with a wet

148

tea towel. As Betty had often done, she sprinkled flour on the bench and patted it over a rolling pin.

He grimaced. In Duluth, Betty's absence had been a sinkhole in his daily landscape. If he wandered too close to it, he unconsciously tightened his lungs, taking the same minimal breaths as he had when he discovered her lying senseless on the bathroom tiles.

'May I have a glass of water?'

'Oh!' An uneven hole stretched in the pastry. 'Sure.' She ran a glass under the tap, and brought it to where he stood. 'Sorry, I should have put a jug in your room. I'm cooking beef. Do you eat beef?'

'Yes.'

She snatched the glass back from him. 'I forgot—we have ice water.' She tipped it into the sink and refilled it from a plastic container inside the refrigerator door. 'Is everything else the way you like it?'

'Yes. It's all fine.' He sat down at the table with his glass. 'Where's . . . Bill?'

'He's in town, mopping up the shopping list. I forgot a few things. I'll get this done and then we can talk. I'm making Beef Wellington. We're in Lower Hutt, but there's no recipe for Beef Lower Hutt! Or Upper Hutt! Although they call this "Hutt City" now, but they're two big towns really . . .'

He'd learnt long ago that it was less tiring to let people run on until they'd finished.

She twitched, and hastily untied her apron. 'I'm such a numbskull, I didn't think, it'll be ages before this is ready to cook.' She sat down. 'Is there anything you're eager to see? There are beauty spots all over. Glaciers and rainforests, side by side. And the Maori culture. We'd love to show you round, but we used up most of our vacation time after Christmas—we have a caravan at Riversdale, just over the mountains, on the coast.' She waved one arm awkwardly behind her back, presumably indicating its direction. 'You could use it if you like, hire a car—do you have an international licence? Unless you have other plans.'

'Actually, Rita, I didn't make any further bookings. To get to New Zealand, that was my only thought.'

She blushed. 'Well, are there places you'd like to go now you're here? The South Island?'

'Maybe. I'll get my bearings for a few days.'

'You're welcome to stay as long as you like.'

'That's very hospitable.' He looked down at his glass, adopting a reflective pose. 'The thing is, Rita, I'd appreciate your opinion on something that's been bothering me. You may recall, in my letter, I wrote about Betty.'

She looked alarmed. 'Yes. I'm so sorry, Leland. Did you get the card on your pillow?'

He nodded. But she, having reminded him, now seemed embarrassed, fluttering her fingers in dismissal. 'She was . . . you must miss her. It's . . . terribly sad she can't be with us.'

He ignored these strained effusions. 'I mentioned in my letter that she has not made this . . . period of bereavement . . . any easier.'

At last, she was quiet.

'You knew her well? I think you did.'

She looked away. 'No. Not well. We roomed together for a few months. A year, maybe.'

'Did she ever . . . evince any tendency to inappropriately withhold information?'

'Um . . . no, I don't think . . . no. Well, I mean, it's been so long . . .'

'What I'm getting at here, Rita, is . . .' He closed his eyes for a moment, pretending to gather strength. 'Betty didn't tell me she was sick.'

She frowned. 'What? What do you mean?'

Now he could unreel his prepared story. 'The first I knew of it . . . we always ate breakfast together after my walk, but when I got back to the house she wasn't in the kitchen. I went upstairs to find her, and there she was, laid out on the bathroom floor. I thought it was a faint, maybe, but she never woke up from it. She was in a coma thirteen days and then she died. I had no idea.'

He tightened his chin. 'I never had a chance to say goodbye.'

'Oh my *goodness*.' Her hand advanced over the red Formica but stopped several inches from his.

He had expected her to ask him to expand, but she dropped her head and contemplated the tabletop.

He said, 'I have no idea why she acted that way. That's why I'm interested in your thoughts on the matter.'

The aroma of sautéeing mushrooms floated around them.

'I'm sure I don't know . . . could she have made a mistake?'

He shook his head. 'She survived thirteen days in the coma only because she was healthy everywhere else in her body.'

'Oh, Leland.' Her sympathy splattered around him. 'Maybe she simply didn't know—did she know?'

Again, a nod. Too wounded to speak.

'Maybe she *thought* she'd told you. Or at first she was scared, and then forgot . . .'

'No. I challenged the oncologists. Threatened to sue. They told me she'd ordered them to say nothing. They'd had her put it in writing—' He blocked out the words in the air with his hand: '"It is my express wish that you not tell my husband, Mr Leland Swann." Couldn't have been clearer.'

It was true. He had the letter in his document wallet.

'Maybe she wanted to protect you. Maybe she didn't know *how* to tell you.'

If he hadn't known better, Rita's nervy enthusiasm might have led him to believe she was talking about a mere outline of a woman, someone with whom she had no connection, but he had reviewed Henry Allerton's notes on her friendship with Betty. He had always been fairly sure that Henry's wilder suspicions were groundless. After all, the music man's judgement in other areas had been lacking. In particular, his harebrained idea that Leland should marry Betty, thus containing her while promoting his career, had backfired.

Notwithstanding, Rita and Betty had definitely been close. But if she did not want to dwell on her association with his dead wife, that would serve his purposes fine.

She said, hesitantly, 'There could be all sorts of explanations . . .'

He decided to move to the second part of his complaint. 'You have a generous, open spirit . . . However, Betty's final deception wasn't her only—'

'Oh darn, the mushrooms!' She jumped up and tended to them, muttering. A clang as she moved the pan to another element. 'Let me . . . *there*. Where were we? Golly, I'm sorry, that was insensitive.'

Better to save the rest for later. He bent his head. 'I find I can't discuss it right now . . . it's all too recent. Let's say . . . it wasn't the easiest of marriages.'

Her eyes widened. She pushed back her chair a little and moved her hands to her lap, looking away. Several times she opened her mouth. At last she said, 'It feels . . . wrong to be talking about her like this, seeing as she can't speak up.'

'I have to tell you, Rita, I was told that many at her funeral testified to her caring nature—you'll understand, I was too shaken to take a great deal in myself—but, to me, her deliberate concealment of her illness seems like a monstrous failure to . . . to *love*.'

The word ballooned between them. He looked straight at her, but she would not meet his eye.

'I'm so *sorry*.'

He smiled as genially as he could. 'Why should *you* apologise? I'm grateful—' And in response to her instinctive, tiresome demurral: 'No, sincerely, thank you for listening.'

In case her sympathy had not been fully awakened, he sobered again. 'It's been a terrible time. When everything one assumes about one's life is . . . turned on its head . . . I feel like I've been scoured out.'

A nauseating humiliation began to rise in him; he had inadvertently reminded himself of too much. He tried to concentrate on her twitters, but he could not help remembering what had driven him to New Zealand.

In the days after Betty's collapse, he had discovered that

152

she'd crammed the cupboards with groceries: further proof, if he needed it, of her deception. A forty-strong selection of My Treat meals-for-one in the chest freezer. Boxes of cereal stacked under the kitchen sink. Eleven toothpaste tubes laid head to tail in the shallow drawer of the bathroom vanity. And, on the vanity's tiny bottom shelf, beside the cleaning fluids and brush, four rolls of toilet tissue squashed into ovoids.

He could not bring himself to learn the art of shopping lists, and so, after Betty had been in hospital for a week and a half, his toilet tissue ran out. Walking bandy-legged to the box of Kleenex on the bedside table, he had grunted in disgust.

This was not *right*.

Nothing was right.

He looked at his upturned slippers under the bed, their rubber soles worn and peeling, and at the carpet, abraded to its roots at the bedroom door. Dust cloaked the bedside lamp. All confirmed the Movement's failure, and the malicious triumph of decay and death. He balanced on a pinhead, darkness whirling around him: a shrunken, cowering nullity.

Turning, he glimpsed the curtain at his neighbour's den window falling into place. He yanked up his trousers and carried the Kleenex to the bathroom. No sir. This was not for Leland Swann. Death, if it must be (though not any time in the imaginable future), but never oblivion. He would prove to God, as God was surely waiting for him to do, that he deserved to sit at His side, to be supremely prominent in the heavenly and temporal regions throughout eternity.

Rita's hands fluttered. 'I can't imagine how it *feels* . . .'

The screen door opened and Bill walked in carrying groceries. 'Afternoon, folks. Here's the loot, love. Good to see you taking it easy.'

Leland would have preferred to tell him later, but Bill could not be fooled. 'What's up? You two look like the sky's fallen.'

Earlier, it had seemed to Leland that his host and hostess were at odds, but now Rita seemed far too ready to talk.

'Bill, Leland's said that Betty didn't tell him she was sick. He didn't find out until she went into the coma.'

He sat down. 'Is that right.'

Leland gazed out of the window while Rita explained. He was uncertain how to hold his features. If he stopped trying to make an effect he might melt away, but he could not strive for an expression of grief without beginning to be overwhelmed by fury. It was imperative that he control himself. He wanted these people to know what Betty had done: telling the story was part of beginning again, of leaving behind Betty's corrosive influence. He pressed his fingertips to his brow.

'Are you all right?' Rita looked concerned.

'I'll pull through. It's . . . a blessing to be in your lovely home. Thank you for listening.'

Now she did, shyly, squeeze his hand. 'Anything I can do.'

Bill leaned back in his chair, his burly arms folded across his chest. 'That's some story. Must have made it hard for you. I have to tell you, it surprises me. Betty always struck me as an open type of person.'

Leland searched his face but could see nothing in it to indicate disbelief. Little sympathy either, though. 'People change over the years. Betty changed.'

'I suppose so. Still, makes you wonder why she did it.'

'It's obvious,' Rita said indignantly. 'She was sick. Even if she did write that letter, it doesn't mean she was right in the head.'

Leland hoped Bill wouldn't wonder too hard. 'I think I'll take a nap before dinner.' He stood, nodding sheepishly to acknowledge his earlier display of emotion.

Rita said, 'It's our privilege to have you here . . . our honour.'

'Thank you.' He smiled at her. It didn't matter if Bill was harder to convince. After he had triumphed, everyone would treat him with reverence.

Reverence, he repeated silently, turning to the door. The woman was dead, after all, her power obliterated. *Keep that in mind*, he thought. He ambled down the corridor, warm pleasure spreading through his belly. He would take one of his pills and sleep well, knowing that Betty's subtle chokehold was loosening at last.

❦

Rita unpacked the groceries, Bill helping with the higher shelves. He looked her way several times, but didn't bring up Leland's disclosure. When they had finished, she thanked him and kissed him on the cheek. After all this talk about death she couldn't be angry, despite his odd behaviour towards Leland. Whatever happened, she would always love him.

Then he said, 'Do you remember that very first letter Betty sent us? About Julius Toller?'

'No. I'm running late with dinner, I need to get a wriggle on.' She saw his surprise, and added, 'Sure I remember what *happened*, but I don't remember the letter. Can we leave it? I've got enough to think about.'

After Bill had gone outside to turn on the sprinklers and take his evening walk through the greenhouse, she returned to the kitchen table and sat for several moments, smiling at her hands, oblivious to dinner's looming deadline. As long as she blocked all thoughts of Betty, she could lose herself in the glow of the conversation's final moments. Leland had treated her as a confidante. He had not said a word about the tract, or their failure to promote People Under God's Command in New Zealand.

Forty years ago, when she and Bill left the Centre, she had lost the assurance, insofar as she had ever possessed it, of a life fully used by God, blessed with the absolute confidence that at all times one was doing the Right Thing. That loss had played a large part in the mental torments she suffered after Stella's birth: Stella, the contrary, troubled baby who, unlike every other child in the coffee group, cried so hard when she was put down on a colourful mat that some days Rita, who interpreted the cries as evidence of her inadequate mothering, did not even get away to

155

brush her teeth; Stella who would not sit quietly on anyone else's knee; who, until she was eight months old, woke to nurse every two or three hours at night and yowled for an age before falling back to sleep.

One morning, shaking up the formula in their old house, Rita had glanced out of the kitchen window at the fence and, beyond it, at the houses on the other side of the gully. For several moments (it was the *time* it took that distressed her) she could not recall that the kitchen was on the ground floor. It seemed likely that it was higher. If she stepped off the windowsill, would she fall?

A friend of Bill's returned from a winter holiday on the Central Plateau and described to them the entirely white landscape he'd looked upon day after day from his cabin. At first Rita had merely dreamed of gazing on a blank sheet of snow that would not, as the chaos in their tiny house did, present her at every turn with manifestations of her incompetence. Later, though, she made real plans: to find time, somehow, to fill the freezer with cooked meals; when that was done, to wait fifteen minutes from Bill's regular phone call announcing his departure from work, and then to leave the house. To watch from behind the bushes until he arrived. Then, once he'd walked through the front door to Stella's wails, to run to the bus stop.

Wafting around this torment was the stink of what lay beneath: her bewildered disappointment at the collapse of the Promise and their ejection from the Centre. And, not least, her guilty, unspeakable suspicion that Betty would never have the chance to excel at what she herself was doing so badly.

She didn't travel to that pristine landscape. She couldn't stop crying for long enough to cook the freezer meals. Bill took her to see a doctor. For the next two years she swallowed tiny orange tablets. They gave her hot flushes and rendered the inside of her mouth permanently dry, but after a while they also forced a little space around the most crushing thoughts, separating them from their disguise as Truth. Stella began to sleep more consistently, and Bill persuaded Rita to take a break from the mothers' group in which all the other babies were crawling and babbling and chuckling and swallowing solids with aplomb.

Bill opened the screen door and reached around to collect an empty ice-cream container from the counter. 'The new beans have shot up—I'll pick some for the salad.'

'Lovely.'

Under the kitchen table, her toes began to tap-tap on the lino. That Leland had confided in her promised something wonderful: a release from uncertainty. Maybe she would end her life knowing she had done something right.

Suddenly, a scene played in her head, fully realised although it had not been there the moment before: Stella and Dan facing one another on a flawless sward of grass, the ocean twinkling behind them. A small crowd, formally dressed, champagne glasses at the ready (Charlie and Zane and Noelle too—how could they miss it?). In the background, waiters hovering with canapés. As Stella and Dan turned from their restated vows, Leland came forward and said something brief and profound about love.

She would put it to Stella over dinner. Truly, it was an inspiration.

She stood and began to work on the Beef Wellington, foreseeing real happiness for all. Later, after the pastry had stretched and broken again, she remembered what Leland had said about Betty. *I hope that's the last of it*, she thought. *Betty's dead. It's a shame. That's all.*

She balled up the pastry and concentrated on perfect rolling.

2

That night, when Bill roused her, it was by flinging his wrist across her thighs. She had been lying on her back, sleeping lightly, and when she halfway understood that she was conscious she smiled dozily to herself, because it was the weight of his arm that had done it. Even though his deep, regular breaths told her that he was still sleeping, later on she could argue that it was *he* who had woken *her*, making it twice in a row. It was their game—which they played only to enjoy its failures—that they would take turns waking one another for love.

Tonight, for some reason that she did not want to remember, she lingered close to sleep while she snuggled up to his chest. Her limbs remained so drowsy that she could only butt her head gently under his chin and lift one floppy hand from the sheets and rub the back of it against him. She felt hot, suddenly, and kicked at the quilt so that it descended to their waists. One of her legs ended up hooked over him. He began to rub his lips over her ear lobe.

After a while he turned towards his bedside cabinet and came back to her with lubricant on his forefinger. She pressed against him. In the darkness it seemed that they were the only people in the world, and this hour the most precious time in history: she often felt this way after she had been angry with him and made it up. He pushed her shoulder gently and she turned over, angling her torso away from him, humming with delight: of all their variations, this gave her the most pleasure. When they had finished, she fell asleep tucked into his lap.

Later, she woke again into the darkness, unable to tell how much time had passed. It was Leland's voice. Angry. Her eyes flicked open. He had heard them making love and now, disgusted, was standing over the bed, chastising them. She couldn't remember whether they'd been noisy. They'd grown unselfconscious since the children had left home, but how could she have let herself forget their guest?

She jerked on to one elbow, peering at shrouded shapes until her heart slowed. The hair at the back of her neck was damp with perspiration. She lay down and moved her legs to a cooler patch of sheet, hoping to lose herself in sleep. Bill gargled something unintelligible, and shortly after came Leland's agitated voice.

She slipped out of bed. In the half-lit hallway she paused by the door to the guest room. It was slightly open. No sound. *Talking in his sleep*, she thought.

Further along, Stella's door remained tightly shut.

The Beef Wellington had turned out perfectly, the pastry light and golden, the meat tender. Rita had served it with buttered, caramelised carrots, new potatoes and Bill's green salad. Leland missed the whole thing, never emerging from his late-afternoon nap. Each time she had looked in on him he was lying in the same position, on his back on top of the quilt in his shirt and slacks, hands neatly folded over his belly. Before she went to bed she crept in and, breathless at her daring, covered his legs with a mauve mohair throw. She left a plate of food for him in the fridge and, on the kitchen counter, a note explaining the eccentricities of their decrepit microwave.

As soon as she'd served dinner, Rita, flustered by the empty chair, launched into her campaign of persuasion: Stella and Dan should celebrate their union with a renewal of vows, to be held at the close of the Harper Family Anniversary Weekend. A recognition of their relationship and a commitment to the future. She twinkled, not daring to look at Bill—maybe Charlie and Noelle and Zane would decide they could make it after all, if they knew they were missing a wedding celebration! And what a terrific opportunity to buy a new dress!

At the start of her mother's promotion Stella had laid down her knife and fork and tucked her chin into her chest. When Rita finally trailed off, she said, 'That's a lovely idea, Mum. I'll think about it'.

Rita sallied forth a couple of times: 'Sweetheart, wouldn't it be fun? Something for you and Dan to look forward to while you're missing each other?' And, trying to sound light and breezy: 'That Fijian chapel served its purpose, sure, but now you're in your thirties, maybe—well, wasn't it kind of touristy and rootless?'

'I was in my thirties *then*.'

Rita ignored the interruption. 'Wouldn't you like your family and friends gathered round to say—' she lifted her fists from the table in a gesture of sporting encouragement that felt wildly unfamiliar '—"We're with you *all* the way, Dan and Stella!" Wouldn't that be terrific?'

Bill spoke up. 'Reet. She's had a tough day. Maybe talk about it later, eh.'

Stella said, 'Mum, to be honest, I'm not sure Dan'll be keen. He's not really into . . . ceremonies and stuff.'

'Sometimes men need time to come round. If he knows it's important to you. You never had anything *formal*.'

'Sure. Yeah. Maybe.'

Rita took a breath but forked some potato into her mouth to keep from speaking again. She swallowed some the wrong way, and Bill had to rise from his chair and thump her back.

Later, while he scrubbed the meat tray, he said, 'Love, I know you mean well.' He dried a hand on his apron, and squeezed her waist. 'But this vow thing sounds like one of your busy-busy ideas. You think you would've come up with it if you weren't so anxious about Leland being here?'

'I'm not anxious! It's not only your Quaker lot who can hear inspiration from God!'

'I know that.' He paused. 'You think Leland might be interested in coming to Meeting? The Movement had a bit in common with the Quakers. Listening together, a political angle—' he laughed '—though you couldn't say they're on the same side.'

'Well, ask him.' She wasn't convinced.

'Maybe I will. Look, give Stella a bit of time to settle, eh? There's something going on there.'

Rita had been disconcerted to hear Bill confirm her earlier suspicions. Now, hovering outside the utility room door, she recalled the determined set of Stella's mouth. Bill was right. Her indifference could not be due to simple fatigue. Something else was occupying her.

Rita's fingers flew to her lips. Was there trouble between Stella and Dan?

Oh, that would be the end. Bad enough a union that began in secrecy, but however much she disliked Dan, she did not want Stella to endure the raw pain of separation and the uncertainty of beginning again. And what would it say about her mothering if one of her children didn't even turn up to the Harper Family Anniversary Weekend and the other's marriage had just broken down?

She tried to calm herself. Stella and Dan were tempestuous types. More likely they'd argued at the airport and would make it up fervently in precisely the kind of mood that would welcome the prospect of a romantic ceremony. Maybe Stella could fly to the Philippines and surprise him with the idea.

'Stop. *Stop* . . . evil mouth.'

She jumped. It was Leland again, hoarse in his sleep, urgent and distressed.

Should she wake him? She padded to his door and gently pushed it open. He continued to mutter.

Who dared to anger him?

Settling on her consciousness like an old story from her childhood came the events of the previous afternoon. That thing about Betty: she didn't want to contemplate it.

She moved into the room. In the light from the hallway she could clearly see the contorting planes of his face. At some time since she last checked on him he had changed into his pyjamas and climbed under the covers. The mohair throw had fallen to the floor.

It was ridiculous, she thought, to have imagined that he might despise them for making love. Why would he? She and Bill had been married almost forty years.

'Stop, Betty. *Stop*. No, Karol. No, you are wrong. Get out, both get out . . .'

He thrashed on to his side, and his breathing became animated by wakefulness. Rita stood stock still. If he opened his eyes he would see her.

It seemed from his tone that he had been defending himself from an angry, accusing Betty. Rita did not want to be any more intimate with Leland's complaints about his wife. A Betty who was angry with Leland stood too close in her thoughts to a Betty who might be angry with *her*.

Karol, though. She had not heard his name for many years. What had Betty and Karol said to Leland in his dream? It spooked her. She listened, trying to judge whether she could safely back out of the room. If she held her breath, she could hear his: even and quiet. She crept into the hallway and stood there, thinking. Would he remember his dream in the morning? What did the day, scarcely declaring itself through the candy-pull glass in the front door, hold for them?

She padded to the kitchen and went to the fridge for milk. Leland's plate of food had disappeared. There it was, empty, on the draining board. Odd, silvery striations caught her eye: had he *licked* it? It was a compliment, she told herself, and stacked it in the dishwasher.

She fetched a small enamel saucepan from the cupboard, thinking of all the other meals she would have to cook for him, and of how her feelings had been spinning since his arrival. She almost wished she could go to work in the morning. It was exciting beyond words to have him in the house, but it might be easier to climb the narrow staircase to Abel Andrews Accounting than to negotiate her tumultuous reactions. The competent, relatively serene Rita they knew in the office had deserted her as soon as his letter appeared, and Rita suspected she would never return.

Rightly so, perhaps. Even after that Rita had bloomed back in the mid seventies, she had always been guiltily aware that her days were occupied with what the Movement would have described as trivia: efficient administration, happy clients. Now, standing by the stove and stirring her milk, with Leland lying not twenty feet away, she thought that it wasn't good enough to be *pleasant*. Pleasant, content, calm, caring—that didn't stop people from flying planes into buildings. Didn't mend broken marriages or give everyone in the world enough to eat.

Nevertheless, for almost thirty years, an office in a squat five-storey block on one of Lower Hutt's lesser business streets had offered her an addictive peace of mind. She had begun applying for secretarial positions a few weeks after Charlie started grade school—primary school, they called it here. Mr Abel of Abel Andrews Accounting liked her on sight, and took delight in her combination of administrative and secretarial skills.

She had never been among such a consistently happy group of people. Mr Abel's daughters (accountant and receptionist) sometimes disagreed, but no one held grudges, and the only time Rita received a substantial criticism was when Mr Abel, his forehead luminously scarlet after a difficult end-of-month, steered her by the elbow into his office and told her that if she apologised one more time he would have to let her go.

'I can't take it,' he said. 'My blood pressure skyrockets.' He mocked her tremulousness. 'Every time you say "*Sor*-ry", ugggh—' fists shaking '—I want to throttle you. I've tried to let it ride over me, water off a duck's back type of thing, but it's *damn annoying*.' He glared at her. 'My doctor's warned me about stressful situations. When you get like that, can't say boo to you without you going sorry, sorry-sorry-sorry-sorry, Rita, *you* are a bloody stressful situation. Excuse my French. No—don't say it!'

For days, she couldn't meet his eye. Bill suggested that she could count to three in her head, slowly, before saying anything at all to Mr Abel. It worked, as long as she made this strategy her number-one priority. Inevitably she slipped up, but all it took was a baleful glance from under his knotty eyebrows and she'd half-swallow the 'sorry' before it came out. A couple of years later, she realised with surprise that her involuntary 'sorries' had all but vanished.

Now and then one of the younger staff would let loose with colourful language or a bad-taste joke but, in short, Abel Andrews harboured nothing that could cause Rita unease. Her only worriment was the involuntary question, needling at her whenever she most relished the sunny, relaxed atmosphere: if she had failed God's Promise, and left the Movement, how could she really be in the *right* place, doing the *right* thing? Would she one day be accused of selfishly wasting her life?

She poured her milk into a mug, and burnt her mouth on it. Leland's presence had erected a barrier right across that narrow staircase. That the youngest accountant had shouted to her on Friday evening, 'Next week I'll dish the goss on Gav!' gave her a twinge of yearning, but Leland had brought God with him— that God in whose Promise she'd once believed. She could not go back to her old life now.

She added some cold water to her milk and drank it quickly, then went to wake Bill. There was only one bathroom, and she didn't want Leland to be inconvenienced. Stella had talked about taking the day off, and would probably sleep in. There was still no movement from the guest room.

Bill groaned when she patted him. She left him to doze and spent a little extra time on her own appearance. In the dining room, she spread a fresh cloth on the table and laid it for breakfast. Later, after she had woken Bill again and, on hearing Leland stir, taken coffee in to him, she began to put together the ingredients for her pancake mixture. Once it was in the fridge, settling, and she had washed up her bowl and mixer, she wandered through the living room.

Stacking a newspaper together, she caught sight of a red and yellow uniform passing by the window. She opened the front door as the courier raised his hand to the bell. 'You're on to it,' he said, and handed her his electronic signing pad. When she had made her awkward scrawl, he gave her a bulky FedEx envelope and jogged back to his van.

Her name and address were written in large slanting capitals with a black marker pen. Someone called Aurelia McClure was the sender. Rita thought she'd heard the name before, but the address, in Belchertown, Massachusetts, didn't help. She carried it back to the kitchen, musing. An old high school buddy, or someone from Lambert's? No. Nor had she known anyone from the Movement by that name.

Patsy Gurner, née Chant, was the only Movement person who kept in touch these days. Rita glanced at the revolving washing line on the back lawn. Eight years ago, when Patsy had toured New Zealand with her husband Everard, she had laughed at the shirts and towels hanging there. 'At home only poor people put their laundry out! Don't you find it gets stiff?'

'I like it,' Rita had replied. 'It smells fresh. It smells of the outdoors. Anyway, when were you ever fat?'

Twelve years of selling exercise videos and motivational diet tapes from her programme *Christ Wants You Slim—Shed Sin for HIM!*™ had made Patsy a millionaire. In a newsletter which had arrived shortly before she and Everard flew in from Sydney, she had announced the formation of her New Vessel Bible Study groups. Rita had noticed the change in her signature photo. She was 'Pastor Patsy' now and instead of smiling into the camera like a mom-next-door, she stood on a forest path and looked gravely through the branches of a cedar, as if in possession of wise secrets. Big hair, bouffant and very golden, topped her angular boniness.

'Oh, I piled on the pounds when I was pregnant with Rosellen,' she had said, still looking critically at the washing line. 'It's *sin*, Rita, it's all sin. It doesn't matter whether we sin a lot or a little, we're still excluded from the light of God. The New Vessel Church will be our path back, our open door, and *Christ Wants You Slim* is our support.'

'It's a church now? I thought you ran study groups.'

Patsy tossed her hair. 'Yes. It's a church, and it'll be a bigger church. In the Lord's time.'

Rita reminded herself to ask Leland whether Patsy had written him. Something to talk about.

From the bathroom came the sound of splashing water and

Bill singing, intermittently, the chorus of 'Over the Sea to Skye'. She found a pair of scissors and cut open the envelope. Inside was a battered-looking uncased cassette tape and, folded within an accompanying letter covered in many loops and swirls, another of those bulletins from Betty's funeral.

Enough, she thought. And, *what now?*

It felt good to fasten on to irritation. She tossed the bulletin into the recycling bin by the screen door, making sure to cover it with a flattened cereal box.

On the tape's label someone had written, in shaky blue pen, 'Rita Harper'. This annotation partially covered a pencilled 'Vivaldi', written by the same person but with a steadier hand. Very carefully, as though it might sense her touch, Rita laid the tape on the table and began to read the letter.

Dear Rita Harper,

Please excuse me for addressing you without any Mrs or Miss, but as I am only a cousin of Betty's I don't know your circumstances. Without wanting to press the point no one else in the family knows who you are either, but luckily Roger (my husband) found Betty's address book and I am glad to be able to finish off this piece of business for her.

I shouldn't have started like this when what this is all about is Betty's tragic passing which hopefully you already know of from maybe a mutual friend and I am not the first to tell you. Knowing me I'll only write this letter out once (I am not the greatest writer) so please accept my apologies for that too. I hope my penmanship is readable.

I have to say as well that please take my word for it I haven't listened to the tape and neither has Roger. I am dying of curiosity though! Which is another reason to get it out of the house sooner rather than later.

You may already know that Betty's funeral was lovely though a bit short for my tastes. I gave the eulogy and I spoke off the top of my head and my oldest son videotaped it. I haven't got around to writing it out yet but I will send you

166

a copy when I do if you want one. At the end of the eulogy although it wasn't officially part of the service I announced an opportunity to give thanks for Betty and several people spoke including one young man who told an inspirational story of how she happened to come into the library when he was a young boy and found him scared and crying behind a bookshelf and she read to him and they talked and over time they got to be friends. His mother had left him there while she went shopping. Now he's a fourth grade teacher and he meditates and he talked about the universal spirit. I like all that kind of thing, I don't know about you. He said that when he grew up Betty told him that the day she found him in the library she had had a 'thought' to go there and into the children's section even though she had no reason to. Betty and her 'thoughts'! I used to see her several times a year and sometimes those thoughts seemed to me like something more mysterious than intuition or good sense.

Leland didn't speak at the funeral. Of course that's not unusual for the bereaved spouse it being too stressful. He didn't ask us back to the house either but wanted Roger and I to go back the next day to deal with Betty's things which we thought was understandable so we stayed a couple of extra nights in a motel. But when we returned we found he had left his keys with his neighbors. I don't know when he's coming back or where he's gone and neither do his neighbors in case you are thinking of visiting though I guess that would be quite a hike from New Zealand. It was a relief to know we would be seeing Betty's house again because I miss her awfully, she was a darling and so kind to me. She knew me my whole life and we talked on the phone every week. We were surprised when she married Leland but I hope she was happy.

I am jumping all over the place so I'll finish up. It is nice to write to you thinking that you were a friend of Betty's and maybe we can correspond with each other and share our memories of Betty. That would be nice. I should tell you that we found the tape in the bottom drawer of her little roll-top

desk *(my daughter is inheriting it)* along with a few other odds
and ends and nothing to say when she made it. So I wasn't
sure whether to send it and we brought it back home with
us but yesterday evening it weighed on my conscience and I
thought oh send it quickly and have sat down to write this to
you. Maybe that was one of my 'thoughts'!

If you happen to come to the States please come visit. You
would be more than welcome.

Yours truly,

Aurelia McClure.

In Rita's hand, the letter began to shake. Her eyes went to the
cassette tape on the table. It was a misleadingly shabby object,
but she knew it to be loaded with accusing cries that only waited
to be loosed upon her, blighting her life.

She tilted her chin and gave the tape her most imperious look.
Keeping this expression steady, she held the FedEx envelope
open at the edge of the table and prepared to sweep the tape
out of sight. It was like Leland had said: Betty had undoubtedly
changed over the years. She had always been headstrong and
opinionated, and may not have been the easiest person to live
with. Rita could not be held responsible for any of her sadness.

'What's that funny look on your face?' Bill stood in the
doorway, towelling his hair.

'Nothing.' She stuffed the tape and letter into the envelope,
shutting it into the cupboard under the sink.

'Is it mail?'

'It's only . . . it's nothing,' she said, her back to him. 'Just a,
you know . . . thing. More junk.'

She heard him move further into the room, and then the radio
came on: '. . . bomb in a Baghdad marketplace killed twenty-
two,' said the newsreader. 'Further south, an airforce helicopter
was shot down—'

'Leland up yet?' Bill asked, raising his voice over the radio.

'I don't know. I'm making pancakes.' She pulled the mixing
bowl out of the fridge.

'I'll look in on him. Stella's got an early brunch date in town. I said we could give her a lift. Have you asked him what he wants to do?'

'In Naballa, British forces took five casualties,' said the newsreader.

'The . . . museum. I thought. And lunch at the cable car. Can you please turn that down?'

'Okay. That sounds like a good plan. Get his mind off recent events.' He lowered his voice. 'If I hadn't heard it myself . . . seems odd that he can talk about Betty like that.'

'We don't know the whole story.'

'No.'

'I need to get on with these pancakes.'

'Right. I'll go give him a knock.'

'. . . said the convoy had been a civilian wedding,' muttered the newsreader. 'Iraqi sources claim twelve children are among the wounded.'

Rita winced and switched off the radio. There were times she could bear to listen to stories of mutilated and orphaned children, but the early morning was not one of them.

A few minutes later, she surprised herself by crying over the pancake bowl. Betty's mother had made such an affectionate fuss of her during that Christmas she spent in Montauk. Aurelia McClure's declaration of family forgetfulness seemed like a fresh rejection, even though (she realised, impatiently wiping her eyes) Mrs Wallace would either have passed on by now or be very old, and if very old likely to be losing her memory.

So that was that.

And it was Leland's business what he chose to do after the death of his wife. And neither Bill nor Aurelia McClure could truly understand him.

Leland and I, Rita thought, *will always have a kind of bond.*

🌿

Stella had arranged her first meeting with Adrian at a central-city café where they could talk like any ex-colleagues who might need to discuss the current market for their skills. For all she knew, that would be the extent of their conversation. She spent the journey into Wellington twisted sideways in the back seat, her plastered foot on Rita's lap, listening to her mother make conversation with Leland about the city's tourist attractions. Judging from Rita's vivacity, there had been some chemistry there, even if it only went one way. Stella smiled to herself—it made her feel protective towards her mother that she had suffered from unrequited love. Leland wasn't worth it, but he was a bit of a dag. It would be amusing if he tried out one of those famous 'Challenges' her mother had mentioned. Probably he had the same cold-reading skills which allowed so-called psychics to fake their insights.

At the café, Bill pushed open the heavy doors for her. She kissed him and, with a pang of guilt, waved to her mother. Until that moment, she had almost forgotten her purpose.

Inside, she pulled a magazine from the racks and found a free table. A few minutes later, she looked up to see Adrian standing in the entrance. He grinned at her, oblivious to those impatient on the steps behind him. Then his expression became serious, full of intent. He was taller than she'd remembered, and handsome in his shirt and tie. Virile, even. He wove through the tables and leaned on the back of the other chair.

'Stella.'

'Hi. Thanks for coming.'

'Have you ordered?'

'No.' She indicated her cast. 'I took a header down some steps.'

'Ouch. Coffee?'

'Not yet . . . I haven't eaten breakfast. Can you get me a bagel with cream cheese and ham? Low fat.' She offered him a ten-dollar note.

'My shout.'

When he returned from the till, he said, 'Gotta tell you straight off, I'm still with Louise . . . Oh Christ, you probably want a project manager. Do you?'

'No.'

'Okay. And . . . are you still with your boyfriend?'

'No. Not for a while now.' Slow and level. He must not think she was desperate.

'Look, I'm assuming—if I've got it wrong—'

Calm down, she wanted to say. No. What she really wanted to say was this: So, any family diseases? Heart? Breast? Huntington's? Alzheimer's? How many other women have you propositioned? Have you been tested for STDs?

Instead, she said, 'Sorry I wasn't in touch after IT-chieve broke up.'

'I didn't expect it.' He laughed. 'Hey, Harper, remember those insane sheep?'

She took a quick breath. Already he was invoking a shared past.

Next to them, two women laboured to lift a table in the direction of the window. It was bolted to the floor like all the rest. At last they gave up and sat down. One jiggled a buggy that was squalling by her knee. If it were *my* baby, Stella thought, I'd cuddle it.

Now he was telling her about his folks, who at seventy-seven and eighty still played croquet every Sunday afternoon, frequently went bush walking outside Whitianga, rose raucous hell at neighbourhood wine-tastings. While he talked he tapped his fingers on the table in time to the music, some kind of African jazz fusion. She wondered if he had musical talent; how many of her lacks his genes might redress, how many of her strengths they'd undermine.

His parents were strong in the church. 'They got me into spirituality, you know? I was in the Christian Union at uni. I've lost the faith since, though. The whole God thing seems kind of out there . . . disconnected from me. You found that too, I remember you saying.'

'Mmm.' When had she ever talked to him about her upbringing?

His folks were each other's best friends, he said. That was all he'd ever wanted. He stopped. He seemed to be waiting for some kind of declaration.

'I've been thinking about you,' she said. 'A lot.' That was true. 'Maybe we could get to know each other.' She rubbed her good leg along his calf.

He frowned. 'It doesn't bother you that Louise and I are still together?'

Was it supposed to? She couldn't tell. Was he going to get virtuous on her now? Or did he want to see evidence of guilt so he could comfort her?

She feigned indecision. 'I don't know . . . I had this impulse to call you.'

He laughed. 'Guess you really have lost that whole morality thing. It's one year next week, you know that?'

'Since when?'

'Back when we were sheep musterers. It's been a hell of a long year.' He smiled to himself and emptied a paper tube of sugar into his coffee, spilling some on the table. 'You didn't seem that keen, back then.'

'No. But . . . you know how it is, I've had time to think. To remember you.' She attempted a winning smile. 'Our jokes by the water cooler.'

He began to talk. Apparently Louise had taken to hiding household items. For every object she hid and Adrian found, she revealed a new, devastating secret. Late last night, after he'd turned the bathroom upside down looking for his toothbrush, it had knuckled his skull from inside his pillowslip. After he pulled it out, Louise had told him that the sea—Wellington harbour, to be specific—depressed her. Pretty bizarre for a girl who grew up in the Florida Keys. Adrian himself would have been happy living halfway up the Desert Road, if that's what she wanted. If it would have kept the woman he'd married—*she'd* been fun, upbeat, sure a little complicated, but sexy-complicated, you know? He would've renounced his windsurfer and kayaks and their million-dollar view of the islands and the yachts and the harbour mouth, and transplanted the whole family amongst tussock and rocks years ago if she'd taken the wraps off that little beauty. It wasn't like he found his work so fulfilling, that he had to stick around. He felt guilty, he said, that he couldn't be completely loyal to Louise in her depression, but she'd refused treatment. He wouldn't have been looking elsewhere if it hadn't gone on so long, wouldn't have said what he said to Stella last year, and hadn't taken a granny's footstep away from his wife since then.

Stella's bagel arrived, bulging and skewered with toothpicks. She pried a slice of tomato out from the layers of lettuce. Adrian's diatribe had erased her hunger. She didn't want the suction marks of other relationships. She wanted him to be without context, so that nothing she did could affect him or anyone else: only her own womb.

She tapped a passing waiter's elbow and ordered an espresso.

When he said 'harbour mouth', he had paused and looked at hers. She pushed her forefinger through the spilled sugar, making a white wavy line close to where his hand lay on the table. 'I had a dream. About us. It was—' she held his eye, trying to assess how much he wanted '—amazing. Almost . . . transcendental.'

'What was it about?'

'Oh . . . um, we were together, on . . . a beach. Rugged. Like an east coast beach. In the early morning. On a dune, watching the sun rise. When I woke up, I had this memory of an amazing *connection*, of being *bonded*, like no one else existed.'

She tried to ignore the tightness in her stomach. The only other time she'd told so many lies was when she had announced her elopement to her parents.

'This is incredible,' he said. 'I never thought you'd . . . I mean, after a year. I'd almost given up.'

'Never give up,' she said, meaninglessly.

He glanced around the café, seeming to grow taller, the hero in a tear-jerking, uplifting story of struggling, fated, glorious love.

'I thought we could . . .' She looked at him from under her eyelashes. 'See how it goes.'

He looked at his watch. 'I've got an eleven o'clock . . . look, I don't want to rush you, but how about I find somewhere for us . . . ? A late lunch. I can take a couple of hours.'

'That'd be—'

'I can't believe you're here, saying these things. We don't need to . . . do anything.' He looked earnestly at her.

'No, it's fine.'

'I mean, how can this be wrong, when it's all working out? She'll be better off without me, right?'

They made arrangements, and he stood, briefly touching her cheek. 'Good thing we'll be moving to private premises. I could get careless, you sitting there looking like that.'

After he left and she began to gather her things, fatigue hit her. She had not anticipated that pulling off the ruse would require such extended concentration. Perhaps, she thought, it was because she had appropriated the process of seduction for her own purposes that she did not feel at all aroused by his ardour.

Did being turned on help you conceive? she wondered.

And would the sex, far more intimate than a mere lunch date, be proportionately more difficult?

❧

Over lunch, Bill asked Leland straight out if he still Listened. As though, Rita thought, he was enquiring after nothing more significant than a golf habit.

Leland nodded gravely. 'Certainly. I try to maintain a constant practice of being in communication with God. It's not only the notebook.'

'Very true,' said Bill. 'I don't often use a notebook myself these days.'

They were in a restaurant at the summit of the cable car,

174

sitting by a curving wall of windows that looked over the city and the sparkling water. From her seat opposite Leland, Rita could see the pine-forested peninsula that jutted into the harbour and, near its tip, the glint of a dead prime minister's white marble memorial. Beyond the peninsula a wide, tricky channel led to the open sea. She tried to let the view infuse her with serenity, but she wished Bill had not asked about Listening.

Bill was oblivious. Between mouthfuls of macaroni cheese, he began to talk about his experience of Listening after the initial years in New Zealand when they had failed to get the Movement going. Those were his words: 'failed to get the Movement going'. Rita expected Leland to interrupt, but he seemed preoccupied by his bowl of onion soup.

Bill said he had found comfort in the hills, going into a sort of meditative state when he walked the tracks, his mind slowing with his practice of taking four uphill steps to each breath— two in, two out. Leaving disquiet in the valleys. How that and digging in the vege garden opened his mind to unlooked-for possibilities.

He paused. 'Hah. I'm telling porkies. That version misses out a chunk of time. Truth is, I stopped Listening altogether for a while. Got cocky. Started thinking the top of my mind knows everything I need to know. And to be honest, I realised that the Movement's politics, no offence, weren't the same as mine. But Listening's where we started out, and I remembered you don't walk away from the place you first stood up in. Then I found the Society of Friends, the Quakers. They'd been Listening the whole time, back since the 1600s. As radical and active as any group of people I've met. Challenged me to put some grunt into my beliefs.'

'You've given your time to them?' Briefly, Leland's interest flared.

'Yes, you could say that. Come with me to Meeting, if you're interested. There's a fair bit in common with People Under God's Command. Listening together, searching for the will of God together. God being the light within us.'

Bill could be more tactful, Rita thought, talking to the man whose Movement had failed.

But Leland didn't seem bothered, nor even to be paying attention. He turned to Rita. 'And you? Are you also . . . ?'

'With the Quakers? No. I went to a couple of Meetings but—frankly, it's not my style.' No less than an *hour* of silence on those wooden benches, without a notebook or pen to occupy her hands, hemmed in by others' breathing and coughing and fidgeting—each time, it had raised her to such a level of anxiety that she'd had to grip Bill's hand to keep from bolting.

She hoped Leland wouldn't ask whether she still Listened. Once, when Charlie was two and a half, he had tipped all the clothes pegs from their plastic ice-cream carton on to the kitchen floor, and spent a quarter hour happily transferring them between his dumper truck and an empty yoghurt pot. Before lunch, it occurred to her to insist that he put them away. She wanted to begin to train him in tidiness.

Later, after they'd picked up the pegs together, she'd realised how those thoughts might have sounded if she'd heard them in a Listening. *Insist that he tidy the pegs before lunch. Help him with the task—make it fun.* Imperative and no-nonsense, like the Listenings she'd transcribed at the Centre. She could hear the two voices in her head: her own voice, fading now, and the 'God' voice.

And then, before his nap, Charlie had emptied out all the pegs they'd tidied. She didn't mind, because he was tired and only learning. She knew that if she'd believed the first thought came from God, she would have felt compelled to make him pick them up again. She knew, too, that more spiritual people might be confident that God wouldn't want Charlie to get upset directly before his nap. They would understand the difference between a Temporary Right Thing and a Permanent Right Thing. They might say that her first thought, in her own voice, came from God too.

It was all very complicated, and she felt weary just thinking about it. She had decided she could only do her best, and stop trying to work out which thought was or wasn't from God. Nevertheless, on and off over the years, driven by guilt, she tried sitting up in bed with a notebook. This would go on for a few weeks but she always became very agitated. Bill called her 'driven' at those times, and the kids hated it. She seemed to have cut herself off from God, even though she could not stop believing in Him.

'What is the Quakers' position on Love?' Leland asked.

Rita held her breath. He had not yet mentioned the furore over the tract, but was he now making a reference to it? Did he mean to imply that Bill had joined the Quakers only because he was dissatisfied with the Movement?

'It's at the heart of it,' said Bill. 'It's about recognising "that of God" in each person, and treating them that way.'

'And are there any particular . . . projects, operating in this country, exploring the idea of Love?'

'I'm not sure what you're getting at—peace projects? Social issues?'

'No.'

Rita hoped Bill would not get started on pacifism. She wondered what Leland thought about the war. He had not mentioned politics yet. Nothing about Communists. Nothing about threats to liberty and the American way of life.

He said, 'It was a mistake, I confess, not to make Love explicit in the Movement. Before the group found me, they had placed Love somewhere around the Three Pillars . . . I forget the original configuration.' He shook his head. 'These days, I believe, people take offence if you advise them on their behaviour.'

Rita and Bill looked at each other. Did his admission count as an apology? Hardly: he seemed to have forgotten Karol Sadowski's vision and the events which had led to their expulsion.

'True,' Bill said cautiously. 'Back then we used to jump in with both feet if we got a whiff of dishonesty, and more often than not got away with it, cheeky enough to carry the other fellow along with us on the path to a better world. I reckon a lot of the time we were speaking from our own pride. But . . . the Three Pillars shouldn't be sneezed at. There's no question the world'd be better off if it took Perfect Truth or Selflessness to heart. Traders organising shut-downs of power plants to drive up energy prices—there's greed and dishonesty by the bucketload. Everyone out for himself, most people waiting for the others to change first. If it wasn't for the Movement, I'd be the same. Still am, most days. The Three Pillars made people . . . think about their obligations to each other. Made them think beyond their own comfort.'

Leland had been eating while Bill spoke, his eyes on his plate, but now he pushed aside his knife and fork. 'I've arrived at the belief that it is Love which enables people to find their way to the Three Pillars. The love of compassion and caring and respect: *agape*, as the ancient Greeks called it.'

Rita gasped. This was a complete change. He was transformed! Never mind the lack of charisma: this was the wiser, mature Leland.

He clasped his hands on the tablecloth, looking intently at them. 'But before I begin, there's something else I want you to know about Betty.'

Her heart jumped. She remembered the tape, now tucked into her underwear drawer. She liked knowing where it was. If she'd tossed it into the rubbish and sent it out of the house, it would have haunted her.

'After the Centre was sold . . . well, to judge from her behaviour, I believe she was overly attached to that grand building. We should have worked hard to rebuild the Movement, but . . .'

'What's your point?' Bill's voice was cool.

Leland paused and seemed to reconsider. He pulled a navy-blue handkerchief from his suit pocket. 'Excuse me. In any case, since she died, I've reflected a great deal on love and respect—on *agape* love, God's love. As Christians, it's meant to be the foundation of everything we do. But the wrong people have co-opted the word for the wrong reasons. My point, Bill, as you put it, is that I believe I still have a public role to play, a legacy to leave.'

The first time Rita had seen 'agape love' written in a church newsletter, she had imagined a woman with eyes and mouth wide open. But that Sunday their minister, like Leland, pronounced it 'ah-gah-pay'.

Leland described his project: to collect stories from ordinary people about loving acts they'd experienced or witnessed and, with their permission, to publicise those stories, so others could be inspired to 'engender *agape* love in their own lives'.

'Like the random acts of kindness thing?' she asked. Her hairdresser had taken that on as a guiding principle, giving blood, organising charity auctions, donating to food banks, wiping rainwater off playground swings and slides, cooking mammoth dishes of lasagne for new parents and the bereaved.

'Those acts would . . . be included, yes. But I'm envisaging a focus on the greater source. Kindness often springs from plenitude. Sacrifice and compassion, however, can manifest in any life, however poor or disadvantaged. I believe I've been led here. New Zealand is a marvellous place to begin. I have some savings, and I plan to set up an office and interview those who have stories to share.'

'That's quite an idea,' said Bill. 'How long for?'

'We'll see,' said Leland. 'I hope to garner some media interest. I hope others will pick up the idea and develop it.' He turned to Rita. 'I'll need assistance. Your . . . skills would be most useful.'

He had not so much asked as told her, but yes.

Yes, exhilarated, the sun beating off the tablecloth into her eyes, she would assist.

❧

Leland finished the onion soup, satisfied with his progress. Ever since he had shouted at his dream-bound, traitorous wife, there had been no more accusations or unspoken, invidious judgements. The two of them, Betty and the old man, Karol Sadowski, had vanished.

When he had sunk back into sleep after despatching them, he had dreamed of this woman, Rita. She had loomed over his bed, glaring, as if she expected him to offer an explanation.

As if she knew something.

As if she had been speaking with the dead Betty and now knew the truth.

But that was ridiculous. Here she was, beaming her accommodating smile across the table, grateful for his invitation, eager to begin work.

At two o'clock the hotel bar was dim, despite the bright sunshine outside. Stella sat in a leatherette alcove, the dregs of her second vodka and lime before her, hoping, in equal parts, that she would conceive immediately and that the actual conception would take place in other, more glamorous circumstances. After she'd finished the drink and wiped the condensation from her fingers, she decided she'd rather conceive immediately. The baby had the rest of its life in which to be polished and beautiful. It didn't matter where the spark ignited.

In the bathroom her cast showed up frayed and grimy against the beige laminate walls. She washed her hands and gave her teeth a quick brush, glossed her lips and ran her fingers through her hair. Limping across the foyer, she pretended to be familiar with the hotel, but when she stopped by the elevator her head floated. The vodka.

In the stuffy corridor she knocked, paused, and knocked again. Waited. She prepared an intimate smile. When he'd texted the room number, he had said he would arrive first.

Her phone beeped: *Held up. With u in 10. Room's in both names.*

She returned to the foyer and tried to look businesslike. The receptionist gave her the key as though it were perfectly normal for guests to arrive without bags. Stella resisted glancing back as she turned again to the elevator.

The room was tiny, the queen-sized bed covered in a silvery diamond-quilted spread that appeared impermeable. She sat on it and applied more lipgloss, then considered the task ahead. It occurred to her: a fortuitous delay. Lying back against the pillows, she pushed her hand under her skirt and touched herself, the living hot slipperiness a universe away from her view of grey pleated curtains.

The first tingles had spread through her thighs and belly when he knocked at the door. For a moment she felt like ignoring him; she had no guarantee of any pleasure if she let him in. But she greeted him and did her best to initiate the opening moves, pulling him down beside her and opening the collar of his shirt. Even so, he detached himself.

'Are you tense? You seem tense?'

'No—nervous. I haven't done this before.'

He let his hand drop and fell backwards on to the bedspread. 'We could just talk.'

'No. I mean, I like talking to you, but—' She touched his cheek. 'I've been thinking about you all day . . . the bedspread's horrible.'

'Ah.' He overdid the mock-relief. 'It's the *décor*, then. Out of the way, Harper.'

He stripped it off the bed, then attended to the buttons of her shirt, kissing her. She tilted her head so she could twist her tongue more deeply into his mouth. Through one eye she watched his lashes flicker against his cheeks. She ran her hands over his back. He slipped his fingers under the waistband of her skirt, and when he touched the KY gel she'd applied in the bathroom she remembered to cry out, even though he missed her clit. Easy-peasy-lemon-squeezy. The heel of his hand pressed against her pubic bone.

'Christ,' he said, convinced of her arousal.

The touching stopped. She opened an eye and watched him stripping off his shirt, bending to unlace his shoes. 'Help me.'

181

She put her arms around him and unbuckled his belt; pushed his trousers over the bulge, briefly excited by its hardness down the length of her hand. The pillowcase smelled of washing detergent and an over-hot iron. He nudged her under her waist, and again, until she rolled over.

'Sorry about the cast,' she said into the pillow. 'It's getting a bit scraggy.'

'Last thing on my mind,' from somewhere above her belly. Now he cupped his hand between her legs, tilted her and planted kisses up her spine. Better than Dan, she thought smugly. Less structure. She could almost let go.

She fell on to her back again. The weight of her cast twisted her calves together. He moved down the bed to untangle them and pushed her thighs apart, his breath hot against her.

'Oh—' remembering the gel, and wriggling up on to her elbows '—come back here.'

'Sure? Hey, what's the scar on your tummy?'

'Nothing. Old stuff.'

He smiled, reaching for his jacket.

'No—' she grabbed his arm. 'I don't need anything, I'm . . . I'm on the pill—'

'Really?' He drew back, looking at her with concern.

'Yes, I'm . . . allergic to them, to latex, my mum fed me too many bananas—it's true, honestly, you have to be careful with babies and bananas—I'm all clear though . . .' She heard herself gabbling, and whispered, 'Come on.'

He closed his eyes, fell back on to her. 'Crazy girl.'

Four years ago it had taken her many months to convince Dan that his cock alone was not enough to make her come. It would be terrible luck, she told herself, as Adrian began to grind away, if he turned out to have read the same instruction book. She tried to convince herself that raging lust accounted for his inaccurate jabs; later, when he had calmed down, he might be more interested in her pleasure.

Or maybe Louise liked this kind of thing. Four years, forty . . . her parents had been together ten times as long as she and

Dan . . . Had it become platonic and boring?

'Is that good for you?'

'Oh—yes, oh, God, yes, yes . . .' But nothing was happening. She tried rocking harder. The friction settled in the right place and her 'yes' rose, but the dragging weight of her cast began to burn her thigh muscles.

What was it like for old people? She couldn't imagine Leland having sex: too austere, too removed from the real world. What had Betty been like? Had she been into it?

She saw Betty standing by the window, rolling her eyes at the bed where Adrian was in full swing, propping himself up with sinewy arms and throwing his head back. 'Girlfriend, what are you *doing*?' she'd say, like a mélange of every chat-show host Stella had ever seen.

If Betty were alive, maybe Stella could have talked to her about this. In high school Stella had written to her about boyfriends and breakups, and Betty had implicitly understood that by the time the letter reached her Stella would be over the worst of it and not in need of her advice. *Dear Stella, I hope last month's ruckus has died down and that the others have come to their senses.*

Subtle, Stella realised, automatically rocking under Adrian. Betty meant, *Don't you be mean, too.* But she never overdid the advice. Betty had faith in her.

She realised she'd been quiet too long, and began to squirm, hoping her 'Ah, ah' didn't sound fake.

Betty had never questioned Stella's account. *Girls can say very mean things.* Even if she knew the whole story about Adrian, Stella thought, she would be wry, not judgemental. She wouldn't behave as though a little deviation from the rules would bring on the end of the world.

After Adrian had finished, an awful thought occurred to her. While she discreetly tilted her hips and watched him dress, she tried to frame her question so he wouldn't suspect anything. 'One of my mates wants to get the snip, now he's got kids. You ever thought about that?'

He laughed. 'God, no. They'd have to knock me out to get me near the hospital.'

Fine. Now she wanted to ask him whether Louise used chemical detergents; whether he habitually rode narrow-saddled bikes in tight shorts or had ever attended a childcare or schooling facility on a site later revealed to be polluted by lead or dioxins, or had been drinking heavily or smoking dope, what with the stress of his marriage. But she only smiled and asked if they could meet again tomorrow.

All things considered, she was off to a good start. Half-convinced she'd hit the jackpot first time, she did the longest victory-shop her ankle could stand, and returned to Lower Hutt. Hopping up the corridor from the front door she heard the chirpy tones of an infomercial.

Leland turned off the television when she entered the lounge.

'Stella. I'd like to talk to you.'

For the sake of her mother, she balanced on the arm of the sofa, shopping bags gathered at her feet.

'You should know, seeing as you were close to Betty. She was ill for a long time; up to six months before the coma, she knew she was going to die. She didn't tell me. I'm not sure why. Why would she have done that? What earthly reason?' He grabbed fistfuls of his hair.

Tumour-related dementia came to mind, but the thing with the hair seemed calculated. She couldn't be bothered.

'Sorry,' she said, 'sorry for your loss.'

'Forgive me . . . my bereavement's very recent.' He swallowed, made a show of recovering his equanimity. 'Your mother and I are initiating a project designed to spread the idea of compassionate love. What do you think of that?'

Trust Mum, Stella thought. She cast around in her memory for Philosophy 101. 'There's no true altruism. Anything that says there is, is only people trying to comfort themselves in the face of death. We have to live for today.'

'Selfish.'

'Sure. I probably am. I give to charity collectors on the street, but mainly so I don't feel guilty.' Was it worth it, to wind him up?

'Ah—you feel guilty.'

Now *that* would be proof of his powers—if he could divine what she'd been up to only three hours ago.

He gave her a generic knowing look: he knew nothing.

She snorted, and covered it up with a cough: she with her fake stoned-student rambling, and him with his earnest, conversion face.

'What's guilt, anyway? The cultural burden of failed expectations. Excuse me, I need to rest my ankle.'

She made her way towards her room, reflecting that before her life with Dan imploded she had liked to think of herself as a basically honest person, had believed that her discomfort over how she'd lied to Rita about the endometriosis and the elopement meant that she had basic integrity. Hah—if she didn't watch herself, she'd start believing that the ethos of women's magazines, that religion of expressyourselfloveyourfamilyan dfriendsliveinthemomentdon'tlookbackbepositivebeselfactua lisedcreategoodmemoriesbelieveinyourselffulfilyourpotential dreambigrespectothersdonoharm, 'spoke' for the ethos of her generation.

She took her washbag to the bathroom and brushed her teeth. Was that it? Was 'do no harm' the extent of one's obligation? From her letters, Betty had seemed like she could never have set out to harm anyone. But maybe she had been *too* nice: why else would she have stayed with Leland so long? Maybe she had been essentially conservative. Maybe she loved him in some way Stella couldn't imagine. But then why did she shut him out from her illness and death?

Stella peered at herself in the bathroom mirror. If 'do no harm' was the ultimate goal, at least her affair with Adrian . . . but then she remembered the two little girls. No. They would never find out.

What would Betty would have said about them? She seemed to really love kids.

Stop fantasising, Stella told herself. Why this preoccupation with the opinions of a dead woman you've never met?

Say her baby was a boy—the chances of one of Adrian's girls encountering their step-brother in a soap-operatic coincidence and incestuously falling in love were far smaller than their chances of being hit by lightning or obliterated on the motorway. In fact, given the reputed paucity of donations to Wellington's sperm banks, with each man's produce spread around several women, if she obtained the necessary semen there, the resulting baby would have a greater chance of getting sinful with relatives than if she continued doing it her own way. So it could be said— listen up, Betty—that she was taking the more ethical route.

She splashed her face with warm water and massaged her wrinkle-deterring creamy cleanser into her cheeks. She had left it on the ledge by the washbasin, and its level in the frosted-glass bottle had plunged down. She was sure her mother had been sneaking blobs.

Wasn't she, in fact, forcing herself to become *more* loving and unselfish by having a baby?

'Sure,' said Betty's avatar, prodded. 'You have to find your bliss. No one's getting hurt. And you can never tell who's destined to save the world! It could be your child!'

Who am I kidding? Stella thought. *My 'bliss'?* She of all people should know better than to turn her desires into some kind of religion. No. She tucked the bottle of cleanser into her washbag and zipped it up. She was too honest for that. It was like this: she wanted a baby, and therefore, on a four-weekly basis, she would fuck Adrian at every opportunity.

At the door, she reconsidered. Then she unzipped the bag, extracted her cleanser and replaced it on the ledge.

3

The current CEO of Abel Andrews was happy to give Rita unpaid leave, as long as she found a suitable temp and agreed to return for confidential meetings. On the same day, a long-standing client, a commercial estate agent, dropped into the office and put her in touch with the landlord of several local shopping malls. Excited, Rita phoned the man, but when she tried to explain the Project, he was suspicious.

'Nothing personal,' he said. 'I've had a few dodgy tenants, so I'm on the lookout. Not to worry. I prefer to make decisions in person. I do have a small office free, as it happens.'

She left work early and picked Leland up from home. The mall was a mere five-minute drive away. She knew it well, its low, wide entrance bracketed by a florist's chaotic with blooms on one side, and, on the other, Rapt, specialising in ribbon and gift boxes, and suffering from the nearby suburbs' lack of gentrification. The core of the mall was a single dingy corridor. A minor supermarket bulged from its end like the head of a hammer. With the landlord, Rita and Leland walked out of the dazzling sun into the gloom, past the dollar-a-ride toddler aeroplane and the stands of sunglasses outside the pharmacy. He waved paternally to Rapt's bored assistant. They passed a key-cutter's and shoe repair shop. Further along was a dressmaking business. Several mannequins stood in the window—Rita had an impression of cinched waists and fitted jackets. A woman inside smiled at her.

The office turned out to be the last retail space on the right, easily overlooked by shoppers who strode in and out of the supermarket's cramped produce section. 'It's not too flash,' the landlord said, unlocking the flimsy door. 'Probably accounts for the quality of my last tenant. You two look all right. You say it's a Christian project?'

Next to the door was a long window backed by a dusty venetian blind. *Scent by An Angel: Aromatherapy and Massage* embellished the glass in cursive gold lettering. He nodded at the sign. 'She began to offer hypnotherapy, not my cup of tea.' The door creaked open. 'Two rooms. No natural light in this first one, but the carpet's in good shape.'

The air smelled still of the aromatherapist's oils: lavender and lemon, and something spicy.

'This will be fine,' said Leland. 'Humble beginnings. Perhaps we can obtain one of those folding boards to put out on the street.'

'I'll get the cleaners in,' said the landlord. 'It'll be ready for you day after tomorrow.'

'Can you get us two desks?' Rita asked.

He snorted a laugh. 'I own an office building. I reckon I can find you a couple of desks. Ten bucks a week extra.'

After the cleaners had hurried through, Rita decorated the worn desks with posies from the garden, and brought in two fans and a potplant. She polished the remaining grime off the window in Leland's office and spot-cleaned the carpet. Leland was eager to make a start, and she persuaded him that until word of the Project got out he might stand on the main street and recruit passers-by. When he appeared reluctant, she suggested a question: 'May I ask, what's the greatest act of love you've ever known?' If they gave him a good answer, she said, he could encourage them to walk into the mall and find the office, where she would be waiting.

On the first morning, she stood in the darkness behind him and listened to him use the question she had provided: he did not deviate from it. A trio of businessmen, young and coarse, guffawed. Leland bristled, and Rita stepped forward. 'We're talking about the love of compassion and kindness—has anyone done something for you that you later understood made all the difference in the world? Think about it. Come back and tell us.'

Later, she heard Leland re-using those lines. But she could not eavesdrop for long. As soon as a middle-aged woman offered to give them her story, Rita had to return to the office. The woman turned out to be a fellow American, hailing from Pittsburgh. She told of how, shortly after her arrival in New Zealand ten years before, a neighbour had invited her to 'tea'. The following afternoon this woman had duly walked next door and drunk a cup of unfamiliar tea, chatting with her neighbour who was peeling potatoes at the kitchen sink. After an hour or so the woman went home, and it wasn't until two years had passed and she and her neighbour had become bosom buddies that she learnt a Kiwi 'tea' meant dinner. The potatoes had been intended for her. How kind of her neighbour, she said, not to draw attention to her mistake when she already felt displaced and strange.

Their next customer was the wife of an Alzheimer's sufferer who extolled the compassion of her husband's underpaid carer: she saw love each time her husband's repeated query about the weather forecast was met by this man's lively reply, as though he had not repeated the information thirty times already that morning. Later, a new father said he now understood what great love his adoptive parents had shown when they allowed him, at fourteen, to move in with his birth mother.

Rita found the work easy. She backed up the tapes with shorthand, and spent hours that evening turning the swirling eddies of talk into typewritten stories, using a dictaphone she had borrowed from Abel Andrews. If she concentrated, she could stave off the thought of the tape in the top drawer of her dresser, secreting betrayals and disappointments between its thin black ribbons.

In the middle of her third consecutive evening transcribing, Bill set one of the chairs from the dining table next to her little computer desk. He sat down and leaned close to her.

'Stop a minute, love.'

'I've nearly finished this interview.'

'Come on, take a break. You need to stretch. Stretch your wrists.'

Obediently, to hasten his departure, she pushed her arms straight, one at a time, and pulled back on her fingers. Then, for good measure, she rolled her shoulders, smiling at him. 'Okay?'

He took her hand and held it on his knee. 'Reet, is Leland paying you anything for this?'

'Shhh!' She glanced behind her, even though she knew Leland had gone to bed an hour earlier.

'He's paying for the office, isn't he?'

'We don't need it! Ever since the house was paid off you said I could stop working, and I never wanted to. Now I do, but it's only for a little while. *And*—' warming to her annoyance '—if I'd volunteered for one of the . . . the Quaker *peace* projects or a social work thing, you wouldn't give a hoot about the money!'

'It's not the money. He . . .' Bill hesitated. 'He should value you.'

She almost retorted, but a sense of the moral high ground stopped her. For some reason, Bill was prejudiced when it came to Leland. He had gotten the wrong idea, failing to understand as usual, and was trying to tell *her* what to do. He'd even gotten what you might call paranoid. The other evening he'd taken out the recycling and walked back in through the screen door waving some paper. It turned out to be that damned bulletin from Betty's funeral, all crumpled and damp from being smashed up against baked bean tins and ginger ale bottles. She'd been momentarily confused, and turned to look at the other one, the one Leland had sent, which Bill had propped up against a school photo of Stella. Where had this one come from? he wanted to know, and she'd said, oh, nobody, an old acquaintance, and he'd asked who, and for a moment she'd panicked that she might have to lie, but Stella had come into the kitchen and distracted him. Later, when he'd asked again, she had her answer ready. Betty's cousin, she said, thinking this piece of the truth would finish it, but he probed. How did this cousin know where to send it? Betty's *address* book, she said, trying to hide her anxiety. Was there a letter? he asked. Sure, she said, a note. A friendly note.

All true.

She was too busy to get sidetracked by his concerns. The Project was doing so well. If she kept smiling at him, and patting his shoulder, like she did now, he'd let her be.

Over the next fortnight, the Project only strengthened. Sometimes two or three people were waiting on chairs in the corridor, filling out the registration form. Leland was forced to cease his salesmanship and start interviewing. He seemed impatient, but Rita told him that the Project was taking off as fast as one could expect in Lower Hutt.

They heard the controversial: a lobbyist for euthanasia who refused to give his name and described a cousin's courage in putting an end to his brother's agony. The physical: a cancer-ridden man given 'new' kidneys through the organ-donation system and living to see his first grandchild. And they had many who misunderstood the question and said something like, 'My husband makes me tea every morning and that's how I know he loves me.' Rita tried to intercept those before they reached Leland.

At the start of the third week a very young, chirpy woman from the community newspaper bounded into the office. She apologised for not ringing in advance but she hadn't been able to get hold of their number. Rita told her the Project deliberately didn't have a telephone: they wanted people to tell their stories in person. The human touch was everything.

Just then a balding man poked his head through the door. Ken Block. Was he in the right place? The journalist interrupted Rita, poking her business card towards him. Did he object to her listening in? Ken Block did not.

His wife Sally, he said, worked as a sound technician and often cycled home late over the hill to Wainui. Last week sometime, he thought it was Tuesday, she'd noticed a cyclist a fair way up ahead who didn't seem to have any lights. Practically invisible in the dark, especially to fast drivers. But when the cyclist turned a corner the red beams shone out. He'd been wearing the light on the back of his helmet, apparently, and his backpack obscured

191

it. So Sally, even though she was tired—their two-year-old's coughing and crying had kept them up the previous night—cycled hard-out to catch him. All the way round the corner and up the hill.

'She could've easily thought, nah, stuff it, can't be bothered. But she's a really good person. I love her heaps, eh. She's been knocked off her bike once already on that hill, scared me shitless, oops, sorry, anyway, if it was *her* cycling without lights and someone took the trouble to let her know, I'd be majorly grateful.'

Rita believed him. He was on the level, not looking for reflected glory like some of their contributors.

The journalist loved it. 'We should *so* run this type of thing more often!' She arranged to meet Ken and his wife back at the Project office to take their photo. In it, Sally Block stood to one side, small and diffident under her bike helmet, while Leland shook Ken Block's hand. But despite the journalist's eagerness she did not serve the story well. Ken's simple declaration of love was missing from the article, as was any reference to Sally's accident. Without his animated mixture of embarrassment and excitement, the tale sounded banal. Leland frowned at the headline: 'Random Acts of Kindness Inspire'.

'It's *Reader's Digest* stuff,' Stella said dismissively. She hopped to the sink and rinsed out four coffee mugs that she'd transported from the utility room on the handles of her crutches. 'She only printed what Leland told her; she didn't even Google him. And really, Mum, I think your contributors are telling you what you want to hear. Love's not that straightforward.'

'It makes a change from the usual blood and gore. The journalist said so.'

'Yeah . . . it's sweet of you to think this will make a difference, but niceness doesn't sell. It's not dramatic.'

Rita suppressed a sigh. When Stella described her as 'sweet' it always felt like an insult.

In some ways, her daughter was an easy houseguest, often going out, returning by taxi well after the older generation had retired to bed. But the other evening Stella had been working in the dining room, the phonebooks inconveniently wedged under her laptop and spreadsheets covering the entire table, when Rita tentatively asked if she could lay it for dinner. Stella had snapped. Later, emptying the bathroom rubbish, Rita recognised transparent tampon wrappers. So that was it. She ridiculed her sudden disappointment: silly to wish Stella pregnant if she and Dan were having difficulties.

'Hey,' Stella laughed suddenly, 'maybe that's why the crucifixion story took off—heaps of love, if you believe it, *and* heaps of gore. The ultimate drama. And if you don't listen up and pay your dues you'll go to hell. There's your audience motivation. They must have had a really ace focus group working on that one.'

Rita tutted, searching for words. 'It's easy to put down the Project, but this is *love* we're talking about. Real love, like . . . when you're in trouble and need someone to show you some compassion. That's what's being married means—especially in the long run.'

'Mum, are you on about that renewal-of-vows thing again? I know you mean well . . .' Stella passed a hand over her eyes.

'Sweetheart . . .'

'Really, please, no more hints. It sounds lovely, but I don't think it's going to work out. Maybe another time.' She gripped her crutches. 'Night.'

Another time? What was the problem with *now*? But Rita knew that Stella never changed her mind through confrontation. She kissed her, feigning contentment. 'Night, sweetheart. I'm glad you're here.'

Stella began to swing down the corridor. After a few steps she turned and squinted. 'Mum . . . is everything okay with you and Dad?'

'Yes. Why wouldn't it be?'

'I dunno. Just wondering . . .'

Rita's discomfort grew while Stella gazed at her. At last she giggled self-consciously. 'Go off to bed. I have to clear up.'

Then she called after Stella's back, 'You and Dan come to the Anniversary Weekend and you'll see! We're fine!'

❧

Stella and Adrian had checked into another hotel at lunchtime on the day after their first tryst, and the day after that. After the fourth time in as many days, Adrian jokily called her 'my little nympho'. On the fifth day, they met in a sushi restaurant. Adrian suggested that they should not touch at all. This was fine with Stella. She had finished ovulating. While she ate nori rolls and salmon, his eyes burned over her.

She pleaded off a couple of dates after that: a physio appointment, a bad cold. Conveniently, he was landed with a sudden work deadline.

Over the weekend, harbingers of her period appeared on her panty-liners: brown dead-blood spots and smears, a warning she'd grown used to since her mid-twenties. When she saw them, a weight settled on her chest. How fervently, she realised, had she wanted to get pregnant straight away. *Endurance*, she told herself. *You didn't think it'd happen the first time, did you?*

While Stella had her period Adrian 'understood', but he booked an Upper Hutt motel for the next Saturday night. She caught a taxi; her parents waved her off.

'What did you tell Louise?' she asked after Adrian had let her in to the unit.

'Work. I'm in Masterton.' He closed the curtains, although it was still light out, and set two glasses on the veneer coffee table.

'What if someone sees your car?'

He produced a bottle of Glenmorangie. 'Want one?'

'Yes please . . . um, no, actually.'

Alcohol, mayonnaise, tiramisu, seafood, soft cheeses—the alcohol she knew about for sure, but she couldn't remember which of the others were proscribed before pregnancy. The childcare and pregnancy sections of bookshops seemed off-limits to her, the domain of women who were going about this in a more conventional way. Only the other day had she got around to buying a folic acid supplement.

Adrian said, 'The way I see it is, we try to manage the risk, but we're kidding ourselves if we think we can make it disappear. There's a point at which you have to say—' he shrugged, settling back on the couch '—so be it.'

He sipped his whisky. He was wearing an indigo turtleneck with jeans. His fringe kept falling over one eye. Something about his little foray into recklessness disturbed her: not that he increased their chances of being discovered—she had nothing to lose—but a certain theatricality, a sense of performance.

'Do you *want* Louise to find out?'

'God. No. Not yet.' He nodded towards some laminated menus on the phone table. 'Hungry?'

'I already ate.' Lamb and potatoes, with a compulsory side order of Project stories.

'Me too. Been parental-support-slash-referee at a six-year-old's birthday party, stuffing myself stupid on cheerios and fairy-bread.' He smiled ruefully. 'Where do your folks think you are?'

'Installing new server upgrades, working till dawn.'

'How about giving me your home number? D'you think I'd go down well?' He wasn't serious.

'Mmm. Could you get me a glass of water?'

'Sure.' He watched her drink it. 'When does that cast come off?'

'Not for ages.'

He groaned.

'What's up?'

'All this . . .' He flung an arm at the pleated curtains. 'This crappy furniture, it's claustrophobic. And we're forced into a motel, for Chrissakes. It's sleazy.' He grabbed her hand. 'I think we have the potential for something really deep.'

She knew that if she looked away from him he would doubt

her sincerity. She laid her palm against his cheek. 'Adrian . . .'

'Sorry. It's just . . . the stress at home. And this is . . .' He poured himself another whisky. 'I'm not complaining. The sex has been . . . awesome. Before, I felt like—' he laughed, rolling his head against the back of the couch '—a neglected car in a garage, and every now and again someone'd come out and tinker with it. Get it going, take it for a ride. Put it away for another few weeks.'

Someone? Did he mean he and Louise were still having sex? Diminishing his sperm count?

He smirked. 'Are you jealous?'

'Um . . . yeah, a bit,' she lied.

'Baby, you know she'll get suspicious if I start . . . denying her. I have marital obligations, okay?' He brushed his hand over her breast. 'It's not like she's on to me every night. Depression is *not* conducive to libido. With you and me, it's more than sex. We have to keep this thing real.'

'Yeah, I know . . . why're you looking like that?'

'Nothing . . . some guys at work were talking about this other guy who's having an affair—he's managed to get his wife together with his mistress, who's also married with kids, and the upshot is they're all off together, happy families, for a long weekend.' He shook his head in disgust.

'Right.' Did he rank himself above the holidaying adulterer in the moral stakes?

'I honestly think we can have something good and pure. Something big. You know what I mean?'

She took a breath. 'Absolutely.' It made it easier to lie to him if she believed some part of him was standing by, watching himself.

'Wow, it's good to talk. With you I have all this energy. You sure you don't want a drink?'

'Go on then.' She could pretend to sip.

'Tell me something. Tell me about your childhood.'

She gave him a stripped-down, misleading version of running away with Petrol, omitting the Three Pillars and Listening, and how she had wanted to figure out for herself what she believed. She tried to pass it off as a stupid, hotheaded escapade, but he was triumphant.

'I knew, that first moment I saw you sitting behind your desk, I knew there was a fire in you. Couldn't fool me with that cool exterior.' His arm around her shoulders now, tight, confident, his fingers playing with hers. 'You're kind of subdued tonight? The way I see it is, we've got plenty going against us. We have to be in this all the way for it to work.' He nodded towards her groin. 'You're . . . all done with for the month?'

It took her a moment to catch on. 'Huh? Oh, yes. The red tide's receded, thank God.'

Dutifully, she snuggled her head against his shoulder. No chance, no chance at all that this would play out like a date movie, the charms of the hapless manipulated victim transforming the schemer's heart.

He asked, 'You want to watch TV? We've only got a 17-inch at home.'

'Sure.' She passed him the remote.

The television blared into life, completing the room's banality. They watched a reality show about scrapping, marginally abusive parents whose offspring perfectly imitated the example they set. So the resident child psychologist would have it, and Stella and Adrian agreed, Adrian providing illustrations of how Louise's behaviour affected the girls.

A baby boy, the youngest of the TV family, bounced in a blue harness hung from a spring suspended in the kitchen doorway. His toes flexed repeatedly against the lino as he propelled himself up; his body slumped a little forward as if he reached for a cuddle. Stella worked hard not to imagine the small arms clutching at her sleeves, the feet bouncing on her thighs, downy hair under her kiss.

Adrian said, 'That woman knows her stuff.' He rubbed Stella's shirt where it stretched over her breasts.

She did not want sex. Her ovulation wouldn't come round for at least another five days, and she had forgotten to look up how long sperm could loiter in her tubes, hoping for a receptive egg. She sighed, forgetting her role.

'You okay?'

'Oh—a bit of a headache. My bed's a torture-rack.'

'You still on that camp bed? Can't your folks rustle up something better?'

'Their guest hasn't left.'

'The American guy? Doesn't he want to get around the rest of the country?'

'He's kind of doing some work,' Stella said, distracted by the pressure of his fingers on her shoulders. 'He and Mum have this project thing . . .'

Adrian sat upright. 'A project? Hang on . . .' He rustled through his briefcase and pulled out the local paper. 'Is your mum . . . *Rita* Harper?'

Oh God. 'Yup.'

'I was reading about it before you walked in. The Agape Love Project. *Neat* idea.' He pronounced it correctly. She remembered his stint in the Christian Union.

'Was your dad into—' he referred to the article '—People Under God's Command too?'

'Yup. That's how they met.'

'That must've been incredible.' His eyes glazed. 'What's he like? Leland Swann? Can you introduce me?'

'No! Are you kidding?'

'Yeah. Maybe.'

Stella kneaded the back of her neck.

'Stiff muscles, eh.' He muted the TV and rubbed his nose against her hair. 'Mmmm . . . .'

His hand slipped under her top, and she felt its heat around her left breast. 'I love this lacy stuff. Louise's underwear looks like a convent's ragbag. What a coincidence, eh? Weird shit.'

She rolled her eyes at the silenced television, but then he reached behind her back and undid her bra, squeezed a nipple. She gasped, and immediately felt like a hypocrite, she, who took pride in knowing herself. Still, like every other time so far, she had to feign arousal once he got started for real. While he thrust back and forth, digging her into the cushions, she watched the psychologist mouthing reassurances at frazzled parents, and tried to figure out which days of the week her next ovulation would cover. She had to borrow some of Adrian's determination and see this through.

A dry, popsicle heat ruled. More than once Rita reprimanded herself for wishing not to be stuck at the tail end of a gloomy mall. Only when she visited the bathroom did she glimpse the distant square of sunlight at the entrance. When she returned, she found a woman waiting in her office. Clipped grey hair, an intricately patterned scarf knotted at her throat, hands loose in her lap, her legs pressed together like an Egyptian Pharaoh's. She seemed unaffected by the heat, and from the start she spoke in complete, measured sentences as though reciting a script in her fancy English accent.

'Before I begin, you must understand that I do not give permission for you to use my story.' She waited for acknowledgement, and Rita nodded. 'I'm here for entirely selfish reasons, but perhaps my story will help you in some way. Categories, or somesuch. I should be honest, though, and say I don't particularly care whether it helps or not.'

A controlled laugh. 'I'll begin then, unless you object . . . ? I'm English, as you've probably gathered. My father died on a hospital ship in 1941. He was ship's chaplain. It was the day before my seventh birthday.' Her accent became more pronounced. 'The ship was unmistakeable, like every British hospital ship, garlanded in green lights . . . painted with red crosses. It was on its way home. They bombed it in the afternoon. The nurses got many of the wounded into lifeboats but a good number couldn't be moved. The ship began sinking, with those men below deck knowing they would drown and . . . unable to help themselves . . . One would suppose they were terrified even after all they'd

199

been through. And sick at heart to be denied England when they had believed themselves safe.'

Rita kept expecting the woman to look away, but she did not. It was a challenge to keep breathing with that gaze fixed upon her.

'My father stayed below deck until almost the last minute, and then he did climb up and ran to the rail, one of the nurses told my mother later, and they were shouting from the boats for him to jump, because you're aware that when a ship goes down it sucks you with it? But he looked over his shoulder, and then turned back and smiled at the nurses, and ran away from the rail. And that was the last they saw of him, although at least another half minute passed before the ship sank. He went down with the wounded. My mother brought me up to give thanks that he had provided me with such an example of unselfish love. The irony is that I did not remember him as an affectionate father, and after that it was worse, because how could he have loved me if he chose to leave me? Can one genuinely love if one does not love the people closest to one? Perhaps I lack the necessary faith. Which you possess, I expect,' she said curtly. 'Did you have your father while you were growing up?'

'Yes.'

'Why are you smiling?'

'Oh—I was thinking about how he died. Sorry.'

'And? How *did* he die?' Sharply, as if Rita intended to compete with her for tragedy.

'Nothing dramatic . . . old age . . .'

'Not a great deal to smile about there. I'm not looking forward to it, are you?'

'. . . contentedly, though. I think he was content.'

'How nice for him.'

'It surprised me.'

Smugly content with crystal-waving, positive-thinking Ianthe in their Florida retirement village. The warmth, he crowed in his few letters to Rita; the delicious, melting, constant warmth. Why hadn't he moved from Minneapolis earlier? Which she read between the lines as, *If only your mother hadn't held on so long.*

Rita said, 'I don't think you're selfish.'

'I beg your pardon?'

'There should be some other word . . .'

The woman, rising from her chair, humphed. 'My daughter likes "self-care". I disagree. We don't need to *try* to "look after ourselves"; evolution has dictated we do nothing else.'

Rita said hurriedly, 'Do you want—?' She wasn't sure what she could offer.

'No. My daughter would like me to "talk to someone". Now I can tell her I have. Don't get up. Goodbye.'

Rita did stand, because it felt like a defeat to be told what to do by this woman, and in any case she had to go into the mall and collect the next interviewee.

But the corridor was empty. She watched the woman pause outside the pharmacy and go in. Behind her, the office seemed uninviting; she hesitated while shoppers tripped past into the supermarket. She hesitated so long that some of them exited with full bags. When she thought about turning around and going back to work, and then home that night, her upper lungs felt filled with balloons. She could not take a satisfying breath.

Is this it? she thought. Was the Project the fulfilment of the Promise? It didn't feel like it. But she could not shake the idea that Leland had come to New Zealand in order to complete the Promise. He must be part of her future, that future in which she would know, finally, that she had done the Right Thing in God's eyes. Even the past, lying coiled in plastic casing in the top drawer of her dresser, could not shake that hope. Her father, happy with Ianthe, had been sure of his place in life. Surely, then, she deserved to be.

Frustrated, she turned and looked at Leland's door. What was he doing in there? He rarely emerged. He wore a suit to work every day, and treated each visitor with cool reserve.

Was she supposed to fall in love with him now? That could not be right, when she had made vows to Bill before God. But maybe Stella and the Englishwoman were correct, and there was nothing straightforward about love.

Not for the first time, she walked to Leland's door and laid her ear against the wood. She could hear nothing. Briefly, she imagined that he might be standing on the other side, listening for her, and then she despised herself for being so silly. She must not expect anything.

But why had he not mentioned the Promise? She must talk to him.

¾

Leland, wandering towards sleep, was uneasily aware of Betty hovering behind the swimming black and orange pools in his eyelids. It was no dream, he was sure of that, because to dream of Betty would mean he cared for her opinion.

Rita had persuaded him to wear one of Bill's sun-hats, a floppy spread of white towelling that covered his nose and ears with shade. But now he dozed, his head tipped against the back of the deckchair, the late sun crashing down on his face. He battled to push his syrup-thick thoughts towards his dead wife, yearning after the complex, well-reasoned speech he knew he was capable of, but he had to repeat each phrase several times, struggling to remember it while he got a handle on the next one.

He coughed. His head swung forward.

'Leland, an iced lemonade?'

The garden flared. Crimson rhododendron blossoms and tomato vines against a white fence rushed at him. With the conviction of the just-woken, he knew that if he could remember his entire speech he could banish Betty forever. He tried to summon the words, but could only bring to mind, 'Don't think that merely because you were closer to God—'

'Leland?' Rita stood over him, proffering a glass.

He accepted the lemonade, took a gulp. The chilled drink hit his worn molar, sending fiery lines of pain up to his left eye socket.

'Agh.'

Why had he bleated such a ridiculous thought to his wife? It was not true that Betty was closer to God than he.

Rita pulled another deckchair to his side, its joints creaking.

'I was worried you might get burned. The sun's still strong at this time of day.'

The straightness of her spine provoked an unexpected memory, as though a force had swivelled his head so he saw what had been at the periphery of his vision. The young Rita: a postulant, a woman in waiting. What did she want? Had it been a mistake to come to New Zealand?

No. That was Betty-thinking again, creeping in with ambiguities and distrust, nudging him away from his resolve. He must be positive. On the whole, these circumstances were far more desirable than those he'd endured in the early years with Karol, when he had been subject to the old man's every whim, unable to pursue ideas that he knew could take the group to national prominence. Even when Karol's lupus made travel difficult, he had continued to drag them around the country with no apparent strategy. Once, leaving Madison, they had driven to March, Wisconsin, for the first of several speaking engagements scheduled over a week in that state. However, the very next morning Alice Maniaty happened to mention that God had spoken to her about her cousin in Striper, the feckless one who'd gambled away his house. Karol insisted that they drive back through the state borders. When they arrived in Striper they discovered that Alice's cousin had been admitted to hospital the previous day. He groaned when they walked into his room and didn't repent before he died. They missed that day's speaking engagement in Wisconsin, and went without dinner and a bed that night in order to get back for the next one. Zigzagging all over the country for years, the few donations wasted on gas rather than food or publicity.

Karol resisted pursuing pledges. They didn't even maintain an up-to-date list of followers. He told people to write care of that cripple Esther Cray if they had a problem, saying God would probably show Himself before he, Karol, got around to replying. He assumed everyone would be as inspired as he was.

Leland knew better. Ordinary folk needed a strong guiding hand. He secretly thought God a fool for leaving so much up to free will: enough, in fact, to have scuppered People Under God's Command. For decades after the Movement's collapse it had been painful to recall how, if they had acted earlier, the mood of the fifties would have borne them along. People Under God's Command would have been a stronger, more widely known and resilient institution, able to withstand the later attacks of a degraded, Communist-controlled media, and thus able to rise again with the new conservatism.

Instead, the likes of Jay Grimstead and Duane Gish had ignored him; the Coalition on Revival made no reference to the Movement; Roy Moore and his simplistic Ten Commandments campaign got all the attention; and intelligent folk believed that Charles Colson's 'worldview training' couldn't be bettered. Even fluffy little Patsy Chant looked set to outstrip him with her plan to transform hundreds of thousands of piously dieting Christians into her very own 'New Vessel' congregation.

Hah.

Before he slept he had mentally compiled a list of men who might help him get this new Project off the ground in America. Men with contacts in the film industry and publishing; men who could distribute the product to church networks. He would need plush offices in a major city. A smooth organisation, attracting funds.

'Would you prefer a coffee? Leland?'

Unavoidable. He girded himself for conversation. 'Thank you, no. I am beginning to understand the harmful effects of even mild stimulants.'

'Oh.'

'Betty became very attached to her coffee. To be frank, it's liberating to be alone . . . a period of real growth, of preparation. Insights that otherwise might not have occurred to me.'

'Uh-huh.' She looked away and fiddled with her hem. After a few moments she caught his eye. 'Sometimes . . . it strikes me how strange this is. I mean, here we are.' She paused, and continued hoarsely, 'It's funny to think I once believed we might end up together.'

This made no sense to him, but he smiled with neutral reassurance. 'Indeed.'

'I have to ask you, Leland . . . I mean, it shook my faith a great deal when . . . when we didn't. Seeing as I thought God had promised me.' She mustered a resonant bass: '*You will marry that man!*' Tittered. 'How could I have misheard Him so badly? But I mean, it's not like I'm unhappy with Bill. Of course not! We're coming up forty years!'

'Congratulations.' He had no memory of her infatuation. She would have been like those ravening girls at his father's church who saw their future in the preacher's handsome son and never spoke of it.

'Well, yes! But . . . I can't make the two things fit together. You know, number one, that God spoke to me about you—I truly believe it, especially now that you're here; and, number two, Bill and I have been married all these years. He's a good man, and I'm very grateful for him, I *love* him, but I've always wondered . . .' She tailed off, blushing, but started up again. 'I've almost gone crazy, wondering if I imagined it, or misheard Him . . . The worst thing is that maybe I failed, somehow, and maybe that's why you told Bill to marry me, and maybe I've been living this kind of . . . second-best life.'

He saw an opportunity. 'You, at least, have a happy marriage. You're very different from . . . you have a humble attitude of service.'

Again, she looked around as though someone had goosed her. It seemed she did not like to hear of Betty, even in allusion.

He gathered his resources. He had never enjoyed reassuring nervous women. 'But we are not talking about love and marriage. We're talking about faith. The problem of faith when one cannot see how God is working. You have mentioned your fear that you failed Him. You're not failing Him now. The Agape Love Project is His.'

'I know,' she said doubtfully. 'I'm grateful for this opportunity . . .'

'Be assured, if you act with good intent and orient yourself towards the sacred, God will work in your life.'

'Do you think maybe He *didn't* speak to me? Do you think I got it wrong?'

Everyone needed to feel special, even the stultifyingly ordinary. He had known this since his earliest observations of his father's congregants.

'I'm touched that you've confided in me, Rita. This brings us to a new level of collegiality. So I say to you, have faith in the . . . Promise that you heard. Just as we have only the slightest understanding of God, so we may fail to understand, until they are brought to fruition, the deeper implications of His Words.'

'Do you mean the Promise might mean something different? From . . . marrying you? It seemed so specific.'

'Pray about it, Rita. Pray with faith.'

'Oh. I will.'

She seemed happier now that she had a distinct instruction. He himself did not feel the need to pray. His own mind, working as inseparably as ever with God's, had already bestowed on him a very plausible idea.

He smiled at her. 'I think I'll try one of those herbal teas. What would you recommend?'

If everything went to plan, he would need assistance into the long term. It was perfectly conceivable that God had, in fact, spoken to Rita back then, intending her to dedicate her life to Leland, and that she had misunderstood Him. It was a reassuring thought: God, wanting Leland to prove Him wrong, had put into place the means by which he might do so.

4

Rita and Leland had begun, on fine days, to walk to the Love Project's office. She calculated that for every stride of his, she took approximately one and two thirds. He did not condescend to slow down, and he always looked straight ahead.

Since their conversation about the Promise she had noticed how, on this morning walk, everything sprang towards her in lustrous colour. Today, trees flung their branches up to the gleaming blue, cars roared back and forth like chariots, feathered swathes of cloud reclined across the margins of the sky. Even the unpainted plank fence they now passed seemed stoic and noble, its irregular whorls and knots hinting at the singularity and sacrifice of trees, and its dust-browned, fluttering cobwebs at the grand cycle of life.

Rita herself felt as sparkly as sugar crystals, marching at speed towards her significant, life-changing work. She had lost weight, too, with this daily constitutional. She had had to buy a stronger deodorant. Life had suddenly become very full.

They reached the mall as the pharmacist was putting out her hoarding on the sunny sidewalk. She told them a young man had dropped in a note for them a few moments ago: 'You'd have caught him if you'd been a little earlier.' Rita read the note over Leland's shoulder, her head bent daringly close to his arm.

'Am purveyor of weekly Monday aft. show on Wellington Community Access Radio. Interview with Leland Swann, say the 18th? Call me.' The broadcaster had scrawled his name—Nathan Kendrick—and his number across the bottom of the sheet.

Leland nodded in satisfaction. 'You see, Rita, this is how it all begins.'

'I can't come,' she said apologetically, 'if it's that Monday. The eighteenth. Abel Andrews has booked me to take minutes in a tricky client meeting.'

Leland indicated that that her absence wouldn't be a problem, and stood to one side, humming at a pyramid of vitamin C jars, while Rita dialled.

Nathan, deep voiced, answered. Great. Right. Wait, she was American too? He could tell from her accent. How long had she been in New Zealand? Right, so she'd been in America while People Under God's Command was going strong? Did she know Mr Swann then? Had she been in the group?

His interest bordered on the prurient. She tried to convey this to Leland as they walked up the mall, but he only asked her how he would get to the radio station on his own, and could not be satisfied until she had found him a copy of the train timetable.

The only person to venture into the Project's office that morning was a cheerful man under the impression that they were running a matchmaking service. Later on, after waiting in vain for other interviewees, Rita paid a visit to the dressmaker down the mall from their office. The woman seemed very pleasant. She made Rita a cup of coffee in her kitchenette, and showed her photographs of beautiful gowns that she had made for proms and weddings. A violet silk with a square neckline caught Rita's eye. Stella, she thought, would look lovely in it.

When she returned, Leland was standing by her desk.

'I'm sorry! I went for a little wander. No one was waiting. I looked out for visitors.'

'That's fine.' He smiled at her. 'I've been thinking.'

'Do you want to sit down? Or—' she remembered her duties '—do you have some dictation?'

'No. This is a conversation between . . . friends.'

Happiness unfurled inside her. He had never entered her office except to make an administrative request.

'I have this to say.' He began to pace across the room. 'It seems to me that, in the spiritual realm, it's as if these forty years have not passed.'

She thought immediately of the Promise, and Leland interrupted his pacing to meet her gaze.

'Metaphysically, it is *sin* that demands that time should pass: time in which the results of our sin can become apparent.'

Her stomach rumbled. She blushed, and layered her hands over her belly.

'I mean to say, sufficient time for reflection, for recognition of the sin and for conviction. Time for a turning to restitution. The *Movement's* sin was leaving Love out of our prescription for the world.'

Wait until Bill heard this. Leland had called his own omission a sin. How could Bill think badly of him now?

'If there was no sin, there would be no need for time. Thus, if we repent, and make good with this Project, and God forgives all sin, doesn't it follow that, in a spiritual sense, the intervening time would also vanish?'

Her mouth fell open. Was he saying God's Promise to her was as fresh as if she'd heard it yesterday?

She said, 'I'm not sure what you're getting at. I mean, I'm married already.'

'Remember what I said, Rita? Have faith in the goodness of God. He won't ask you to do anything wrong. All will be well, and all will be well.'

The night before, she had heard a young man say that on one of Leland's tapes. Briefly, she wondered if Leland had realised she would recognise the little prayer, but the thought vanished beneath a swell of delight. Leland seemed to be suggesting that the future would incorporate everything: her marriage to Bill, what good she had managed to make of her life after leaving the Movement, and fulfilment of the Promise. It couldn't be better.

'All will be well,' she echoed.

Leland attempted a wink. 'Hold on to your hat, Rita. We're on the verge of something big.'

♨

A few days before her next ovulation, Stella, working late, made a strategic mistake.

'I need to see you,' Adrian said when she answered her cellphone. 'Why didn't you answer before?'

'I didn't hear the phone. The cleaner's vacuuming.'

'I need to see you.'

'Um, okay. Sure.'

'Where are you?'

'Work.'

'I'll be there in fifteen.'

'Tonight's not that good for me . . .' She redeployed the application. The data wasn't appearing at all now.

'What?'

'It's, it's a bit . . .' She clicked the save button, watched the stack trace fill up the console, Googled the error. 'I'm pretty busy.'

'What the fuck? I'm in a crisis here!'

'Um, okay.'

'*Okay?* Who the hell have you turned into? I thought we had something! I tell you I'm in a crisis and you come on to me like some shrivelled prune.'

She exhaled. 'Calm down, Adrian.'

A thud, and the line went dead.

She weighed her phone in her hand, looked through the bank of windows at the orange-tinted city sky. In an hour she could walk—well, hop—into the bar across the street, assess her options. But it was a long shot. If she let Adrian go, and hit her ovulation having forfeited her best chance, she'd hate herself.

His phone rang all the way through to the message. She hung up, checked a couple of promising articles and tried again two minutes later. He answered on the fourth ring.

'I'm really sorry, babe.' She had never before called anyone babe.

Nothing.

'You know what it's like, I've been here all day and I haven't spoken to anyone since five, and my mouth hasn't caught up with my brain.'

'You said "I" or "my" four times.'

'Um, okay. Sorry.'

'Are you there for me, Stella? If you're not, forget it. This has got to be more than a stupid pash. I'm living a real life over here, I've got problems. You have to be with me all the way.'

Mollification wasn't working. She ramped up. 'Hey, lose the gloves! Or, what, do you get off on being angry?'

A silence. Then he said, 'I'm in the playground near our house. She's lost it.'

'Really? Are the girls all right?'

'Yeah. Fine. Fast asleep. They're all asleep.'

'But . . . shouldn't you get back there?'

'Christ, I know how to look after my own kids, okay? I don't need a fucking social worker. She's never hurt them.'

'Mm-hm. What happened?'

'She tried it on with me a couple of times.' The surliness hadn't left his voice. 'She doesn't hit hard enough to bruise.'

So how do you know your kids are safe? Stella thought.

'Last week when you were playing the "I'm-so-unavailable" game she finally agreed to see a shrink. In the waiting room she says she needs the loo, so she gets the door code from the receptionist and goes into the stairwell, and ten minutes later I go to find her and she's buggered off.'

'Where did she go?'

'That's not the fucking *point*. Down six flights and off to the railway station. Whatever. I was worried sick about her.'

This struck her as resoundingly insincere.

'Are you listening?'

'Yes.'

He sighed, whether at Louise's incorrigibility or her own failure to commiserate she could not tell.

'Today I got her to go to the doctor's with me. Naturally, she bungs on an act for him and he assumes I'm overreacting. "Oh yes doctor I was a bit depressed after my daughters were born and recently I've been a bit tired . . ." *Tired*. Shit.'

She held his buzzy voice away from her ear for a few moments and scanned the next page of results.

'. . . and while she's paying he tells me that if I want to talk, if I have further issues to discuss, I'll have to make an appointment on *my own behalf*.'

Far below her on the street a truck ground its gears.

'Tonight when I get home she's turned everything, every bugger-last stick of furniture and box and jar in our bedroom, upside down. Like some stupid student prank, except, at this . . . manic level. The coat hangers. All through the wardrobe—we've got a walk-in—she's unscrewed the poles from the wall, and threaded the coat hangers on to the poles so they're hanging from their . . . triangular bits. Then put the poles back up. Our clothes are all over the walls, hammered on with carpet tacks, upside down. The wallpaper's wrecked. And in the ensuite she's buried the toothbrush heads in Blu Tack and they're standing under the glass like some . . . weird . . . aquarium thing.'

She moved the phone away from her ear again. She had heard of cases in which couples were unable to conceive because the woman was allergic to her partner's sperm. Maybe she was allergic to Adrian.

'And there's a bloody great hole in the bedroom wall where a bed leg's gone through. When I said what the hell's going on she did this freaky smile and shrugged, and I told her to come and help me put it back so we could go to bed, and she said put what back, and I showed her the bedroom and she said what's wrong with it? Then she stopped talking.'

'Where's she sleeping?'

'Spare room. Which you might think was her purpose, except I had to . . . persuade her to go there because she was going to crawl into the space between the upside-down bedhead and the floor. Jesus, I don't know what to do.'

She imagined Louise squeezing, head first, into the dusty recess. Louise smiling in the dark while she levered herself along the carpet with her elbows. It was not a mad smile.

'Do you think she might be winding you up?'

'Of course she's bloody winding me up!'

'No, I mean . . .'

'Christ, Stella, I know my own wife, okay?'

'Yup. Mmmnh.' She would not say sorry again.

'I need to know you're on my side.'

'I'm listening, aren't I?'

He sighed again. 'Her friends encourage her. Not in a good way. Bunch of moaning minnies. Sit around and angst over coffee. That's what I like about you. You do stuff. You make your life happen.'

He seemed to be waiting for an answer.

'Well, thanks.' She kept her voice neutral.

'You're not going to offer, are you. So, can you meet her? Discuss stuff?'

'*Meet* her? Are you kidding? What the hell would we discuss? Your sexual prowess?'

'Is that all you think about?' His voice broke. 'You know my shit. And even though Louise rarks me up, I care about her and I *thought* maybe you could help. As a mate.'

Stella thought she would, in fact, like to meet someone who had gone to such lengths. Then she recalled her goal. 'It's crazy! Why would you want me to meet your wife? We'd be . . . inviting disaster. It'd be nuts.'

'Why? You'd hold it together. Look, she hasn't made that many friends here. And if we're going to make a go of things, it'd be the right thing to do, wouldn't it, to leave her in a better state? If she's not going to help herself, I have to do something.'

Really? she wanted to ask. What *will* you do? Drop a comment into the breakfast cereal, betraying your intimate knowledge of Louise's new best friend, and enjoy your starring role in whatever chaos ensues?

'No. I don't think so.'

'You don't get it. I'll spell it out. If she stabilises I can leave her.'

'Mmm.'

'Don't sound so enthusiastic.'

'I just don't think it's wise.' She looked back at the screen, wondering if the server configuration was the problem.

'Why the hell not?' His voice rose. She recalled that he was, apparently, alone in the middle of a playground. 'What am I for you? Some kind of side dish?'

'Don't shout.'

'You're bloody frozen, aren't you? Do you have any feelings?'

There was a tragic ring to his voice; she imagined him sweeping an arm towards the empty slide and limp swings.

She didn't call him back, but the following evening, when she noticed the first signs of her ovulation and reached for her cellphone, she remembered the tone of his voice. He didn't answer. He didn't return her messages. Not the next day, nor the next.

Every time she went to the toilet she examined her panty-liner, checking for the stretchy clear mucus that would herald her ovulation. She tried not to think about how few eggs from the remaining ovary might yet make the journey down her scarred tubes; she tried not to think that the egg currently making its way out of her body might be one of her last.

On the morning of the Project's seventeenth day, as he and Rita walked to the office, Leland noticed labourers working around a wooden shed wedged between two single-storey shops. Going home that evening, they saw a huge truck backed up on the sidewalk. Its wheels had shattered the asphalt. The shed had been hoisted on to the truck-bed and fastened with cables. Brown dust and cobwebs covered its lower boards. Leland and Rita were forced to step on to the deserted land to get past. The air smelled of damp earth and rotting wood. He almost tripped on one of the chunks of asphalt that jutted up at the edge of the sidewalk; the weight of the truck had shattered it.

'Why all this fuss?' he said to Rita, annoyed. 'Why not demolish it on the site?'

'Oh,' she said, 'They're saving it! It was probably an old workman's cottage. A railway cottage, maybe.' She gazed at it. 'When Bill and I got here, I felt like that house looks. Ungainly. Out of place.'

A house? He frowned at the infeasibility of it, that someone might have considered this shack an adequate shelter.

When had he given up hope that this earthly life would fill him with what he needed? Long before he met Karol, he had known that for sure. Nothing in his parents' limited existences had made him confident that he would be *seen*. They would have relished the privations of a house like this one. They would have squashed him into it: they always wanted him smaller.

Luminous yellow and orange reflectors had been nailed to the building's lower corners. She touched the tip of her forefinger to one. 'Sometimes . . .'

He thought, then, that the time might have come to reveal his idea, but before he could get started she laid a hand on his arm.

'Leland, what you said in the office last week, about God's forgiveness . . . um . . . eliminating time? So that it's as if the last four decades haven't passed?'

He nodded, wishing she didn't feel the tedious need to clarify. He could not move fast enough—get into larger waters, have others take over the talking, the explaining. Nevertheless, he must stay in this place long enough to give the Project a sure foundation.

'So . . . I shouldn't worry about how long it's taking for the meaning of the Promise to come clear?'

'You could conclude that.'

She lightened. 'But still, I don't see how . . .'

'Let's go on.' Gingerly, he placed a hand in the small of her back, and they began to move slowly down the street. 'I have a proposition for you. As for whether it fulfils the Promise, I believe only time will attest to that. Time and prayer.'

'A proposition!' She waggled her head merrily. 'Do tell me.'

He concentrated on his speech. 'When you told me about your Promise a fortnight ago, I confess it startled me.'

'Oh . . . you didn't show it.'

With effort, he suppressed his irritation. 'I considered it prayerfully. After some days God showed me . . . Do you recall me speaking of Holy Marriage at the Centre?'

'Um . . . maybe. I think so.'

He did not believe her. They turned into the next street.

'You know, I've started at the wrong end. This is my weakness, to be theoretical where I should pay attention to the practical. The Project is developing well, and in due course I aim to appoint others to carry on here. I will be based in the States, putting the model into practice there. The US Project is likely to grow quickly. I'm thinking a book development, a documentary. I'll require someone to smooth the way. I believe it's God's will that you should come to the States for six months. We understand one another on a spiritual level, as the Promise demonstrated, and you've developed the Project here. You'll be able to explain it to others.'

She said nothing.

'Naturally, you'd have your own living quarters.'

'Could Bill come too?'

'Of course. I'm eager to sell the Duluth house. So long as we're close to a major airport it doesn't matter where we go.' He pulled something from the depths of his memory. 'Seattle's renowned for hiking, I've heard.'

'And . . . I don't mean to be . . . *mercenary*, but could you pay me? You know how it is, we have to think about our retirement, and Bill's worried . . .'

'Be assured, the means will be there to support everyone. Prosperity always follows the Lord's will.'

At last, she stopped asking questions and clasped her hands in front of her bosom. 'Oh, I can't believe . . . this feels like the fulfilment of *everything*! When do you want to go? Because, we have to stay for our anniversary—the Harper Family

Anniversary Weekend. I'm sure Stella's going to get enthusiastic about the ceremony and there's lots of work to do for it.'

'Naturally. To everything there is a season. What is your schedule?'

'For the weekend? It's . . . my, how time flies, it's coming right up! Leland, we wish you'd come. We'd hate it if you stayed in Wellington while we were on holiday. Bill and I wouldn't be married if it wasn't for you. Stella and Charlie and Zane wouldn't exist! It'll be a wonderful time, and I really think that when Charlie and Noelle hear about Stella's renewal of vows they won't be able to stay away.'

She was babbling. He said, firmly, 'Be assured, we will not leave New Zealand until some months after your weekend. I have several months left on my visa. We need to build momentum. Be known in every household.'

'Oh, that's wonderful . . . do you mean you'll come?'

'Come to what?'

'To our weekend! The Harper Family Anniversary Weekend!'

He grimaced. He had another subject still to cover, and all he wanted was to get back to the house and retreat to the silence of his room. 'Yes, I will come. Another thing. I've mentioned the idea of Holy Marriage. That's a concept I'd like to promote once the Project gets on its feet in America. Spiritual partnership. A spiritual union in which both participants live for the glory of God. Betty did not adapt to it easily. She was not ready for it.'

Rita took a sharp breath and began to walk faster, grinning anxiously over her shoulder at him.

He raised his voice. 'Perhaps it is our *working* partnership in this spiritual realm which God referred to when He . . . made the Promise you heard.'

She nodded avidly, and stopped, allowing him to catch up. When they were side by side she said, staring straight ahead, 'I don't mean to be insensitive, but could you stop talking about Betty? I find it hard to hear about her.'

He said nothing. She took his silence for agreement, and

217

perked up. 'I like what you've said about this "working partnership" being spiritual. I can't imagine not being married to Bill! You know, it'll be the most amazing thing to know I wasn't hallucinating when I heard the Promise. And to know I'd done okay before I die.'

Maybe, Leland thought, he would have done better to marry this one. A good administrator, naturally obedient. He cast around for the right comment.

'You need never have doubted it,' he said at last.

Why did God put him in these situations where he had to simulate fellow feeling? He knew it was part of the payoff, the uneasy alliance he had with his Maker. He lifted his hand, and after a moment's awkward hesitation, patted her on the shoulder.

'Let's continue. What are you going to cook for me this evening?'

5

Rita resolved to reorganise her dried herbs and spices. It took her most of one evening to throw out the stale mixtures, refill, polish and relabel the jars, then shuffle them on the racks. The task was not as absorbing as she had hoped. When she was done, she wandered into the living room. Stella and Leland were sitting at opposite ends of the dining table, Leland going over transcripts of the Love Project interviews with a blue pencil, and Stella working on her laptop, her back unsociably turned towards the lounge, where Bill was reading one of his journals.

Rita adjusted a couple of knick-knacks and walked behind Bill's armchair to close the drapes. Then she jumped—Bill had reached backwards and taken hold of her wrist. 'Come here, love.' He pulled her on to his lap and wrapped his arms around her, playfully squeezing the air out of her lungs. 'Take the weight off your feet.'

She squirmed. 'I'm squashing your magazine.' She leaned forward and pulled it out from under her, ripping the cover. 'Darn.'

It was one of Bill's current affairs publications. He folded back the torn page, revealing the headline: 'UN Demands Close of Guantanamo'. Rita stared at it. The day before, a young woman who had heard Leland was American had come into the office and politely requested that they 'carry home the message of peace' to the US Administration. 'Children are dying,' she had said. 'Children are being orphaned.' *I know*, Rita had wanted to say, *it's heartbreaking*, and, *I didn't vote for them*. Instead she had said, 'We're not political in that way. We're trying to change things from the ground up.'

The woman had argued some more, and then Rita had thought to say, 'But when we take the Project to the States, we'll be a stronger force. We can get people to listen to us then. In a few months.'

Bill said, 'You all right?'

She shook back her hair. 'Sure.' She hadn't found the right moment to tell him about Leland's invitation.

The doorbell rang. She leapt off his lap, untying her apron. 'Goodness, well, I guess we have a visitor!'

Leland put his pencil down and watched Rita as though she was about to announce something that pertained to him. Stella didn't look up.

'You expecting someone?' Bill asked.

'You never know! I'll go see.'

At the front door, she kept her voice low and cordial. 'Hel-*lo*! Thank you for coming! We're so excited!'

'Hi.' The dressmaker carried a large sports bag. Rita approved of her outfit: navy slacks and a white shirt. Businesslike. Nothing Stella could despise.

'You can drop your bag in here.' She led the dressmaker into the main bedroom. 'So you and Stella can have some privacy! Oh, give me a peek! I love pretty materials.'

'I left my calico samples along in the car. I can get them if she's interested.'

'Women want *calico* gowns?'

'No. They're mock-ups.' The dressmaker produced swatches of silk and satin. 'Have you thought about what you'll wear?'

Rita rubbed a floral linen between her fingers. 'My, this is gorgeous. I don't know . . . I'm not good with fashion.'

'Maybe something you can use again.' The dressmaker held up a square of turquoise, a weightless, slubbed wool. Rita made loud appreciative noises, hoping Stella would hear and be curious. 'Well, come through to the living room. She's working too hard, she needs a break.'

Bill looked up. 'Knock me over with a feather! Evening, Florence! What brings you to our neck of the woods? Do you need me to sign something?'

'Are you two acquainted?' Rita asked.

The dressmaker looked at her with delight. 'So *you're* Bill's wife! He's talked about you a lot.'

Bill had stood. 'Florence comes to Meeting, love. You're not here on Quaker business?' he asked her.

'No. I'm here about your daughter's dress.'

'Okay. Stella?'

'Mmm?'

'Florence is here about your dress.'

Rita held her breath.

'What dress?'

Bill turned to Florence. Florence turned to Rita.

'Yes! Surprise, sweetheart! Florence is a designer, a friend of your dad's, and she works next door to the Project office!'

Stella twisted, frowning. 'So?'

'And when I bumped into her the other day I thought it would be just perfect! For someone local to make your dress!'

'Mum. What are you talking about?'

Suddenly, Rita wanted very much to move herself and Florence and Stella into the bedroom, away from Bill, who looked as though he knew precisely what she'd done and why.

'Florence can design your dress for the ceremony, sweetheart. The renewal of vows . . . I know you said you weren't . . . but I thought once you saw her *lovely* fabrics . . .'

Stella slumped over her laptop. 'Oh, *God*. Jesus *Christ*.'

Leland looked up, tapping his blue pencil against his lips.

'Stella,' Bill said quietly. 'Let's talk like civilised people.'

'Dad!' She spread her hands. 'I don't need a dress!'

'I thought it might help you get in the mood, sweetheart. If you *think*, you'll see what fun it could be. And—' Rita moved closer '—if you act excited, Dan might rise to the occasion. You could even propose . . . fly to the Philippines and surprise him!'

'But I'm *not* excited. Anyway, I'm not sure how to get in touch with Dan.'

Rita tried to fend off the gloomy import of this statement. 'What do you mean? Didn't he leave a number? Doesn't he know about your ankle?'

221

'That's not the point.'

'He doesn't know?'

'Yes, *okay*, he knows.'

Florence cleared her throat. 'Maybe this isn't the best time.'

Rita had forgotten her. She tried to speak brightly. 'Why don't you go get those calico pieces. You can lay them out on our bed.' She stalked into the hallway as if she intended to fetch the samples herself. 'Don't worry, she wasn't expecting you, is all. We'll be with you in a jiffy.' She led the dressmaker all the way to the front door.

Marching back to Stella, she hissed, 'Won't you even look? It'll be fun. Relax! Forget yourself! Even if things aren't great between you and Dan, if you start acting *positively*, with some *hope*, that'll help! The longer you leave things . . . fermenting, the harder it'll be to patch them up.'

The front door closed. Rita glanced over her shoulder. Florence had been very speedy. Was she in the bedroom, trying not to listen, or in the hallway, listening carefully so she could report their dissonances to the Quaker congregation?

'Mum.' Stella screwed her lips into a tight knot and looked away, breathing hard. 'I appreciate that you want me to be happy. And . . . I want *you* to be happy, and I'm sorry I wasn't clear about this earlier, but . . . it's really unlikely that this renewal of vows thing is going to work. Tell the woman thanks but no thanks. Please.'

In a flash Rita saw her mistake: she hadn't given her daughter the guidance she needed. Ever since the teenage Stella rebelled, Rita had been scared off by her confidence and sarcasm. If she had been a stronger presence in her life, Stella might now be listening with respect.

Rita saw how it could have been: her daughter on a porch, arm in arm with a square-jawed, forthright husband. He waved at Rita, leaping over the railing and advancing towards her across a smooth lawn where her grandchildren played. 'Mother Harper! Welcome!'

Dan was not that man. But Fijian chapel or not, he and Stella were joined in God's eyes. She glanced down the table. Leland was watching them, as passively engaged as if Stella were a TV. She imagined a renewed Stella telling this story for the Love Project: '. . . and then my mother really laid it on the line . . . if it wasn't for her . . .'

No: she would not let this marriage, however tainted its beginnings, dissolve because of an ill-timed business trip and a silly grievance.

'Sweetheart, marriage is . . . you can't simply give up on it, like a pair of shoes you don't like any more. Even—' she laughed a little '—if the heel's given way or they're wearing through on the sole, you know, there are places you can go to have them fixed!'

Bill sat down opposite Stella.

Stella rubbed a hand over her face. 'Stop. Please.'

Her daughter's expression, tired and sad, scared Rita. Stella pressed a few buttons on her laptop. It glowed brighter, then shut down. She closed the lid and shoved it aside.

'Dan and I are pretty conclusively finished. No amount of counselling is going to help. He's gone. As in, when he does come back to New Zealand, he won't be coming back to me.'

'Love.' Bill patted her arm. 'I'm sorry.'

'Yeah, well . . . it's better like this.'

Better?

'But why? What happened?'

How could Bill accept this disaster? Tears ran down Rita's cheeks.

'There wasn't any particular thing. We both changed, not in the same way. Different values, different priorities.' Stella sighed. 'I couldn't make him happy any more. I'm really sorry, Mum. Don't cry.' She gave a hard laugh. 'And no, before you say it, it wouldn't have made any difference if we'd been married in a real church.'

Leland got up. Gathering his papers, he left the room.

'I wasn't going to say anything about church—but you *did* make vows. Why didn't you tell us? I never would have invited that woman over. I'm so humiliated.'

223

'I knew you'd be upset. Please don't cry, Mum.'

'Reet. It's okay. Everything will be okay.'

She pushed Bill's hand away. First Charlie's defection, now this terrible shock, and in neither case did he get it: how her life would be left hanging, incomplete, with nothing to show.

'It's not too late, Stella! If you speak honestly to Dan, and apologise for your part in what went wrong . . . he's had time to think it over, he's probably waiting to hear from you!'

The dressmaker spoke behind them. 'I'll be going.'

'Oh.' Rita half rose. 'Sorry to have inconvenienced you. Leave your business card on the hall table. Leave two!'

'It's okay. See you at Meeting, Bill.'

Rita thought they might wait to resume their talk until the front door closed, but Stella did not seem to care what the dressmaker thought of her.

'Believe me,' she said, 'Dan's *not* waiting.'

'But this could be a turning point for both of you! Finding some humility, learning to seek the right way together . . .'

'Look, I know you and Dad have that, I know, and I would love to have what you have, but it's not going to happen with Dan. He was a mistake. It's my fault.'

'Are you saying you'll get divorced?'

Stella hesitated. 'I guess so.'

'I don't want you to begin your life with a divorce!' Tarnished, she almost said.

'I'm almost thirty-seven. I'm not exactly "beginning" my life.'

Rita tutted. Even more reason not to let the marriage go.

'I'm really tired. I'm off to bed. I'm sorry. I'll move out soon, I promise.'

'No hurry, love.' Bill patted the laptop. 'I'll pack this lot up for you. Sleep well.'

After Stella had steadied herself on the crutches and hopped down the passage, Bill laid his hands on Rita's shoulders and kissed her forehead.

'Bit of a shock, eh? A hard thing to hear.' He pulled her up.

She stood stiffly in his arms. 'Might be all for the best. We kept giving him the benefit, but he never impressed me.'

'What do you mean, "impressed"? A husband isn't ... something you *buy* at the supermarket! Not like ... deck furniture on trial! It's a *marriage*! And what happened to "there's something of God in everyone", like your lot are always saying.'

Bill half smiled. 'True. But that doesn't mean he's good enough for my daughter. At least we'll have her to ourselves over the anniversary weekend.'

If Stella still wants to come.

'It's not about personalities,' Rita mumbled into his shoulder. She stepped around him and went to brush her teeth.

Later, after Bill fell asleep, she cried. After she cried, she reflected on Stella's words. *I couldn't make him happy any more.* She was left with a single conviction: the separation hadn't been Stella's idea. Dan had wielded that poisonous, final knife, and Stella had stubbornly let him. Worse still, tonight Bill had proved himself weak enough to let it pass. She shuffled to the edge of the mattress, as far as possible from his slumbering back.

This sundering of a marriage did not fit with God's Promise finding its way into the light. How could a God who had made that Promise, and had brought Leland here to fulfil it, also think it was all fine and dandy for Stella and Dan to break *their* promises?

And because it did not fit, she knew it could not be. She felt anointed to act. Her job was not yet done.

Stella's flat pink thermometer showed a dip in her temperature. Later that morning she made her way to the offices of the software company where Adrian worked. She expected a receptionist, but when the lift doors opened she found herself at one side of a very large room. The five people at desks lined up against the far wall did not look up. She walked across the bare expanse of carpet until she caught someone's attention.

'I need to speak to Adrian.' She made sure to sound very sombre.

The man pointed towards the end of the room, where a corridor led into further reaches of the office. 'First on the left.'

Turning the corner, she saw Adrian sitting behind his desk; a woman in a sharply cut green suit was sitting in one of the other chairs, a pink folder in her lap.

'We need to see more progress,' he was saying. 'Give them the hard word.'

His glance flicked to Stella. He laughed, as if he'd proved a point. 'Hah!'

'Hi. I'm sorry, I've got bad news. It's your Uncle Mort. He died this morning. Heart attack.'

'Uncle Mort?'

She could have killed him for that note of scepticism. She shifted her weight on the crutches. The woman in green was not making this easy for her either. She looked at Stella coolly, her hands pale on the closed folder.

'Yes. Ann really wants you there.' She turned to the woman: 'Sorry to interrupt.'

The woman said nothing. Adrian's mouth had set into a line. *He wants me to beg, the bastard.*

'Um, I'm sorry I didn't get in touch earlier about him being sick. I've been preoccupied . . . neglecting my friends. Sorry.'

Adrian smirked. 'No worries. Stella, this is Louise, my wife. Stella's mum happens to run that Love Project I told you about.'

'Uncle Mort. What an unfortunate name. Prescient.' Her accent was soft, relaxed.

'Yeah. It's sad.' Adrian's eyes glinted.

Stella still could not judge his intentions. Would he sell her out? Only her crutches and the distance to the lift prevented her from bolting. She imagined Louise striding after her, bringing her down with a sharp tackle.

'Stop it, Lou, I know what you're thinking. You're getting

the wrong end of the stick. Again. "Uncle Mort" is Murray. From IT-chieve, remember? We called him that for being such a gloom-meister.'

'I worked there too,' Stella ventured.

'He treated me like a son.'

She felt sick. He would blow it.

'Your boss?' Louise cocked an eyebrow. 'You always said he was a nerd.'

'He wasn't that bad . . . after I left we used to get together sometimes, have a beer. You wouldn't remember, you were going through . . . you know.' Adrian leaned back in his chair, half-closing his eyes.

Louise said, 'That doesn't sound like much of an obligation. You're meant to take the girls to netball tomorrow.' She turned to Stella. 'How come you're the messenger? Why didn't the wife ring Ade?'

'She might have tried,' he said. 'I've been out all morning. Ann doesn't like leaving messages. She won't be coping . . .'

Louise frowned at Stella. 'Aren't you going to the funeral? You can represent the company.'

'Um, no. I can't go. Work stuff.'

Adrian stood. 'Sorry, darl. And tell the principal to pull her finger out. The fees we're paying should cover legions of classroom support. Stella, do you need a lift back to your office?'

'If you're headed that way.' She had left her overnight bag there.

'I'm going home,' he said. 'The other direction. Got to pick up my gear.'

'Don't worry then. I need the exercise. Give my sympathies to Ann.'

An hour after she'd got back to the office, breathless and sweaty, Adrian picked her up. They headed out of the city in the sluggish Friday-evening traffic. When they reached the motorway, Stella said, 'She knows.'

He laughed. 'She's like that about everything. She thinks

Holly's teachers are conspiring to hold her back. She visits me every day to make sure I'm not shagging any of the office girls.'

'You should have told me. "*Ade*".'

'Nah, it doesn't matter . . . on one level she realises she can't take all her suspicions seriously. She's too intelligent for that.'

It sounded plausible. 'You didn't tell me she's American.'

'Yeah, I did . . . She's all stirred up about Holly at the moment. Problems with her reading.'

She seems nice, Stella almost said, but stopped herself: the last thing she wanted was to discuss his family.

He said, 'That was great. It was a close one.'

'Mm.' She could not pretend to be excited by their recent danger. Her story had been pathetically thin. She saw that if the affair were to continue, she'd have to plan for more than just her ovulation dates. It was getting complicated. She sighed.

He glanced at her. 'What's the go?'

'Nothing.'

In Martinborough they stopped at a café for dinner. The owners had painted large mock-tapestry scenes on the walls, and a dark-haired man was playing a soft, plinkety tune on a harpsichord. A waitress showed them to the one free table. Adrian had grown sullen; he had again demanded that she befriend Louise, and when she refused he clammed up, lounged in his chair and chewed on the bread rolls.

'Come on, this is meant to be fun.' She laid her hand over his.

'You're incapable of taking this seriously.'

She almost nodded. What a relief it would be to confirm his accusations and chuck the whole thing.

Nearby, several tables had been pushed together to accommodate a large group. A woman dinged a fork on her glass and began to speak about Bevan. They'd miss him but he'd raise hell in New York. From the direction of their smiles Stella worked out that Bevan was the balding young guy with his back to her.

'Hello? Earth to Stella? God, you don't give a flying fuck about me. When you came to the office I thought, At last, the woman's prepared to take a risk. But you've turned into the bloody Sphinx again.'

'We're different personalities, that's all.'

The waitress set Adrian's soup down. He didn't touch it.

Bevan the Resourceful and Reliable returned from the bathroom, wearing a black T-shirt that read 'I Survived the Equity Team'. His colleagues cheered.

'How can you be like this? Your mum and dad must be passionate types. People Under God's Command was full on.'

'What makes you such an expert?' She didn't like the thought of him knowing anything about her parents.

'See, the minute I start to know you, you go septic. You refuse to let me in. This isn't going to work. I'll phone a taxi to take you back.'

For a moment she could not think what to do next. Then she yanked on the tablecloth. His soup bowl teetered. She pulled the cloth again, more strongly, rising to her feet at the same time. The hot liquid cascaded over the edge of the table, but he had stumbled up already.

'*This* is me!' She grabbed a wine glass and smashed it on the tiles. She had begun by faking anger, but once she got started the lost ovary loomed before her on the white cloth, red and cystic, swollen with evil intent. She snatched up a fork and stabbed at it. Adrian lunged at her, pinning her arms to her sides. She tripped on a chair leg and they crashed on to the floor.

The café owner stood over them, yelling. Stella lay on her side with her face pressed against an enthralled diner's handbag and wept. Adrian stroked her hair. When they stood, Bevan the Resourceful and his team stared and murmured.

The owner made her wait outside while Adrian paid for the damage with his credit card. She sat in the car and bit her thumb until she stopped crying.

Adrian opened the driver's door and got in. He sat without speaking for a few minutes.

A couple left the café and peered into the windows on their way past the car.

He said, 'Nosy buggers. We need to talk.'

'I don't want to.'

'Is it Louise? That I'm still with her?'

She shuddered. 'It was hard seeing her. Proof that she's real.'

He laughed. 'God, I'm glad you did that. I was going spare, wondering how you felt.'

He drove a little way and left her in the car while he went into a supermarket. She redid her mascara and lipgloss. When he opened the door, he tossed a bag of pistachios into her lap. 'Gangster nuts. Throw the shells over your shoulder and you can hear the assassin's approach.' He handed her two bottles. 'Lanson Black Label. Don't say I don't spoil you.'

They found a room at a dingy bed and breakfast. He started by pouring the bubbly into the toothpaste glass, but finished the night drinking straight from the bottle. Before they fell asleep, he came three times inside her.

In the morning she woke to see him by the dresser, his fingers sorting through the contents of her toilet bag.

'What're you doing?'

He whipped around. 'Got any painkillers?'

'They're by the mirror.' She pointed.

He swallowed two and came back to bed, resting his head on his arm, looking at the ceiling. 'The way life turns, eh Harper? The way life turns.'

'What're you on about?'

'D'you want a wake-up call?' He pushed his hand between her legs and began to stroke her. 'Can't fully participate this morning. Head's a crusher. How's this?'

'It's . . . good.' It was. 'Yes. There. There.'

He licked his finger and put it back.

'Oh—yes.'

He knew when to pause and when to begin again. When to slip his fingers all the way in, stroke, stop, wait for her to call out. She clutched at his shoulders. He sat her up between his legs and drew decreasing circles on her breast with his fingertips, gave her more.

230

Later, though, he turned down her requests for a repeat. He wanted to visit a micro-brewery he'd heard of. After the visit, although it was only lunchtime, he drove her home.

He was tired, he said. He didn't want to raise Louise's suspicions.

⁂

The community radio station was housed in a flat-roofed, squat building on the corner of two traffic arteries. Leland found pea-green double doors that opened on to a windowless stairwell. A cacophony of screeches and drumbeats filtered down to him. He began to climb the stairs and saw a young man on the landing. Rows of small badges ran down both lapels of his ill-fitting suit jacket. The youth extended a hand.

'Leland Swann. I'm Nathan Kendrick. You only just made it, man.'

Leland followed him through more double doors. Inside this room, a woman was standing on an old office chair, trying to pin a poster to the wall. She had shining blonde hair, tied low on her neck, and although she wore unsightly dungarees something in the curve of her arms and the way she thrust out one hip brought Betty sharply to mind. Leland shuffled sideways, trying to see her face.

Nathan Kendrick glanced over his shoulder. 'Gotta keep going. We're on in a couple of minutes. D'you want a coffee or something?'

'A glass of water.' Leland looked back, thinking to catch a profile of the woman, but she had turned away and was climbing down from the chair. Then she disappeared, walking towards the stairwell.

He followed Nathan Kendrick through another door with a window in its upper half.

The boy told him to sit at a wide table. Headphones, microphone. The water. Then he dashed around to the other side and held a headphone to one ear while he pushed some buttons. He switched to a deep drawl. 'Pounding Sheep . . . they're playing Indigo tomorrow night. A great gig will be had by all. Ka pai. This is Nathan K with you till six. I'm interviewing Leland Swann, a self-styled American religious leader—that's self-styled *religious* and *leader*, I'm pretty sure he's authentically American . . . anyway, welcome to the show.'

Leland thanked him. He had the measure of this upstart boy. Facetious comments could not bother him. Like the newspaper article, this interview was only the beginning of his media campaign—a warm-up.

'You're from Minnesota, correct?'

'Yes, I've lived there most of my life.'

'And now you're in . . . Lower Hutt? Conducting research via your "Agape Love Project", getting people to tell you stories of when they've experienced acts of, um, genuinely unselfish love, right? Tell us more about that.'

'Well, Nathan, we called it the Agape Love Project because—'

'Ah—gah—pay,' Nathan intoned slowly. 'Is that Greek or something?'

'Yes. In the English language, Nathan, we have only one word for love. But if we say "I love chocolate-chip cookies" it doesn't mean the same thing as "I love my wife". The Ancient Greeks had four different words for love. For example, *eros*, which is the subject of most "pop" songs.'

'*Eros* as in erotic.'

Out of the corner of his eye, Leland saw a blonde head pass by the window in the door. He cleared his throat, and forced himself to remember his notes.

'Correct. And *phileo* is the basis for the suffix "-phile": "bibliophile" and "francophile". It describes the feeling of liking something or someone; of personal affection that expects affection in return.' He tried to modulate his voice so he did not sound too dry. '*Storge* is team-feeling, found among soldiers in battle, sports teams, and so on.'

'*Agape* is the fourth?'

'Yes. *Agape* is arguably the highest form of love—'

'Hang on . . .' Nathan ruffled through papers. 'I've got a fifth kind. *Thelo,* is, um, the desire to be prominent. Sounds more like ambition than love.'

Leland's mouth was very dry. He took a sip of water. 'Well, Nathan, you're correct. That's why I don't include it.'

The boy snickered. 'Right. What would Wikipedia know.'

'We're asking people for stories of Agape Love because it's Agape Love that makes the world go round. It's unconditional, compassionate, doesn't expect anything in return.'

'Was Agape Love part of People Under God's Command?'

The swerve took him by surprise.

'This was back in the late 1950s, 1960s, right?'

'Yes. It's interesting you should bring that up, Nathan.' Leland saw how to step ahead of him. 'As you may know, the Three Pillars, which were the basis of our philosophy, along with Listening to God, did not include Love.'

He tried to catch Nathan's eye, but the cowardly boy had tilted back his chair and was gazing off to the side.

'I view this Project as a step in a spiritual journey—'

'Right, yeah, the Three Pillars . . . for listeners who aren't aware, those were Perfect Chastity, Perfect Truth and Perfect Selflessness. So, Leland, "People Under God's Command" has kind of a militaristic ring to it, doesn't it?'

'No. We weren't associated with the military.'

'I didn't suggest that. And you're in Aotearoa New Zealand to publicise your group.'

'No. The Agape Love Project is an entirely separate enterprise.'

'People Under God's Command is defunct.'

'We want to do what we can for the future.'

'Who's "we"? In 1969 the People Under God's Command Centre in St Paul, Minnesota, was sold due to dwindling funds.'

Leland made an involuntary rattling noise at the back of his throat. 'Messages about sexual purity and selflessness will never be universally popular.'

'The Hare Krishnas get by . . . What do you say to accusations that your group was a cult?'

'Have you done any in-depth research, Nathan?'

'People Under God's Command is listed on a whole bunch of websites—usually in the archives—that warn about cults. Although, I, um, recognise that's a controversial term.'

'Anyone who promotes the idea that man should follow the Will of God is going to encounter opposition.'

It did not tax him to come up with this defence. During the 1970s he had written many pamphlets. Later, he composed several chapters of a book with the working title *America's Necessary Transformation*. Many times he had imagined himself on a television panel or a talk show; he had imagined his *comeback*. Until he realised the extent of Betty's mental sabotage, he had believed it was imminent. He believed it was what God wanted.

He looked towards the door. The blonde head had not reappeared. Betty was dead. He would not think of her.

'Do you stick by what you said in 1967, in a speech that many religious commentators mark as the beginning of the end for your group, that—'

'I was quoted out of context.'

'Let me finish, please. Do you deny that you said, "I thank God for removing Martin Luther King"? Did you mean that you thanked God for King's *murder*?'

'Like almost every other reporter before you, Nathan, you are quoting that statement out of context.'

'You could have explained yourself at the time.'

'Well, Nathan, if you would be courteous enough to allow me to explain now—'

'You didn't want to talk about it then. You refused interviews.'

'I don't have the text of that speech with me, but as I recall, Nathan, what I said was . . . what you quoted, and about John F. Kennedy, I said because it seemed to me that America was becoming addicted to personality, to mortal personalities, and therefore the population couldn't keep its eyes on God, but got preoccupied with the idea of one or two people as saviours.'

'So, you'd deny a charge of racism? It was a challenge to the cult of celebrity?'

'Yes. That's correct.'

After the donations had dried up, and those who remained in the Centre had gathered in Leland's study, Gus Driver said, 'Here's the thing. If we sell now, and I've checked this with the lawyers, we'll be able to keep enough of the income from the sale to give some to each of the people sitting around this table.'

Leland had believed the group would come together in another location. But once he and Betty had completed on a single-storey, one-bedroom cottage on a back street in Duluth Heights, they discovered none of the others was even staying in Minnesota. Martha Sands took her roomful of belongings right down to Florida, to live with her younger sister in Tallahassee. Cynthia Chant likewise fled to family members, spending her allocation on a tiny apartment in Maryland. Henry Allerton bought an RV and announced his intention to compose a piece of music for each of the national parks.

'Why New Zealand?' Nathan asked. 'Don't your fellow Americans need to hear about Agape Love?'

'Surely.'

'So . . . you're trying it out on us? You've heard about our reputation for early adoption of new technologies and you thought you'd see if it'd transfer to, um, spiritual stuff?' He had reverted to his bored drawl.

Who was this boy to question his motives? Leland sensed Betty's spirit at work. Self-pity began to rise in him. Why must he always be dogged by one who suspected him of the worst?

'Forgive me, Nathan, for asking you a personal question . . . but have you ever been deeply bereaved?'

Nathan's eyes narrowed, and Leland saw that he had, through divine discernment, touched on the thing that might turn the interview.

He continued, 'I have, you see . . . I lost my wife recently, and if you have suffered a bereavement, Nathan, you may know . . .' Yes. He had silenced the boy at last. 'You may understand how a bereaved person may make sudden decisions that seem inexplicable to others. Luckily for me, coming to New Zealand has been a wonderful thing.'

Nathan looked very tired, just as Leland felt after this unnecessary exercise. Rita should have warded off the interview, he thought. She should have perceived the boy's intentions.

'Yeah . . . I'm talking to Mr Leland Swann, people, and he's talking to me about his late wife, and how he's ended up in Aotearoa collecting stories about love. That's *agape* love. If you wanna talk to him, get yourself out to Lower Hutt. You know that painting on the ceiling of the Sistine Chapel, God reaching down with his big white hand, his pointy finger touching Adam's pointy finger? So Mr Swann, right, *he* and God are like, none of this fingertip rubbish, slip me some skin, man. Go talk to him about your troubles. Or love. Whatever. But not sex or friendship. Go figure. I'm gonna play the White Stripes now. Enjoy.'

'Thank you, Nathan,' Leland said, but the boy had turned off his microphone. He raised an ironic palm. 'Yeah. Check ya. But it's not over, mate. You know that, eh. We've got enough homegrown types like you already. Don't need imports. You keep going, you'll find the *Dom Post* on your back, then there'll be a bit on the TV news. People here don't like religion getting mixed up with politics. You try and ally yourself with one of the right-wing parties, everyone'll think you're being sponsored by the Bush administration. Or do you enjoy being unpopular?'

Leland considered replying in combative tones: *It depends on with whom I'm unpopular.* But now that the microphones were off, there was no point. He saw the uselessness of it all, and the flimsy thinking that had given rise to this trip—why had he imagined that he could build a flourishing movement in such a small country?

Leaving the rundown building, he reflected that in the United States, if you won over only a very small percentage, you could build up enough momentum to keep going. You would not be known and discussed in the way of an errant family member with whom everyone is familiar and whom no one can take seriously. And the boy had been right in pointing out the political differences.

He looked out for the blonde woman. His eyes flicked from side to side in case she was standing on the sidewalk. She did not appear among the skateboarding teenagers and the shoppers, but by the time he reached the taxi stand he had persuaded himself that the difficulties presented by the interview had been of a divine nature: had helped him, in fact, to see that his work here was almost finished. He and Rita should leave for the United States as soon as possible.

When they arrived at the Project office the next morning, their first visitors were already waiting. A man lolled in the seat closest to the office door, his arm slung over the back of the seat next to him, which was occupied by a much younger woman. Stringy blonde hair hung around her moon face.

The man addressed Leland. 'We flew from Hamilton. Had to get a shuttle from the airport. You should be putting on transport.'

'Open the door, please, Rita,' Leland said remotely. During their walk that morning he had been reluctant to talk about the radio interview. She had tried to tell him that no one listened to that station—that she, in fact, could scarcely remember what the interviewer had said.

She apologised, and hurried to unlock the door. Then she said to the waiting couple, 'I'll get you a registration form. How did you hear about us?'

'Fate. My nephew's a champion under-12 swimmer, my sister sent the clipping. You lot were on the back. Some crummy story about a woman cyclist. Was that Leland Swann who went in?'

'Yes.' She darted into her office and picked up a clipboard.

'Rita,' Leland said from his room, 'I don't want to see that man.'

'No. I think he's with his . . . daughter, anyway.'

She returned to the corridor and handed the clipboard to the man. 'Your name and address, and the gist of your story.'

When he had completed it, she asked, 'Do you want to come in together?'

He nodded.

'This way then.' She led them into her office.

The man looked around. 'Where's Leland Swann?'

'I'll be interviewing both of you.'

His face reddened. 'That's crap. We didn't come all the way down here to see a secretary.'

'You can see him, sir, if you prefer to tell your stories separately.'

'No. It's about family. So you see men but he doesn't see ladies? How's that work?' He jerked his head towards Leland's door. 'He's sitting on his arse in there.'

'Dad. Come on.' The girl sat down.

Rita read their registration form. Todd and Kylie Jones. Underneath the request, 'Please provide a brief summary of your story (2–3 sentences)', he had written, 'THE STRENGTH OF ONE FAMILY'S LOVE'.

Todd Jones laid his hand, palm down, on her desk. 'Why we're here is, Kylie was raped last year.'

After a moment, Rita recovered her voice. 'I'm very sorry.'

'Yeah. Scum . . . you going to turn that thing on?' He pointed at the tape recorder.

'Oh . . . yes.'

He raised his voice. 'Todd Jones here. This is our story. The strength of one family's love. My daughter Kylie was raped. She's sitting next to me. We're not religious. What I believe in is life. You gotta love what's given to you to love. Basically our story is, it's our family's love that gave life to my granddaughter Tiana.' He spoke loudly, glancing from time to time at Leland's door.

Rita asked, '"We" is . . . you and Kylie . . . and your wife?'

'Yep. Simone.' He gestured at the clipboard. 'Put her name on the form. She couldn't come, she's babysitting Tiana.'

'She's not my mum,' Kylie said.

Todd looked exasperated. 'That's irrelevant, Ky. Stay focused.' He stretched out his legs. 'You'll want to hear how we did it, right, how we made Kylie see.'

Kylie's face was blank, with no suggestion of how she felt about having been made to see.

'We reckoned she was in shock, so we gave her a love bath, that's what we called it, me and Simone, and after we found out she was pregnant we started talking to the baby too, in the womb. We said, we love you, we love you. We love your baby, we love you, we love *you* baby, and we love you *and* your baby. If we were both at home, like at the weekend, then one of us'd talk to Kylie and one of us'd talk to the baby.'

'Kylie, do you want to add anything?' Rita wished the girl would look at her.

'No.'

'Tiana's a sweet name.'

Todd said, 'The scum doesn't get a look in. He'd *like* to be a dad. In his dreams. We don't refer to him as "the father". He's "the sperm". Cos that's all he is, far as Tiana's concerned.'

Kylie glared. 'You could shut your mouth about him.'

'The healing power of family dialogue, Ky, remember?'

Rita imagined that she might take Kylie aside, after the interview, and say something quiet and profound. Then the girl might talk to her, and this knotted feeling would lift from her chest. 'Do you have a photo of Tiana?' she asked.

Todd's hand whipped around to his back pocket. 'Does the pope shit in the woods? You're not Catholic, eh.' He pulled a photo out of his wallet and passed it over the desk. 'That's Simone there. Outside our house.'

The photographer had stood some distance away. Kylie held a blanket-wrapped bundle in her arms. She looked down at it, and her hair dangled over her face. Todd stood on one side, grinning, his chest thrust forward. Simone wore sunglasses.

Rita looked closer, trying to find a defining feature. 'She's got dark hair?'

'Yep,' said Todd. 'Takes after me.'

'*He* had black hair,' Kylie said.

Rita asked her, 'Is the nursing going okay?'

She frowned. 'I'm not a nurse.'

'I mean, um, the feeding. Does Tiana wake a lot at night?'

Kylie said flatly, 'I never knew before how you can feel two things at the same time. Opposite things.'

Todd pushed back his chair. 'No offence, but this doesn't fit my vision.' He strode to Leland's door and rapped on it. 'Hello? Leland Swann?'

'Um, Mr Jones?' Rita stretched an arm towards him.

Todd tried the handle and pushed the door open. 'Gidday. You should hear this story. You won't find another story like ours. For showing the sheer power of love. It's like the Christmas story. There's a baby at the end of it.'

'Mr Jones.' Rita was behind him now, but could not see Leland over his shoulder. He had braced one hand on the doorframe and his other was propped on his hip, so that the crook of his arm formed a barrier.

'Sometimes it takes someone to insist on love, maybe where there's another person concerned who's not as advanced, and you have to fight against that person and make sure love wins? That should be a central point in your documentary. You'll probably want us all on camera.'

'I'll play him the recording,' Rita said.

'You could listen to it now,' he said, ignoring her. 'Ask me supplementary questions.'

Kylie came to Rita's side. 'You got other people coming this morning?'

'Yes . . . probably.'

She shoved Todd's shoulder. 'Dad. Did you hear that? There's other people coming. I got an idea. You write it down and send it in. I'll write too. I like writing.' It was her longest speech.

He looked at her. 'Yeah. Not bad.' He said to Leland, 'She won a prize, at school.'

'What a good idea,' Rita said. She touched the girl's arm. 'Good idea, Kylie.'

Kylie rolled her eyes.

She'll never do it, Rita thought.

'Let's move, Dad. There's a train in ten minutes.'

Todd said, 'You got our contact details. You'll have the story by next week. I'll follow up. You fellas should get a phone. What's your home number?'

'It's not . . . you leave your number with us. We'll be in touch.'

They left at last. While she was seeing them out, she heard Leland close his door. Afterwards she slumped into her chair and ate cheese crackers from a package in her bag. The Jones's registration form lay in front of her. The strength of one family's love.

The tape recorder clicked off. Her munching was preserved for future generations. She wrapped the crackers up, oddly humiliated.

There was no sound from Leland's office. She thought about the tapes she had transcribed that week. His most frequent comment was 'hm'. Sometimes, in a long pause, he repeated the last words spoken. 'My dad got diagnosed with prostate cancer and my youngest sister had a breakdown . . .' Leland: 'Ah, a breakdown.' If the interviewee had fallen silent for longer than a minute, he'd say, 'That was difficult for you,' or, 'That must have been rewarding.'

They were not looking for counselling. They only expected that you would listen.

She would have listened to Kylie. She would have been sympathetic, but Kylie had not even looked her in the eye. *How is she coping?* Rita wondered. She had no idea how one would, because (thank God) she had never been raped, and neither had she known anyone who—

But at this thought she got up and went into Leland's office. He

241

had his elbows on the desk, fingers clasped over his knuckles.

She asked, 'Did you see the girl? Kylie?'

'No.'

'She was raped. That man's her father. He and his wife persuaded her to keep the baby.'

'Commendable.'

She could not answer that, so she said, 'A story like that really makes you think.'

He began to revolve his thumbs, one around the other, and said with a note of surprise, 'He went right ahead and opened the door.'

'If you look at it from the girl's point of view,' said Rita. Her heart beat faster. She could not predict, herself, what would come from looking at it from Kylie's point of view.

Betty would have been all right, she told herself. *Her . . . uncertainties were all finished with by the time she married him.*

On his desk lay a paperweight given to Leland by an admirer, a rectangular block of glass the size of a large club sandwich, containing in its core an impression, formed from bubbles, of two preening birds on a branch. An image flashed, disappearing so fast that she wasn't obliged to notice it: that she would grip Leland's shoulder and repeatedly stab the paperweight's sharp corner into the soft tissue of his temple.

'Is there anything else?' he asked.

'I don't know what to think about them coming in. It didn't seem like it was her idea.'

Betty would have been fine. Just fine. No reason to think otherwise. (But then why had she made the tape?)

'I'm tired,' he said. 'Write it up and I'll consider it later.'

Rita left the room, closing the door behind her. She sat at her desk, her elbows pricked by cracker crumbs.

Then she sobbed, neither knowing why, nor caring who might see her from the mall.

6

Close to midnight on a Wednesday, Rita met Stella coming out of the bathroom. They had hardly spoken since Stella broke the news of her separation from Dan, and Rita, who had unwisely drunk a mug of hot tea before bed, was not expecting to see her now, wan in a white nightie decorated with champagne bottles, balancing on one crutch, a small spongebag in her other hand. The hallway night-light showed up a shaded puffiness around her eyes.

'You're crying? What's wrong?'

'Nothing.' Stella clumped past her into the kitchen.

'Can I get you anything?'

'No thanks.'

Rita followed, turning on the light. 'You *have* been crying.'

'I'm sore, that's all. I've got my period. Cramps.' She ran a glass of water and tossed a couple of white tablets into her mouth.

Rita had never known her daughter to cry from pain. Her hands began to tingle. Her anger, when it blew in, turned and flew straight back out of her mouth. She trembled as she spoke. 'You can't let him get away with it. He should have to *answer.*'

Stella looked weary.

Rita knew she had guessed right. 'Oh, sweetheart.' She wanted to comfort, to speak of women who bore children well into their forties, but Stella was chewing her bottom lip and looking towards the door. How could she be so resigned? Rita's hand turned to a fist that she pressed hard into the counter.

'He let you think you were the one! If he had doubts he should have said, so you two could work them out. Or at least he could have let you go earlier so you could've found someone else, had a chance!'

243

'Mum . . .'

'I know it's none of my business, and you don't *like* me knowing your business and you don't want to talk about it—about anything ever with me—but I can't bear to see you cry! You never cry.' She herself was crying now.

'I'll be okay.' But Stella's eyes were teary, too, and she pressed her lips together.

'I can't bear to think of that man waltzing away with all his options open. He can do anything he wants! He hasn't lost anything. It's not *fair* on you! I could . . . call him *names*!'

Stella sniffed, and laughed. 'Go ahead.'

Rita wanted only to step forward and clutch her, to find in Stella's strong, rounded arms, in the heat of her neck, the assurance that everything would be all right.

'Does he even *realise* what this means for you?'

She gave an exhausted shrug. 'Maybe.'

'But if he gave *up* without trying!'

'Shhh, you'll wake Dad.'

'*Well*—'

Maybe Bill should be woken. Maybe he should be forced to recognise the true consequences of this breakup, rather than brushing it off with 'good riddance'. Naturally, left to himself, he would never consider what it meant for a childless woman of Stella's age to be abandoned (for that was how Rita now thought of it). For a moment, Bill, in his indifference, seemed as culpable as Dan.

'I'll be fine. It's the cramps making me a bit tearful. Don't tell Dad, okay?' She paused by the door. 'Mum? . . . Dad said Leland asked you to move to America.'

'Not move. Only for six months.' Rita struggled to hold Stella's gaze, because since she had spoken to Bill, Leland had said that they should leave soon, after the Anniversary Weekend, and had made a further suggestion—that for the next few years she might divide herself between New Zealand and the States. Six months here, six months there. Promote and organise the project, vacation with the family in between.

244

She hadn't told Bill, or Stella, that part yet. Perpetual summer. Perpetual assurance that her life had purpose.

'What about Dad?'

'He can come too. There's lots of great hiking . . .'

'What if he doesn't want to? He hasn't even reached retirement. You wouldn't go without him?' Stella searched her face with the kind of intensity Rita usually longed for in their conversations.

'We'll see. Don't worry. Everything will work out.'

'Mum, sometimes I think you're living on a different planet . . . Is Leland leaving before the Harper . . . Anniversary thingie?'

'Sometime around then,' she said vaguely, and, with more determination, 'When will *you* move out?'

She regretted it immediately. Why that snark in her voice? If she knew next to nothing about her daughter's heart now, how much less would she know when Stella was gone, in touch every few weeks if they were lucky?

She watched Stella retreat, imagining what she might say if she knew about Leland's most recent offer. Typical that she would take her mulish father's side on that topic, when it was her mother who best understood the significance of Dan's betrayal.

Rita had told Bill about Leland's initial invitation three nights ago, while fixing her rollers. He had been standing at the wardrobe, hanging up his clothes. In the mirror of her dresser, she could see only his back and the movement of his arms.

'For six months,' she had said. 'Maybe you could get some extended leave.'

'Do you want to go?'

She tried to keep the excitement from her voice. 'I haven't Listened yet, but it feels like the right thing. You're always saying God speaks to us outside of Listening, too.'

She could hear him chewing his tongue. Then he said, 'Do you think . . . fair enough, the Agape Project's highlighting a lot of good in people . . . but do you think Leland's the man for it? The right man?'

'Why wouldn't he be? You're so . . . mealy-mouthed about him. Hypocritical. You *do* still resent that he made us leave the Centre.'

'Reet, something's not right with him. He's missing some kind of responsiveness . . . some part of his humanity.'

'*Humanity*? What are you talking about? That's nonsense. He's changed, so what? He's gotten older, we all have. And he's grieving. No wonder he's quieter.'

'I'm not talking about whether he's different now to how he was at the Centre.' Bill hesitated. 'Even back then, maybe he wasn't the man we thought he was.'

'So now he's a liar?'

'I didn't say that—it's hard to tell whether he understands himself.'

'Bill, you are *not making sense.*'

He looked at her, then brushed past and walked into the corridor. 'Come on.'

In the living room, he opened the bottom drawer in her desk, stood and faced her. 'Betty's letters.'

She attempted indignation. 'Have you been reading them?'

'Don't be dotty. You've always kept them there.'

She huffed and protested, but he was immovable.

'So what?' she said. 'What's this got to do with anything?'

'Read her first letter, the first one she wrote after we came back.'

'Why?'

'If you still think it's right to go, I won't make a fuss.'

'The light's too dim. I can't see.' Nevertheless, her fingers riffled through the pile of envelopes until they reached the bottom of the box.

He said, 'Let's go back to the bedroom.'

He followed her down the corridor without touching her. As she passed her dresser, she felt the presence of Betty's tape. What would Bill say if he knew about it, and that she hadn't listened to it? What was its message? Had Betty railed at her for casting off their friendship or, worse, guessed that Rita had been in possession of information about Leland that might, if she had shared it with Betty, have dissuaded Betty from marrying him? And, if so, how could Rita ever make it up to a dead woman?

She sat on her side of the bed, next to the lamp, the wall a few inches from her knees. Bill sat beside her. 'Read it out loud,' he said.

'All *right*.' She wanted to get it over with. She began. She threw each word away as it left her mouth, and afterwards she tossed the letter down on the quilt where Bill could not easily reach it.

23rd April 1964
Dear darling Rita,

I meant to write you the morning after you left but something dreadful happened. Julius Toller died on the front steps. He drank poison—he still had the bottles in his pockets. He must have arrived early, because Margot found him wet with dew when she went to sweep the porch. He looked terrible lying there.

Everything's been crazy. But the Centre's felt strange ever since you left. I wish I could talk to you. How are you finding married life? Do you and Bill tell each other all your secrets? I don't know what to expect. I know important people will tell Leland secrets and he'll have to keep them from me, but it feels weird to start out with Mr Toller's suicide hanging over us.

No one's talking about it. Leland hasn't told me anything. In Sharing, Henry Allerton announced that Mr Toller had left a letter expressing infinite gratitude for Leland's work. I was with Leland in our room when he read that letter. Rita, he went yellow around the mouth. I've never seen him look so sick. He said something about the wages of sin. Henry took the letter away from him. I probably spoke too soon but I said maybe we could hold a memorial service. Leland said no.

We went to his funeral yesterday. Miss Leonora cold-shouldered Leland afterwards, and when I asked him why, he didn't say anything.

Henry said we should go ahead with the first performances as planned. He said the public would sympathise.

It's funny to think only ten days ago we were all in the chapel getting married and I was Listening on how to get Leland to include Love in the Pillars. It seems more like a year. I miss you something awful.

Sorry I'm so gloomy. I'll write you with more cheerful news in a few days.

Write me back,

All my love and hugs, Betty XXX

'What's this got to do with whether we go to the States?' She wound herself up to outrage, for of course she never had written Betty back, nor had she told Bill all her own secrets either then or now. 'My whole life, practically, in *your* country, I'll probably die here, the least you could do—'

'I'll be happy to go back, for the right reason. Tell you what, I'll ask the Friends for a Meeting for Clearness. Get some perspective on it.'

'Why do you have to talk to the Quakers? Why can't you talk to *me*? What's so wrong with getting people to think about unconditional love?' She had rehearsed that last line.

'Nothing. But listen to me, Reet. I think Leland refused to see the old man. Toller wrote to him quite a few times. I don't know the whole story, but . . .'

Despite herself, Rita remembered meeting Leonora Toller outside the Secretariat. Cynthia had turned down her request to meet with Leland. Had Leonora intended to persuade Leland to see her brother?

She renewed her attack. 'You think this, you think that, but if you don't even know for sure what happened . . . !'

'Julius Toller believed he needed Leland's forgiveness.'

'What for?'

248

Bill's mouth skewed. 'Nasty goings-on before he met the Movement . . . with little girls . . . we found negatives in his desk.'

'So what? Leland's not God. I mean, maybe he has a particular distaste for that kind of thing. Who doesn't? You can't blame him for not wanting to see Mr Toller again.'

'I'm glad you think he's not God,' Bill said.

Rita thought he might smile, but he didn't. He continued, 'If it was only the Toller thing . . . but he had . . . an inflexibility about him. I don't get the feeling he's put it right. I don't like the way he talks about Betty.'

'She didn't tell him about her illness! He never got to say goodbye!'

'He's angry with her for more than that. He doesn't seem very well, Reet. I didn't see that when I was young and keen—or maybe I didn't want to. But now . . . I'll be a monkey's uncle if I let him take our life away.'

She caught hold of the distraction, bouncing across the bed to create some righteous distance between them. '*Our life?* Maybe if you paid *attention* to our life, our family, you'd notice what's going on with Stella? But no, you think it's *dandy* her husband's left her. It's a pattern,' she said triumphantly. 'You didn't like Dan, so in your book it's marvellous that he's waltzed off. And you have some weird prejudice against Leland, so he must be wrong too! So much for *something of God within everyone.*' She kicked off her slippers and tussled with the quilt, hunching her back towards him. 'Turn off the light, please.'

In the morning she looked like she'd been dragged through a bush backwards. She'd forgotten to put on her hairnet.

Now, she remembered that last 'family' shot she had fired at Bill. It filled her with a sense of virtuous duty. The light from the kitchen threw her shadow down the corridor, a squat, foreshortened monument pointing towards their bedroom, but she did not follow it. Instead, she went into the living room and found her notebook.

Stella had never revealed Dan's work or cellphone numbers, but Dan, holding forth during tense Sunday lunches, had often mentioned the name of his company. Rita had marked it down at the back of her notebook where she hoarded snippets of information about the life of her uncommunicative daughter— names of friends and workmates, cafés she frequented, films she'd seen, even the birthdays of her in-laws. Anything that would bring her nearer.

It wasn't until she'd looked up Kyros Architectural Associates in the directory and had the phone in her hand that she recalled the time. The office would be deserted.

She couldn't stop. She switched on the computer and Googled Daniel Reed together with Kyros. At first she forgot to set quotation marks around his name, and the random results bamboozled her. Then she remembered, added 'architects' for good measure, and right up there on the screen was the information she needed.

Kyros award-winner reports from Manila
Daniel Reed, a senior associate at Kyros, describes his innovative work with our partner firm. In a project designed to reconfigure . . .

She looked up the Manila firm's website and rang without checking the time difference. No one would answer, but she didn't care: she only wanted to touch Dan's whereabouts, to haul him closer to hearing what she thought of him. At least she would be sure of the number.

'Aahh . . . Alcoba Planners and Architects.'

Startled, she said she was ringing from New Zealand.

'You're lucky.' The man's accent made each word distinct. 'I happened to be walking through the lobby. But it's late, you know, most of our people have left.'

'Yes, sorry.' Her heart beat faster as she asked for Dan.

'Hah. He's in my office actually.'

'What's your extension?'

'Um—6482—but I'll transfer you if I can figure out these buttons . . .'

She jotted down the number while she waited. Click, the phone said. Click click. She held it to her ear until she was sure she'd been cut off.

She curled up on the couch and slipped her feet under a cushion. An old resentment began to weaken, juddering loose from the memory of how her mother had treated Bill when Rita had taken him back for inspection. All the predictable questions—how would he provide for her, his prospects—delivered with enough stiff reserve to turn Bill beet red. When the conversation creaked on to lighter topics, Hilary Daley didn't once address him directly and never made good on that omission, not even on her daughter's wedding day, nor two days later, when Rita and Bill left for New Zealand.

Now Rita thought that her everlastingly angry mother would understand Rita's need to speak for Stella, whose dreams had been skewered by a careless, selfish man. *I'm doing this because I love you.*

She dialled the number, replacing the last four digits with the extension she'd been given. Dan answered after two rings.

'Daniel, it's Rita Harper.' She instinctively stood, aiming for an unfamiliar poise.

Silence. 'Rita . . . ?'

'Stella's mother.'

He breathed heavily. 'Eugene said it was a Kyros person . . . we're pretty busy here.'

'Do you know that Stella broke her ankle?'

'No.'

'After you left. She's staying with us.'

'You rang to tell me that? Presumably she informed you we've split.'

'Yes.'

'We're under a pretty stringent deadline. I can't chat. What time is it? Isn't everyone in bed?' He sounded amused.

Rita imagined his colleague sitting back in a leather chair, watching him. White-lit drawing boards and long rulers.

'I know you don't care what I think of you. You never did, not even when you and Stella were . . . together.'

'Right, so, okay. You're angry, for some reason. But look on the bright side. Must be nice for you to have Stella around.'

'I want her to be happy!'

'Good for you.'

'Don't you feel cowardly, running away?'

'This trip was scheduled months ago.'

'You have *obligations*. You made vows. You're still married. Shouldn't that have some priority?'

A pause. 'Did Stella ask you to ring me?'

'Stella's not feeling . . . Dan, I can't answer for her tastes, but I know she wants you back, and don't pay heed to my grouchiness. I'm sure if you and I were honest with each other we'd find plenty in common and may even end up liking each other. You're both such live wires, I can't believe you're giving up! It's not fair on her!'

'Hold *on*. Have you talked to Stella?' He laughed. 'Shit. I'm telling you now, you absolutely should talk to Stella.'

She flushed. 'You may find this situation comical, but . . . as you may know, Stella's not an especially *confiding* sort of person . . .'

'You can say that again.'

'I've watched her over the last few weeks . . .'

'You're getting emotional, Rita.'

At 'emotional', she imagined him winking at the invisible Eugene. Tears sprang to her eyes. 'You wait a minute! You . . . you need to drop your act and truly think about what I'm saying!'

'You're not saying a lot, to be frank.' And while she said, 'Why do you have to be so *rude*!', he talked over her: 'Find someone else to harangue. I'm putting down the phone now.'

Hilary Daley sneered at her. *Where's your vim? Where's your vigour?* Rita pressed redial.

He answered on the first ring: 'Daniel Reed.'

'Dan, I'm sorry I got upset.' She kicked the couch—why should she apologise? 'We're not done. Stella's too stubborn to make the first move . . .'

'Stella . . . Fuck it—' he exhaled loudly '—you don't have a clue. If I hang up again, will you keep harassing me?'

She tried to sound devil-may-care. 'If you mean do I intend to make you see your obligations, yes.'

'Obligations. Right. I don't have any obligations, and since your lying daughter'll probably never come clean with you, I'll tell you why.'

He asked her if she was sitting comfortably. She remained standing and told him to say his piece. The first time round, she didn't listen; she was waiting her turn so she could get on with persuading him to come home. He had to repeat himself.

'All we did in Fiji was . . . swim and eat.' A muffled snort in the background. 'We faked a marriage so you wouldn't give us a hard time about living together. The photos are a put-on. The ring was cheap. Ask her.'

It was his tone, as if he didn't care whether or not she believed him, that tightened the muscles around her heart. 'Stella doesn't lie. She wouldn't lie to me.'

'Yeah, right. So she restricted her lies to *me*; told me she didn't want kids and then tried to trick me into "fatherhood". The monster in your bosom. If she tells you it's not true, you'll have to decide who to believe. Ciao.'

It couldn't be true. Stella had no reason to lie. Didn't she have enough faith in her mother's love to be honest with her?

The answer calcified, pitiless: no, she didn't. Those lists at the back of Rita's notebook attested to it.

She wrapped her robe around herself and turned on to her belly; she pulled her knees up and covered her head with her arms. She wished she could go to Bill for comfort, but what kind of comfort could she find with him now? She lay curled on the couch for hours, but she could not make herself small enough.

🌿

When Stella entered the kitchen in the morning, she knew from her mother's face that one of her lies had been discovered. Frozen in panic, she couldn't strategise, couldn't calculate which lie or omission (the elopement? the affair?) was most likely to have come undone. But Rita glanced pointedly at her left hand and said with shaky sarcasm, 'You've taken off your *ring*, at least. I guess you and Dan have been laughing at me all these years.'

She dropped her face into her rigid fingers. 'Oh. God.'

'Dan sounded . . . pretty amused at my expense.' Her mother's words came in strained bursts.

'You talked to him? When?'

Rita, crimson on her cheekbones, raised her chin. 'Last night. After I saw you crying. A mom can ring her son-in-law any time, I guess, only he's not, so . . . I guess it's *my fault*.'

'Oh shit. Oh God, you were never meant to find out. We did it to protect you.' Even as she gave the excuse, she heard its untruth. 'And Dad. Oh God, have you told him?'

'Stop your blasphemies!'

'Mum . . .'

'You shut your mouth if you have nothing but . . . but blasphemies and lies . . . I couldn't sleep . . . how could you hurt me like that?' Her hands grasped at the air.

'I didn't mean to. We should have told you straight out. It was Dan's idea, he's a total waste of space . . .'

'Don't blame it on him! He's nothing to do with me! You're my daughter!' Rita swiped at her tears, glaring.

'No, but . . .'

'Don't you dare open your mouth to me if you're going to sound like one of those politicians or . . . or *sports* people who say they're sorry but they made a "mistake", they "misjudged"— no, they don't even use the word "sorry", they say "regret", like they weren't there or adult enough to know what they were doing. You knew what you were doing was wrong . . . my heart hurts!'

She gazed at Stella, imploring, her fists pressed against her breastbone, shoulders tight. 'It's hurting, and . . . all down to my fingers.'

'Mum?'

'Ah . . .' Her mother began to cry freely now, stretching blindly until she touched the back of a chair, collapsing into it.

'Mum, please, I'm sorry.'

You *bastard*, Stella thought. Right at this moment, while her mother suffered, he was probably fucking some call girl in a hotel room. She longed to throw herself across Rita's lap, but her cast ensured that she kept her distance, propped awkwardly behind the chair, and nervous because if her dad came in now he'd be ropeable—

But it was Betty she involuntarily summoned, standing in the kitchen doorway, arms folded, looking at her with heavy disappointment.

Well, said Betty, who had always believed from afar in Stella's fundamental goodness. *I didn't know that.*

Stella swallowed rising tears. Briefly, she felt convicted. She alone had wrenched these gobbeting sobs from her mother's chest.

But the Three Pillars—unbearable! ridiculous! their stifling morality had *forced* her—and only *you*, dumb-Mum, would make such a stupid fuss you're so predictable, this is why I didn't tell you in the first place . . .

Betty tossed her hair, sniffing. *Don't even think about it. Don't start off down that path.*

Get a grip, Stella told herself. Enough of dead women.

'If I'd ever thought you'd find out,' she said, 'but he promised not to tell, and I kind of thought we'd last . . .'

Rita slammed a palm on the table, whirling around to face her. 'Do you know what I went through after you told me you'd gotten *married* in *Fiji*? How it pained me you hadn't even wanted me at your wedding? You made me doubt myself as a mom!'

She rose and stumbled into the living room. Stella tried to breathe; could not imagine what would happen next. Rita returned with the framed 'wedding' photo of Stella standing on a pier, holding flowers, her feet bare, Dan a little way behind her.

Her eyes were dry now. She slammed it down in front of Stella, breaking the glass. 'Get rid of it.'

Then she ran, her dressing gown flapping desolately.

With difficulty, Stella fetched the dustpan and brush from the cleaning cupboard and swept up the shattered glass.

Bill came in. 'What's going on? Your mum's in tears.'

It seemed from his frown that he already knew. 'I . . . Dan and I . . . we didn't elope. We lied. We weren't married. We pretended.'

She wanted him to ask for reasons, but he only said, his face hard, 'She just found out?'

She nodded, and he went.

That morning she left the house as soon as she could. She almost packed her bags, but did not want her parents to think her cowardly as well as a liar. After work, however, she called Adrian and arranged to meet him in a bar. They started with martinis and moved on to whisky. She matched him drink for drink, asking him about Louise and listening carefully to his complaints; she offered opinions. They ate spiced potato wedges and aioli. Relieved, buoyed up by the bar's conversational, laughing roar, and the mellow alcohol, and the memory of how he had pleased her during their most recent session, she decided she might even like him.

When he turned the conversation to Leland Swann she became loquacious on the subject of People Under God's Command and the ideal of perfectly moral behaviour. Without attending to how he received her stories, she related what she knew of the St Paul Centre, although she avoided talking about her parents' involvement. He listened in silence. Forgetting that she had already told him about running away to sea, she gabbled a rambling version.

He cocked an eyebrow. 'Shame about your dog.' He turned

his glass around on the coaster several times before speaking again. 'D'you reckon you never had what it takes?'

'What?' She sensed the nature of his question, but could not understand it. Weeks of forgoing alcohol had lowered her tolerance.

'Nothing.'

'No, no, what do you mean?'

'D'you reckon maybe some people are born to find something that's true . . . and most other people don't understand . . . they can't deal with it?'

'God, I don't know.'

'I'd better take you home. Get a bit of shut-eye. Tomorrow's a working day.'

'I'll . . . stay here.' She fumbled for her wallet.

'Don't be stupid. Come on. I'll call a taxi.'

'Wait. I need the loo.'

It pleased her that the alcohol had not affected her crutch technique; it seemed like some kind of integrity. On her way back from the bathroom she bought two Smirnoff Mules.

'I'm not paying if you chunder in the taxi,' Adrian said when he saw them.

'I've never thrown up from vodka.'

That was true, but after she'd finished one bottle and let the empty slide to the taxi carpet, she fell asleep, and woke only when Adrian heaved her on to her parents' driveway. In the clean, fragranced night air she felt much drunker than she had been in the bar. The thought that she should enter the house alone occurred to her as an abstract proposition, the kind she might consider while watching a movie about someone else's life.

Adrian told the driver to wait, appropriated her bag and found her house keys, opened the door and propped her ahead of him on the step. Her crutch banged on the doorframe. She giggled. 'Shhhh! Shhhh!'

'Where's your room?' he whispered.

'Up there.' After a few steps she swung into his chest and

prodded it hard with her forefinger. 'Oi. We can't. Fuck. Here.' She snickered.

'Shut up.' He pushed her further down the hall. 'Is this it?'

Somehow, they made it through her door. Stella smelled something spicy. Laundry powder, she thought.

Then, foggily: *Mum. Poor Mum. Shit.*

'Where's the other one?' she asked him.

'Other what?'

'Gimme my bag.' She fell on to the bed and dug around until she found the second vodka. 'Open it.'

'You're not planning on drinking that.'

'Whaddarya, some kinda . . . health fascist? I'm not . . . oh— it's a screw top! C'mon, lover boy. Dare you.' She lay down.

'Can't. Taxi's waiting.'

She shut her eyes and hung her arm over the edge of the bed, the bottle dangling from her hand, the alcohol in her blood softening every edge.

After a few moments Adrian said, 'Sleep tight.'

She thought she replied.

In the bathroom, Leland swallowed two of his sleeping pills. Then he went to the kitchen and fixed himself a cheese sandwich so that they might be more quickly digested.

Buttering the bread, his hands trembled. Several times he looked behind him. The dream had forced him from sleep and from his bed, and still he felt its fearsome miasma; the spirits that had informed it hovered over him.

Carrying his sandwich, he switched on the deck lights and stepped into the fresh night air. The potted daphne by the sliding doors rolled its louche and drunken scent towards him.

Yesterday's scenes in this unsettled household had stirred him up. He must leave soon. When he returned to his guest room he would open a window and turn on the light.

But he could not shift the dream. He remembered every word.

Karol had made him dream it. The old man had been in the dream and behind the dream. Through the dream he had said, *I know everything, now. I know what God told you to do.*

Leland stood by the deck table, unable to sit down. Close by, car tyres crunched on gravel and a door slammed. It gave him no comfort to know that others were awake.

The dream had taken him back to his mother's garden. He was twenty-four. It was spring. Karol, wrapped in scarves and shawls, sat next to him in a wheelchair. Through that window was the sickroom his mother and Martha had made in the parlour.

In the remembered garden, Karol had said in his husky voice, 'You seem never angry. Sometimes I wonder that you are maybe dishonest. But I think this is my own sin: I am proud, I insist always on the opportunity to forgive. I myself must be the Messiah!' He laughed; it sounded as though his throat shredded.

The sun had shone on Mrs Swann's roses. A cream-coloured lichen grew on the flagstones by Leland's feet.

'Not so many ideas from you as at the beginning,' Karol had said. 'Not so many great ambitions for the group. What is in your heart?'

Leland had gazed at the lichen. 'I've learned a lot, I guess.'

On the night-bound deck, Leland growled in frustration. He dragged out a chair and thumped its arms as he sat down. He should not be forced to remember that meeting in the dream's context of judgement and misunderstanding. He chomped on the sandwich with exaggerated movements of his jaw, trying to push the dream away. But it kept coming to him, and with it the full memory of that morning.

Karol had said, 'You also have the sense that God wants this group small?'

'Could be,' Leland said, although every atom of him disagreed.

'Not everything in this grand country must be big. Capaceeous. Prodigee-ous. I like this word, "ineffable". Another name for God. He will not fit in our hands. You have been angry with me sometimes?'

Leland had not met Karol's cloudy gaze while he lied. 'I was afraid you didn't love me the same way you love the others. But . . . God's will be done.'

'So. You will be God's small man who leads?'

That line had featured in the dream, and the dreaming Leland had cringed and woken, grabbing his robe and escaping the bedroom. Now, his fists resting before him on the table as if his wrists were handcuffed, he told himself that Karol and Betty did not understand. An exceptional man must wrestle with God like Jacob wrestled with the angel, must prove himself. They did not understand that a man might be so close to God that God misunderstood him.

In the garden that morning, Leland had wanted something more definite from Karol. He had wanted Karol to affirm his superiority amongst men, but in issuing the invitation to lead the group, Karol had spoken lightly, his head turned to look at a sycamore. Leland had no intention of being a 'small man'. Bending, he had picked up a twig and dug a path through the lichen. But a more insistent thought had arrived in his head.

No, it told him. *Say no. It is not the right thing. You are not the man for the job.*

He had pretended to cogitate while he found the strength to ignore the thought. Karol waited patiently. Then Leland straightened, taking on a sombre look.

'If it is God's will, and your will, then I will.'

Karol had laughed. 'God's will is enough, I think.'

Leland believed that it did not frighten him to think that he had disobeyed God. He had always known he would prove God wrong: furthermore, that God *intended* him to do that very thing.

Now, the deck lights shone into his eyes. He wished he had not turned them on. He did not want to return to his room until the pills had begun to take effect. He went back into the kitchen and found a covered plate of mashed potatoes in the refrigerator, glossy with butter and cream cheese. Standing by the open door, he worked his way through it with a dessertspoon.

He could not pray. Since that day in his mother's garden he had never been able to talk to God. This, too, did not matter. As soon as he had made his point, he would be joined with God in a way few mortals had known. After death, the likes of Moses and Jacob would consult with him. Together they would direct the future of the world, and the world would remember them.

After a while fatigue laid a heavy weight on his forehead. He experimented with shutting his eyes, and decided he could safely go back to bed.

He moved through the stillness of the house. Entering his room, his first thought was that Betty's corpse had manifested. The dark form covered by a rug was unmistakably a woman's. His breath caught in his throat, but in the silence he heard the form give a gargling sigh. Then, with horror, he understood that the dream had passed into reality: here was Betty, ready to continue Karol's message. She had lain here waiting for him while he ate cheese and mashed potatoes.

He began to speak, to order her from his room, but did not continue, because whether she was chill and ghostly, or warm and corporeal, if she brushed him as she passed through the doorway his heart would stop.

He was sure she sensed his presence. Why did she remain silent? Why did she not charge him with spiritual corruption and hubris, as he had always known she wanted to?

'What do you have to say to me,' he asked in a low voice, 'Betty Swann?' He said that to remind her that she had once belonged to him, or should have behaved as though she did. 'Why have you come?'

She did not stir, and it was too dark to see her face, but he knew she watched him. What malevolent powers might she have brought from beyond the grave?

'You could not have known what passed between me and Karol in the garden,' he said. 'But the way you behaved, you seemed to. If you had trusted me, we might have conquered together.' It came to him suddenly that God was, after all, overtly on his side, and had struck Betty down in order that he might complete his work. He hissed, 'You could have been spared this disease, but you sabotaged me with your doubt.' His words filled him with righteousness, and he drew closer to the bed, his face averted. 'Answer me.'

She sighed again, and jerked. 'You came back!'

Her tone was triumphant, but she slurred her words. He realised that she had returned in her tumour-ridden state. Her incapacity did not encourage him, for it meant that she had brought death with her.

'What do you want?'

Her hand shot out from the bed, grasping the hem of his pyjama top. 'Whaddya think?'

He wrenched it free, panting hard and chilled with sweat. She muttered something contemptuous.

'Speak. We will finish this here.'

'Nah. You're addicted to me.'

The curtain flapped. Uncertainty grew in him, but he had no space in which to recognise it. From a safe distance, he rallied himself.

'Indeed, I am not. Rita is my helpmeet now. She's coming back to the States with me. A far more able support than you ever were.'

A long pause. Then: 'Fuck's sake?' Her voice clearer. She rolled upright, shaking off the cover.

He wanted to slap her, and found it hard to control his breathing. 'Stella. You have sorely grieved your parents.'

'Screw you, Leland. You're messing up everything . . . Mum'll never go with you.'

The fear in her voice strengthened him. Karol receded. Now all he wanted was to get her back to her own room and let the pills do their work. But she continued to rant.

'You're a fraud. The Love Project's a piece of shit. You want to understand love, look at Mum and Dad.'

'Love takes many forms. It changes.' He pulled hard on her

arms to lift her from his mattress. Even though he knew this was not Betty, he shuddered at the feel of her skin.

She stood in front of him, wobbling and furious. 'Lemme *go* . . . You don't know jackshit about love. You act like you never loved Betty. She was wonderful, a lovely lady, and I bet she had a bloody good reason for not telling you she was sick.'

His grip tightened. His instinct told him to throw this polluted, impious woman to the floor, but the imperative was to get her back to her rightful bed. For the moment, he could not think of how to do it, and she seemed to have run out of steam, so they stayed in their repellent embrace.

A movement in the doorway. '*Stella?*'

She jumped in his arms, then slumped, lolling her head back. 'Oh, great.'

The light came on. Leland flinched. Had Rita heard the conversation? She came forward, her nightdress rippling around her knees, and touched her daughter's shoulder.

'What are you doing in here?'

'I know what you're thinking, calm down.'

'No. You don't know what I'm thinking.'

Rita's level, authoritative tone seemed to shame Stella.

'I've . . . had a bit to drink, so shoot me . . .' She sat down on the bed.

Rita said, 'There's a wet patch on the carpet. And a bottle.' She said to Leland, 'I'm sorry about this.'

He concentrated on benevolence. 'That's fine. It's true what they say: when you have a child your heart walks around outside you.' A visitor to the Project had told him that.

Stella made a disgusted sound. Even Rita did not seem impressed. She picked up the bottle and looked at him as though she were assessing a side of beef. But then she said, 'Leland, I'm ready to go any time you are.'

'Go *where?*' Stella said belligerently.

Rita continued, 'I need a new start, and this seems to be what God wants . . . I was mistaken to think I had any unfinished work here. I'll buy my ticket tomorrow.'

'*Mum!*'

Mentally, he thanked the wayward girl for giving Rita her final impetus. 'What about Bill? Does he want to come?'

'I don't know. Maybe. Well, I'd better make sure Stella gets back to her room.'

The girl did her best to stalk away. He heard her squawking at Rita, and Rita's single, low-voiced reply.

He removed his robe and slid into bed, hoping the disruption would not decrease the pills' effectiveness. After lying for a few minutes he got up again and padded down the hall—the house already restored to silence—to the bathroom, where he swallowed two more. Only four left in the little brown tube. Indeed, it was time to return.

The first, unexpected thought to pass through Rita's mind when she saw the shape of Stella in Leland's arms was, *It won't work. She can't get pregnant with him.*

And then she had to ask herself why she had thought such a thing. Oh, not the fact that Stella wanted a baby—that was now obvious. But the probability that Leland was infertile. It seemed to her she had been thinking of it yesterday, rather than hiding from it for decades.

She laughed silently. All those years of guilt about Betty, and only because as a naïve young woman preparing for her own surprising marriage, she'd had some kind of misplaced sense of responsibility, some idea that she should have warned Betty that maybe Leland could never have children. In her jealousy, she hadn't told her, and she'd felt like a rotten person ever since, especially since Betty and Leland never did have a family.

Well, even if Leland's infertility was a fact, and he'd been callous enough not to tell Betty about it before they married, it didn't stand to reason that it was Rita's fault or that Betty would be angry with her.

She could go and listen to Betty's tape right now, confident that it would offer only love. Betty might be mad at her for not writing, but she'd been a generous person. Even if, by some twist that Rita couldn't imagine, she had guessed that Rita knew about Leland's infertility, she would never hold a grudge and, on her deathbed, wish to make a person feel bad.

She would listen to the tape in the morning.

She felt a new, resolute calm. Stella couldn't hurt her now.

In the laundry room, she tucked Stella into the camp bed with no superfluous conversation. But after she'd closed the door she stood outside it and unconsciously stroked her lower ribs. Something didn't feel right.

I can be at peace now, she told herself. There wasn't anything else that might have hurt Betty.

The image of straggle-haired Kylie, barely grown herself, holding baby Tiana, passed through her mind.

A tremor ran down her spine.

No. It was too much to contemplate.

She returned to her bed, where Bill slept on, oblivious to the night's dramas.

Part 4

1

Three days before the Harper Family Anniversary Weekend, Stella took a call from Bill in the minimalist grey-toned living room of her new apartment. He told her that he and her mother would make the five-hour drive north in separate cars: he with Stella, Rita with Leland.

'For your ankle, your mum reckons. In case you need space to do some of your physio.'

'My ankle's fine. She's still mad at me. *God*. I can't believe Leland's coming. It's meant to be a family do. Is she still planning to go to the States with him?'

'Weekend after next. She's resigned from Abel Andrews and bought her ticket. It's not you, love. Don't worry about it. How's your new place working out?'

'It's fine. Thanks for helping me move.'

'Must be nice to sleep in a proper bed again. You bought a new one?'

'Yes. Can't you say anything to her?'

'Not much . . . she's not going to change her mind because of anything I say.'

'I'll apologise again. Over the weekend. She's been "too busy" to meet me for lunch.'

'Good on you.'

She heard in the timbre of his voice that he did not believe she could stop her mother from leaving, and she resolved to prove him wrong. Her apology would be humble, but limited to lying about the 'elopement'. Not marrying Dan was nothing to be sorry for.

She firmly believed that signing the six-month lease on the apartment, a business-district office conversion, had marked a fresh start. During those six months she would find and buy the impossible house: an affordable, sunny, spacious dwelling close to the city, with fewer than thirty steps and a level, fenced garden. It was easy to think clearly now that she'd finished with Adrian. She wished she had contrived to end the affair before moving into the apartment, but he had rung her cellphone the day after and insisted on meeting her there.

He had been taciturn when he arrived, and she thought he was going to break it off before she could. Then he made her sit beside him on the couch, and while he reminisced about their time together he began to repeat the nimble tricks he'd used during their weekend away. They ended up on the kitchen counter, on the coffee table, in the shower, beside the bed. She had given up on his potency and so—in light of his newfound commitment to her pleasure—let herself relax. It was the most fun they'd had.

Nevertheless, when he buzzed the intercom the following evening, and she recognised, after a few moments, that he intended to dump her, she could only be relieved. He insisted on remaining in the hallway while he delivered his monologue about their 'misalignment' and his 'realisation of a greater purpose'. Stella vowed that the next guy she hooked up with would be the last: a good bloke, with none of Adrian's showmanship or Dan's sarcasm.

She packed for the Anniversary Weekend with a sense of burgeoning maturity, reflecting that shock and panic had led to her liaison with Adrian. If she had her time again, maybe she would wait for a better prospect, and try not to wonder whether the scarring in her tubes would get too much worse before this new man arrived. But she would not waste her energy on regrets. What was done was done, and now she must focus on persuading her mother to stay.

When Bill picked her up, though, she was shocked by the effort behind his smile. He moved as though weights were attached to his shoulders. The thought of him eating alone, washing dishes alone, reading his botanical journals alone, sleeping alone, brought pity to lie heavy on her chest, although she could not imagine that he would feel sorry for himself.

Once they had reached the motorway and begun to travel along the belt of coastal towns, she asked him if he could get some leave and go to the States with Rita.

He took a while to answer. 'I've thought about chucking in the job. But even if I could . . . it doesn't seem right. I can't picture . . . us *being there* . . . the same way I could never see you and Dan going on. Last week I had a Meeting for Clearness with some of the Friends about whether I should go. Same result.'

'The Quakers? Is that the thing where you pick a few people to listen to God with you?'

'Yep, or you can ask the Meeting to pick people for you. That's what I did.'

'And they said for you not to go? What about keeping your marriage together?'

He nodded. 'I know. But you can only do the right thing. You can't fix everything.'

'So, will you two . . .' She tried not to sound too anxious.

'She says we'll still be married,' he said briskly. 'She and Leland'll live in the same house over there, but they won't . . . it'll be some kind of spiritual partnership.'

'"Spiritual partnership"? Is that what she said?'

'Actually, I've heard Leland call it a spiritual marriage. A Holy Marriage.'

'*What*?'

'He said Gandhi had one, with a married woman, his soulmate. Gandhi hoped to remake India with this woman, solve its problems, but his son and advisors didn't understand. They made him break it off.'

'Mum and Leland aren't soulmates!'

'She says I can go over any time, and she'll be home after six months. It's my fault if we're separated, according to her.' He said this without bitterness. 'Then she'll stay at home six months, then it's back to the States.'

'Oh, God. She's really serious about this.'

'Seems that way. How's your ankle doing? You need to do some of those exercises?'

'No. It's fine.' Stella hesitated. 'Do you really think she'll come home?'

'She says so, but once Leland gets it up and running in the States, I reckon he'll be done and dusted with the Kiwi side. Don't know what she'll do then.'

'He's such a fraud.'

'No need to be rude.'

Stella thought there was every need, but she loved her dad for his civility, and her pity for him deepened. She said, 'She's been in such a tizzy ever since he got here, it's like she's been cranking up for this, or something.'

'There's stuff we don't know about, I reckon. There's a tape . . .'

'What tape?'

'Last week. I was putting away the laundry—'

She cracked a smile. 'You're such a sensitive new-age guy, Dad . . . Seriously? What's on it?'

'I think it's from Betty. She hasn't listened to it.'

'How do you know?'

'I asked her.'

'Did you *tell* her to listen to it?'

'No . . . Could be years old, anyway, from the looks of it.'

'But why hasn't she listened to it?'

'I don't know. Could have nothing to do with all this.' He glanced out the side window. 'Chronic erosion around here.'

He was right. The lower slopes of the nearby paddocks looked as though they suffered from a skin disease.

In the next town they stopped for fish and chips, and ate them at the edge of a sports field while the air grew cool. Once, her father said, 'They'll be there now,' and she knew he meant her mother and Leland who had left Wellington before them.

She said, 'They didn't have anything going at the Centre, did they, Mum and Leland?'

He threw a chip at some dusty pigeons. 'Leland always seemed too busy for romance. There wasn't much of it around anyway.'

'Not the sex-crazed cult-leader type.'

'No. In fact—' he looked surprised, as if he'd just remembered '—you could've knocked me down with a feather when he and Betty got engaged. They announced it the day after your mum and me. Must've been something in the air.'

'Yup. Must have, to make her think he was a good deal.'

They could not finish the clammy fish, and deposited its wrapped remains in a rubbish bin. On the car radio, Stella found a station playing sixties music. For the rest of the journey she let the topic of Rita and Leland rest.

The closer they got, the more tightly Bill gripped the steering wheel. It was dark when they found the road leading to their rented house, and Bill drove up and down it three times before they spotted the name, *Parehua*, on a gatepost. They turned in. At the end of the tree-lined, meandering lane, a copper-shaded outdoor lamp lit up the portico and shrubbery.

'Where's Mum's car?'

'Maybe she put it in the garage.'

They parked, and Bill tried the front door. It was locked.

'They're not here,' Stella said, unnecessarily.

'Doesn't look like it. Maybe they've gone out for takeaways.'

'In these parts? The only place open back there was a kebab shop.'

He turned over a rock, then a stone cat. 'Seem to remember your mum said the owners were leaving the key by the door somewhere. Yup. Here we are.'

Stella followed him over the sill and switched on a light. They found themselves in a large, unnaturally tidy kitchen. 'They haven't been here,' she said. 'Look, there aren't even any drops in the sink. Mum would've made tea. They left before us, right?'

'I waved them off. Then it was a good twenty minutes before

273

I was ready to come and collect you. I reckon they had at least an hour on us.'

'Call her.'

Bill pulled out his phone. 'Here we go. Oops. Battery's flat.'

'Use mine.' She gave it to him, and he dialled.

'No answer.'

'She thinks it's me calling . . . maybe she doesn't want to spend any time with me. Maybe they've gone straight to Auckland and they're not even going to say goodbye. I'm so sorry, Dad.' She pushed her hair back from her face.

'Calm down, love. She's turned hers off. It went straight to message.'

'Where *are* they, then?'

'There'll be some explanation. We'll give them another hour or so. Could be all sorts of hold-ups, what with people leaving town for the weekend. Let's find the bedrooms and have a wash and think what to do.'

On the ground floor, two twin rooms opened through french doors on to private patios lined with potted lavender.

'Leland should be comfortable here,' Stella said drily.

In the other direction, a long living room was divided in two by a tall wooden screen made of three hinged panels, each covered with an embroidered scene of sailing ships.

'It's the kind of place that looks good with not much in it,' Bill said. Stella saw what he meant. Groups of furniture sat far apart from each other on white rugs, and wide waterways of blue tiles flowed between them. In one corner, next to a window, an antique brass telescope stood pointing into the dark garden. 'There's a spa pool out there, apparently,' said Bill. 'Under the gazebo. And a trampoline.'

'God, it's huge,' said Stella. 'Why didn't she scale down after Charlie said they weren't coming?'

He didn't look at her. 'Maybe she hoped they'd change their minds.'

She remembered the renewal of vows. 'Nothing's the way she wanted it, is it.'

'I don't know, love. You and me, we're here.' He turned away from the window. 'And Charlie and Noelle have done their best—I've got their thing.'

'What's with the marine theme?' She pointed to a model schooner that sat near them on a low table.

'The sea's pretty close. Your mum said.'

'Oh . . . does Charlie know? About Dan and me?'

'They know you've split up.'

She took from this that they did not know about the non-elopement. Noelle hadn't been on the scene four years ago but Charlie had given them a 'wedding present' of placemats and coasters. She and Charlie had always got along, at least after he left his evangelical phase behind. He would be disappointed in her.

She put him out of her mind. 'Check out that huge stereo.'

'Reminds me, did you bring the presents?'

'We'll need a skip to take away the polystyrene. Can't beat electronica for unnecessary packaging.'

'Good. Let's see what's upstairs.'

It took them a minute or two to find the way. At last Stella opened a door leading out of the kitchen, and they walked along a dim, narrow passage at the end of which was another door. On the other side of it, they found the stairs.

'Odd arrangement,' said Bill.

The master bedroom glowed with multiple inset lights. Standing at the window, they could see the tops of bushy trees.

'Orchard,' said Bill. 'Look, apples. Lit up.' He walked to a corner of the room and paced along the length of one wall, then another. He stood for a moment, and said, 'I could fit eight vege patches in here. And a chook house. And a barn.'

Stella laughed. 'Stop reverting, Dad. Hey look, you've got an ensuite. You don't have to worry about Mum going off with Leland. She won't want to leave. There's a marble basin.'

'Yup . . . I think the room next door's ensuite, too.'

'God, I can't wait for a bath. My apartment's only got a shower.'

'Look, love . . .' He had sat down on the bed. 'Do you mind . . . ? Thing is, I'd like some time alone with your mum. It being our anniversary and . . . everything's that's gone on.'

'Yes?' She didn't get it.

'There's a bath downstairs.'

'Oh, yuk, I mean, I don't mind being downstairs, but . . . next door to Leland?' She shuddered.

'That didn't appear to be a problem three weeks ago.'

'What? *Dad*. I was drunk.'

He laughed.

'I don't see how you can be so . . . when she and Leland . . . they could be anywhere. They could have had an accident.'

'No.'

They returned to the kitchen. Stella boiled the kettle, and they made tea with the complimentary teabags. Bill laid his phone on the table. 'I didn't bring the charger. Maybe she's trying to ring me.'

'Try with mine again.'

He did. 'Nope. Nothing.'

'Shall we ring the police?'

'No . . . maybe they've broken down not far away. I could drive back for a bit.'

'Not happening, Dad. I'll hide your keys.'

She saw that she needed to keep him busy. 'You go brush your teeth. Spruce up. Here, I brought some candles. Nice ones, smelly. Put them round the bedroom, make it romantic. For God's sake, when she gets here, don't mention chook houses and vege patches.'

He gave a crooked grin. 'All right.'

She watched him move slowly along the passage towards the stairs, and almost cried.

In her room she lay on the bed and watched TV with the volume muted, flipping distractedly through the channels. What if her mum *had* run off with Leland, preferring not to spend a weekend around an unhappy husband and deceitful daughter? If they were planning to embark on a spiritual marriage, she

276

thought, that would make their disappearance a spiritual elopement. Ironic.

Outside, tyres crunched the gravel. She sat up and lifted a corner of the curtain. In the yellow light she saw her mother close the driver's door and look towards the house. Leland emerged from the passenger's side.

Stella dropped the curtain and fell back on the pillows. Since she'd left her parents' house, the morning after she'd fought with Leland in his room, she hadn't spoken to her mother face to face. She'd apologised over the phone, but the apology only produced an unsatisfactory, stiff gratitude.

For a few days, Stella had managed to whip up some anger of her own. Hell, she'd apologised. What more could she do? She set aside her remorse while she shopped for a new apartment and dealt with change-of-address forms. But now the sight of her mother by the car, drooping with tiredness, brought back her talcum-powdery smell and the sound of her voice. Stella wished she could pretend to be asleep, but she stood and fluffed her hair.

They were already inside the kitchen, Leland leaning with one hand on the counter, frowning at her mother.

She saw Stella. 'Hello.' Her mouth twitched a little. The lines around it were deeper, her cheeks mottled and heavy.

'Hi, Mum.' Stella kissed her quickly, so she couldn't recoil. 'Dad must be snoozing. I'll give him a yell.' She walked past Leland without acknowledging him, and took a few steps into the passage. She heard Leland say, 'In Phase Two we'll establish networks, look at distribution.'

'Dad! They're here!' She got her shouting over with quickly, but her mother must have made a quiet, short response, because Leland spoke again: 'Phase *Two*. I outlined it in the car. I thought you were listening?'

Bill trotted down the stairs, nudging Stella on the way past. 'Reet! Did you get a flat tyre?' Stella followed him into the kitchen, glad to see him march right up to his wife and kiss her. He cupped the back of her head in his hand. 'We were getting worried.'

'Sorry.'

Leland was still frowning. He said, 'I need to call someone. Is there—?'

'In the lounge.' Stella jerked a thumb over her shoulder.

'I'm sorry we're late,' her mother said, after he'd disappeared. 'We'd just set off and Leland said he needed to visit with someone who'd been to the Project. Pastoral care. So I drove him there and went back home. He was there over an hour.'

'How rude!' Stella exclaimed.

'Why didn't you ring?' Bill asked.

'I don't know.' Rita rested her forehead on his shoulder.

'You look all done in.' He said to Stella, 'Are you all right to show Leland his room? I'll take this one upstairs and tuck her in.'

Leland was by the far windows in the living room, talking on the phone, his back to the door. Stella slipped in and stood next to the screen, in plain view, should he happen to turn. No one could claim she was hiding.

He said, 'The plan now revealed to me . . . yes, in the first instance you should tell your story to the two of us. Yes, at first. It should seal the decision. No turning back. And then you will return with us. No room for doubt.'

A second recruit, she thought. Another middle-aged lady, probably, looking for meaning in life.

Leland said, 'Good. That's settled.'

When he had hung up, she said, 'If you're *finished*, I'll show you your room.'

'Eavesdropping, Stella? That doesn't surprise me.' He followed her. 'You are the very essence of deceit.'

'That's your room. The bathroom's through there. The toilet's at the end of the hall.' She went into her room and closed the door.

Birdsong woke her at six. She dressed in sports gear and entered the damp garden through her french doors, but had not taken five steps before she began wishing for a strong coffee. She resisted, breathing deeply, testing her ankle, visualising oxygen flowing through her bloodstream. Her virtue gave out halfway across the neighbouring paddock, and she dragged herself back, eyeing the upstairs windows and wondering what her parents had said to each other during the night. Leland's curtains were still closed, but that meant nothing. Maybe he was watching through a slit. She flicked a finger in the direction of his room and went back to bed.

She did not wake again until mid-morning. As she stumbled into the kitchen, eyelids gluey, she heard Leland asking, 'Are you ready?'

He was standing near the other door, watching her mother wash dishes.

'Where are you going?' Stella asked, alarmed.

He affected detachment. 'We have an appointment to see one of our Project visitors.'

'Up here?'

'Vacationing in the area.'

Rita said, 'It slipped my mind.'

'We discussed it in the car, I'm sure. A remarkable case: repentance leading to a deeper understanding of love. And a practical contribution, if I'm not mistaken. You may not labour long alone, Rita.' He smiled paternally at her. 'It's fitting you should meet now.'

'I'll come in and say hello, but I'm feeling a little . . .' Rita didn't meet his eyes. 'I'll drop you off, and maybe he can bring you back.'

'No. Your presence is necessary.'

'Sorry. I found yesterday's drive . . . tiring.'

'You'll feel different when you're there,' he said.

Stella asked her, 'Will you come straight back?'

'Yes.' Her mother gave Leland a weary half-smile. 'A few days' rest and I'll be raring to go.' She dried her hands and picked up her purse.

'Come right back, Mum. We need to talk.'

She showered quickly and went over her notes. She had written out her apology to ensure it was unambiguous. Bill knocked on her door to ask if she wanted coffee. The proper stuff, he said. He'd found a plunger. They sat in striped deckchairs on the patio and sipped without speaking. There was nothing to be said. Only two conversations mattered, Stella thought: her apology; and the other one, in which Rita might say goodbye.

That was her task: to make sure the second conversation didn't happen.

2

The morning after she had discovered Stella drunk in Leland's room, Rita had woken to find that she did not want to listen to Betty's tape, after all. In the following days, while she sorted and packed and ferried carloads of old clothes to the Salvation Army, she had thought occasionally of it. Always, she decided to leave it until tomorrow: make some quality time, have her own little ceremony. Perhaps she might even write a letter to Betty and read it aloud someplace in the open air. Light a candle or plant a sapling.

But there was never any time tomorrow, or the day after.

It was not that she was avoiding it. Maybe she should carry out her ceremony once she'd arrived in the States. That would surely be more appropriate, seeing as Betty had never visited New Zealand.

When Bill found the tape in her drawer, she did not tell him that she had felt it pushing at her every time she passed. She said it wasn't any of his business, and, surprisingly, he seemed to agree. Perhaps, she thought, the revelation of Stella's lies had shocked him into realising that she couldn't turn down Leland's invitation to help people understand Love when Stella hadn't loved them well enough to tell them the truth, and maybe they hadn't loved Stella well enough either.

She let herself forget about the tape.

While she returned the audio equipment and sorted out her papers at Abel Andrews, she knew that she had already left her pre-Leland life. She felt as if she lived on the cusp of an indrawn breath. Everything that really mattered lay in her future. She wrote in her notebook:

What I know:
The Prophecy—a 'spiritual partnership'—God's direction
(finally!)
Stella doesn't trust me or need me
I can see Charlie and Zane on the way to and from the States
L needs me for the Project
Bill could come if he wanted to

That night she had difficulty falling asleep. While she dozed, a big desk appeared, with the word *Project* engraved into the leather right across its centre. *Leland* was underneath it; *God* across the top, in bigger letters; and *Charlie and Zane* slightly to the side. She opened a drawer in the desk and found a notebook labelled *Stella*. Bill's notebook was in the next drawer down.

She took this to mean that Stella was beyond her help, and Bill too, unless he agreed to come to the States, in which case his name would appear on the desk's surface, right up there next to . . . she wasn't sure where, exactly, but she knew *Bill* would be written big, even if he could never comprehend her decision to leave.

After that, she thought with pleasure of the desk and the way it set everything out in such an organised fashion. At last, her life made sense.

Then, three days ago, she had begun to pack clothes for the Anniversary Weekend, and lifting a camisole out of her dresser she uncovered Betty's tape.

Last night, surrounded by lavender-scented pillows and cushioned by an expensive mattress, she had slept only four hours and then lain awake, listening to Bill's little noises. Now she stood by the back door of their borrowed house, hugging herself, watching her husband and daughter dozing in sun-loungers. Her fatigue gave her chills, even on this hot day. She would have preferred to hide in the bedroom, but she knew that one of them would come to find her, for this 'talk' of Stella's.

It was apparent from their relaxed postures that Bill hadn't given a thought to challenging his daughter about her behaviour. Rita moved impatiently, knocking the corner of a blue ceramic wind chime.

Stella's head shot up. 'Mum?'

'You all right?' Bill said. He came towards her and took her arm. 'It's getting hot out here. Let's go in. Can you make some more coffee, Stell?'

Rita let herself be led. It was a relief to sit down on one of the plush white sofas. Bill sat beside her and squeezed her hand. Stella came in with the coffee and mugs. Hers was already full. 'What've you got there?' Bill asked.

'Green tea,' she said. 'Not so much caffeine.'

She gave a mug to Rita. Rita took her hand out from under Bill's so she could warm herself on the hot china.

Stella began to speak, but Rita said, 'No, I want to say something first.' She cleared her throat. 'I'm not changing my mind.' She wanted to appear steadfast: if she convinced them, she might believe it, too. 'I believe it's the right thing, for me to go to America and help Leland with the Project. Everything that's happened over the last couple of months adds up to a very clear signal for me, the clearest since . . . since almost always.'

Bill's elbows were on his knees. He had clasped his hands together and laid his forehead on his knuckles.

She said to him, 'You can still come. It's not too late. We're going to be living in Seattle, like Leland said. And we'll see Charlie and Zane on the way over.'

He took a breath to speak, but Stella spoke first. 'Do you guys mind—can I say this before everything's decided?'

Rita noticed that her cheeks looked a little fuller than usual. She seemed nervous. 'I know you've already heard me apologise, but I want to say it in person. I'm truly really sorry I lied to you both about getting married. I hurt you most of all, Mum. You probably think you can't trust me any more. I wasn't thinking about . . . what you deserve from me. I told myself it didn't matter if there was this thing between us. I told myself you'd combust if you knew the truth. That it'd be better to pretend we were married. But really I didn't have the guts to face you. I'm sorry.'

It was more than Rita had expected. She knew this apology was prompted by her imminent departure: that Stella would try to persuade her to stay. Still, here at last was the confiding daughter she'd longed for.

'Well,' Bill said, and stopped. 'Thanks, love. It helps to hear that. How about we leave it for a while and move on to some birthday celebrations?'

'My birthday's not until next week,' Rita said.

'This was always meant to be your birthday party too. We've got . . . stuff.' Stella got up—she was still limping a little, Rita noticed—and left the room. Then she put her head back around the door. 'Where is it, Dad?'

'Side pocket of my bag. Next to the wardrobe.'

They heard her climbing the stairs.

Rita said, 'I'm sorry, I've got a card for you, but I didn't manage to get a present yet.'

He squeezed her hand again. 'Not to worry.'

They sat in silence until Stella returned, carrying several wrapped, rectangular packages. Rita did not see how they could have fitted into the side pocket of Bill's suitcase. Stella put them down on the coffee table. 'Hang on a minute.'

She left the room, and after a couple of minutes came back in carrying a plate with six chocolate-iced muffins, each stuck with one candle. She started singing as she came through the door, and Bill joined in, *Happy Birthday, Happy Birthday*, his voice determinedly loud and gruff. When they had finished, Bill took the topmost package from the pile, a flattish square, and handed it to her.

'A couple of other folks who'd like to say hello.'

She didn't understand, but she opened it. 'A CD,' she said. There was a card pasted over the top of it: 'To Mum, with love from Charlie, Noelle and Zane'.

'It's a DVD. Here.' Stella took it from her and went over to the television. In a few moments music came through the loudspeakers and yellow cursive writing appeared on the screen, surrounded by dancing, cartoonish balloons: 'A Very Happy Hawai'ian Birthday!'

'Amazing what they can do, these days,' Bill said. 'With the editing.'

And there was Zane wearing a tiny lei, sitting on Noelle's knee outside their house in Maui, Charlie next to them. 'Happy Birthday, Mum!' Charlie called, and, 'Aloha!' Noelle said. She smiled so that her eyes almost disappeared under her straight black fringe, and lifted up Zane's pudgy hand and waved it. He was naked except for the lei and a diaper, and had the sweetest, plumpest cheeks and, when Charlie tickled his tummy, a huge toothless smile, like a sideways serif 'D'.

'Look how much he's grown. He's got your nose, Bill,' she said. She ached to hold him. A three- or four-day visit every six months could never be enough.

The camera toured through the house. They saw Zane's nursery, walls painted a pale green, a frieze of orange parrots around the ceiling. Zane lay on his tummy, dribbling gleefully. Zane rolled and batted at stuffed toys hanging from a baby-frame. Zane ate solids—mashed yam and banana, his face and hands covered with yellow mush. Zane was thrown in the air, and laughed.

He would never be that age again. Even if she arrived in Hawai'i tomorrow, Rita would miss this. It hurt to think like that, but it was better than thinking of everything else. *I'll see him soon*, she told herself. *On the way to the States. I am going to the States.* She must not let herself falter.

There wasn't nearly enough of Zane: they kept showing her Charlie's home office, or Noelle's artwork, or both of them surfing (who was holding Zane?), or Charlie strumming his guitar. Towards the end Zane hardly appeared. Finally, Charlie turned up with his guitar again, Noelle crouched beside him, Zane once again on her knee. Charlie said, 'Time for a last song, Ma, and then Dad's going to deliver the next part of our gift.' *Happy Birthday, Happy Birthday*, with Noelle waving both of Zane's arms in time to the music. Bill sang along under his breath, and even Stella hummed.

The room seemed much emptier after the DVD had finished. Bill must have felt it, too, because he said, 'Right, what's next!' and fished another present from the pile, a small box. She peeled off the tape and folded away the paper.

'Go on, look at the present, don't worry about the paper!'

Rita didn't understand the picture on the box, or the name. A web-cam?

'It's a camera, Mum, for talking to Charlie and Noelle. They've got one too. You can see Zane every day, if you want. It's from them. Their idea. You clip it to the top of your laptop. There's stuff in that other box to make it work.'

'That's lovely,' she said. Did they think she wouldn't be seeing Zane in person at all? Had she failed to persuade them that she was really going with Leland?

Bill and Stella looked at each other. 'Time to make a call, I reckon,' he said. He walked to the phone, which sat on a low wicker table underneath one of the windows, pulled a piece of paper from his pocket and dialled a long number. She could guess who it was, and she smiled widely, to get some happiness into her voice.

'Hello,' Bill said. 'It's me. Yup, a bit earlier than we said. Are you all there? Is Charlie home?' He turned from the phone. 'We're in luck. They're in. Come over, Rita. They want to say hello.'

She took the handset, nervous. The sunlight was beating into this corner of the room, and instantly she began to perspire. Did Charlie know about her plan to join Leland in the States? Would she need to defend herself to him, too? But she was hardly required to speak. First Charlie and Noelle sang the birthday song again, their voices tinny over the line. Then she only had to say, 'How's your work, Charlie?' and he gave her a summary of everything he'd done during the last two months. They put Zane on. She thought she heard him breathe. In the background, Charlie said, 'Zane! Say "ga"! Say "ga"!' There was a pause. Charlie came back. 'We've coaching him to say

"Grandma", but he hasn't mastered "Ma" yet.'

She laughed. It was, actually, easy to feel happy if she thought exclusively of the fact that Zane existed.

'And how's your work, Mum? What's going on with that Project thing Dad mentioned?' His voice was too light. They had told him, and now he was patronising her.

'It's going fine,' she said. 'It's very exciting. I'm looking forward to seeing you.'

'Sure. Dad too, yeah?'

'Maybe.'

'Is Stella there?' he asked.

Rita gave her the phone and took a few steps away from it, into the shade. She kept her eyes on two plastic penguins which bobbed in a box on the windowsill. They were riding surfboards, surrounded by a violently blue, viscous liquid.

'Hi,' Stella said. 'Thanks . . . yeah. I'm okay. Yeah, it's in the city, pretty convenient. I can walk to work . . . No, about two months ago.'

Was she talking about her ankle or Dan's departure?

'The Philippines.'

Dan, then.

'I'm going to put you on the speaker phone,' Stella said. She glanced at Rita while she hit the button. Her cheeks were crimson. A low whooshing sound came from the machine. She turned around again, speaking into the handset. 'I'm sorry to interrupt the birthday stuff but I need to tell you something.'

'What have you done now?' He sounded jovial.

'I lied to everyone about me and Dan being married. We didn't get married, we only pretended. I'm really sorry, Charlie, I didn't think about what I was doing'

It seemed to Rita that despite the apparent sincerity of her earlier apology, only now, talking to her brother, did Stella feel shame. *It doesn't matter*, she thought, with some surprise. It was part of Stella and Charlie being young together.

'Are you serious?' Charlie asked. 'Why the hell'd you do that?'

Stella sighed. Bill moved forward and stood behind her, laying a hand on her shoulder. 'It just seemed easier. For us. I had this thing in my head about how . . . Mum would react.'

'So, what, the whole thing in Fiji was just a sham? That photo of you two on the dock, and everything? With flowers?' The white noise from the speaker phone seemed to have increased, as if Charlie's agitation hissed and shushed around them.

'It was just . . . to support the story.'

'So this whole time, you've been lying this whole time? Five years?

'Four.'

'And what, have you only told us now because Mum and Dad have been asking questions? You would have gone on with it if no one asked?'

'I don't know. I'm really sorry, Charlie . . . I've still got the placemats, if you want them back.'

'I don't want the bloody placemats!' He continued in a quieter tone. 'I can't believe it.' Then he blew out loudly, and tutted.

'*What*?' Stella was beginning to sound testy.

'I'm thinking, man, poor Mum. Is that why she's taking off? Mum, are you all right? Do you know what you're doing?'

That's enough, Rita thought. She'd forgotten about Charlie's self-righteous streak. If only everyone would understand that she wasn't 'taking off' out of hurt pride.

'I'm all right,' she said, directing her voice into the speaker. 'I did feel very upset when Stella told us.' She kept talking over his interjection. 'But . . . I can't feel bitter. It wouldn't be right. Because I haven't been completely open with you all about why I have to go with Leland.'

If she told them, she thought, maybe she'd feel more certain about the rightness of leaving.

'Especially—' she turned over her shoulder and spoke to Bill '—I haven't been honest with you.'

He blanched a little.

'What was that?' Charlie said. 'What did you say? You have to speak into the phone, Mum.'

288

'I know. I was saying, I haven't been honest with your dad.'

If only she could transfer the knowledge into Bill's head instantaneously so he did not have to worry for another second about what she meant. She cleared her throat. 'Back when I met the Movement, the very first evening, when my mother took me to see *The Divine Instruction*, afterwards, when I was listening to Leland speak, I heard God say, *You will marry that man*. And there was a silence around those words, throughout the whole hall . . .'

'Everyone heard it?' Charlie asked.

'No . . . the words came out of nowhere. They jumped into my head, as if someone was behind me, talking to me. I felt them . . . vibrating through my whole body. Every limb. It was completely convincing. I'd just completed my first Listening. And—'

Stella leaned her elbow on the windowsill, wrinkling her nose in a humorous, slightly patronising way. 'Not to point out the obvious, Mum, but you didn't marry him. You married Dad.'

'What was that?' Charlie didn't wait for an answer. 'So what's your point? You didn't marry him.'

Rita sighed. She was aware of Bill behind her. 'No. And I love your dad.' She turned and spoke to him. 'You know I love you.'

After a beat, he nodded.

'What did you say? Have you got some crazy idea that God wanted you to marry Leland?'

'No! Well, definitely not after your dad and I were married.' She could finish being honest with Bill later. The kids didn't need to know about her early doubts.

Charlie said something lengthy and incomprehensible. Someone—Noelle, probably—exclaimed. Then he said clearly, 'Noelle says it sounds bizarre . . . ah, and she also wants to say that it'd be fantastic to have you *both* here, any time you want to come.'

'Mum,' Stella said. 'You can't seriously let something you

think you heard, like, forty years ago, influence you now!' She had picked up the penguin box and was shaking it so that the penguins flipped and surfed, the ugly blue slime breaking into droplets around them.

Rita said, 'I haven't finished. I always wondered if I'd gotten out of sync with God's plan, somehow. Even though I was always happy with your dad. I wondered, on and off.' Her neck had stiffened, talking down into the speaker.

'Ergo, God's plan didn't include me and Charlie,' Stella said. 'God can get stuffed.'

'Let her speak,' said Bill.

She said, 'When Leland arrived, it all came back to me.' Now it was her turn to be truly ashamed. Bill would know how much she had withheld. At the same time it was easier to confess, to repeat her rationale, than to begin to think about why she might *not* go to the States. 'And then, after a while, I told Leland about it. About how confused I was.'

'Confused about Dad?' Charlie said.

They were refusing to understand.

'Well, and then Leland—and I'd been working on the Project, and everything—he thought about it a while, and he said he'd always believed in this ideal of spiritual partnership. Working together, but not in the *married* married sense.'

Her cheeks heated up at having to clarify to her children that she did not intend to have sex with Leland.

'This was just before he asked you to go to the States, to be his assistant, that you told him,' Stella said, witheringly.

Rita said, 'It just gives me so much peace, about my whole life, to think this could be the meaning of the Promise. Because it means everything in between has been right as well.'

'But how could you think being with Dad, and us . . . that all that was wrong?'

'Reet,' said Bill, slowly, 'you know how you always doubt yourself. You always think you've done the wrong thing.'

'I know I'm not wrong about this,' she said, feeling desperate. 'It makes sense.'

'This spiritual wotcher-ma-call-it,' said Charlie's disembodied voice.

'Yes,' said Stella. 'Has Leland said whether he had one with Betty?'

'That's beside the point,' said Bill.

'I'm a bit out of my depth here,' said Charlie. 'I'm missing out on half the conversation.'

'The thing is,' said Rita—a pressure had risen in her chest at Stella's mention of Betty—'if your dad would come with me, maybe he'd understand. I can't describe it. It's a spiritual thing.'

'I don't get it,' said Charlie.

Elsewhere in the house, a door closed. They turned and looked down the long room. Leland appeared under the archway. There was someone behind him. Rita could see past them both into the kitchen, and through the kitchen window a black SUV with tinted windows.

'Hullo?' said Charlie. 'Are you still there?'

'We need to go,' said Bill. 'Leland's back.' He picked up the handset. 'We'll call again later. No. It's not like that. I'll let you know. Bye, son. Love to Noelle and Zane.'

Leland's companion followed him a little way into the room, and Rita recognised him as the Project visitor she had met, briefly, that morning when she went to drop off Leland. She had forgotten his name. His face was bright with anticipation, like a chat-show guest ready to meet the public.

Bill began to move towards the pair. Stella moved faster, stopping only a few inches from the tall stranger's T-shirt. She asked, in a low, loaded voice, '*What* are you doing?'

A wordless misgiving began to clot and curdle in Rita.

The man grinned over Stella's head. 'Hi again, Mrs Harper. You must be Mr Harper. Congratulations on your anniversary. It's amazing, it's brilliant to see two people stick together. Forty years, right?'

'And you are?' Bill asked.

'I'm Adrian.'

Stella said, urgently, 'Come outside.'

'You two already acquainted?' Bill said.

Rita watched Leland nod, satisfied. Her exhaustion hit her again. She gulped and stumbled to the sofa. If only she did not think about the tape, she would be all right.

'Yup. We know each other.' Adrian sidestepped Stella. 'Mind if I—?' He made himself comfortable next to Rita. He smelled of fresh sweat.

Bill sat down heavily on a facing armchair. 'You're . . . one of the Project's contributors?'

'He's going to work with me,' said Leland. 'In America. He's relinquished his sin.'

'It's a new life for me and my family,' said Adrian. 'I'm incredibly excited. I'm full of energy. I've lost all my cynicism.'

'*This isn't about you,*' Stella said, pale, speaking to him as though no one else were in the room. She had moved to stand behind Bill's chair.

'It's all good,' Adrian said to her. 'Leland and I Listened.'

'That's right,' said Leland. He had not sat down, but stood at one end of the long coffee table, seemingly ready to intervene.

'Why don't you tell us what's up,' Bill said.

Adrian took a ruminative breath. 'It's quite a story. Stella and I know each other very well. She might not recognise me, though—she might not believe what's happened to me. I met Leland through her. I went to see him at the Project, after she'd talked about him. He showed me my sin.' He took out his cellphone and laid it on his right knee. The screen displayed a single line of text, but Rita could not read it.

'I know it's not cool for people my age to undergo instant conversions, but I see it as a matter of logic. The world can't go on like this, everyone out for themselves. I was part of it, and I have to stop living for myself. But that's not all. It can't end with me.' Adrian spread his hands, palms up, looking at Bill as though he expected approval. 'What's the use of me stopping my sin if my inaction allows others to continue?'

'Adrian.' Stella seemed to have no other words.

'You're off the mark, mate,' Bill said. 'This is a family do. If

292

you've got a score to settle, you should wait until you're back in Wellington.'

'I don't have a grudge, Mr Harper. That's the thing. This *is* a family do, and what I'm about is family. Family's where healing should start.' He became grave. 'My folks split up when I was ten. I can't visit the same anguish on my own kids.'

'You told me your parents were happily married!' Stella exclaimed.

'That wasn't the whole truth. I apologise. I'm as much to blame as you are. We used each other. Leland reminded me about what mattered. I needed that. I'd been messing around, kidding myself that I was a dude. Deluding myself.'

It struck Rita that this was close to what her daughter had said about her own behaviour. None of it surprised her. The affair seemed a foregone conclusion, in retrospect. Given who Stella was. Given her current circumstances.

Bill stood. He said to her and Leland, 'How about we leave them to it? This isn't our business.'

Wake up, Rita thought.

Adrian said, 'You should stay. Look, this might seem like I rate myself, but you could understand this as a kind of divine intervention. If you're into the God as personality thing. Like in California, where people stage interventions for friends who're headed towards disaster. I want to give Stella a chance. We were irresponsible. We thought we didn't answer to anyone. But now I realise I'm accountable for my family's happiness. Accountable to God, too. I think I almost believe in Him again.' He smiled at Leland.

'What are you getting at?' Bill asked. He sat down. Rita knew how much he distrusted people who could not make their point. She felt a deep sadness for him.

Adrian said, 'Tell them, Stella. Begin the healing.'

'Hang on,' said Bill.

'The thing is, she needs to admit her sins. When my daughters say sorry, we make them say what they're sorry *for*. There's a reason for that.'

293

'What about Louise?' Stella jutted her chin at him. 'Did you confess to *her*?'

'You're married?' said Bill. He twisted around to look at Stella. 'You slept with a married man?'

He's behind, Rita thought. *No wonder—he doesn't know how much Stella wants a baby. He probably doesn't remember how early my change came.*

'You want to see where Louise is at on this?' Adrian pushed a button on his cellphone. 'Ask her yourself.'

The phone beeped, and the line of text disappeared, replaced by a little picture that Rita couldn't make out. She assumed he was ringing his wife. She did not understand until she heard the door open.

Young voices. 'Daddy?'

'In here, princess.'

A very thin woman came into the room, ushering two girls before her. The smaller one wore silver fairy-wings over a pink dress, the other embroidered jeans and an oversized bush shirt. The woman had light brown hair, parted in the middle and tied into a ponytail. She was wearing a denim skirt and a red lacy camisole that did not flatter her complexion. While Adrian made introductions, she looked only at Stella. It was not an accusing look, but restrained and unfriendly, as if she understood that she could not bring all of herself into the room.

Does she know? Rita wondered. *How can she bear to be here?*

Adrian said to Stella, 'There you go. All yours.'

Bill said, 'Wait a blimmin' minute, this isn't right.' He asked the older girl, 'What's your name? My name's Bill.'

'I'm Holly,' said the girl, with immense self-importance. 'I'm six and three quarters. This is my sister. She's four and a half.'

'My name's Dinah,' said the smaller girl. '*That's* my grandmother's name too.'

Bill crouched next to them. 'It's a pleasure to meet you, Holly, Dinah. Would either of you like a chocolate muffin?' He took two from the plate. 'There's a trampoline outside. Look, through this door.'

Adrian tensed. 'Dinnie's too young.'

'Chill *out*, Ade,' his wife said in a tired, detached tone. She told the girls to make daisy chains, promised to join them in five minutes so they could bounce. Holly demanded to wear her mother's watch.

They're used to disappearing, Rita thought.

Stella came to kneel beside her. '*Mum*.' She ignored Adrian, who smiled at the top of her head.

Bill said to the wife, 'I'm sorry we have to meet under these circumstances.' He sounded exhausted. 'Have a seat.'

'Rita,' Leland said, 'last night it appeared that your commitment was wavering. We decided it was better for you to know the truth.'

Adrian said to Stella, 'Do you have anything to say to Louise?' He touched her shoulder. She started, and her curls shook. 'Get off!'

Rita vowed not to respond with the shock and grief they wanted from her. She suspected that the young man, in particular, hankered after fireworks. She would not satisfy him. If she started to cry, she might not stop, and they would get the wrong idea.

Stella looked over her shoulder and said to Louise, 'I'm sorry for being party to your husband's deception.'

'Betrayal,' Adrian corrected.

'You could use any number of terms,' Louise said drily.

Bill asked her, 'How long have you known about this?'

'About an hour. Yesterday afternoon my husband decided we all needed a holiday. Up in these parts. He likes to get away.'

'You don't seem . . . distressed.' Bill shook his head. 'I have to say, I'm deeply ashamed. More than deeply. We didn't bring up Stella to do this kind of thing.'

Leland said with authority, 'Louise is a very forgiving woman'.

Louise raised her eyebrows for a fraction of a second.

Why aren't I more upset? Rita thought. But she let the question lie. It was easier to watch the drama than to consider why she welcomed the distraction.

Louise said to Stella, 'So. Do you consider yourself a home-wrecker?'

Stella replied without sarcasm. 'I don't know. Is your home wrecked?'

Rita understood that her daughter might like this woman— like her better than Adrian, whom she had looked at with such repugnance.

'When did all this take place?' said Bill. 'Stella?'

'We finished about a week ago. It started in February.'

Rita remembered Stella's musing face, when they had arrived home from the airport three months ago and found her sitting on the steps.

Bill grimaced. 'While you were in our house?'

'No!'

'You could say we've sinned against all Three Pillars,' said Adrian, pleased with himself.

Rita doubted whether Leland had picked up on his new recruit's note of irony.

Leland said to Stella's back, 'Do you wish to express full repentance?'

Rita saw how her nostrils flared.

He said to Rita, 'It's up to her now. Naturally, you feel greatly shocked. But you should perceive these events as a crucial part of God's plan. Have you told them about what God said to you? The Prophecy?'

'. . . The Promise. Yes.'

He was gratified. 'Bill. This is difficult for you to grasp. Nevertheless, we hope you find it in yourself to come with us.'

'A Prophecy?' Adrian said. 'What was that about?'

Louise sighed.

'It was a long time ago,' Rita said with finality.

'Did it relate to . . . this?' He gestured at the others, at himself.

'No.'

'*Mum.*' Stella leaned closer.

Rita had been sitting for some time in a state of utter clarity about Stella's situation. She had detached herself, let herself relax. Perhaps this was why long-hidden memories now quivered, and against her will something expanded to give them room. She sensed, through increasing panic, that if she wished she could let these memories be at home, as they had always wanted to be: what she had learnt when she went to propose to Leland after the disastrous meeting with her parents; the secret that Betty had revealed later that evening.

A call came from the garden. 'Muuuu-um!'

Louise asked, 'Am I still needed here?'

Adrian said, 'Well, hun, y'know, there's *stuff* . . .'

'Right then. I'll see where the girls have got to. Don't be long, Ade.'

She was almost out of the door when Stella said, 'Louise.'

She turned.

'I am sorry.'

'Okay.'

It was a transaction.

Leland shook his head in disapproval.

Rita remembered that the last time she had talked to him about Stella—it felt like years ago—she had been furious. Maybe he thought she still was. During their drive north, after he had tried to engage her in conversation about the Project's future, he had raised once more the subject of Stella's deceit. (How little they knew of it then. How silly her reaction looked, given what she knew now.) He had said she was a wilful girl, like a young Betty; in need of correction but—unlike Betty— with the potential for spiritual growth. Rita knew he was pandering to her with that last comment. He talked about 'muscular' love, and said she should not let herself be taken for granted.

Now she wondered for how long he had known about the affair. Known, and failed to tell them.

297

In the car she had not listened well to him, because she was thinking about Betty's tape. That afternoon, when he had suddenly announced that he needed to meet with one of the Project visitors, she had dropped him off at an opulent house in the hills and then returned home. The house must belong to this man, she realised. This Adrian.

There had been nothing left to do at home while she waited for Leland to call. She wandered through the rooms for a while, thinking how soon she would be gone. *A fresh start*, she thought. *Leave the past behind*. She found Betty's tape and carried it to the little radio-cassette player in the kitchen.

It began with a muted hiss, and then, shockingly familiar, Betty's voice. '*Hi*, Rita.'

Immediately, Rita longed to be back in their room at the Centre, laughing over some kitchen mishap.

'Gosh—' a little laugh '—I only have to say your name and I get stopped. Well. Okay. I'm not going to rewind again.' A sigh. 'Where do I begin . . . I'm sitting here at my little desk . . . I'm very tired.'

Long pauses. And then, as if she'd only just thought of it: 'Maybe you've moved!'

A click, and another; her voice more muffled now: 'Did I start this yesterday? I can't remember . . . It's snowing today. I've missed you.'

. . .

More strongly: 'For a long time I guess I tried to figure out why he didn't . . . act like a normal husband. He seemed angry, right from the start. Like he thought I was his conscience and he had something to hide. He would go on and on about how Karol Sadowski had handed over the leadership to him. Like he expected me to argue.'

. . .

'I guess you were angry with me too? For marrying him? Or maybe you're one of those "out of sight, out of mind" people. But I could never get myself to believe that. We were good friends, Rita.'

A clicky tapping, as though Betty had fiddled with a pen against the edge of her desk.

'Last year, I finally thought about starting a new life. A truer life. You could say that now I've got definite plans, huh! Do you think I would have gone through with it?'

She gulped. The tape clicked again.

She resumed in a more reflective tone. 'Are you there? Or did I decide not to send this?'

. . .

'I guess I had inflated ideas about how much I could help him. On the one hand. And I thought it was God's will. And there was my pride, too. I didn't want to be wrong about him.'

A long pause, and then her voice starting again, wavery: 'But he didn't seem to . . . want me. Never has.'

. . .

A shaky laugh. 'All these sex therapists nowadays, advice in this and that magazine . . . none of it would have helped. Not that he wanted help. When he did do it,' she said with more energy, 'it was like he was marking his territory . . .'

. . .

'I'm having a good day . . . my head's clear. I've never told anyone before. Maybe I'm not telling, if I don't send this.'

. . .

'What got to me was wondering whether, you know, it was my fault. Because of the attack. Whether it had killed something in me . . .'

A hiss that went on so long Rita thought Betty had walked away from her desk.

But she began again: 'You could say I'm behaving badly, not telling him I'm sick. It's not a Christian act, not a forgiving act. The way I'm thinking of it is, it's my last gift to him. Something real that he can be angry about.'

The next hiss ended with a click. Immediately, fevered violins leapt into the gap. Rita listened to the end of the tape, hoping Betty's voice would resume, but the violins continued unrelentingly until the play button on her tape recorder flicked

299

up and the room filled with silence. She played the other side, turning the volume as high as it would go, listening to the hiss, rewinding and replaying sections of static in case it was Betty whispering, whispering a recantation of all she'd just said.

After Louise left the room, they sat without speaking. Adrian breathed shallowly beside her. Finally, he said, 'I feel like I've moved to a higher plane. Leland, can you tell me more about this "spiritual partnership" thing?'

'Yes,' Stella said. '*Do* tell.'

Bill looked at her sharply.

Rita's hands lay in her lap. Her panic had passed. She had never felt so calm. The memories she had shut out for so long were growing in her like unborn children, kicking and jostling. She knew she could contain them.

Leland, hands clasped behind his back, mentioned St Augustine. He invoked the early church. He quoted from Paul's first letter to the Corinthians, Chapter 7: '*Now concerning the things whereof ye wrote unto me: It is good for a man not to touch a woman.*'

They burst forth, those memories. They began to climb up inside her.

3

The door to Leland's den was ajar. Rita knocked; heard, 'In.'

Here was the octagonal room Margot had described during Rita's first week at the Centre. It was murky; green velvet curtains were drawn across three of the four tall arched windows, and the only artificial light came from a squat lamp on a desk by one of the bookcases. But from where Rita stood, she could see the dais extending from each wall far into the room. In a shallow octagonal pit at the centre a leather sofa and two armchairs were arranged around a coffee table covered with newspapers and copies of *Life*.

Leland was not sitting in the high-backed chair behind the desk, nor in either of the lower chairs placed opposite. Rita thought she might have imagined his call. But then she saw him in a far corner. He had lifted the edge of a rug and was staring at the floor beneath it. He did not look towards her when he spoke.

'I hid Leonora Toller's letters, and now I can't find them. They're a liability.'

'I don't deal with letters.' Her quick thinking surprised and delighted her. She had talked herself into an enchanted, holiday state, like a girl on a dare. Here she was, venturing into Leland's den! When she'd knocked on the mansion's doors nine months ago, she never would have believed herself capable of such boldness.

He dropped the rug and walked to the desk. Gathering her courage, Rita moved towards it and sat in one of the low chairs. Various objects were ordered before him: a blotter, a pen holder, the lamp, a vase of jonquils. He sharpened pencil after pencil, and as he finished each one he added it to a row which was arranged so that the lead tips pointed at Rita over the near edge of the desk like tiny missiles.

'Those look like terrific pencils,' she said, prompted by nerves. 'Do you have a good eraser? I hate it when the eraser catches the paper.'

The wood shavings and granules of lead fell away.

'That looks like a good, sharp—sharpener.'

He said, 'I have no dictation today.'

'I'm not in the Secretarial Team. But I take minutes for the Playwriting Committee . . . I'm sorry about this morning . . . falling on you like that. When I was with my parents.' She tried not to think of how his soft, cloth-covered thing had given way under her fingers. 'And about the gravy during the Senator's dinner. I hope your trousers cleaned up okay.'

'Why are you here? Do you have information for me?'

'Um, yes. Actually I do.'

'Under which category?' He opened a drawer and extracted a single sheet of blank blue foolscap, which he placed on the blotter in front of him, straightening it with the edges of his palms.

'Pardon?'

'Which category?' He waited. 'Questionable behaviours. Potential revenue. Security. Expansion. International activity.'

'This is different,' she said, beginning to feel the power of the Promise. 'It's about you. From God,' she added.

He started. The veins at the sides of his neck stood out. 'God has given you information about me.' His face was grim, unreadable.

She wanted to, but could not say, *About us. Not just you.*

'He told you what passed in my mother's garden? He told you what He said to me?' His lips were tight, as though more words were dammed up behind them.

She could hardly speak into this. 'It was right at the beginning, when I first met the Movement . . .'

He stood, thrusting back his chair with a bang. It tipped a little and he slapped it upright. He stalked to a window. 'I have done my best. Powerful men respect us. Every day we make new inroads.'

Uncertain, she stood and walked a little way around the

desk towards him. 'I don't know anything about the garden. The Movement's . . . given me purpose. We all look up to you.' She went closer. 'You show us the way to God.'

'You know nothing about the garden.'

'No.' She wished he would change the subject. Anxious to make small talk, she scanned the room for ideas, and saw two large framed embroidered texts hanging side by side on the wall to her left. The first bore a title in elaborate, Latinate lettering: 'CHARITY, I COR XIII'.

> v1: Though I speak with the tongues
> of men and of angels,
> and have not charity,
> I am become as sounding brass,
> or a tinkling cymbal.

A small, involuntary noise of recognition escaped her.

He came nearer, speaking in a low, forceful voice. 'I *know*, even as I am known.' He pointed to a verse in the second frame.

> For now we see through a glass, darkly;
> but then face to face: now I know in part;
> but then shall I know even as also I am known.

'Yes,' she said eagerly. *Face to face*—she recalled it from Sunday school. It had always felt like a promise of limitless affection.

He repeated, insistently, '*I know*, even as I am known'. *Now*, he seemed to be saying. *Now* I know. I don't have to wait until after death.

'Who embroidered this?'

'Martha Sands. When I donned the mantle of leadership.'

'It's about love, isn't it? What love is.' Wanting to demonstrate her understanding, she said, 'I guess Martha was thinking of the Roof of Love. I mean, before you included it in the Pillars.'

'Indeed. Love *is* included in the Pillars, primarily the Pillar of Selflessness.'

She looked again at the text, with its evocation of a self-denying, self-effacing, patient, hopeful and calm person. It annoyed her, but she did not want to tell him that.

'Don't you think . . . love might have a special place in marriage?'

He looked at her without comprehension. He's tired, she thought, burdened by the needs of America, of the world. For whatever reason, God had not yet planted love for her in his heart. She took a shivering, shallow breath.

'It seems kind of appropriate, talking about this. Because . . . I heard a Promise from God, that we would marry. You and me,' she added, in case he understand. 'When I came to *The Divine Instruction* with my mom. He said, *You will marry that man*. I was looking straight at you. And afterwards there was a silence. Like God had made everything quiet so I would take notice.'

'Marriage?'

'Yes. I guess God may not have spoken to you yet about marrying me.'

He bent to pick a loose thread from the rug and wound it tightly around the tip of his little finger, the thread cutting off the circulation until the skin turned purple.

'I've never heard anything so clearly in my life.' She giggled nervously. 'I guess it's pretty well unheard of for a woman in the Movement to propose to a man. But I thought, since it's a Leap Year, although it's not Valentine's Day . . .'

She prayed for his eyes to light up. But he was silent, gazing at a point behind her left shoulder.

'Patsy told me about how you can't be a father, so I want to say, if you're worried about getting married with that kind of . . . trouble, I don't mind, truly I don't.'

After a few moments he said thoughtfully, 'It may be that you will take the message of Holy Marriage to the women.'

He strode to the bookcase by his desk, his vitality renewed, and took from it a thick leather-covered volume. 'Herein, *other* words that Paul wrote to the Corinthians. No woman has heard me speak of these matters before now.'

He read as though heaving a leaden sack down a flight of steps, laying a slow, thumping stress on every second or third word: '"Now concerning the things whereof ye wrote unto me: It is good for a man not to touch a woman."' He held up his index finger. 'It is *good*. For a man *not to touch*. Further on Paul says, "For I would that all men were even as I myself. But every man hath his proper gift of God . . ." and *so on*.' He slammed the Bible shut. 'Paul's followers did not have the necessary *discipline*. Therefore, wanting them to "avoid fornication", he was forced to recommend marriage to *all* of them. But *we* are the Three Pillars. We are the new church. Paul said, "I would that all men were even as I myself." Hah. He might be surprised to see what we have here. He might be *humbled* to see what modern, God-led leadership can achieve.'

He went to the desk and scribbled, mumbling to himself.

'Maybe we should Listen together? Or—' she was inspired '—maybe you want to Listen first with some of your friends? Because I know I heard God's voice. It was spooky.'

'Did you not hear what I said? God intends only *Holy* Marriage for those under His command.'

'What's Holy Marriage?'

'Marriage without fornication. A spiritual union.'

'But . . . how would people . . . make babies?'

His lips twisted in distaste. 'Holy acts of procreation, directed, purified by God—that is not fornication.'

She doubted that he believed his own words, and her uncertainty increased with his next statement.

'I must tell you, Miss Daley, in response to your proposition, I believe it's God's will I should enter eternity unblemished by any carnal sin.'

'You just said that . . . making babies by God's will wouldn't be wrong!' She blushed to be talking so freely with him.

'I don't expect you to understand.'

'But what about the Promise I heard? What about God

saying, *You will marry that man?*'

He stared at her. 'On reflection, I charge you not to speak outside this room of Holy Marriage. I might have overestimated the moral strength of my people.' He raised his hand. 'You should go now.'

She hesitated, unable to believe that this was how her story would end.

'Go, Miss Daley.'

In the narrow corridor she had to lean on the stone wall. What did the Centre hold for her now? Surely the untouchable, distant Leland she had just encountered was not the real man.

'Rita?' Cynthia Chant stood before her, eyebrows raised. 'What are you doing down here?'

It took her a moment to find her voice. 'I'm not feeling well. I guess I got confused.'

'Indeed you did.' Cynthia looked at her watch. 'Patsy and the others will be in the kitchen.'

'I'm feeling nauseous.' It was true.

'Go lie down then. I'll tell Patsy.'

Lying on her bed, she tried not to think of what the future held.

Betty came in after dinner. 'Where've you been? I hunted for you after lunch. I've been dying to talk to you.'

As if she'd heard it second hand, Rita remembered how Henry Allerton had attacked Betty during the Playwriting Committee that morning, and Betty's reaction. She wished, now, that she had never told her about the Promise. Certainly, she would never tell her about its humiliating end. She recalled her promise to listen to Betty's troubles.

'I wasn't feeling well. Sorry.'

'Oh, you poor thing. Did you lock yourself in the bathroom?' Betty threw herself down on the other bed. 'Thank goodness you're here now. I don't think I can hold this in another moment.'

She tried to raise some sympathy: Betty might get curious if she seemed too distracted. 'Mr Allerton was hard on you.'

Betty swallowed and rolled on to her stomach. 'That's not

306

the thing . . . I thought the Movement would show me the answer. But I haven't given my whole heart to it. So many of my Listenings, I haven't shared with anyone because I would have had to tell. I have to tell you now, Rita. The reason I got so upset this morning.'

It had happened in her summer semester at college, she said, in the late evening, on the long gravel path that ran between the drama faculty's small theatre and her dorm.

He was in her theatre class, a freshman like her. In previous weeks she'd turned him down twice. She had to study, she was helping a friend—perfectly regular reasons. But she saw him all the time, and it was awkward. That night he walked out from behind a bush and startled her.

You expect better than this? he asked after the first few minutes, growling hotly into her ear, a deep, Laurence Olivier voice she knew he'd cultivated. He dragged her across the lawn towards the shelter of oaks. They stood in the shadow of a wide trunk.

She couldn't answer: he had jabbed one knee between her legs, forcing her to stand with her feet apart; he clamped a hand over her mouth, pressing her head against his chest. There was an ache across her breastbone and up her neck. With his other hand, he twisted her arm behind her back.

After you turned me down cold, in front of my friends?

He began to wrench at her arm, emphasising his words.

I'll make you see you can't treat me like shit.

Thin voices rose in the distance, but he jostled her further into the trees.

Tell the truth now. You want me, don't you? That's why you're playing hard to get.

'I didn't understand what he meant. I hadn't done anything before then.'

Tears spilled down her cheeks. She tucked her knees underneath her, her fists bunched above her knees. 'I haven't told my folks. They're . . . happy people. They think the world's a good place.'

Rita sat up. She had forgotten about Leland. 'Tell me.'

She hesitated. 'I peed my pants.'

He'd said to her, *You're wet for me, I know you are.* And suddenly the hot flux poured out of her. At the same time she began to cry, her lips shaping *Mommy, Mommy.*

His thigh, still jammed between her legs, collected most of her urine. He shoved her so hard she barrelled into an oak, scraping her chin on the bark. 'That's how I got—' She rubbed the scar under her chin. 'I thought he might let me go then. But he didn't.'

You filthy girl. You take off those panties now. Do it.

'Did he—'

'No. He did . . . things to himself with my panties, and he hurt me with his fingers. That was the first time I heard the word, you know? When he said it.'

I'm not going to rape you. You're too dirty for me. I'm going to make you feel how dirty you are.

It was getting darker by then. He lit matches, instructing her to remove her girdle and her brassiere.

Without taking off your dress, he said. *What're those dresses called?*

Shirtwaister.

I've seen chicks do it. One strap off, then the other, then oops! Right out of a sleeve, abracadabra! Yep, just like that, honey.

'Funny, I hate thinking of that the most. I'd done it often enough. Once even with a man, though we didn't get any further. But that's the thing. Because he made me do it, he tied that night into my whole life. Like . . . no one had ever hugged me or kissed me, or smiled or cooked or flown planes or danced or raked leaves or made something work. It made me angry. I tried to be scornful. Thinking he couldn't hurt me. But I couldn't stop shaking. He went around campus like he hadn't done anything. Once he even came up and talked to me. I had to leave.'

She chuckled. 'That play. *The Divine Instruction.* It was terrible, so unnatural I almost died laughing. But when Gus said to Listen, I Listened. I thought, This is it. This is how I can be happy again. When I was writing down my Three Pillars, God said, *Go with these people. You'll learn what real love is.* I leapt at it, 'cause I felt so *stupid* that this thing had got me down . . . So I guess I assumed I had a deal with God. All my energy, all the wishing for stuff I thought I'd been entitled to. Fun. Popularity. I'd give that to Him. And He'd give me peace. Except, I don't think I meant peace. I meant forgetting.'

She shivered. 'I'm so cold.'

'Get under the quilt.'

Rita tucked her in.

'Were you thinking about this when you looked so washed out? After Mr Allerton said you were wrong?'

'Yes . . . it makes me wonder why I'm here! Don't tell anyone, they'd only say I was a sore loser. But after Mr Allerton said that, it was like some stagehand had been lurking in the wings with a big bucket of all the fear and . . . *sadness* about that night, and the bucket tipped up over me—'

She hugged her knees and cried for a long time, unselfconscious sobs that Rita envied.

Uncertainly, Rita knelt by the bed and laid a hand on Betty's shoulder. After a while she began to rub her back. Everyone else in the Centre would be preparing for bed or praying or already asleep in the frosty darkness; no one would suspect that Betty held this ugly story within her. It did not belong in the Centre. If Betty told it in Ladies' Sharing, someone would suggest she should forgive the man. Watchful Mrs Chant would ask her whether she had flirted with him, or if she had been wearing anything provocative that night.

'Would you pass me a tissue, please?' Betty blew her nose several times. 'Sometimes I think this'll never stop. Maybe I was wrong to want the Movement to give me an answer. Maybe I'm too selfish and stupid to understand it.'

'Are you planning to leave?' Rita tried to keep her voice level. If Betty left, she would have to leave, and what would happen to her then?

'I don't know. My feet are frozen.'

Rita untucked the foot of Betty's bed and fitted her own woollen socks over Betty's feet.

Betty laughed through her shivers.

'You're a hoot. You're the best friend I've ever had. Like a sister. I guess no one else knows me so well now.'

Rita smiled awkwardly. Betty's description of her failed deal with God—the decisive action, the anticipated divine erasure of former unhappiness—had aroused an apprehension in her that she did not want to name.

Betty looked sleepily up from her pillow. 'Do you hate me for telling you?'

'No. It's awful, I can't imagine what kind of man would do something like that. You're so brave.'

She did, indeed, think it was awful, and she hated to think of Betty enduring it. But she moved restlessly around the room, tidying the bureau top and adjusting the curtains.

Where was the confident, breezy Betty who would help her to navigate the unpredictable path to union with Leland? And what on earth did Rita possess, beyond socks, that could help her friend?

'Could you pray with me?'

'Oh—sure.' Rita smiled as if God truly was her strength and refuge in times of trouble. She knelt beside Betty's bed, looking straight ahead of her at the mounded quilt.

'Dear . . . God.' She could not bring herself to call him anything more intimate. 'Please help Betty.' And then, in a burst of true feeling, 'She doesn't deserve to feel like this. She loves You and wants to serve You and she'd be able to do that much better if You'd give her some peace.'

Betty stretched out a hand and briefly stroked her hair.

'For ever and ever, Amen.' Rita lifted her head, relieved.

'You're a pal. Thanks for rooting for me.'

'Will you be able to sleep?'

'Mmm. I think so.'

Betty seemed calmer at breakfast, and afterwards Rita didn't see her until the work session directly before dinner. They met in the library, where they were to make a start on cleaning the leather-bound volumes. Rita climbed on to the portable wooden steps and wiped each book with a damp cloth before handing it down to Betty, who laid it out on a trestle table.

Two men were working close by, making notes from newspapers. Rita imagined that when they left Betty might want to discuss her feelings once more, but when the men did fold up the papers and close the door behind them, Betty said, 'I've had an incredible day.' Her face, turned up to Rita, was luminous with intent. 'I had a thought in Listening this morning that I should go talk to Martha.'

Martha Sands had been stuck on the second storey for several days, confined to her bed by a badly sprained ankle. She had turned it outside on an icy step and had bruised her backside as well.

'I didn't feel like obeying. I didn't go until after lunch. But it was odd—as soon as I walked through her door, I knew I'd come to ask her about the tract. You know? The one you showed us in the Playwriting Committee.'

I didn't mean to, Rita wanted to say. *It was a mistake.*

'She was pretty grumpy, not in the mood at all for sympathy, so I got right down to it and asked her about the Roof of Love and what Karol had said about it.' Her forehead wrinkled. 'I'm still working out what she told me . . . somehow . . . it doesn't make sense, when you compare it with what the Movement stands for these days.'

'We should keep working,' Rita said. She turned back to the shelf, but Betty's low, earnest voice continued.

'Martha said Mr Sadowski never talked about the Three Pillars without changing them somehow. The ideas stayed the same, but whatever type of person he was talking to, the Three Pillars would be represented by different things. Once he described Chastity and Truth and Selflessness as three great

311

mountains, and Love was the atmosphere surrounding them. Like the oxygen.'

'I don't get it.'

'Well, without the oxygen the mountains—the Three Pillars—would be barren, nothing would grow on them and anyone trying to climb them would die. The other one she talked about, the Three Pillars were redwoods, and Love was the sap that drove through them and gave them life. And sometimes the Three Pillars were growing up from the soil, which was Love, and sometimes they were solid, and sometimes they were water, and she said it got confusing but she liked it that way.'

Betty stopped talking. Rita had kept on passing books to her, and now she had quite a pile in her arms, but she did not turn to the table.

'Wow,' said Rita. 'That's really interesting. You should write a history of the Movement, or something.'

'At first I felt kind of frustrated, but then I thought, *Well, Betty, what else do you need?* And my feet took me straight from her room to Leland's den.'

Rita almost dropped a book on her head. What if Leland had asked Betty to comfort her room-mate whom he had the day before rejected?

'At first I didn't know what to say to him. I mean, he must have been there when Mr Sadowski made those analogies, right? But I had the thought to tell him straight out what Martha had told me. He didn't say anything but he listened and never took his eyes off me—you wouldn't believe how dark it is in that room, I guess it helps him pray—and when I was done he said he didn't remember Karol describing the Three Pillars like that. And *then*, Henry Allerton walked in, and I felt like running away! But Leland asked me to repeat my story.'

She looked over her shoulder, and whispered, 'If I hadn't told you what I told you last night, I would have lost my nerve. But I felt strengthened, like that memory had been poisoning me and now it's lost its poison. Sitting there in Leland's den, I realised that Mr A's not so bad, after all. Just cranky.'

Henry had asked her—with respect, she said—how, in her opinion, the philosophy of the Movement should be changed. He took notes.

'I hadn't gone in there with any plan, but I said, put Love at the centre of things. Like Karol Sadowski did. Measure everything against it. Not romantic love, but, you know, love where people look after each other. Care for each other. Like you looked after me last night.'

Leland had thanked and dismissed her then, seemingly distracted by some papers on his desk.

'They're busy as all heck, I guess. You know what, though, I left feeling as though maybe something real had changed. Through you and Martha and everyone else, and I was just the mouthpiece.'

Listening, Rita surmised that Leland had not told Betty about his idea of Holy Marriage. This gave her a little fillip; if no other woman knew, she still had a special relationship with him.

'I'm sure we'll be able to include Love in the play now,' Betty said. 'Gee, I've had so much energy today. I can't believe how different I feel. You're a pal.' She put down the books and hugged Rita's calves.

At the next Playwriting Committee meeting, it turned out that Bill loved Karol's images too, and so did Nadine.

Betty could not say that Leland had given unequivocal approval for the inclusion of Love, but he had seemed to listen to her with approval, so they decided to write a trial draft and perform it as a surprise reading. Bill came up with a new, Love-related variation on the plot: that after his initial conversion, the union leader, fearful of losing his family's respect, and jealous of a younger rival's abilities, would disobey a Listening: specifically, a divine instruction to step down from the leadership of the union. His disobedience was the major turning point in the story: it would lead to problems in the family, and so on. The moral was that you had to show your love for God by obeying Him, and, without obedience, you couldn't Love others properly or get the Three Pillars to work in your life.

They put as much effort into the 'trial' as if they were to premiere it on Broadway. Alice Maniaty, taken into their confidence, forgot her worries in her enthusiasm for the story. Writing sessions and run-throughs were punctuated by her chirrups of 'The play's the thing!'

During those weeks, the atmosphere in the Centre was urgent. New members were joining daily. Distracted by the frantic activity and the rehearsals for the play, Rita could almost forget Leland's rejection of her proposal. At last, she was the cheerful and energetic young woman she'd always aimed to be.

They presented the play after a Sunday lunch, leaping from their tables at Bill's signal and singing Henry's opening song, 'A Trustworthy Man'. Betty, Nadine and Gus Driver, their sole recruit, carried the tune a cappella; they had told Bill and Rita to mime. Some of the Chorus joined in from their seats.

Alice stepped forward, her cheeks pink. 'Your indulgence, dear people!'

Behind her, Nadine tied a scarf around her hair and Gus collected a wrench from underneath the lid of a serving dish. At the Long Table, Henry Allerton and Leland were expressionless. Rita took one last look at Leland and hotfooted it with Bill to the old butler's pantry. There she had hidden props for their parts of the factory owner and his wife, and index-carded notes of their lines prefaced by the dialogue immediately preceding them: 'the Shakespearean method', Alice had said.

In the dining room, Nadine and Gus began the 'kitchen scene', set in the home of the union leader. Betty, their flirtatious, self-centred daughter, tried to get their attention.

Rita put on her hat. 'How do I look?' she whispered to Bill. 'Can I pass as a rich matron?'

They had closed the pantry doors. In the dim, brown light she could not see his face, but the lumps of his shoulders heaved up and down. He took a small box from his pocket.

'You need this.' He picked up her left hand and removed from it her notes, laying them on the counter. She felt him slip a ring on to her fourth finger.

In the dining room, Nadine cried, 'Who's eaten my apple pie! You're for it!'

'Rita,' Bill whispered, 'will you keep on being my wife after this is over? I mean, can we get married? While we've been working together . . . love just waltzed into that committee room and laid itself over me like snow. Jeepers, I'll probably never get that poetic again. Alice's Shakespeare must be getting to me.'

She felt mortified on his behalf. Laughter rose from the dining room. Betty must have started to complain about her boyfriends.

'I talked to Leland last night,' Bill added hastily. 'And Henry and some of the other men. We Listened. There's a general consensus you're the right woman for me, Rita. I can't imagine marrying anyone else. Leland told me to go ahead and propose.'

Leland approved? Was he testing her? Or getting her out of the way so she did not embarrass him further?

'Keep it on for now,' Bill said. 'I won't tell anyone it's real unless you say. Pretend it's a prop.'

With the tips of her thumb and pinkie she wiggled the ring a little, pushed it up to her finger's first joint and back, felt its slender circle and tiny sharp-edged pebble.

She understood, suddenly, that she would be linked to Leland if she followed his wish that she marry Bill. Maybe she would be his *spiritual* wife and, seeing as he would never marry, no other woman could be more of a wife to him. Of course, she was not the only fiancée to be approved by Leland, but she was the only one bound to him by a Promise from God.

'We're coming up,' Bill whispered. He laid his hand in the small of her back, nudging her out of the pantry, but at the door he paused. 'We're a good team,' he said, and smiled a lopsided smile, his face close. His hand on her back moved a little, and she shivered from the base of her spine to her shoulders.

In the dining room, while she argued with his character about whether they should allow their son to date Gus-the-unionist's daughter, she caught herself imagining what it would be like to touch that hollow between his collarbones. Her next, unbidden

315

thought was to hope that he hadn't been entrusted with the idea of Holy Marriage.

The play seemed to be a great success, even though Gus dropped his notes and they all lost their places and had to be prompted by Alice, and, once, Nadine began to giggle. The third act was dominated by Gus's character, Jack, who had to argue with God and his conscience about whether he should resign from the leadership of the union.

Rita, back in the pantry with Bill, listened to Gus's speech. She wished she could see Leland's face. How meaningful it would be for the Movement to use this story. Leland was Jack's opposite: he had undeniably been mandated by God.

As she returned with Bill to their temporary stage in order to act out 'the battle of the families', she made a point of not looking towards the Long Table. The final scene followed: Jack confessed his disobedience to all, and sent a written blessing to his younger rival. The play ended on a note of quiet satisfaction.

When the cast lined up and bowed, most of the dining room gave them a standing ovation. Rita bobbed up and down, the blood rushing into her head. After the applause died down, and the cast members began to grin at each other, Rita looked over to where Leland and Henry had been sitting. They weren't there.

'Where did Leland go?' she asked Betty.

Betty frowned, wrapping her scarf around her hand. 'They left just before you and Bill came back on. Leland got up and walked out of the room when Gus was giving his "repentance for disobedience" speech. Mr Allerton followed him.'

Rita was disappointed that they had not seen the final act, but her growing delight could not be sullied. Someone found her lovable—someone had given her a diamond ring! 'Maybe they're due somewhere. Lunch doesn't generally run this late. We didn't get to check Leland's schedule, remember.'

'Maybe.'

During the afternoon, she found that if she imagined herself into a box with Bill, a small dim box like the pantry, and drew a single line from it to the Promise, and through the Promise to

Leland, then she could imagine being happily married. She tried to Listen, but it was like tuning a radio to static. Surely, she thought, she had been given sufficient signals.

As folks were finishing their dessert that evening, Bill walked over to Rita's table and crouched to tap her shoulder, giving her a private, excited smile that sent gladness bursting through her. She stood. He dinged a fork several times against her water glass. It seemed to Rita from the joy on the faces turned towards them that everyone must know what he was about to say.

His voice was strong and happy. 'When I met Leland and his crew at that bus station, I had some inkling I was in for the ride of my life. But—' he squeezed her hand, and lifted it, showing her off, so it felt, to the crowd '—if I'd known what . . . riches and beauty I'd find, and that this lovely lady would agree to be my wife, I'd . . .'

Even Rita couldn't hear his next words over the hail of cheers. All the men at her table shot out of their seats and vied to pump Bill's hand. Another group set off a chorus of the wedding march, 'Da da daa da da daaaah', and the rest of the dining room followed. Betty ran up and gave her smacking kisses on both cheeks.

'I had no *idea*! Who can tell what God's got up His sleeve, huh. Bill's such a doll.'

Rita smiled and giggled. She and Bill were the focus of this rejoicing. She was popular.

Later, in their room, Betty asked, 'When did you begin to think that what you heard at *The Divine Instruction* maybe wasn't . . . ?'

Rita shrugged. 'It was just, you know . . .', and Betty seemed satisfied with that.

The next day, Henry Allerton called Betty out of a lunch-preparation session. Rita did not see her again until they were seated in the dining room, when Patsy jogged her elbow and pointed.

'Betty. At the Long Table!'

Rita looked first at the very end of the Long Table, where

the least important sat, and so had not spotted her by the time Henry Allerton rang his fork against his glass and stood, calling for their attention. Then she saw her: there she was, sitting between Henry and Leland, her smile quivering.

Afterwards, as soon as Betty emerged from the crowd of well wishers, she came straight to Rita.

'At first I didn't know what to *say*!' she whispered. 'I wanted to Listen with you before I gave my answer, but Henry said we had to announce it straight away, because Leland's meeting an important Republican this afternoon and Henry said it could make a big difference to his chances if he's engaged to be married, and so we just Listened right there, the three of us. And it seemed *arranged*, you know?'

Rita held her face still.

'Like God saying, now that you've let go of your fear of the bogeyman, I can get things moving. Isn't it amazing how He managed it? Getting Bill to propose *first*, so you could discover that *he* was the one, and so it could be clear to me that God wants this for me. And you two are so cute. Hey, we could have a double wedding! Margot can be our matron of honour, what do you think?'

Rita had the sensation of falling forward, endlessly. With both hands, she held on to the edge of the table.

'Careful, Rita,' said Alice Maniaty, who was chaperoning. 'You're pulling at the cloth.'

If Leland had chosen Betty, that meant he was not thinking about *her*. He did not hold a special, spiritual place for her. Betty would take up all of his feelings.

It was as Rita had suspected: she would never be the special one, lifted above criticism, eternally approved of.

And she had lost her friend.

'Rita? Are you all right?'

She smiled. 'Sure! Wow. It's . . . overwhelming. Everything changing so fast.'

No, she had thought: she had not lost Betty.

She had never had Betty at all. She owed her nothing.

4

In the living room of the holiday house, Leland had begun to disprove St Paul's thesis in much the same terms as he had used forty years before. Only Adrian was taking much notice of him. Rita could not listen. Bill had turned his head away and was scanning the bookshelf. Then he rose and, fetching a large volume from a lower shelf, began to riffle through its pages.

When Leland paused for breath, Bill said, 'In verse 5 of that chapter, Paul wrote, "Do not deprive each other except by mutual consent, and for a time, so that you may devote yourselves to prayer." Then he talks about needing to come back together, so Satan can't tempt you. Doesn't sound much like Holy Marriage to me.'

Stella murmured, 'The purpose of sex being to insure against temptation, then. Great. Oh, and for *procreation*, right. Super.'

'Do you believe in Satan?' Leland asked Bill. 'You and your Quaker friends? That would surprise me. But what you've quoted is at the heart of the matter. A man who is completely under God's command—who is so closely allied with God that he travels *beyond* temptation—'

Bill said, 'You make man sound like God.'

'You're hardly even alive,' Stella said.

Leland said to her, 'You have a lot to say for a girl who gave such a poor apology to the woman she has mistreated. And your mother is in despair over you. Look at her.'

Adrian said, 'The sex *was* wrong, the use we made of it. Life without morals doesn't work. I've proved that. So have you, Stella, if you look at your life honestly. What you want, how you've been trying to get it. That's no foundation for living.'

She said, 'The lying was wrong. You broke your promise to Louise, and I helped you—that was wrong. The sex we had was probably wrong. God knows it wasn't that much fun—'

'Is that right,' he said.

She ignored him. 'But sex *isn't wrong*. Mum. You can't work for someone who thinks sex is wrong.'

Bill, whose chin had descended to his chest, lifted his head and spoke to Rita. 'If you thought you were meant to marry Leland, why did you say yes to me? You couldn't have known Leland was going to ask Betty.'

Why had she married Bill? What could she tell him?

Adrian said, 'In a *spiritual* marriage—'

'Shut up.' Stella, despite her bravado, looked like a child again, gazing wide eyed at her mother, waiting for her answer to Bill's question. Waiting to hear something that could change the colour of her life.

But there was no question.

Not, why had Rita married Bill?

There was only the knowledge of what she had done to Betty.

Her legs were not steady. She had to balance her hand on Stella's head to remain upright.

'Mum?'

All of her concentration went into each step: out of the room, through the kitchen. Up the stairs, her mouth dry. In their room, she sat on the embroidered window seat. She could not tell how much later it was that Bill came—one minute, or twenty—thumping along the carpeted corridor, hesitating at the door. Trying to joke. 'Crumbs, I'm not that bad, am I?'

She turned to him, and he came towards her.

'Come on, let's have a hug. Why are you crying? Are you trying to tell me you're leaving? I've been an idiot. I'm sorry. Whatever you want, Reet, I can't come right now, but maybe later.'

She shook her head.

His voice thickened. 'You don't want me there?'

'No. I do, I mean—'

'What, then?'

She began to sob. Her words came out in jagged gasps and cries. He stroked her back until she could speak.

'I didn't warn her . . . a whole life without . . . *this*.'

Her hands had been pressed flat against his chest, and she twisted them outwards and patted her palms against his upper arms, squeezed them to make him understand. 'This . . . kindness. And she *needed* it.'

She could think of no other word for it: this kindness she had known since their wedding night. In the early months of their marriage, Bill had sometimes tried to joke with her about it: had there ever been another woman who cried so much on first sharing a bed with her husband?

Leland had not spoken to them, even when the Centre hosted a lunch for Betty's and Rita's families during the wedding preparations. Straight after the performance in the dining room, he had shut down any further development of Bill's play. Henry Allerton had fired them all from the Playwriting Committee and said he would compose the script himself. When Leland rose to make his speech during the wedding reception, Bill turned to Rita and kissed her on the cheek. 'Don't worry,' he whispered.

Mr Wallace, on Rita's right, also leaned towards her. 'We're very thankful,' he said, 'that you were Betty's room-mate. She's told us you had a lot to do with bringing about this happy day.'

Mrs Wallace shushed him.

Several other people had already made speeches, joking about the characteristics of the four newly-weds, praising them, making happy predictions for their married lives, so the fact that Leland didn't describe his feelings for Betty, or congratulate Rita and Bill, did not strike the general audience as odd. They had become used to his businesslike approach. That was how they would have described it, Rita had thought, listening to him talk about the future of the Movement.

But she knew something was coming. Something bad. She dreaded it.

When Leland delivered his judgement, in about the third minute of his speech, it was far worse than she had imagined.

She and Bill were to leave the Centre and go to New Zealand. And start up the Movement there.

'He's thrown us out,' she cried to Bill, as soon as they were alone together. It had been hell, keeping a smile on her face during the intervening hours, condoling ruefully with Betty as if the tragedy of Leland's decision was that they would be separated. 'He's getting rid of us.'

'New Zealand's a good place to bring up kids,' Bill said, but she didn't pay any attention. Somehow she got through brushing her teeth and changing into her nightgown. She hardly noticed Bill pulling down the quilt and squeezing in next to her.

There were no double beds in the Centre. Cynthia Chant had counselled Rita on how to fight and vanquish symptoms of inappropriate lust. Bill had mentioned a similar session with Henry Allerton. Their single beds were to be separated by a bedside table or a chair. She should change into her nightgown in the bathroom or underneath a bathrobe. She and Bill should wait for God to tell them when to begin a family.

Jammed up against him, inhaling the smell of his new cotton pyjamas, she cried and cried. Gradually, she became aware of how strange it was to be next to anyone in bed, let alone a man. If it wasn't Bill, she might have been frightened, but Bill would never hurt her. Even though she still could not stop crying—all was fractured, ended—there was still a kernel of gladness in her that he didn't care for Henry Allerton's rules.

He tried to comfort her with words. It would be all right. It was a new opportunity. Sometimes the best changes in life began with what seemed like a terrible time—like how he had come to America after his troubles in New Zealand.

At the mention of that unknown, unpromising place, she sobbed even harder and, thrashing under the quilt, turned her back on him. He tucked an arm around her waist and held her tight. Later, he began stroking her back, her hip. She tired of crying and lay quiet, hiccuping occasionally, her chest jerking. Sometimes, though, she could not help falling once more into despair, and then her tears would start again.

She dozed, and immediately entered a dream of Leland. All he had to do was stand in the doorway of his den and look at her, and she cried once more. She woke whimpering. Bill bent over her and kissed the side of her mouth. Her pillowcase was damp and hot. It was a relief to unpeel her cheek from it, turn her head and meet his lips. They kissed briefly, and lay for a while on their backs, his arm beneath her neck, his fingers buried in her hair.

He said, 'This probably sounds like a bad excuse, but I'm hot. Do you mind if I take off my pyjama top?'

At first he only distracted her. Sometimes she still cried. Finally, though, he distracted her beyond distraction.

Now, on the window seat, she said against his shoulder, 'She needed it . . . even more than me. She was hurt.'

'Who? What are you on about?'

Her breath came in shivers. 'Betty.'

'Betty? Needed what? A hug?'

'Yes . . . and . . . everything else.'

'I'm not getting you, Reet.'

'Touching . . . loving.'

He was silent for a few moments. Then, 'Is this something to do with Leland's spiritual marriage thing? That he was talking about just now?'

She had intended to tell him; nonetheless, she hated to hear him make the connection. She nodded, biting her lip. 'Holy Marriage. He told me about it. At the Centre. When I went to talk to him about . . . what I'd heard.'

'What had you heard?'

'The *Promise*. God's Promise.'

'That you thought you'd marry him?'

For a moment she could not speak.

'Reet?'

'When I told him about the Promise, he told me his idea, about Holy Marriage. And then he told me not to tell anyone. But I should have warned Betty. Because Patsy had said that maybe he was infertile, so . . . but I was jealous. Furious with her.'

'With Patsy.'

'*No.*' Why did he refuse to understand?

'Oh, you were jealous of Betty, so you didn't say anything to her. Hang on—that means . . . if Leland thought he couldn't have children, and sex could only be for . . . are you saying there was nothing? During their entire marriage? Come on, that can't be right.'

'Almost nothing. The . . . tape. She said so on the tape.'

'You listened to it?'

'After you'd left to pick up Stella. And Leland was visiting with Adrian.'

'Good Lord . . . why did she stay with him?'

'I don't know. She said she'd been planning to leave. But she got sick.'

'Hang on. Did you know? Did you know Adrian was coming today?'

'No. I dropped off Leland and went back home. Then I listened to the tape. But I couldn't take it in. I was trying to make it be all right. Make everything hold together.'

Another pause.

'Have you been . . . unhappy?'

She shook her head. 'I was happy but . . . I don't know, I couldn't . . . trust it. That somewhere, someone—God—wasn't looking resigned, saying, well, if that's the best you can manage . . .'

'God didn't think I was up to scratch?'

'Not that, I didn't mean that. But I hadn't . . . followed His plan, hadn't managed to do the right thing. Live the right life.'

'This God's opinions seem pretty much in line with what your mum thought of you.'

'I feel so bad.'

'I'll forgive you. If you stay.'

'No. I feel bad about Betty. About what she went through.'

'Ah. The Holy Marriage thing is very sad, but she could have bailed out. And Patsy wasn't exactly a reliable source, eh?' He kissed her jaw line where the flesh had long begun to sag. 'You don't know—Betty might still have married him. Or he could have told her. You're not more responsible than everyone else. Are you still planning to take off with Leland?'

'If I'd *told* her, though, at least she would have known! She didn't know what she was getting into.'

'Reet, are you going to start with the sackcloth and ashes?'

She could not answer. Guilt was her only certainty.

'You keep it up, and I'll be the one leaving. It's the only thing I don't like about you, this . . . beating yourself with sticks. Betty'll know you're sorry.'

She had said sorry to Betty, over and over during the drive the night before, while Leland talked.

Her lips were level with the weathered dent at the base of Bill's neck, her safe, redemptive place, and she touched them to it, felt its pulse.

He sighed. 'Reckon Stella needs you here as much as I do. She's knocked me for six, that one. Where did she get the idea that it's all right to . . . my own daughter.'

For the first time she understood the danger and dullness of her mind: that she could make some guilty connection between Stella's adultery and her own deceitfulness; if she wished, could commit herself to endless remorse on Stella's behalf. She turned away from it, and used words she'd heard from Bill.

'She'll come right. If those two—' Adrian and Louise, she meant '—have problems, they're not all caused by her.'

'The kiddies, though . . .' He sighed again, and kissed the top of her head.

'We can't do anything.'

He looked into her eyes. 'Are you going with him?'

'No. I can't. I was mixed up before.'

'Thank God for that.' He kissed her on the mouth, and on the second, longer kiss pushed his tongue between her lips— how shocked she'd been the first time he did that. His stubble scratched her chin.

'I'm lucky it was you.'

'You're right there.' He kissed her again, and moved one

hand to the nape of her neck. 'Henry Allerton was considering potential brides at about the same time, I remember.'

'Urgh.'

When, distantly, the clock in the living room rang eleven, he broke off. 'Can't believe it's still morning. I'm exhausted.'

'You could nap.' She did not want to consider what might be happening downstairs.

Bill did not seem to care either. He rose from the window seat, still holding her hand. 'Reckon I will. Come and have a cuddle. I need to get to know you again, now you're not leaving.'

She could not refuse, but once they were lying down he pulled her blouse out of her waistband and unhooked her front-fastening brassiere, stroking the lower curve of her breast. Rolled closer and kissed her harder. Then he hitched up her skirt and began to tug at her stockings.

'Bill . . . *Bill*! You can't—they're all in the house. And the little girls . . .'

He leapt off the bed and latched the window, pushed the door shut, but she sat up on her elbows.

'No. They'll still hear.'

He regarded her for a moment. 'Wait. Don't move.' He tucked in his shirt and left the room. She heard him thudding down the stairs as fast as his knees would allow, and then, within seconds, beginning the ascent again.

'Right. This window: shut. Girls miles away on the paddock. Hall window: shut. Door at the bottom of the stairs: shut. Door to the kitchen: shut.'

She laughed at his silly-spy imitation. He sat down next to her, kissing one earlobe, then the other. With the tip of her forefinger she touched his belt-buckle. He chuckled—it was an old joke—and nudged her further on to the mattress.

Despite Bill's precautions, she planned to restrain herself. She had not lost the habit of caring what Leland thought, and who could tell how thick the walls were.

However, as he moved around her body, she drifted away from this resolution—it was, after all, a very well constructed house. And their bedroom was located at the opposite end from the living room and kitchen. They would never hear her. No doubt they were talking. Debating. Arguing. She didn't really care.

As soon as Bill went upstairs to check on her mum, Stella left Adrian and Leland alone. In her room, she pulled the long curtains against the sun and lay on her bed, eating seaweed crackers from her bag and working out strategies for whatever might happen next. She tried not to dwell on how little she wanted to see Louise again. What mattered was keeping her parents together, but that was looking less likely than ever.

Halfway through her first packet she stopped crunching for long enough to hear the faint, occasional sounds coming through the ceiling. She propped herself on her elbows and, gazing up at the stippled paint as though it might reveal the noise-makers, tried to remember the layout of the house. Were Adrian and Louise having make-up sex in the spare upstairs bedroom? She couldn't imagine it. She pulled back a curtain. Sure enough, there was Louise, walking with her daughters alongside a distant hedge. The older girl was skipping.

The noises seemed to have stopped, but *there*—another one. Louder.

When she moved into the corridor, she couldn't hear them so well. Adrian and Leland were sitting in silence at either end of the kitchen table. They were not looking at each other, and Leland's eyes were half-closed.

Adrian smirked when he saw her. 'You've had time to think?'

She moved past the table and opened the door to the other corridor. Had she imagined the cries? The door at the top of the stairs was shut. She crept up and opened it, and returned to the kitchen, grinning.

'Listen. Hear that?' She waited until the next cry came,

and lowered her face towards Leland's. 'That's the sound of a woman in *pleasure*.'

He turned his head away, as if she smelled.

'You should leave. Mum's not going anywhere.' She caught Adrian's expression. 'What's the matter? Can't hack the thought of oldies doing it? At least they love each other.'

He said, 'So, Harper, did it work? Are you pregnant with my seed?'

She had no time to figure out how he knew. 'Fat chance. Oh—and how likely is it you'll be observing Perfect Chastity, let alone Holy Marriage? Have you told Louise about that one?'

He clasped his hands together on the table top, looking at her earnestly. 'You wouldn't understand—I want to live for something else. I got bored with myself.'

She did get it, but she would never tell him that. 'Have you done the whole Listening thing? Restitution and repentance?'

'I've made a start.'

'She won't go with you. You'll lose the kids.'

'Too right she will. We've talked about it.'

His bluster made her smile. 'Go on. Tell me. What's she done now?'

He hesitated, and looked at Leland. 'My passport's missing. Only since last night.'

'Very good! Perfect Truth! She's hidden it?'

'It's temporary. An adjustment thing. She wants to talk, then she'll bring it out.'

'Yeah, unless she's flushed it.'

Another, more violent cry wafted down the stairs.

Leland made a sudden movement as if to stand, but sat again. He said hoarsely, 'Bill knows I have no objection to him coming.'

She was almost hysterical. 'That's good!'

'You have such a limited mind,' Adrian said.

She shrugged. 'You guys can take Leland back to Wellington. He can't stay here.'

She left them and walked through the living room into the courtyard. From its far end she could see Louise sitting cross-legged on the grass, daisies in her hair, the two girls dancing around her. Louise seemed to be conducting them, her arms long and sinuous.

'Hi! Adrian's ready to go.'

Her arms descended. 'Yippee,' she said. 'We'll meet him round the front.'

Stella returned to the kitchen. The cries had stopped, but she gathered from Leland's expression that while she had been out of the room they had reached their crescendo.

'Louise'll meet you outside. You don't want to keep her waiting.'

Adrian looked at Leland. He said, with some desperation, 'She's right. You can come with us.'

'If Rita's intentions have altered, she needs to tell me herself. She gave an undertaking.'

'Dad said she finished transcribing all the interviews.'

This seemed to make some impression, but he stayed in his seat.

'You can't stay here. They wouldn't have—' Stella waved a hand towards the stairs '—if they hadn't sorted things. And they wouldn't have sorted things if Mum was still thinking of going with you.'

He thought about this. 'I have clothes in your guest room. Some papers.'

'Mum gave you a key. Leave it under the mat.'

The head of Adrian's younger daughter poked up through the open window. 'Daa-aaad. Mum says to say we're in the car. It's *hot*.'

'Five minutes,' he said.

'I'm *hungry*,' said the girl. 'Can I have another muffin?'

'There aren't any more,' said Stella. 'Sorry.'

Leland rose. 'Tell your mother I'll trademark the Project. Internationally. She'll be—' he seemed to be searching for the words '—in breach if she uses the stories.'

She wanted to sneer at his deluded ambitions, but she knew his world did not admit self-doubt. She said, 'I'm sure she'll abide.'

'I need to call America.'

'Use my cell.' Adrian handed it to him. 'I'll go make room for your bags.'

'And I need to eat,' Leland said. He looked at Stella.

'Um, we'll get something on our way,' Adrian said.

Leland nodded, and carried the phone into his room, closing the door.

Stella congratulated herself on her self-control. She had almost said, *God. Your poor wife. Poor Betty.*

Leland was standing by Adrian's jeep, supervising the loading of his bags, when Rita and Bill came towards him. Bill's arm was around Rita's shoulders, and she had the full-cheeked look of someone who had just woken, squinting as the sunlight hit her eyes.

He was munificent, working hard to overcome his antipathy for what they'd done. He had been practising this speech since he finished the call to America. 'You see, Rita, your resignation opened the way for the true plan. As so often happens. While I Listened in my room, God gave me the thought to ring Patsy at her New Mexico compound.'

Adrian called over his shoulder to his wife, who was standing a short distance away, watching them, her arms folded. 'Hey Louise? Get that? We're going to New Mexico. Desert as far as you can see.'

Her expression didn't change.

'Oh,' said Rita. 'Patsy Chant? I mean, um, Gurner?'

'Yes. She's very happy to be gaining my experience. And, of course, the prospect of using the Agape Project stories.'

Bill looked confused. 'For her diet business?'

'No. She has moved beyond that. A new church, a promising

new church, has grown up from the roots she laid down. The New Vessel Church. I will bring invaluable experience to it.'

The younger daughter, who was in the jeep, kicking the back of the seat in front of her, began to chant in a sing-song voice, 'I want an ice *cream*, I want an ice *cream*.'

Perspiration trickled down Leland's chest. He wished he had taken off his suit jacket.

Patsy, when he got through to her, had said, 'Let me see . . . the primary functions are filled. But I think . . . oh sure, Leland, we can find a place for you.'

When he got there, he would make her see. He would exert himself.

I want an ice *cream*, I want an ice *cream*.

Bill moved towards Adrian's wife. Leland heard him say, 'You've been very gracious. I can't tell you how much this horrifies me. We brought her up right. Not to hurt people.'

Her eyes slid over to where Adrian was rearranging the bags in the back of the jeep. She said, 'He was always going to do something bizarre.'

Immediately, Bill looked at Leland, and this gesture made Leland realise that Adrian's wife could as well have been referring to Adrian's conversion as to the adultery with Stella.

Was she another Betty? Would he never be rid of these undermining women?

Rita scuffed the toe of her sandal against the gravel. 'Well, I hope it works out for you.'

He wanted to say something about the inevitability of God's plan, about how he was only a vessel, or somesuch, for God to use as He might; but he felt weary of talking. He wished he might never need to make conversation again. In Patsy's new church he planned to be a near-silent spiritual guide making occasional, highly significant pronouncements to small audiences.

Rita stuck out her hand, startling him. 'Give Patsy my best.'

He shook it jerkily.

'Let's get this show on the road!' said Adrian.

Leland did not like getting into the back seat, jammed next to the older girl. She smelled of something overly sweet and chemical.

Bill raised a hand to him through the open window. 'See you, Leland.' He turned to Rita. 'How about a snack? I'm peckish.'

In the passenger-side mirror, Leland watched his erstwhile hosts turn their backs. When the jeep turned, he peered over his shoulder. Before Adrian had steered around the first bend, Rita and Bill had disappeared into the house.

🍂

Rita offered to stack the dishwasher after lunch, but Bill said he'd do it and instructed Stella to take her mother for a walk.

Stella led her across the courtyard and down a path that went through a small gate and around the edge of a field. She was silent, and at first Rita assumed that she was trying to figure out how to apologise for this latest scandal: her affair with a married man. But Stella swung her arms and looked around at the scenery as though she feared nothing.

Back in the house, Rita wondered, *was she only upset because she believed Adrian would wreck her chances of changing my mind about the States? Does she care at all about what I think of her behaviour?* She began to breathe more heavily: it would be easy to raise some anger over this. But she couldn't think of what to say, and anyway, she was too excited.

'This is a nice walk,' she said.

'I saw it this morning,' Stella replied. She left the path and climbed a low hill. Rita followed her. Below them, skeins of cloud-shadow moved across the grass.

Stella shaded her eyes and said, panting, 'There it is. There's the sea.' A thin slice of polished cobalt was visible over the edge of the headland. She took a deep breath, and another. 'I didn't realise this area was so high up.'

'That's good for it,' said Rita, stopping below her.

'Good for what?'

332

'Breathing deep like that,' she said, feeling a foreign, delighted complacency. She tilted her head back, the better to watch her daughter's reaction. 'Breathing into your diaphragm. Sending the oxygen around.'

'Around *what*?'

'Your body. Your bloodstream. You haven't told that man, I guess.'

Stella gaped.

Ah, Rita thought, and paused to relish the moment before continuing. 'When I was carrying you, I used to walk around the block four times a day, breathing deep. I've always thought that's why you're so smart.'

'Not that smart,' said Stella, with uncharacteristic melancholy. 'How did you know?'

'Oh, you've been laying your hand over your belly. Like you're protecting something. And once you touched your chest like it was sore. And . . . a mom's intuition, I guess. There's a look about you.' She did not remind her of the night she saw her crying outside the bathroom.

Stella blew out like a runner trying to recover her breath. 'Whoo. I thought I had a few more months to work out how to break it to you.'

Rita wanted to get in the questions before Stella remembered to clam up again. 'How far along are you?'

'Not far. About five weeks . . . they count it since the beginning of your last period. But it might not stick.'

'Is that man the father?'

'Yes . . . don't tell Dad yet. Please.'

'You need to talk to him.' *And me.*

'I know he's upset.' Stella's voice was pleading. 'I don't think he should deal with it all at once.'

'No. But you should tell him. Did you ever . . . love that man?'

'Adrian? Are you kidding?' Then she looked shocked, as though understanding what she had confessed to.

Rita stared at the strip of sea. Back at the house, Bill might be expecting her to tell Stella off, and indeed she was tempted to pronounce judgement. It seemed the lowest kind of deception to use the act of love without love in order to make a man into an unknowing father. And there was so much undoing that must follow: they could not be silent while Stella hid the existence of her child from Louise and Adrian, however unpleasant a man he was.

She tussled with herself: if she did not speak, would it be only because she feared losing Stella altogether? It was, too, a little humiliating that Stella had not asked her if *she* was upset; had not seemed afraid to set out on this walk with her.

Stella began to descend, treading carefully between the tussocks. She pointed at the narrow, uneven paths, no wider than the span of Rita's hand. 'Sheep tracks. Remember how Dad used to explain them every holiday, like he'd forgotten we'd seen them a hundred times already?'

She was avoiding the subject, Rita realised. Stella was too clever not to be worried about the future: who would want to be forever linked to someone like Adrian?

'Don't leave it too long to tell Dad about the baby,' she said as Stella passed her. She started down the hill. She thought, *I don't know myself well enough, that I can know what to say at a time like this.*

Even so, a red-faced, raucous little person popped up before her. He was standing on a plinth and holding a scroll—wearing a toga, for some reason. He waved the scroll back and forth, exhorting her to convey its message to Stella. He made her laugh.

Stella turned. 'Why're you laughing?'

'Oh . . . nothing.' But Rita stopped on the path.

Behind the little man there was an amorphous, greenish mass made up of her desires. She leaned forward, trying to see inside it.

Stella was waiting for her at the bottom of the hill. She had picked a long blade of grass and was carefully shredding it with a fingernail. Her face was closed, unreadable.

Rita had not quite reached her before she asked, 'Are you planning to stay in Wellington?'

No, that wasn't it.

She thought again, and moved a few steps closer. 'When this baby's born, I want to see a lot of it. My grandchild. Our grandchild. Are you listening?'

She waited until Stella met her eye, and said, 'I want to be a real grandma. I want the baby to laugh when it sees me. You'll let me do that, Stella. You will.'

Acknowledgements

Thank you to my writing and reading friends: Naomi O'Connor, Carl Shuker, Anna Smaill, Peter Hall-Jones, Abby Letteri, Laura Kroetsch, Jared Gulian, and Jane McKinlay; and in particular, Tim Corballis, Kate Duignan, Ingrid Horrocks, Rachael King and Katy Robinson.

Thank you to Creative New Zealand for the generous grant which arrived at a crucial time.

Thank you to Fergus Barrowman, Jane Parkin, Heather McKenzie and Anna Brown for being brilliant at your jobs.

Thank you to those in the know: Dr Marion Leighton and Quentin Abraham, Jamie Reid, John Peek of Fertility Associates, May Sahar and Brian Molloy.

My love and thanks to all my family, especially Richard and Joy Pearce, and Hal Wilkes. Most of all, thanks to Patrick, whose support made this book possible.